Fic Bon
Bond, Nancy.
Truth to tell

D0031661

DISCARD
LIBRARY
TELLURIDE M/H SCHOOL
725 W COLORADO
TELLURIDE, CO 81435

TRUTH to TELL

Also by Nancy Bond

A STRING IN THE HARP
(1977 Newbery Honor Book)

THE BEST OF ENEMIES
COUNTRY OF BROKEN STONE
THE VOYAGE BEGUN
A PLACE TO COME BACK TO
ANOTHER SHORE
(Margaret K. McElderry Books)

TRUTH
to
TELL

by Nancy Bond

LIBRARY
TELLURIDE M/H SCHOOL
725 W COLORADO
TELLURIDE, CO 81435

MARGARET K. McELDERRY BOOKS
New York
Maxwell Macmillan Canada
Toronto
Maxwell Macmillan International
New York   Oxford   Singapore   Sydney

This novel is a work of fiction. Names, characters, places, and incidents are either the product of the author's imagination or are used fictitiously. Any resemblance to actual persons living or dead, events, or locales is entirely coincidental.

Copyright © 1994 by Nancy Bond
All rights reserved. No part of this book may be reproduced or transmitted in any form or by any means, electronic or mechanical, including photocopying, recording, or by any information storage and retrieval system, without permission in writing from the Publisher.

Margaret K. McElderry Books
Macmillan Publishing Company
866 Third Avenue
New York, NY 10022

Maxwell Macmillan Canada, Inc.
1200 Eglinton Avenue East
Suite 200
Don Mills, Ontario M3C 3N

Macmillan Publishing Company is part of the Maxwell Communication Group of Companies.
First edition
Printed in the United States of America
10 9 8 7 6 5 4 3 2 1
The text of this book is set in 10 pt. Times.

Library of Congress Cataloging-in-Publication Data
Bond, Nancy.
Truth to tell / Nancy Bond.—1st ed.
p. cm.
Summary: In 1958, having been dragged by her mother to a decaying mansion in New Zealand, fourteen-year-old Alice thinks that she has stumbled on a shocking secret involving her long-dead father.
ISBN 0-689-50601-5
[1. New Zealand—Fiction. 2. Fathers and daughters—Fiction.] I. Title.
PZ7.B63684Tr 1994
93-11248
[Fic]—dc20

For Margaret, editor and friend

Acknowledgments

I owe special thanks to Joan de Hamel, in Macandrew Bay, New Zealand, for willingly answering a variety of questions and, best of all, becoming a valued friend; to Dorothy Butler for making the introduction; to Mr. Dangerfield for sharing his knowledge of the Dunedin-Christchurch rail service; to my friends Kit and Kate for their companionship on my last trip to New Zealand; and— always—to my sympathetic and supportive family.

Kate glared at her. "All right," she said, "go on."

Mrs. May looked back at her. "Kate," she said after a moment, "stories never really end. They can go on and on and on. It's just that sometimes, at a certain point, one stops telling them."

Mary Norton: The Borrowers

Contents

1. The Beginning: 1958 — *1*
2. Mr. Tatlock — *10*
3. "I'm Not a Bleeding Chauffeur!" — *24*
4. Murdoch, MacInnes & Holt — *32*
5. A Mistake? — *41*
6. A Telegram and a Letter — *54*
7. Interview at Saint Kat's — *65*
8. New Girl — *77*
9. No Secrets — *87*
10. A Visitor to Florestan — *100*
11. The Terrible Two — *112*
12. Odd Socks — *119*
13. "I Don't Like Children." — *130*
14. A Tramp at the Door — *141*
15. Excavating the Dining Room — *154*
16. "I'm Off to My Love with a Boxing Glove, Ten Thousand Miles Away." — *165*
17. *Nepenthes ampullaria* — *180*
18. A Guest for Tea — *193*
19. Inside the Studio — *207*
20. Miss Fairchild Requests the Pleasure . . . — *217*
21. Fathers and Daughters — *230*
22. Rhododendron Sunday — *240*
23. Desperate Measures — *251*

24.   Carried Away   *258*
25.   Now What?   *270*
26.   53 Bessant Street, Christchurch   *279*
27.   Humphrey Tucker   *290*
28.   It's Not That Simple   *306*
29.   Telling Stories: 1976   *317*

— 1 —

The Beginning: 1958

Alice first came to Florestan at the beginning of September 1958: the dregs of winter in New Zealand. It was cold and rainy when she and her mother, Christine, finally reached the city of Dunedin after almost two whole days of traveling: by train, then ferry, then train again. Less than a week before, they had disembarked from the steamship that had brought them from Liverpool to Auckland, and they had barely had time to get used to the feel of solid ground under their feet after four weeks at sea, much less to orient themselves in a strange country. Christine's original plan had been to spend a couple of weeks in Auckland, getting used to things, then to make the journey from the top of the North Island to the bottom of the South Island in easy stages, sightseeing on the way, taking as much as a month to reach Dunedin, when she saw how their money held out. That would give them time to settle comfortably into Florestan, accustom themselves to grand surroundings, get to know the rest of the staff, become familiar with the city, before the house's owner, Miss Emilia Fairchild, returned from India, ready to begin work on the book she had hired Christine to help her write. By that time, too, Alice's stepfather, Len, should have caught up with them.

Instead, they had had to come south as quickly as possible, summoned urgently by Mr. MacInnes. As Miss Fairchild's solicitor, it was he with whom Christine had been corresponding since Miss Fairchild had set out on her latest expedition, so Christine wasn't surprised to find a letter from him waiting in Auckland, but its contents were unexpected. Apparently Miss Fairchild had been forced by illness to cut her travels short. At that very moment she was on her way home from Borneo, several months early. Would Mrs. Jenkins kindly make arrangements to travel to Dunedin immediately and inform Mr. MacInnes of her plans? "Botheration!" exclaimed Christine. "This was supposed to be a holiday."

"It's not fair," Alice protested. "You said we'd have a fortnight in Auckland and we've only just got here." It wasn't that she liked Auckland; it seemed to her raw and ugly, used as she was to the narrow streets and mellowed age of Cambridge. But ships that sailed from England to Auckland sailed likewise from Auckland back to England, and she had a fear of being sucked into the country, deeper and deeper, as if it were quicksand, when all she really wanted was to go home again. "Anyway, she won't be well enough to start working, so she won't need you right away."

But, "There's nothing for it," said Christine. "We'll have to go straight south. It can't be helped, Alice." And two evenings later they boarded the Limited at Auckland Station. Mrs. Royde, wife of a retired bishop living in Wellington, had promised to meet their train there and look after them until their ferry sailed. That had cheered Alice a little: the thought of seeing a familiar face halfway along.

They had shared a cabin on the ship with Mrs. Royde. She was English herself and had made the voyage a number of times to visit family. She knew the ropes and took Christine in hand. They spent many days sitting companionably in deck chairs while the ship churned steadily south, and Mrs. Royde passed on much valuable advice. She was a comforting, solid kind of person, and Alice was reassured to see her again, waiting on the Wellington platform for them. But at the end of their day in the city, when Mrs. Royde saw them off at the ferry dock, they were on their way, alone again, to Dunedin.

Most of the actual trip took place at night: from Auckland to Wellington by train, and Wellington to Christchurch's port—Lyttelton Harbor—on the ferry. Unable either to see anything of the country they traversed, or to sleep properly, Alice had nothing to distract her from the shapeless fears of her imagination. She was filled with the certainty that they were getting hopelessly and irretrievably lost. It was the kind of anxiety that she knew her mother would not understand, and that prevented her from responding to Christine's efforts at conversation. Eventually, her mother gave up trying to talk and absorbed herself in a secondhand copy of *Barchester Towers* she'd bought in Auckland.

On the train they had spent the first night upright, slumped against rented pillows, napping on and off in such a way as to make the trip seem endless, while a constant parade of people tramped up and down the aisles, and children who didn't appear to belong to anyone ran back and forth. Waking once in the dingy light, Alice looked at her mother asleep beside her and thought, with a sudden upwelling of pure, cold panic, How did I get here? Who is *she*? Even after her breath came back and her heart slowed, she could find no satisfactory answers. Over the past few months it had become increasingly clear to Alice that she did not know her mother as well as she had always assumed she did.

In Christchurch there was a missed connection, which meant waiting around at the station, and by the time they reached Dunedin, it was dark. Through the rain-smeared windows of the train, Alice had watched with dismal horror as a gray landscape rolled past, and ached for the security of what she knew. At least, at *least,* she told herself, we're expected. Somebody knew they were coming. There would be proper beds, a hot meal, warmth and light and welcome. Mrs. Mofford, her mother had said. Mrs. Mofford was the housekeeper at Florestan.

"I suppose, after the delay in Christchurch, it's too much to hope there'll be anyone on the platform to meet us," said Christine with a sigh. "There are bound to be taxis. Have you got everything, Alice? This must be it." They climbed stiffly down from the train. Other passengers were being claimed with smiles and hugs and glad exclamations. No one took any notice of Christine and Alice. Christine smoothed her coat, and commandeered a porter.

The taxi driver he found for them was far from reassuring. "You sure about this? You want to go to Florestan?" He gave them a long, doubtful look from under his cloth cap, taking in their travel-weary clothes and the steamship labels on their luggage.

"Of course I'm sure," snapped Alice's mother. "Perhaps you're unfamiliar with it?" She did not like being scrutinized by strangers.

"Oh, I know the house well enough. Well, I mean I know where it is. I just thought you might not—"

"Good." Christine cut him off. "Then you'll take us there, please. And by the shortest route, if you don't mind," she added crisply.

They set off through the rain-glazed streets, the driver humming to himself. Alice saw that he glanced frequently at them in the rearview mirror, but her mother, wrapped tightly in her winter coat and her own thoughts, didn't seem to notice. Pulling up at a traffic light, he said conversationally, "That's the Southern Cross Hotel up ahead. If you want to change your mind, I could drop you there. It's clean and reasonable."

"Thank you," said Christine in a voice as chilly as the evening. "I do not want to change my mind. We're expected at Florestan."

The driver shrugged and went back to humming. Alice twisted a lock of hair around and around her finger; she had a dry, stale taste in her mouth. They drove through streets of shops, closed and desolate-looking, hunched figures at a bus stop, people hurrying purposefully under umbrellas—all of them quite oblivious of Alice and Christine. Alice shivered. They started up a long, steep hill lined with houses, curtains pulled against the dark, families safe inside, at home where they belonged. The taxi stopped, its lights picking out a pair of wrought iron gates set incongruously in a chain link fence. Alice's stomach tightened unpleasantly; she could see nothing through the window, except the gates and slivers of rain slanting through the headlights. The driver opened the gates—they were not locked, but he had a bit of a struggle shifting them.

"Mum—?" said Alice, her voice sounding thin.

But Christine shushed her as the driver got back in and nosed the taxi gingerly along an unpaved, rutted drive, deeper and deeper into a black tangle of shrubs and trees. He stopped again, and this time switched off the engine. They were smothered in silence. Ahead of them bulked a huge shape. Its windows were blank; not a light showed in any of them.

"You sure you're expected?" said the driver.

"Yes. That's what I was told." Christine paid him and climbed out before Alice could move to stop her. Leaving the taxi door open, she marched up the wide front steps and pulled a knob set in the wall beside the door. The only sound Alice could hear was that of rain dripping off uncountable leaves. There was not even the faint rumble of traffic. The rest of the world had been snuffed out like a candle.

"Don't think there's anyone here," called the driver after a minute or two. "The old lady's away—gone off to foreign parts. Want to think again about the Southern Cross? It's on my way—I'll turn the meter off."

Oh, yes *please*! thought Alice fervently. Her mother only pulled the knob again. Somewhere far away Alice thought she heard a hollow chime. "There," said Christine, a note of triumph in her voice. "Someone's coming. Just unload our luggage, if you please. Alice?" There was a sharp click and a scraping, wingeing noise. "About time," she exclaimed crossly to the doorway. "It's raining."

"I know it's raining. Been raining all afternoon," retorted a rough voice. "You come all this way to tell me? Who are you?"

"Mrs. Jenkins, of course. Who else would I be, arriving on this date by taxi? Mr. MacInnes told you I was coming."

"Didn't hear no taxi. You should've come round back. No one but her uses the front door."

With enormous reluctance Alice left the haven of the taxi. The driver finished piling their bags on the wet, weedy drive. "Well, if you're all right then, I'll be off." With every atom of her being Alice willed her mother to say she'd changed her mind, but Christine waved in dismissal. He spun the taxi around, scattering gravel, and bounced off. As his taillights winked out, Alice experienced a cold, sinking sensation.

"Right," said Christine to the crack. "You are—?"

"Tatlock. And I've left my tea getting cold."

"If you wouldn't mind giving us a hand—well, really!" Christine said crossly. "Don't just stand there getting wet, Alice. Bring something inside." Christine gave the door a firm push; it groaned inward, sounding like the haunted house at the funfair, on Bank Holiday. Except that there Alice had chosen to be scared, knowing it wasn't real and could do her no harm, and in a short time she and Len would be out in the daylight being silly and eating ice cream. Her mother came down the steps and picked up the two largest suitcases. Alice unwound her fingers from her limp hair, collected the smaller bags, and followed. The entry hall was flagstoned, even danker than the air outside. Suspended high overhead was a brass chandelier that cast a grudging light on the middle of the space and filled the remainder with sinister shadows. The walls, she saw with dismay, were stiff with weapons: crossed pikes, rosettes of broadswords, studded shields, wicked curving knives. Above the doors hung tattered banners like shreds of cobweb.

"But—" said Alice, "you said—"

"I know what I said. That's what I was told. Just leave those and close the door, Alice, will you? I want to find Mr. Tatlock."

She pushed into the darkness, following a tiny dribble of light that leaked out of some distant room. Alice resisted the childish urge to catch hold of her mother's coat to keep from losing her. Stretching away on all sides were unknown spaces full of shrouded shapes, lumpy pieces of furniture, and a thick, stale, musky odor. It filled the hollow, high-ceilinged room they crossed, like stagnant water. The suggestion of a staircase ascended into denser shadow, and there was the black gap of a cavernous fireplace. Alice caught her breath. On either side of it stood a still, pale figure. She blinked rapidly and exhaled. Statues. At any moment she expected the floor to tilt, or a cackling laugh to explode from under her feet, a fluorescent skeleton to drop down jiggling in front of her, or bats on strings to fly into her face. In fact, any of those things would have been a relief; they'd prove she needn't take this place seriously.

The kitchen, when they found it, was a cube of welcome light. At a large round table in the middle sat a person, invisible except for the gnarled fingers, nails ragged and black-bordered, grasping the edges of the *Otago Daily Times*. Alice saw the newspaper twitch at the sound of their steps. On the bare tabletop were a teapot covered with a green knitted cosy, a cup without a saucer, a pint bottle of milk, and a paper doily with the remains of a slightly squashed chocolate loaf cake on it. A small electric fire glowed orange on the floor next to the chair. Alice shivered again, yearning for heat and food, for comfort.

Christine cleared her throat. In a carefully controlled voice she said, "Mr. Tatlock? Mr. Tatlock, I didn't mean to sound abrupt just now, but we've been traveling since Tuesday evening and it's been an extremely tiring journey. I had been expecting something rather—different—at the end."

The paper twitched again, then came down. "Well, there's no blaming me for that. I've done what I was asked. Been waiting here since four, I have. Just about given you up." Mr. Tatlock was a small, leathery man, his face hazed with stubble, his hair grizzled and wispy. He wore a plaid flannel shirt, with a frayed collar, and brown suspenders. His eyes glittered deep in their pouchy sockets, shifting suddenly from Christine to Alice, who had been staring at him. "Forget to put my teeth in, did I?"

She looked quickly away, her cheeks hot. After an awkward pause Christine said, sounding conciliatory, "Is there enough tea in the pot for two more cups? Or shall I make fresh for all of us?"

He grunted. "Fresh."

"All right." Christine stood a moment, sizing up the territory. She frowned at the sight of the enormous black range, its face covered with doors and dials. On the counter beside the sink was a small electric hot plate with a kettle on it and an open packet of Roma tea. She took off her coat and hung it carefully over the back of a chair so that it would dry without wrinkles. Giving Mr. Tatlock an inquiring look, she said, "Alice, you can look for cups." But Mr. Tatlock sat impassive, offering no help, so Alice began to open cupboards at random. In the second one she found the most incredible collection of pudding basins and jelly molds she had ever seen. She thought very likely she was hallucinating; she felt numb and slightly dizzy. They hadn't eaten anything since lunchtime, more than five hours earlier, and that had been only limp cheese-and-tomato sandwiches—her mother distrusted the ham and chicken ones—warm lemonade, and slabs of dry fruitcake, purchased hastily in a railway café at one of the train's frequent stops. As the kettle began to steam, Alice found cups and saucers, and even a sugar bowl half full of sugar.

Her mother removed the cosy from the teapot. Inside, the cosy was brown with ancient tea stains; the pot itself was fluted bone china, decorated with tiny pink rosebuds. She looked about for somewhere to dump the old leaves.

"Mulch."

"I beg your pardon?"

"Just heave 'em out the back door," Mr. Tatlock advised. "Good mulch."

Christine hesitated a moment, then to Alice's surprise, did as he suggested. A waft of cool, earth-smelling air followed her back into the kitchen. When the tea was made and the cosy replaced, she sat down. Alice perched herself on the edge of another chair, as far from Mr.

Tatlock as possible. Pointedly she did not remove her coat. "Now then, Mr. Tatlock," Christine began. "Perhaps you'd be kind enough to tell me why Mrs. Mofford isn't here."

Pushing his cup across the table, he waited while she filled it. "Couldn't really say. She didn't tell me her plans, just packed up and left. We weren't that friendly."

"Packed up? Do you mean she's gone for good?" Christine cleared her throat a little too loudly. "When was this? Does Mr. MacInnes know?"

Mr. Tatlock took a long, slurping swallow. Alice watched the Adam's apple bob in his wrinkled, scrawny neck. Deliberately he set his cup down. "Oh, must've been five or six weeks back, I'd guess. Mr. MacInnes knows all right—asked me to keep an eye on things, till Mrs. Jenkins gets here, he said." He gave Christine a narrow look and rubbed his chin with a sandpapery sound. "He didn't mention a kid. Just Mrs. Jenkins, and Mr. Jenkins to follow—that's what he told me."

"Then there's been no one but you in this house for more than a month, is that right? There's no one else here now?"

He shook his head. "Not that I know of, missus. And now that you've come"—he stood up—"I'll be off. I still got chores."

"Off?" exclaimed Alice in alarm. Even Mr. Tatlock was better than being left alone.

"But," said her mother, rising abruptly, "what about food? Is there any in the house? We haven't had dinner—"

"In the pantry. Mr. MacInnes asked would I lay in a few things. Didn't know there'd be two of you, of course, but there should be enough to hold you till tomorrow, if you're not big eaters. You can have the milk that's left," he added generously, as he pulled on a yellow oilskin and settled a shapeless felt hat over his ears.

"Mr. Tatlock—" There was a note of desperation in Christine's voice. "Where are you—where can we find you again?"

"In the lodge, down by the back gate," he said, and disappeared into the rainy evening, abandoning Christine and Alice to Florestan.

— 2 —

Mr. Tatlock

There was sun spangling the wet leaves outside the window when Alice woke, and a bird singing, clear and cheerful, quite close. She could hear none of the sounds she was used to, of a city winding itself up for a busy day. Lost, she closed her eyes tight, lay still, and counted slowly to ten. When she opened them again, she knew where she was: scrunched over on one side of a soft, musty-smelling double bed, in a large, unfamiliar bedroom, upstairs in the house called Florestan, somewhere in the city of Dunedin, on the South Island of New Zealand, in the Southern Hemisphere, half a world away from where she wanted to be. She and her mother had been traveling toward this place for well over a month. This was what Christine had forsaken Cambridge for, leaving behind their comfortable little semidetached house on Courtfield Road, with Mrs. Hollings on the other side of the wall, the shops only a few streets away, the bus just at the corner. Everything Alice knew and cherished: her room overlooking the grassy little back garden; the private school she'd attended the last seven of her fourteen years; her best friend, Audrey; the beautiful and solid permanence of Cambridge with its colleges, and gardens, crooked streets, ancient buildings, and river. . . .

A longing for home so strong it was like a cramp seized Alice. The window swam and her eyes stung. Her mother, tired and edgy last night, had told her to stop complaining, it would all look better in the morning.

The provisions Mr. Tatlock had left them were sketchy: a loaf of bread and some butter, a package of cornflakes, and a tinned steak-and-kidney pie. There was no way of heating the pie—Alice would have eaten it cold; she was so hungry by that time, she felt ill. But Christine distrusted tinned pies. "There's no knowing what's in them. They use all the bits they can't sell otherwise." So Alice had tried to placate her unhappy stomach with slices of bread and butter and the remains of the loaf cake. She didn't like tea unless it was full of milk and sugar, and there was little milk and the sugar in the bowl turned out to be a solid, yellowy lump. Christine drank sugarless tea and had a cigarette. She disapproved of smoking; it was a habit she had picked up during the war and had never managed to break. She smoked now and then to calm herself; Alice and Len recognized it as a warning signal.

After this unsatisfactory meal they faced the problem of finding a place to sleep. As Christine said, in a house that size there must be any number of bedrooms. But in order to locate one, they had to leave the light and comparative safety of the kitchen and venture into the unknown. Alice sensed a reluctance in her mother almost as great as her own. They crept through the house like burglars, close together, whispering, fumbling for unfamiliar light switches, most of which didn't seem to work. The staircase creaked alarmingly as they climbed it, making Alice wince at each step. All the doors on the floor above were shut—there was no way of telling what lay beyond, except by opening them. It's like the story "The Lady or the Tiger," she thought grimly.

Neither of them was in a mood to explore, so they claimed the first bedroom they came to: a large, bleak, brown one with a double bed in it and massive dark furniture crouched against the walls. The sheets Christine found in a cupboard were damp and the blankets smelled.

There was no hot water for washing faces, much less for the long, soothing baths Christine had promised. They had no choice but to undress as quickly as possible, climb under the covers, and hope for swift oblivion. Alice ached with weariness. Even though they'd had berths on the ferry the night before, it had been too rough to sleep. Instead, she had lain awake, listening to one of their strange cabinmates snore, wondering what it was like to drown, and wishing she hadn't eaten all those chips for tea.

In the double bed Alice turned her back on her mother, relieved that she was close enough to touch, bitterly angry that she had brought them to such a dreadful place. Outside the casement window the rain tapped like fingers on the ivy. Christine's breathing slowed and steadied. Alice lay rubbing her cold feet together, so tired her eyelids felt stiff and gritty and refused to stay shut, resentful that her mother could have fallen asleep so easily.

When Christine had first begun to talk about a trip, back in April— ''I must get away'' was the phrase she had used—Alice had not unreasonably assumed her mother meant a holiday somewhere. The summer before they'd had a fortnight in Devon, all three of them, and it had been quite successful even though Christine grumbled about gaining weight on cream teas and insisted on going around every church, cathedral, and country house she could find. Successful enough that Alice hoped they might attempt something more exotic: the Channel Islands, perhaps, or even France or Majorca. ''Audrey's father took them to Greece last year,'' she told Christine brightly. ''Audrey said it was super. They found this inn on Corfu—''

''What are you talking about?'' said Christine. ''Greece?''

''She said the water was lovely and warm and the sun shone every day. They came back all brown and healthy. There are lots of package tours, Mum. And Len would love the birds. We could arrange it and surprise him when he gets back.''

''But,'' Christine pointed out, ''we don't know when that will be, do we?''

"Well, no," agreed Alice. "But he said the job was just for the summer. If we waited until the end of August—" Len had taken a job the month before in the engine room of the Dover-to-Ostend ferry. It paid very well, he said; he couldn't afford to turn it down. He'd sent them a postcard of the White Cliffs scrawled with a brief message: "Im fine—hope you are to." On the front he'd drawn little specks with wings in the sky and written "bluebirds." Christine hadn't smiled. "I suppose we could go without him," Alice said doubtfully, "but it wouldn't be as much fun."

As if she had just that moment made up her mind about something, Christine said, "No. I can't afford to wait for your stepfather, Alice. If he isn't here when we're ready to go, that's his lookout. He'll simply have to come on later."

"Later?" echoed Alice. "How long are we going for? And where?" She was beginning to suspect that her mother had more in mind than a fortnight in the sun.

"I'm not sure. A year at least, maybe two." Christine gave her an almost defiant look. "Alice, we're going to New Zealand."

"New *Zealand*? But that's—" Alice's mind raced. She tried to remember. "That's the other side of the *world,* Mum! How can we possibly go to New Zealand?"

"By steamer." Christine deliberately misunderstood the question. "It takes four weeks—four lovely weeks of doing nothing but sitting looking at the sea and being fed four or five times a day. That will be the longest holiday I've ever had."

"What about school? What about your job? And the house—who'll look after the house?" Alice stared at her mother in disbelief. If it were Len saying all this, she'd play along with him, knowing it was nonsense, an elaborate joke of some kind. But Christine did not talk nonsense and seldom joked.

"I mean to give up the lease on the house. There's no sense paying rent for something we're not using. When we come back, we'll find another place. Anyway, I'm tired of living in someone else's house. I told Len that some time ago. And you needn't worry about school, we won't leave until the term's over. As for my job''—she lifted her chin—''I intend to give notice next week.''

Alice felt winded, unable to absorb what her mother was saying. There was an unfamiliar light in Christine's eyes. Not only did she mean every word, she had been thinking about it for some time and Alice had never guessed.

For her own part Alice had only a vague idea of where exactly New Zealand was: a short pink line, hyphenated by the sea, somewhere near Australia. The other side of the equator, which meant the year was upside down: winter when it ought to be summer, Christmas when it felt like June. When she was much younger, she used to wonder why people living below the equator didn't fall off the world. Len said they wore special boots.

''But then—if—we *have* to wait for Len,'' she protested. ''We can't possibly pack up and just go away like that without him. What'll he do? How will he even know where we are?'' She pictured him coming back to Courtfield Road only to find someone strange living at Number 15. ''Oh, no. Mrs. Jenkins and her daughter left some time ago. No, they didn't—no forwarding address that I know of. I'm not sure, but I believe they went away—Australia, someone said. Or was it New Zealand? One of those places . . .''

''We aren't sailing tomorrow, Alice,'' said her mother calmly. ''There's a great deal to be done first. Len could very well be back before we go, and if he isn't, we'll leave word for him. He'll have the address, he can follow on.''

''What address?''

''Ours, of course. For pity's sake, Alice, you don't think I'd go off without knowing where, do you? I've had offer of a job in Dunedin— a very good job, as it happens. I'd be a fool not to take it. I'll be helping to write a book, doing research, editing, and writing instead of typing and filing and fetching tea. I've been considering this for some time and

I've decided I can't afford to turn it down. I'm forty-one years old and I've never set foot outside of this country."

"Well, I'm only fourteen," retorted Alice, not seeing what her mother's age had to do with any of this, "and I'm quite happy where I am."

"At fourteen," her mother returned, "you're too young to be stuffy. It's more than time we both had some new experiences."

Now as she blinked back tears of self-pity, Alice couldn't believe these were the experiences her mother had had in mind. Christine's side of the bed was cold, the covers smoothed into place, her nightgown folded neatly on her pillow. Alice was amazed to realize that she had actually gone to sleep sometime during the night and had slept soundly enough not to hear or feel her mother get out of bed. Struggling upright she shook the dark hair out of her eyes. The wardrobe door stood open and she could see that Christine had hung clothes inside. On the dresser she had set out her toilet articles, the travel clock—it said ten past eight— and two photographs. Alice recognized them immediately.

The one in the Woolworth's frame had been taken last summer outside Exeter Cathedral by an obliging Dutchman. Len had his hands pressed flat together as if in prayer, and was giving his best impression of a saint while Alice made a face at him, and her mother stood in the middle ignoring them both, smiling with the sun in her eyes. In the silver frame was the photograph of a croquet match—young women dressed in summer frocks, Christine among them wearing a straw hat, young men in white flannels, sleeves rolled up. The man on the far right, with a thatch of fair hair falling across his forehead, was Toby Underwood. Alice knew the photograph by heart; it was the only one they had of her father, taken years ago, before the war. Toby Underwood had been killed in Corsica in World War II, without even knowing that Alice was expected. He and his daughter had never drawn breath at the same time.

Barefoot, Alice padded over the mushroom-colored carpet to the open window. Below, to the right, were the front steps up which they'd come the night before, drifted with wet leaves. The stone urns on either side were half full of black-looking water. The weedy gravel circle beyond was rutted and puddled. As Alice watched, a blackbird flew down and drank, then flew into one of the matted shrubs nearby and began to sing again. Further to the right lay a sloping expanse of unmowed grass stretching down to a solid bank of trees. Nowhere could Alice see anything to indicate that she was in the middle of a city. Could she have dreamed it all—the railway station, the shops, the traffic, the people? The blackbird disappeared, taking its song with it, and suddenly Alice was the only living thing in the world. All around, leaves rustled and dripped, and she shivered. The room was chilly.

Outside the bedroom door she paused. She was on a balcony that ran the length of the great hall; there was a similar balcony opposite. At one end steps led down from either side to a central landing and the main staircase. The great hall rose up through the center of the house to a heavily timbered vault, a space filled with silence. The rank, musky smell Alice had noticed the night before lay heavy on the air. It reminded her of something she couldn't quite place. It was very unpleasant. She shouldered her way through it, anxious to find her mother, and at the foot of the stairs caught a reassuring whiff of burned toast.

In the kitchen Christine was sitting at the table with a cup of tea and her shabby little book. Without looking up, she said, ''Good morning, love. You weren't stirring when I woke, so I thought you might as well have a lie-in.'' She raised her eyes and frowned a little. ''Isn't that the same blouse you were wearing yesterday—*and* the day before? It's got spots down the front.''

''What's the point in putting on a clean one until I've had a bath?''

Christine pursed her lips but didn't argue. ''You'll have to manage with tea this morning, I'm afraid. And that's the end of the milk, so the cornflakes are useless. I did find a toaster, at least.''

''That?'' It had sides that opened down, and a frayed cord. Beside it on the counter was a heap of charred fragments.

"Either that or plain bread and butter. If you use it, you'll have to keep an eye on it."

"We didn't have a proper supper last night, either," Alice pointed out.

"I know that, but there's nothing I can do about it, Alice. You'll just have to make do with what's here until we can get ourselves organized and do some shopping."

"Whatever for?" asked Alice in alarm. "You aren't thinking of *staying* in this house."

Her mother lifted her chin. "Certainly I am. Where else would we go?"

"To a hotel for a start. What about the Southern Cross? And there's Mrs. Royde in Wellington. She said if ever we needed anything—"

"Alice—"

"Well, we do. We need *everything*. This house isn't fit to live in."

"Alice, what did I tell you? There's your toast burning, and that's all the bread there is."

Alice retrieved her two slices of blackened toast and sat down, glaring at her mother. There were shadows under Christine's eyes and tight little lines at the corners of her mouth, as if she hadn't slept as well as Alice had thought. Pushing aside any twinge of sympathy, Alice said, "It doesn't look better in the daylight, does it? It looks worse."

Christine shifted irritably in her chair, and picked up a postcard to mark her place in the book. It was the White Cliffs, Alice noticed.

"This isn't at all what you said it would be like. You said there'd be people—"

"I thought there would be."

"What if something had happened to us last night? Suppose there had been burglars—or a fire? No one would have even known we were here, except that taxi driver. He tried to warn you."

"Don't dramatize. We aren't cut off from the world. There's a telephone in the hallway, and there's Mr. Tatlock."

"Mr. Tatlock!" Alice snorted. "I think we imagined him. I could imagine all sorts of unpleasant things in this house."

"We did *not* imagine Mr. Tatlock, believe me," said her mother dryly.

"Pity."

"Once you've finished your breakfast, you can prove it to yourself by going to find him. And mind you're polite. We need him."

"For what?" Alice was disbelieving.

"Hot water for a start. I've been making a list of questions—"

"Then," said Alice rashly, "why don't *you* look for him?"

"The first thing I must do is telephone Mr. MacInnes to let him know we've arrived. I'll ask to see him this morning, the sooner the better."

"I still think you should have telephoned him last night. He could have found us somewhere else to stay."

Christine sighed. "Alice, I told you I saw no point in ringing Mr. MacInnes until we'd had a night's sleep"—Alice noticed she didn't say a *good* night's sleep—"and had a better sense of the situation."

"You mean," said Alice, "until we knew the worst. Well now we do. He should at least have told you about the housekeeper."

"Perhaps he just forgot, or thought he'd mentioned it earlier."

"He knew you wouldn't come, that's why he didn't say. It was dishonest."

Not meeting her eyes, Christine said, "Ask Mr. Tatlock to come as soon as possible, will you, Alice?"

"I don't know where he is."

"In the lodge by the back gate. You heard him. I'm sure you're clever enough to find your way." Christine filled the kettle again and put it on the hot plate. "I'll do the washing up. I don't suppose you made the bed—?"

Outside the scullery door Alice paused and looked around. To her right was an enclosed, scruffy little yard across which were strung clotheslines, slack and punctuated with weathered pegs. Something had built a nest in the clothes-peg bag: wisps of bleached grass stuck out of it. The morning was damp and cool; flecks of vivid blue winked among the leaves overhead, and a pair of little birds looped past her, flashing yellow, black, and red. They looked like the goldfinches Len coaxed into the garden in Cambridge with millet. But how could there be English goldfinches in Dunedin?

And where is Len? she wondered, staring blindly after the birds. Perhaps if he hadn't left Cambridge they'd all still be there now, carrying on with life as usual. It wasn't until he'd gone to Dover that her mother had made up her mind about New Zealand, Alice was sure of that. She remembered watching her mother systematically reduce their possessions to the essential, which she put in storage, and the portable, which she packed to take along. "But we won't have anything when we come back," Alice had protested. "We'll start over. New" was the brisk response. "I'm tired of all this." Was she tired of Len as well? Had she meant that without actually saying it? The question crept, unwelcome, into Alice's chaotic thoughts as they set out from Cambridge, but she couldn't bring herself to ask it.

Then for four sun-dazzled weeks aboard the *Cassiopeia* life went into a curious state of suspension. During that month there was nothing but the ship and its passengers. Except when the storm in the Indian Ocean disrupted things, the days had a comforting, monotonous, unthinking rhythm, measured off in hours between meals. Alice earned a little pocket money looking after two small boys for their pregnant young mother; she learned to play shuffleboard and worked on an enormous jigsaw puzzle in the lounge. She explored the decks with a gloomy young man from the Midlands who was being sent against his will to work on his uncle's sheep station in Australia. Christine spent her days reading and sitting and talking to Mrs. Royde. Her face lost its pinched look, and the lines at the corners of her mouth turned up; she enjoyed her meals, and only once or twice mentioned putting on weight. She played whist in the evenings. Without discussing it, for four weeks she and Alice declared a truce, putting the past and the future away temporarily, living in a kind of enchanted bubble. Looking back on the voyage now, Alice could hardly believe it had happened.

She heard a rapping on the window behind her that made her jump, and saw her mother frowning and gesturing at her with a soapy hand. She pulled her cardigan close around her, wishing she'd put on her coat, and set out, taking the brick-edged path that led into a wide courtyard. On the far side, enclosing it, was a long, low, L-shaped stone building that looked like a carriage house and stables. Instead of water, the horse trough in front was filled with dirt, and tufts of grass thrust up between the cobbles. In spite of the formidable padlocks on the double doors, the green paint was peeling and several of the shutters hung askew. Like the house, it had a depressing, derelict feel to it.

An overgrown, muddy track led out the other side, tunneling through mounds of dark, wet foliage. Some of the shrubs were in bloom, hung with clusters of complicated, vivid red flowers unlike anything Alice had seen before. She eyed them with deep suspicion; they didn't look civilized. Rounding a bend, she entered a sunny clearing in the middle of which stood a small greenhouse. In contrast to everything else, it looked neat and well tended. Through the foggy glass Alice saw blurs of color. She tried the door and found it unlocked. Inside, the air was like thick, rich soup, spicy and fragrant. On the right was a double row of brilliant, boisterous geraniums, overhung with baskets of fuchsia that dripped lurid purple and cerise flowers, and Busy Lizzies that exploded in all directions. Alice was dazzled. She was familiar with their restrained English relatives, blooming sedately in pots and orderly garden borders, but these flowers had cut loose and thrown themselves into a wild frenzy of growth and outrageous color: crimson, salmon, hot pink, magenta, mauve, royal purple, scarlet. They seemed to her the flowers of a nightmare, uncontrollable. She backed out and closed the door hastily.

The track went on and on, twisting like a snake through the wilderness. Behind the dense screen of leaves, on either side, Alice heard noises: rustlings, cracklings, squeaks, and chirps, and she knew she was being watched. Branches swayed, twigs snapped, sun glinted on wet surfaces. Self-conscious, anxious, she hurried along, stumbling over roots, stepping into holes. The breeze maliciously shook showers of last night's rain onto her head and down her neck, and she was seized with a sudden fear that she was in reality going nowhere, just around and around in mazy tangles. Ready to give up and turn back, she burst out into blinding sunshine. Ahead of her was a wide green meadow dotted with flowering fruit trees and, set among them, a miniature half-timbered cottage with a steep red-tiled roof and twisted chimney pots. Climbing roses, like bushy green whiskers, half smothered its mullioned windows. It looked like something straight off a ''Picturesque England'' calendar, with primroses and daffodils shining out of the long grass, and chickens staggering about. The only incongruous note was struck by an old black motorbike slouching under a tree, like a delinquent boy on a street corner.

As Alice stood transfixed, a large black-and-tan dog came bouncing and barking around the cottage, ears and tail high, scattering the chickens in noisy disorder. She stiffened, forcing herself to stand still and keep her hands at her sides as Len had taught her. If the dog bit her, she'd have to believe she wasn't dreaming.

''Kipper! Hi, you—Kip! What're you after, eh?'' The voice came from somewhere behind the cottage. The dog paused to consider, then trotted up to Alice and began to sniff her legs. Its whuffling breath tickled her bare skin.

''Hullo?'' she called, keeping a wary eye on the dog. ''Does it bite?''

''What?''

''Does the dog bite?'' she called louder, twisting hair between her fingers.

A hoe over his shoulder, Mr. Tatlock stumped into view. ''You ought to know that by now. You bleeding?'' He pushed his hat back and squinted at her. ''This is private property. You got no business here. Who are you?''

"I'm Alice Jenkins, of course. We came last night."

He grunted. "Got to get my peas in."

"Wait!"

But he'd disappeared the way he'd come, leaving her alone with the dog again. Kipper's long pink tongue dangled out between rows of gleaming white teeth; she thought he was laughing at her. "I'm not afraid of you," she told him crossly, and followed Mr. Tatlock's trail through the wet grass. Behind the cottage was a large garden plot fenced with chicken wire. Most of it was bare turned earth, with here and there a row of seedlings pushing sturdily up, and at one end a raised bed covered with straw. Mr. Tatlock was inside the fence, although there didn't appear to be a gate.

"Mr. Tatlock—" Alice began, trying to sound firm.

"You still here? I thought you'd gone." Without looking at her, he folded himself stiffly onto his knees.

"My mother sent me to find you. She wants to see you."

"Whyn't she come herself then? Here I am." He poked and patted at the dirt, making little holes and dropping in seeds, then covering them up.

Kipper came and threw himself onto the ground, rolling luxuriously with little grunts of pleasure, his paws digging the air. Alice watched Mr. Tatlock work his way methodically to the end of the row, then sit back on his heels and survey it. "Have a good night, did you?" he said after a few minutes.

It was on the tip of her tongue to say, "No, of course we didn't," but she caught herself. He knew perfectly well what kind of night they must have had alone in that empty, unwelcoming house. "It was all right, considering," she said instead.

"Considering, eh?" He heaved himself to his feet and dusted his hands on the seat of his trousers. "What's she want anyway, your mum?"

"She didn't say. You'll have to ask her."

"I knew it. Been here less than a day and already she's making trouble for me.'' He scowled, then bent back the end of the fence, climbed out, closed it up again, and headed purposefully toward the cottage.

Alice hoped he was going to clean up a little but had her doubts. "Where are you going?"

"Mebbe you've got nothing better to do than puddle about all day. I got sheep to feed."

"Sheep?" Startled, Alice glanced over her shoulder. There were no sheep in evidence. When she looked back, Mr. Tatlock had vanished. From the rear the cottage looked far less quaint. In fact it looked rather like a slum. Tacked onto it were several lean-tos, making no attempt to blend in. The yard was cluttered with piles of lumber, fence posts, rolls of wire netting, old fruit baskets, bales of hay. There were three wheelbarrows—one upside down and one without a wheel—coils of hose, a ramshackle hen coop, and any number of barrels.

Mr. Tatlock reappeared from one of the lean-tos, carrying a bucket of brown pellets.

"What'll I tell Mum?"

"Tell her what you fancy" was the unsatisfactory reply. "Stow it, will you?" he said crossly to the dog, who was running in circles, barking happily. Kipper paid no attention.

"But she said—"

"I'll stop in when I've finished my chores. Tell her not to hold her breath."

He headed off, through the long grass, in the opposite direction from the house.

— 3 —

"I'm Not a Bleeding Chauffeur!"

"Well? Where's Mr. Tatlock? Alice, don't tell me you couldn't find him after all this time?" Christine was up to her elbows in soapy water at the kitchen sink when Alice got back. She was doing laundry; Alice recognized her nightgown being sozzled up and down.

"I found him. He pretended not to know who I was at first. He was surprised we stayed the night."

"And you told him I wanted to see him?"

Alice nodded. "But I couldn't make him come, could I? He said he'd be along when he finished his chores. He *said* he was going to feed his sheep."

"Sheep? Oh, Alice, really! He was having you on," exclaimed Christine.

"I'm only telling you what he said. He's got chickens—I saw them. And a dog—a big one with lots of teeth."

"Well, chickens—that's different. You could keep chickens in the city, I suppose. But not sheep—"

"I did what you asked me to. If he doesn't come, it's not my fault."

They glared at each other. Then Christine said, "All right then. While we wait, you might as well make yourself useful and hang these out. I've propped up the clothesline."

It was half past ten before Mr. Tatlock put in an appearance. The laundry was hanging limply in the little enclosure outside the kitchen, and Christine had begun to survey the contents of the pantry. There were shelves full of ancient-looking tins: some of them bulging, many of them rusty, a number without labels. There were jars full, or half full, of peculiar-looking substances that had darkened with age, or crystalized, or gotten damp and congealed. The sugar in the cannister marked Sugar was no better than the stuff in the bowl—it had set like cement and would have to be chipped out. The flour was full of weevils. Christine told Alice to dump it outside in the shrubs. Crates of empty wine bottles were stacked on the floor. Their feet made gritty, scrunching sounds as Alice and Christine carried the bottles out to put beside the scullery doorway. And everything they touched was covered with a thin, tacky film of black, like damp paint.

"Anyone here?" Mr. Tatlock stuck his head through the door.

"It's *filthy!*" exclaimed Christine. "Nothing's been cleaned in months—just *look!*" She held up her black hands.

"Soot," observed Mr. Tatlock sagely.

"I *know* it's soot!"

"Chimney fire, that was. Four or five months back. Stupid woman."

Christine took a deep breath and Alice watched her compose her expression carefully. "Thank you for coming, Mr. Tatlock," she said, quite pleasantly. "There are a number of things I need to ask you about the house."

"House is none of my job, missus."

"What *is* your job?" asked Alice, frankly curious. She ignored her mother's threatening glance.

"I'm the gardener. I look after the grounds. And I keep an eye on the house when she's away. Out of the goodness of my heart, that is."

"But surely you must know a great deal about it," said Christine.

"Mr. MacInnes said you've been working here for years. He said you came in Mr. Fairchild's time."

"Mmmp." Mr. Tatlock stood squarely on the doorstep, making no move to enter the kitchen. His wiry eyebrows met in an uncooperative tangle across the bridge of his nose. Alice did not think, looking at him, that flattery was going to work, and her mother was evidently coming to the same conclusion. She said, "All right, Mr. Tatlock, let's not waste each other's time. We haven't any to spare. Mr. MacInnes has told you, I suppose, that Miss Fairchild is on her way back to Dunedin at this moment?"

Underneath the brows his eyes narrowed, but he said nothing.

"He couldn't tell me precisely when she'll arrive—he hadn't heard—but she was taken ill, in Borneo, I believe. She's coming home to convalesce, so the house will have to be in reasonable order. To be honest with you, I had no idea there'd be so much to do and no one here to do it. I was specifically told there'd be a housekeeper in residence. But I don't suppose that's your fault." She didn't sound entirely convinced. "So we'll just have to do the best we can, the three of us working together." Emphasizing the last word, she looked from Alice to Mr. Tatlock and waited.

After a long pause Mr. Tatlock said grudgingly, "So what're you asking for, missus?"

"Well, for a start, there's the boiler—"

With a command Mr. Tatlock left his dog lying in the sun outside, lazily snapping at flies, and reluctantly crossed the threshold. "I'm not spending all day here," he warned. "I've my own affairs to see to, understand."

When he came grumbling up the stairs from the cellar, the best part of an hour later, Christine had a pot of tea waiting. She avoided mentioning the condition of his hands as he sat down, though Alice knew it was a struggle for her, and said only, "I'm sorry I've nothing to offer you with it, Mr. Tatlock, but you know yourself the state of the larder."

For good measure Alice added, "We finished the cake last night—I was ravenous." While Mr. Tatlock was still in the cellar, she'd watched her mother add a couple of teaspoons of water to the last drops of milk and swish it around in the bottle. He peered at the pale liquid suspiciously as he tipped it all into his cup. "You'll have hot water in a bit, missus. Some of the taps haven't been used in a while—they'll be stiff and you'll get rust in the pipes. You'll want to let them run."

"Thank you," said Christine sincerely. "I don't know anything about boilers."

He grunted. "That'll be Mr. Jenkins's job, will it?"

"Yes, my husband will be able to cope, of course. He's an engineer."

Engineer sounded very grand for what Len did, Alice thought. Mr. Tatlock slurped his tea, evidently not impressed. "Coming along in a day or two, is he?"

Christine's mouth thinned but her voice was level as she said, "It may take him a bit longer than that, actually. When you've finished, Mr. Tatlock, would you be good enough to drive us into the middle of the city? I rang Mr. MacInnes this morning and made an appointment to see him. And I've several other errands—"

"Drive you?" The brows came across forbiddingly.

"When I spoke to him, Mr. MacInnes told me there was an automobile for the use of the staff."

"That's right. Green Ford, in the garage on the end. Mrs. Mofford used it last. I expect there'll be petrol in it. Bit of a bugger to start, as I remember. Don't use it myself."

"Yes," said Christine, "but unfortunately I don't drive, Mr. Tatlock. We didn't keep a car in Cambridge, you see. My husband knows about them—"

"Sounds like a useful sort, this husband of yours. When he's around. Tell you what, missus. You go out the front gate and turn right. There's a bus stop. Can't miss it."

"Mr. Tatlock," said Christine, working to maintain her control, "I would really appreciate it if you would drive us, at least this once. It would be an enormous help—we don't know our way around Dunedin yet. I'm sure we'll quickly learn, but it would save a great deal of time—''

"*Your* time, maybe, not mine. I'm not a bleeding chauffeur," he grumbled. "All right, missus. I'll do it this time, out of the goodness of my heart. Then you're on your own, eh." He stood up. "I'll get the Ford out and you be ready. I'm not hanging about while you spend hours primping.''

"Primping!" exclaimed Christine after he'd gone. She let her shoulders slump and rubbed the back of her neck wearily.

"Look," said Alice, "why don't we pack our things and bring them along? The laundry can go in a shopping bag. Then we wouldn't have to come back.''

Her mother straightened up. "I need my handbag. Alice, go along and tell him I'm coming, will you? At least tonight we can have proper baths.''

The double doors at the far end of the L-shaped building stood open. Kipper sat carelessly on one hip by the horse trough, grinning. Alice peered warily into the cavelike gloom and saw a pair of baggy trousers sticking out from under the bonnet of an elderly automobile. Mr. Tatlock seemed to be being devoured by a mechanical crocodile. The air was dark and oily and the cement floor was stained black with grease—or perhaps the blood of earlier victims. Perhaps that was what had actually happened to Mrs. Mofford—

There was a clank followed by an indistinct curse followed by an angry whirring noise. Red-faced, Mr. Tatlock emerged hastily from under the bonnet and slammed it so hard the Ford rocked on its tires. "Blasted machine!" he cried. "I hate them!''

"You have a motorbike," Alice pointed out.

"Too right." He scowled fiercely. "But just because I use them doesn't mean I like them." He wiped his black hands on his trousers.

"I thought there'd be horse stalls in here, and carriages." She frowned into the murk, disappointed. Looming beside the Ford was a much larger automobile, dark red, dully gleaming. "From the outside it looks like a stable."

"So? And the lodge looks like a bleeding fairy tale. He would've had it thatched could he find someone to do it. He was always making things out to be other than they were meant for. Where's that mother of yours? Said she was in such a hurry." He didn't wait for an answer, but levered himself into the front seat and fiddled with the dashboard, muttering to himself. The engine gave a sudden, startled roar, and the car shot forward six feet. Alice leaped nimbly clear of the door, but the car made a strangled sound and died in its tracks. "Damn and blast your eyes!" cried Mr. Tatlock in a fury.

By the time he'd bullied it into life again, Christine was waiting. She was wearing her good kid gloves and the little green felt hat she saved for best. "I'll drive you to the Octagon—that's the middle—and wait for you there," Mr. Tatlock told her. "I'm not messing about in traffic. If that's not good enough—"

"That will be fine, thank you," said Christine, bracing herself against the right rear door as they jounced and bucked along the driveway. There was a sudden great thump as the underside of the Ford made contact with the ground. "Shouldn't you try to avoid the ruts?" she asked. She and Alice were in the back; Kipper had the passenger's seat next to Mr. Tatlock. Christine had given him a hard look as she climbed in, but declined to comment.

"Like to see you try—it's *all* ruts," he retorted.

At the gates Alice got out and heaved one side open. There was just enough room for the Ford to scrape through. It obviously had before: there was a long scratch in the paint down its length. She had not quite gotten her door shut again when the Ford shot out onto the street, causing a red-haired boy on a bicycle to swerve into the curb, almost losing his balance. Alice fell back against the seat. Mr. Tatlock pounded the horn with his fist and yelled, "Whyn't you watch where you're going?"

The steering wheel gave him a lot of trouble; he wrestled it around corners, his fingers knotted and white. Each time he changed gears they made a furious gnashing sound, causing Alice to think of the crocodile, and evidently the brakes were effective only if he stamped on the pedal suddenly, with great force. Alice wedged her feet against the seat in front to keep from catapulting headfirst onto Kipper, who was having trouble keeping his own balance.

"See?" Mr. Tatlock shouted over his shoulder, pulling out to pass a green-and-white bus as it began to accelerate away from a stop. "That's the one I was telling you about. Take you right to the Octagon."

"Yes," said Christine, "I see." But Alice noticed that she had her eyes closed just then, and Mr. Tatlock had to wrench the wheel violently to keep the Ford from plowing into a delivery van on the opposite side of the street. Alice glimpsed the driver's startled face and heard Christine hiss softly.

Ordinary things lurched past: a woman with a pram, a cat asleep in the sun on a doorstep, a bright splash of red and yellow tulips, a postman taking letters out of a pillar-box. Normal, reassuring things. After the night at Florestan, Alice was relieved to find they still existed. The Ford swung right, its tires screeching on the asphalt, and plunged down a very steep hill. Alice remembered going up it, much more slowly, in the taxi. They sped to an abrupt, unambiguous stop at the bottom, where the Ford shuddered violently several times and stalled. Mr. Tatlock uttered a cry of rage. After three or four tries he jerked it awake and it shot out into the river of traffic flowing along a wide main street. Behind them Alice heard the squeal of brakes and the bleat of a horn. "He didn't look," muttered Christine through clenched teeth.

They proceeded erratically from traffic light to traffic light. Filled with dismay Alice stared out her window; the strangeness of Dunedin overwhelmed her. The buildings looked harsh and unlovely in the daylight; she knew she would never learn to like it, no matter how long they stayed.

The Octagon proved to be a round green space, like a bull's-eye, in the city's center. It was cut into quarters by two busy streets. Mr.

Tatlock swerved right, around the edge, and rammed the Ford into an open parking place, just beating out another, rather more cautious driver. The engine spluttered into indignant silence, and Christine leaned back and took a deep breath.

"Running a bit rough," observed Mr. Tatlock. "You'll need to get this husband of yours to take a look at it—*when* he gets here, that is." He settled down in his seat, tipped his head back and his hat over his eyes. With a grunt Kipper curled up on the seat beside him.

"I wonder if he did that on purpose," said Christine as she and Alice stood on the curb, waiting to cross the street. "I wouldn't put it past him."

"What?" said Alice, but the light changed and the traffic stopped, and Christine was off.

— 4 —

Murdoch, MacInnes & Holt

Number 17 Bath Street was a squat, unimpressive building, painted a dingy, flaking yellow. At street level it housed a shoe repair shop and a Citizen's Advice Bureau, its window screened from the street by faded orange curtains and an enormous philodendron that pushed hungrily against the glass. "This can't be right, can it?" said Alice dubiously, but Christine disappeared into a doorway at the far end. A narrow flight of stairs ended at a door with a frosted glass panel that said MURDOCH, MACINNES & HOLT, SOLICITORS in black-and-gold letters. Christine paused, peered at her face in the glass, brushed something off her right cheek, and gave Alice's coat a sharp twitch. "And for pity's sake, Alice, try not to fiddle with your hair."

Inside, through another door marked Enquiries was a reception area, its walls lined with volumes on the law. The carpet was dark red and the chairs looked suspiciously comfortable, as if meant for lengthy waits. Behind a desk a young woman with crimson lipstick and matching fingernails was typing with great speed, her eyes fixed on the pad propped beside her machine. Fascinated, Alice watched her turn the hieroglyphics into words. Without looking up she asked, "May I help you?"

"Yes," said Christine, pitching her voice above the clatter. "I have an appointment with Mr. MacInnes. I'm rather late—I'm afraid it was unavoidable. My name is Christine Jenkins."

The fingers froze on the keys, and the young woman swiveled in her chair. "Mrs. Jenkins! Of course. I'm sorry but Mr. MacInnes had to step out for a few minutes. He'll be back directly. He's asked me to look after you in the meantime. I'm Angie." She smiled, her mouth a wide red slash. Her hair reminded Alice of an old-fashioned leather pilot's helmet: short and smooth, a glossy brown. It curved forward symmetrically to a point on each cheek. Alice wondered if it tickled. "Do sit down, will you? Can I get you a cup of tea or coffee? Mind you," she added, lowering her voice confidentially, "it's not very good, the coffee. I'd have tea, if I were you. There are some biscuits—"

"Thank you. We'll just wait," said Christine. Alice regretted the biscuits; breakfast, such as it was, seemed far in the past, but she guessed it would be unwise to discuss it further with her mother. They sat in chairs on either side of the arched window overlooking the street, Christine very precise, her ankles crossed. Slowly she removed her gloves, finger by finger, then smoothed them across her knee. People came and went, the telephone rang, Angie returned to her typing between interruptions. Every now and then Alice caught her giving them a curious, sidelong look, in much the same way as the taxi driver had the night before. It filled her with a sense of foreboding. They seemed to know something that Alice and her mother did not, but ought to.

A craggy, silver-haired man with a leather attaché case came in, and Christine's hand stopped stroking her gloves, and Alice shifted expectantly. But Angie gave him her crimson smile and said, "Good morning, Mr. Saunders. I've put Palmer Shipping on your desk for you." "Ah, have you, Angie. Good girl." He disappeared through another door. With a sigh Alice settled back.

Angie started on her third sheet of paper. Christine glared at Alice, and Alice found that somehow, without her realizing it, her fingers had embedded themselves in her hair. Apologetically, she hastily unwound them and sat on them. Line after line accumulated on the page in Angie's machine. Just before she reached the bottom, a man came bounding in. He had a pink, boyish face and lots of springy ginger-colored hair, and he filled his brown suit like a well-stuffed sausage. "Hallo, Angie. What's up, eh? Anything for me?"

Angie nodded her head significantly in Christine's direction. "Mrs. Jenkins to see you, Mr. MacInnes."

He spun around suddenly and beamed. "Mrs. Jenkins! Well, well, we meet at last! What a pleasure this is!"

Christine rose, very much on her dignity, and took his outstretched hand. "Mr. MacInnes."

"Has Angie been looking after you? I am so sorry I wasn't here when you—" His eyes shifted to Alice. "And this is—?"

"My daughter, Alice."

"Your *daughter*—goodness me! I'd clean forgotten you had one. How careless of me! Here I'd been expecting Mr. Jenkins, not—Alice, is it? How do you do, Alice?"

Awkwardly Alice put out her hand and he pumped it up and down vigorously. The backs of his stubby fingers were covered with ginger fuzz, she noticed. "How do you do," she mumbled, feeling her mother's eyes bore into her.

"I do hope you haven't been waiting long, Mrs. Jenkins. A necessary errand, I'm afraid. I had to pop round to the Courts. Do come along to my office and make yourselves comfortable. I'm afraid it's a terrible muddle just now—I've been working on an estate and hardly had time to come up for air! You know how it is—deadlines! Right along there, that's it—here we are. Now—" He swept armfuls of papers off two chairs and dumped them onto a laden table. They fell like autumn leaves onto the flowered carpet. "Not to worry—Angie can sort them out later. Angie's an expert at sorting things out—wonderful girl! Do sit down.

Alice. I've a daughter about your age. She must be—what? fourteen or fifteen last birthday. I'm hopeless at keeping track—my wife's always after me—birthdays, anniversaries—her name's Margery. She's at school near you—Saint Katherine's. It's only a street or two down from Florestan. An excellent school, by the by, Mrs. Jenkins—not too big, you know. Good reputation. You'll be looking into schools, I expect?''

Alice curled up inside. School implied permanency. It meant having to start from the very beginning with a whole crowd of strangers, feeling your way to safety through shoals of unknown dangers, learning the rules written and unwritten, starting at the bottom of the heap. She'd had to do it when she was seven and her mother had gotten her into Woodhall, but then she'd figured she'd never have to go through it again. Shuddering, she heard her mother say, "Yes, of course, Mr. MacInnes, but—"

And Mr. MacInnes: "No buts at all then! I'd be delighted to put in a word for you—truly. I'm on the board of governors, for my sins. The last term of the year's just started, but it wouldn't hurt to go along and see what's what, would it, Alice. Give you a leg up on next year. I'll just make a note to ring Mrs. Sinclair—she's the headmistress—a rather formidable lady, I might say, but first-rate.'' He shuffled the papers on his desk and wrote a few words on one. "That's settled!'' He gave Christine a pleased smile. "Now, where shall we start, Mrs. Jenkins?''

"I think we'd better begin with the house, Mr. MacInnes, if you don't mind. It's not quite what I'd been led to expect.''

"Oh, yes indeed! I know just what you mean—it's overwhelming, isn't it? Nothing like it in New Zealand. Extraordinary! I remember the first time my father took me there with him—he handled the Fairchild affairs until he retired. Mr. Fairchild knew exactly what he wanted and he spared no expense to have it—bringing an architect all the way from England. And not just any architect, mind you, he had to have the most distinguished. I know for a fact that Edwin Lutyens never designed another house in New Zealand. Then Mr. Fairchild filled it with treasures from all over the world—he was a brilliant collector, C. R. Fairchild. Do you know Florestan has the finest billiard table in the country? They used to hold championship tournaments—''

"It isn't the billiard table I want to talk about,'' interposed Christine firmly. "From your letters, and Miss Fairchild's to me in Cambridge, I had the impression that there was a domestic staff looking after the house. But when we arrived yesterday evening—''

"Oh, my dear Mrs. Jenkins! I am so sorry. Please accept my apologies. I did pop round to see Arthur Tatlock after you rang me from Auckland. I told him when you'd be coming and asked him to have things ready for you. Don't tell me he wasn't there? How awful for you!''

"Actually he was there, but—''

"Ah. You found him a bit gruff, I suppose. He can be rather difficult. I hadn't been up to see him in some time—I've had a lot on my plate recently. But then that's it, isn't it? We're none of us getting any younger, and he must be in his seventies by now. Been at Florestan since before I was born. C. R. must have hired him nearly forty years ago.'' He shook his head in amazement. "He moved into the lodge after Mr. Fairchild's death. My father advised Miss Emilia on that— better to have someone living there than have it stand empty. It would be more convenient if he had a telephone, of course, but he simply refuses. Won't have it. Says it's a modern inconvenience. He keeps an eye on things when she goes off on one of these expeditions of hers. I asked Arthur to lay in a few groceries—to tide you over just until you could find your way around. He said he would—?'' He gave Christine a hopeful look.

Alice waited for her mother to tell him exactly what sort of groceries Mr. Tatlock had laid in for them, but she didn't. Instead, she said, "That's the entire staff then? Mr. Tatlock and the housekeeper you wrote me about? Mrs. Mofford, I believe her name is?''

"Well, of course there *used* to be lots of servants, when all the family lived in the house—a cook, parlormaids, even a proper English butler called Simpson. He used to terrify me when I was a lad—he was immensely tall and always had a drop on the end of his nose. I believe Mr. Fairchild had a valet, too, at one time. More servants than Fairchilds, my father used to say.'' He chuckled. ''Oh, it was very grand. I wish you could have seen it then.''

Alice tried to imagine how it would feel to be outnumbered by your servants. It would mean never having to make your own bed, lay the table, or wash up after meals. . . .

''I'm interested in *now*, Mr. MacInnes.''

''Now?'' He blinked. ''Oh, now there's only Miss Emilia, and she will keep going off to remote parts of the world—'' He sounded rather annoyed.

This is a remote part of the world, thought Alice.

''I did warn her about Mrs. Mofford—not a good idea to leave a woman of her temperament alone in a house like Florestan. It's such a responsibility.''

''Was there something the matter with her?'' Christine frowned.

''Her nerves weren't good—she had quite a fondness for port, if you see what I mean,'' he said with a glance at Alice, who saw quite well that she wasn't supposed to understand. But she had helped shift all those crates of bottles out of the pantry. ''And there were the cats. One for company, what's the harm in that? But she must have had nine or ten. And when Miss Emilia was away, she'd give them the run of the house—they were quite destructive. I thought she'd gotten rid of them after the last row, but apparently she hadn't. Arthur Tatlock informed me—''

''That's the smell!'' exclaimed Alice. ''Cats. It's like Mrs. Hollings's back entry, only multiplied by ten.''

''Mrs. Hollings?'' Mr. MacInnes raised his eyebrows in inquiry.

''Never mind,'' said Christine with a quelling look at Alice.

''She didn't even give notice. She simply left. It was unfortunate, but there was absolutely nothing I could do. She went just about the time you sailed—I had no way of letting you know. I did try to find someone to go in and do a bit of cleaning—hoover a few rooms, dust a bit, make up a bed for you—but it's impossible these days. You simply cannot find girls willing to do that sort of work. I don't know what they expect—and by the time you rang from Auckland—well, you'd already come so far, I couldn't see the point in worrying you with domestic problems before you'd even set foot in the house. I'd only just had the telegram from Miss Emilia about her change in plan—" He spread his hands apologetically, his forehead pleated like a venetian blind. "I thought the best thing would be for you to come straight on and take charge. I felt sure you'd soon have everything under control, Mrs. Jenkins. You didn't by any chance see Dr. Inchcape's letter of recommendation, did you? Well, let me tell you, it was impressive. He simply raved about your common sense and organizational skills— truly! He said you were wonderfully efficient and capable."

"That's all very well, Mr. MacInnes," said Christine, "but he was not recommending me as a housekeeper. You must understand that I haven't come all the way from England to replace Mrs. Mofford. I've been hired to assist Miss Fairchild with her history of Florestan, and I don't think—"

"Oh, my dear Mrs. Jenkins, I do realize that! Of course I do. But this is something of an emergency—you do see that? You're my angel of salvation!" He beamed at her. "If Miss Emilia ever actually gets around to—I mean, of course, *when* she begins work, your help will be invaluable, I know it will. In the meantime, well, it's all hands to the pumps, in a manner of speaking! Not that the ship's really *sinking*—"

"I hope not," said Christine. She did not answer his smile. "Do you know when we can expect Miss Fairchild?"

"As a matter of fact—" He turned and stared hard at a calendar hanging on the wall beside his desk. On it was a photograph of the new Auckland Harbor Bridge, which Alice recognized because they had sailed under it into port. "As a matter of fact, I really don't. I've only had the one telegram and that wasn't at all specific. She's inclined to be a bit—self-willed, you could say. *You* must know, I'm sure."

"I'm afraid I don't. You have the advantage, Mr. MacInnes—I've never met Miss Fairchild."

"Mmm." He chewed his lower lip thoughtfully. "She's actually quite a character. Between the two of us, Mrs. Jenkins, I'm really not that surprised by this turn of events. She's far too old to go gallivanting off to the far corners of the globe by herself this way. Suppose she'd actually *died* in Borneo, eh? Just thinking about the complications turns my hair gray! She says she has to travel to paint flowers, but that's nonsense. She could paint flowers perfectly well at the botanic gardens here in Dunedin. *I* can't tell her that, naturally, I'm only her solicitor. But her nephew, Clem, now—you'd think being family, she'd listen to him." He shook his head disparagingly.

"Does he live in Dunedin? Miss Fairchild never mentioned relatives in her letters."

"Clem? He has a house in Port Chalmers. He runs the family brewery, Armstrong and Fairchild. His mother and sister left Dunedin—oh, it must be ten years ago now. They went back to Australia—Mrs. Fairchild still has family there. They haven't spoken in years, Miss Emilia and her brother's widow—no love lost between them. If there's one thing I've learned about the Fairchilds, it's that they're stubborn. You *could* say intransigent." Changing the subject abruptly, he said, "I'm sorry that Mr. Jenkins wasn't able to travel out with you. I trust he's not far behind. You must have found it difficult coming all this way alone."

"I wasn't alone, Mr. MacInnes. Alice was with me, and we had quite a pleasant voyage, didn't we?" Alice nodded in agreement. It had been so pleasant, in fact, that she was ready to repeat it in the other direction as soon as possible. But her mother went on: "Now if you don't mind, Mr. MacInnes, I've got a list of questions I must have answers to—about the house and Miss Fairchild's business accounts—" She took a small notebook out of her handbag.

"Dr. Inchcape was certainly spot on!" he said with a laugh. "Fire away, Mrs. Jenkins."

Twenty minutes later they were finished. Christine had ticked off everything on her list and written down the information Mr. MacInnes gave her. He saw them to the door at the top of the stairs, saying regretfully that he'd have been delighted to take them to lunch, but he had an urgent appointment. Perhaps next time—? The word *lunch* gave Alice a sudden sharp pain. "I hope you're finding Dunedin to your liking, Mrs. Jenkins. It's the friendliest city in New Zealand—no question. Of course, you could say I'm biased, but I'm always happy to get home after I've been to Wellington or Auckland. We're not as modern down here perhaps, a little slower—but I like that. Do remember—anything I can do for you, don't hesitate to pop round and let me know, or give me a ring. And as soon as I have word from Miss Emilia, I'll let you know." With a wave of the hand he was gone, loping back toward his office. Christine stood looking after him for a minute. "Hmmm," she said, and started down the stairs.

— 5 —

A Mistake?

At the central post office they stood in line behind two women involved in a discussion of interior decoration. Would tangerine accents pick up a primrose room, or would lettuce green be better? Food again, thought Alice glumly, fidgeting from foot to foot. The clerk at the counter, a young woman with her cardigan buttoned up wrong, favored the lettuce herself. She didn't care for orange in a room, it wasn't restful. Alice could feel the impatience rising in her mother like steam in a kettle coming to the boil, but she held the lid down. When the two women finally left, nothing decided, the clerk went to check for letters. She returned empty-handed. "Sorry, love, there's nothing for you today."

"Are you quite sure?" said Christine in a sharpish tone. "Handwriting can be difficult to read."

Especially Len's, thought Alice, picturing his lumpy, wandering letters.

"Isn't that the truth," agreed the clerk, nodding. "Here, I'll have another look, if you like. Just to be sure. Wouldn't want you to miss your letter. You did say Jenkins, love?" This time she brought back a sheaf of letters and sorted through them while Christine watched. "Jones, Jablonski—from New Jersey, that one a place called Hoboken. Isn't that odd? That's in the States—" Christine tapped the counter with her fingers and the clerk went back to sorting. "Jackman, Kelly well, that doesn't belong here, does it? Jorkin—"

"May I see that one?" Christine practically snatched it from her. Alice held her breath. But the handwriting on the envelope was the model of clarity: "Mr. Peter Jorkin," it said, and there was a New Zealand stamp in the corner.

"Sorry," said the clerk, taking it back. "That's it for now. You could try again this afternoon—it might be in the next post. Here on holiday, are you?"

"No," said Christine shortly. "Business. We must get back to Mr. Tatlock, Alice."

But outside the post office she hesitated, glancing up and down the street as if not sure where to go next. Taking advantage of her mother's indecision, Alice suggested lunch.

Christine shook herself. "We'll buy a few things to take back with us now, and I'll ring the shops with proper orders this afternoon," she decided. "According to Mr. MacInnes, they deliver. They probably charge the earth for it, too, but that can't be helped."

"I'm very hungry," said Alice. "I might faint on the street."

"I'll have to chance that," said Christine.

Alice sighed. When her mother had her mind fixed on something, she disregarded details that other people considered essential, like being tired or hungry or uncomfortable. Alice had known her to go all day without stopping for meals if she was concentrating, and she had little patience with Alice and Len, both of whom liked to eat at regular intervals. Part of it was metabolism. In spite of everything they ate, Len always looked undernourished, and Alice was almost always hungry. For her, hunger was like a faint but irritating itch in a place she couldn't reach. Like Len, she never got fat—they joked about her taking after the Jenkins side of the family, and Christine would give them sour looks. She complained that she had only to pass a bakery to gain weight.

Christine took a string bag out of her purse, and on the way back to the Octagon they filled it with groceries. Alice found herself left to make most of the choices; her mother seemed oddly withdrawn, ignoring the pleasantries offered to her by shop clerks. She didn't even seem to hear them. She paid automatically while Alice nodded awkwardly and answered "Yes" and "No" and "Thank you very much, I'm sure we will." At the greengrocer's Christine actually forgot to wait for her change, and a stubble-headed boy in an enormous apron had to come flapping after them with a handful of coins. Without counting them, she dumped them into her coin purse, saying an abrupt thank-you.

By the time they reached the Octagon, Alice was feeling decidedly uneasy. Her mother's preoccupation must have to do with Len. There should have been a letter from him—something to tell them he knew where they were, and was on his way to find them, reassuring Alice that she and her mother hadn't vanished off the face of the earth after all, as she had begun to fear they must have. When she thought about Len, she found it alarmingly impossible to place him in the vast distance that separated them.

"*Now* what? Where can that man possibly have got to?" exclaimed Christine, shattering Alice's thoughts. Alice was about to remind her that it was she who'd left Len behind, not the other way around, when she realized that Christine wasn't referring to Len at all. They were back again where they'd left Mr. Tatlock. Alice remembered the statue of Robert Burns—he still had a gull on his head—and there was the Ford, its front tires hard against the curb—

"That dreadful person! *Blast* him!" This was as close as Christine came to swearing; when she blasted something or someone, Alice knew she was truly angry. Mr. Tatlock was not in the Ford. Alone in the passenger seat Kipper sat up alertly, ears cocked, watching them with bright, suspicious eyes.

"Well," said Alice, glancing around, "he probably hasn't gone far—"

"He said he'd wait. That's what he told me—Alice, you heard him," Christine cut in, her voice oddly brittle. Turning to look at her, Alice saw she'd gone pale: the scatter of imperceptible freckles across her nose stood out startlingly. The last time Alice had seen them was during the storm in the Indian Ocean, which had felled all but the heartiest passengers, like Mrs. Royde—and, surprisingly, Alice herself. They had been kept busy ministering to the wretched with basins and damp towels, seasick pills, and bouillon. But now the sun was shining, the ground was firm underfoot, the horizon held steady.

"We've been gone quite a while, Mum. Perhaps he thought we'd gotten lost and went to look for us?" On the whole unlikely, but she tried to sound grown-up and calm.

"But I don't drive. He knows that. We can't get back without him."

"We only have to wait—he won't have left his dog. We can sit in the car." Alice felt a twinge of fear. Her mother's eyes were dark and unfocused in the pallor of her face. What was she talking about? Only last night they'd taken a taxi up from the station, and Mr. Tatlock himself had mentioned a bus. All around them people spoke English. It sounded a bit strange, but it was English. They weren't stranded, alone and helpless in the wilderness— She put her hand on the door and Kipper leaped up and began to bark, displaying a great many teeth. "Oh, shut up!" Alice wanted to smack him. Her mother stood still, fingers clenched on her handbag. In desperation Alice said, "Why don't I go look for him, Mum? You can stay here in case he comes—"

"No!" The word was sharp as broken glass. It startled them both. Christine let out her breath and said in a tight voice, "You'll only get lost yourself. You don't know this city—neither of us does. He could be anywhere. We'll simply have to wait for him—it's the only thing." Going over to an empty bench, she lowered herself carefully onto it, still gripping her handbag as if she expected someone to come along and try to wrench it from her. "I don't know what possessed me," she muttered, not to Alice. "He was so enthusiastic, so convincing—I'd be sorry for the rest of my life if I didn't—" She closed her eyes and shook her head. "Nothing's gone the way it was supposed to. I don't know what to do."

Twisting and twisting her hair, Alice sat down, too. Her knees felt shaky. The sudden emptiness in her stomach had nothing to do with hunger. It was a return of the panic she had felt on the train, when she'd looked at her mother and seen a stranger. It was one thing for Alice to believe her mother had made a mistake in bringing them here; if her *mother* believed it, they were lost. She was the one who always knew how to take care of everything.

Pigeons waddled and pecked on a patch of bare earth, muttering deep in their throats; traffic churned past; two men walked by, arguing, and a limp-looking woman with a baby straddling her hip. A crowd of young people jostled along the pavement, laughing and chattering, looking for all the world like Cambridge undergraduates. Flooded with homesickness, Alice felt her eyes blur.

She blinked to clear them, and saw Mr. Tatlock. Relief made her giddy. He was stumping stiff-legged toward them, across the street, unmistakable in his squashed hat and baggy trousers. He paused at the corner and looked in their direction, then quickly away, and ran a furtive hand over his chin. "Look, Mum—there he is. There's Mr. Tatlock."

Alice's mother was staring fixedly at Robert Burns's feet. After a moment she wrenched her head around and stood up. Alice waited for the explosion, but there was none. All she said was, "We've been waiting for you."

"Had an errand myself, as it turned out," Mr. Tatlock replied. Not meeting her eyes, he climbed into the Ford. Kipper thumped the seat with his tail and lay down, his forepaws draped carelessly over the edge. He made no objection to Alice and Christine now that Mr. Tatlock was back. Once inside, Alice was aware of the mingled smells of cigarette smoke and the warm, yeasty aroma that Len always brought home with him from a pub. "Find what you wanted, did you?" Mr. Tatlock inquired as the engine gave an indignant yelp and ground its metal teeth.

"Yes," said Alice when her mother didn't answer. All the way back to Florestan Christine sat in silence, staring out the window, oblivious of the jolts and squeals and the blat of horns. In the courtyard she left Mr. Tatlock without a word. He scowled after her, and Alice heard him say crossly, "Thanks very much, I'm sure!" as she hurried after her mother.

Christine was standing at the sink, drying her face with a tea towel. She hung it up and smoothed her hair before unpacking the string bag, item by item, frowning at each as if she couldn't think how it had gotten there. "Mr. Tatlock?" she asked, without looking at Alice.

"He's gone."

Christine nodded. "At least he's got the boiler started, that's the important thing." Her voice sounded almost normal. "I don't think we need bother him any further today. Alice, why on earth did we buy three packets of biscuits *and* a Swiss roll?"

As they sat down to a late, scrappy lunch, Christine began making shopping lists. "You must order whatever you need, Mrs. Jenkins, by all means," Mr. MacInnes had said. "I'll leave that entirely in your capable hands. You ladies know much more about that kind of thing— I'd only have gotten it all wrong if I'd tried to do it for you. My wife says I'm hopeless." He'd given her the names of the merchants with whom Miss Fairchild had accounts. "If there's any question, just ask them to give me a ring—I'll set them straight."

Watching her mother, Alice discovered her appetite had disappeared; the cheese was sour and dry in her mouth, and the sausage roll made her slightly ill. She wanted to ask what had happened down at the Octagon, and what her mother meant to do about it.

"Bread," said Christine, as if it hadn't happened at all. "Two loaves, I think. Would you rather marmalade or jam, Alice? And more tea— hot chocolate for you. It's not very satisfactory not being able to see what the choice is, but this should keep us for a few days. Next week I'll go down and visit the shops myself."

"Next week?" echoed Alice thinly.

"There wasn't time this morning—not with Mr. Tatlock waiting for us—or so I thought." Her pencil hovered, then struck.

"Mum—"

"Sugar and milk, of course. I must see about getting the milkman to stop. For now I'm afraid we'll have to rely on things we can heat up in a skillet or a saucepan: eggs, bacon, porridge, soup, tinned stew, spaghetti—" The list grew. Pausing, she glared in annoyance at the enormous kitchen range standing impassive behind Alice. "Len's auntie Millie used to have one of those stoves—nothing like so complicated, of course. I'm not messing about with it. He can have the pleasure himself when he gets here."

Taking a deep breath, Alice said, "But there wasn't a letter."

Christine looked up and frowned. "What do you mean?"

"He ought to have written. You thought there'd be a letter at the post office. Was that why—"

"I hoped there would be, yes. And I'm surprised Gillian hasn't written—she promised she would. Actually, she's far more likely to than your stepfather, Alice. You know as well as I do how bad he is about letters."

It was true, Alice acknowledged to herself, her mother's friend Gillian was unquestionably more reliable than Len, but aloud she said, "He sent that postcard from Dover. Maybe he hasn't written because he's not coming. Is that what you think? Is that why you were so upset?"

Christine put down her pencil and gave Alice a long, level look. "I've known Len since I was younger than you are now, Alice. It may take him awhile to get here, but he'll come. You'll see. As for the other, I'm tired. We're both tired. We've come a very long way to a strange place. It takes time to adjust, that's all."

I don't *want* to adjust, thought Alice in panic. I just want to go home.

"You said you'd made a mistake—"

Christine shook her head. "No, I don't think so. You must have misheard me, Alice. Now, shall I chance ordering a piece of fish, do you think? I suppose chops might be safer, sight unseen. . . ."

Studying her face, Alice saw that the freckles had disappeared and the color had come back to her cheeks; her eyes had lost their frightening blankness. She'd become her normal, competent self again. Whatever had caused her to stumble, she wasn't going to talk about it.

They had hot baths that night, and got into bed in clean nightclothes, between sheets that had aired that afternoon in the sun, spread across a couple of bushes beside the long, flagstoned terrace. It was an improvement, and it helped a little to have seen by daylight where they were, but Alice did not like the house any better than she had at first and did not sleep very well. In the morning her mother complained that sharing a bed with Alice was as bad as being tossed about by the Indian Ocean. "Perhaps we ought to have separate rooms," she said. "Heaven knows there are enough in this house so that we needn't continue to share a bed."

"Oh, I don't think so," protested Alice in dismay. "I mean, I think it's better to stay together since we're here alone. In case one of us gets ill in the middle of the night, or something."

"Hmmm," said Christine, but dropped the subject, to Alice's relief.

After breakfast they toured the house, from the dank, shadowy cellar where the boiler with its single burning eye squatted like a cyclops, to the bare, drafty room in the tower at the top of the house. The steps up to it were drifted with dead flies that scrunched revoltingly underfoot. They spoke very little. Alice watched her mother, trying to guess what was going on in her head, behind the considering, impenetrable expression. She was disturbed to find she hadn't a clue.

Everywhere Florestan showed signs of neglect and decay, like a mouthful of bad teeth. On the ground floor all the carpets were rolled up, the chairs and sofas shrouded in dust sheets, the heavy drapes pulled tight against the daylight. The reason so many of the light switches didn't work was that the fixtures were empty; someone had removed most of the bulbs. In the dining room the single dim electric light revealed a long, formal dining table fenced with straight-backed chairs and piled high with mounds of yellowing newspapers, periodicals, and catalogs, many still in their brown wrappers. There were heaps of letters, lists, receipts. Suspended from the center of the ceiling was an enormous chandelier that seemed, in the bad light, to be clogged with cobwebs. Alice shuddered.

Behind another door was a brown room: walls, floor, bookshelves, drapes, desk, leather armchairs—everything was brown, even the air, which was heavy with ancient cigar smoke and moldering leather. In the large drawing room Alice wrote her name in the dust on the lid of the grand piano. As soon as she'd done it, she was sorry. There it was, in capital letters: ALICE JENKINS, as plain as if she'd signed it in a guest book. Hastily she rubbed it out with the heel of her hand. Her mother caught her at it and frowned.

They found the billiard table Mr. MacInnes had spoken of so proudly. It stood in the middle of another tobacco-smelling room, on the second floor. The walls here were covered with crimson flocked wallpaper, racks of billiard cues, and sporting prints, including one huge painting of a fine-boned, fiery-eyed chestnut horse posed against a turbulent sky. The table itself was hidden under a fitted cover of heavy, dark material. Christine did not linger; she pulled Alice out and closed the door firmly.

The rest of the rooms opening off the balconies were either bedrooms or bathrooms. The grandest bedroom had its own suite of dressing rooms and bath, and a balcony with French doors. Water had seeped in around them: the wallpaper on either side was discolored and scabby, and there was an ominous stain creeping across the moss green carpet. The mirrors were clouded and flyblown, the clocks—there were dozens of them, all shapes and sizes—had stopped at different times, and dust lay thick everywhere. In the bathrooms the washbasins and tubs were streaked with rust and the old-fashioned fixtures had turned dull green. The hot water burped and spat and ran the color of stewed tea before settling to a scalding trickle. In one WC, the cistern above the toilet had cracked and leaked water down the wall, making a mess on the tiled floor.

At the far end of the opposite balcony they found an odd little room that looked like a nursery, with a high, narrow bed and white painted furniture, a well-worn rag rug on the floor. The bookcase was full of old children's books—*Treasure Island, Kim, Robinson Crusoe, Swiss Family Robinson, Five Children and It, The Magic Pudding*—much read, by the look of them, and a collection of battered paperback murder mysteries. "Whose room is this?" asked Alice curiously. "There aren't any children, are there?" It was the only room they'd come to that actually felt lived-in to her. Christine shook her head. "Miss Fairchild doesn't like children—she's made that clear in her letters." "Then what about me?" Alice said. "I wonder what's in here," said Christine, rattling the handle of the door beside the bed. It was locked. So was the next door off the balcony. Alice wondered what awful secret lay inside.

The crowning horror, however, was the little sitting room under the main staircase, just off the great hall. The stench of cat was overwhelming, thick and nasty, like half-set jelly. A swollen sofa and two bloated easy chairs filled the small space; the arms of all of them were shredded and bits of stuffing oozed out. Just beyond the two windows, dark, stiff green leaves clawed at the glass, as if trying to get in, blocking the light. Alice couldn't tell at first what object sat under the large bell jar on the table in front of the sofa. As her eyes accustomed themselves to the gloom, she could make out an animal with upright, triangular ears, and long, pale whiskers, a fluffy tail wound over its toes. It sat on its haunches, one paw raised. She stared, transfixed. "Oh, Mum, it's a cat," she said faintly. Her mother said nothing at all; she marched across the room and wrestled one of the windows open. The hinges gave an agonized metallic shriek.

They spent the rest of the day cleaning the kitchen: sweeping and scrubbing and scouring, turning out the pantry, investigating the cupboards. There was a strong room off the pantry, with an impressive lock. When Christine found the key on a hook under one of the shelves, what they discovered inside made Alice think of Ali Baba. Ranked floor to ceiling was a vast array of crystal and silver: goblets, serving trays, compotes, decanters, candelabra, punch bowls, ladles, fruit baskets, cruets, coffee services. The effect would have been dazzling if all the silver had not been blackened with tarnish and the glass filmed with gray. "Well," said Christine finally. "I shouldn't have thought it wise to leave all this in an empty house. I wonder if Mr. MacInnes knows it's here."

"The house wasn't supposed to be empty," Alice pointed out. "What do you suppose this is for?"

"Heaven knows. Put it back and come out so I can lock up again."

In one cupboard Christine discovered a cache of odd saucers so crusted with dried cat food she didn't even attempt to clean them. She simply threw them into the trashbin. "On the whole," she said consideringly, "I'm just as glad that Mrs. Mofford's gone. I doubt that we'd have gotten along at all."

By the time the afternoon light was fading and dusk had settled into the kitchen, they were both tired and grubby, but Christine was satisfied that the room was at least habitable. The air was chilly because she'd had the door and windows open for hours, and the tabletop was still damp from repeated scrubbings, but everything smelled of soap, and the floor no longer felt gritty. The trashbin was so full the lid wouldn't stay on, and beside the cartons of bottles there were half a dozen bulging bags of rubbish. Christine made a pot of tea, and Alice opened the Swiss roll as a reward for all her labors. The vanilla cream oozed out of the chocolate sponge cake as she cut herself a generous slice. Sitting across from her mother, licking her fingers, she said, "Admit it, Mum. You didn't think it would be like this at all, did you?"

Christine rummaged in her handbag for her cigarettes, took one, and sat back, crossing her legs. The first match she tried broke; the second had to be struck four times before it flared, but her hand was quite steady as she held it. She shook it out, inhaled deeply, and gave a little cough. For a minute she sat watching the smoke unravel, then she said,

"Dr. Inchcape told me that Florestan was an extraordinary house. He said there wasn't another like it in the Southern Hemisphere, so far as he knew. Of course it's years since he was here himself—that was before the last war, when Mr. Fairchild was alive. If I'd thought—it was bound to have changed." She was talking as much to herself as to Alice, thinking out loud. "He'd always meant to come back, he said, but somehow he never found the time. He got involved in the architectural histories. He was very excited when Miss Fairchild wrote to him, proposing a book about the house and asking his advice on an assistant to help her. He said he thought of me at once—I'd always regret it if I didn't take the job, he told me."

"It seems to me Dr. Inchcape has a lot to answer for," declared Alice. She'd always been rather afraid of him. Her mother had been doing typing and research for him for several years, outside of office hours. Dr. Inchcape was a highly respected don, engaged in writing an endless series of books about the architectural history of England. He was tall and stoop-shouldered, with fierce, jutting eyebrows and a great beak of a nose.

"No, it's Mr. MacInnes, I think. He's not been entirely straight with me," Christine said thoughtfully. Her distant gaze suddenly focused. "Alice, do stop twisting your hair like that. It wants trimming, doesn't it? That's something else we must do."

Sunday was fine and mild. Expecting another day of drudgery, Alice was pleasantly surprised when her mother laid aside her lists and declared herself disinclined to clean anything. Instead, she suggested exploring Dunedin. "We must begin to learn our way around the city, don't you think?" "Oh, yes," said Alice, only too happy to get away from Florestan. They made their way by bus down to the botanic gardens Mr. MacInnes had spoken of, and strolled among the crowds, admiring the gaudy displays of tulips and flowering fruit trees. Christine even agreed to having tea at the kiosk, although she was critical of the currant scones. "Too heavy," she pronounced, picking at one while Alice gratefully consumed the rest, not minding a bit about their heaviness. A brass band played nearby, instruments gleaming—marches and songs from operettas—while children tumbled on the fresh grass and chased one other, and their mothers and fathers watched indulgently, talking and enjoying the sunshine. Couples promenaded hand in hand, or arm in arm. Alice found she could almost forget she was a world away from where she wanted to be, the park looked so peaceful and ordinary.

They walked back to Florestan, detouring through the university grounds. It looked very new and unprepossessing to Alice's critical eyes. A shallow, unimpressive trickle of water ran through it, trapped between high cement walls, not like the Cam with its graceful bridges and soft green banks. When she expressed her opinion that the red-and-white Victorian clock tower looked more like an inferior railway station than a university building, her mother replied crisply that Dr. Inchcape said the University of Otago was a very good university indeed. "You mustn't close your mind, Alice. Cambridge isn't the center of the universe."

Shocked by this betrayal, Alice lapsed into silence. Her father—her real father, not Len—had been a fellow of Clare College, with a promising career ahead of him. Until the war had cut it short. Her mother had hungered for a Cambridge education, and been denied it by circumstances outside her control. All her life Alice had heard the virtues of Cambridge extolled. It was understood that she would one day be an undergraduate there; she would take the place her father had prematurely vacated; she would distinguish herself as he had begun to, and as her mother had not been allowed to. Now here was her mother suddenly throwing that all away.

— 6 —

A Telegram and a Letter

Monday morning, as they were getting breakfast, a deep, melancholy *bonggg* suddenly reverberated through the house. Alice dropped the plate she was about to put on the table, and Christine splattered herself with boiling water as she filled the teapot. " 'Strewth!" she exclaimed. "Alice, do be more careful, will you?"

"What was it?"

Christine ran cold water on her fingers. "It sounds like the front doorbell."

"But—" There was another *bonggg*. "Who could it possibly be?"

"I won't know that until I've gone to see, will I?" She wiped her hands on her apron, took it off, and straightened her skirt. Alice listened to her firm footsteps cross the bare floor of the great hall, then there was silence. Suppose it was a tramp? Or a suspicious character come to have a look around, to find out who was in the house? She thought of the little room full of crystal and silver, the gilt-framed paintings, the ornamental clocks, the glass-fronted cabinets full of treasures—suppose her mother didn't come back? How long should she wait and what should she do? There was the telephone in the hallway—she could call for help, but it would be ages before anyone came. She thought of Mr. Tatlock—he had that dog—but even supposing she could find him, she doubted he'd be much use in an emergency.

But suddenly her mother was back, with a yellow envelope in her hand. She put it down beside her plate.

"Who was it?" Alice was frantic with curiosity.

"Telegram."

"And?" prompted Alice. "Telegram for who? Not us—no one knows we're here, except—" She felt an explosion of hope. "Is it from Len? It is, isn't it, Mum?"

"No, it's nothing to do with Len. It's from Miss Fairchild. She's arrived in Auckland and she expects to be here on Thursday. Fetch the milk, will you? After breakfast—"

"Thursday? *This* Thursday? That's only—I mean, I thought she wasn't—"

"Alice, do stop nattering and eat your egg. I need to think. As soon as we've finished, I shall ring Mr. MacInnes, and I want you to go and find Mr. Tatlock."

"Oh, no," said Alice. "Not again. What do you want him for?" They hadn't laid eyes on him for two days, and Alice wasn't sorry.

"He works for Miss Fairchild. There's a lot to be done, and he can jolly well make himself useful."

Alice sighed. "Oh, all right. Is she very ill? Does it say? Perhaps she'll have to go to hospital instead of coming here." A new idea occurred to her. "It may be months before she's well enough to work on her book, have you thought? There won't be any point in our staying on here. That's what you came for, after all. . . ." She stopped, catching her mother's eye, and busied herself with the lump of cold, rubbery egg on her plate.

Mr. Tatlock was not in his garden, although it seemed a good morning for it: cool and overcast but dry. The motorbike was propped under its tree, covered with an old tarp, so unless he was off tending his make-believe sheep, Alice was afraid he must be home. She had left her mother talking to Angie at Murdoch, MacInnes & Holt; Mr. MacInnes, it appeared, was not in yet and might not be until afternoon. Christine did not look happy.

There were no signs of life at the cottage, no movement behind the windows, no smoke from the chimney; eyeing it, Alice considered going back to tell her mother she'd been unable to find him, but at that moment Kipper began to bark inside. There was neither a bell nor a knocker that she could see, so she rapped on the front door with her knuckles. The barking got louder, sounded just the other side of the wood, but nothing else happened. She pounded with her hand. "Mr. Tatlock? Mr. Tatlock!" Still no answer. She tried to peer in one of the windows, but only got her cardigan snagged on rose thorns; the room beyond was dark, and she couldn't get close enough to see past her own reflection.

He was not in any of the lean-tos around back. Alice tried thumping on the kitchen door. She heard Kipper come bounding through the cottage from front to back, still barking. It suddenly occurred to her that something might have happened to Mr. Tatlock—he was an old man. He could have had a heart attack, or fallen down the stairs. Perhaps that's why they hadn't seen him all weekend? Suppose he was lying unconscious—even dead—and Kipper was trying to tell her? She put her hand on the knob, preparing herself for the grisly worst, when without warning the door jerked open and she almost fell across the threshold.

"Well?" barked Mr. Tatlock, sounding fiercer than his dog. "What d'you want?" His eyes were screwed up against the light and his face was gray with stubble. There was something odd about his mouth. He was wearing a long-sleeved undershirt and his suspenders hung in loops from the top of his sagging trousers.

"You shouldn't do that!" gasped Alice, her heart like a cork in her throat. She caught her breath. "Why didn't you answer me before?"

"Thought you'd take the hint and go away. Well? What'd you come for? House on fire?"

"It would have burned to the ground by this time," Alice retorted. "Mum wants you."

He nodded. "Guessed as much. I knew she'd be trouble, soon's I heard she was coming. Just you go back and tell her she can bleeding well take the bus this time. I got better things to do with my time."

Kipper thrust his black-and-tan head around the door and gave Alice's hand a lick, then cocked his head and grinned up at her. Mr. Tatlock scowled at the dog. "What d'you think you're doing, eh?" Kipper wagged his tail.

"How do you know that's what she wants?" Alice wiped her fingers on her skirt.

He grunted. "Go tell her I'm poorly."

Alice was looking with disapproval past him, her eyes growing accustomed to the dimness beyond. She could see a table covered with oilcloth, and a cluster of brown bottles—there was a crate of them by the door—and a cooker with a kettle and a blackened skillet on it. The air was greasy with the smell of fried potatoes. "No, I won't," said Alice unsympathetically. "You can tell her yourself, when she comes looking for you. She's not in a very good mood, either."

"Nor me, you tell her. She's got no right to bother me—I don't work for her."

"You work for Miss Fairchild, though."

"What of it?"

"She's coming back."

He shrugged. "She lives here."

"Thursday."

He thought about that for a minute, sucking his gums. Slowly he pulled up his suspenders, hunching his shoulders under them. "How'd you know that?"

"We got a telegram this morning," said Alice smugly. One up to her.

His hand made a rasping sound as he rubbed his pouchy face. Then before she could object, he stepped backward and shut the door in her face.

"Well, of all the—you can't just—" she cried indignantly. But he had. She snapped her mouth shut. He really was the most horrid person she'd ever met.

"Oh, good, Alice, there you are." Christine looked up from her lists. "Did you find Mr. Tatlock?"

"Yes," said Alice, "and I'm not going back there again."

"What do you mean? What happened?"

"He was in his undershirt, he hadn't shaved, he had no teeth, and there were beer bottles all over his kitchen."

Christine's jaw tightened. "Did you give him my message?"

"I tried. I told him Miss Fairchild was coming back on Thursday and he slammed the door in my face."

Christine drew hard, black lines with her pencil—a whole precise row of them. The point broke and she put it down. "Thank you, Alice. I shall deal with Mr. Tatlock myself. Now—" She opened her handbag and took out her purse. "Here's some money—that should be enough, I think. I want you to take the bus down to the city center. There's an envelope to collect from Mr. MacInnes's secretary—you remember the way. And you might check at the post office to see if there's a letter."

"You mean go on my own?" Alice's voice rose.

"Of course that's what I mean. For pity's sake, Alice, you're not a baby! Here, I've written out the address for you—"

Glowering, Alice took the money and the address and stuffed them in her skirt pocket. "It won't be my fault if I get lost."

Her mother glanced up, eyebrows raised. "It most certainly will be. If you need directions, you can always ask. The people here do speak

English. And while you're at the post office, will you ask to have our letters sent on here in future? I meant to do that Friday.''

"Tell them we live here?" Alice was horrified.

"Yes, of course. We *do* live here. Go on, Alice, the sooner you go, the sooner you'll be back, and I need you.''

It did not cheer her at all to discover that the bus that stopped just outside Florestan's gates took her straight down to the Octagon, just as Mr. Tatlock had said. The driver greeted her with a grin and a friendly, "G'day," and helped her sort out the fare, making it obvious to everyone else on the bus that Alice was a stranger. She felt them staring at her as she made her way to an empty seat and fell into it. She laid her hot cheek against the cold glass of the window and pretended to be invisible.

When she got off at the Octagon, her eyes lit briefly on the bench where she and her mother had sat Friday afternoon, waiting for Mr. Tatlock. She glanced quickly away, not wanting to remember. Instead, she tried to recall the way to Murdoch, MacInnes & Holt, and wished she'd paid more attention. All the other people on the pavement knew exactly where they were going and how to get there. Alice hesitated at the corner, frowning anxiously, while the light changed and changed again.

"Lost, are you, love?" said a voice by her elbow. "Can I help?"

She jumped. A man with frowzy gray hair peered at her through thick spectacles. "Um—no. I'm not, actually," said Alice, saved by the light, which changed again. She set off, purposefully, in what she hoped was the right direction.

In the end she did have to ask. She picked a safe-looking, grandmotherly woman in a rose wool hat. "Bath Street? Oh, I couldn't say, dear. I'm up from Invercargill myself. I'm visiting my daughter—now *she'd* know. She'll be along soon if you don't mind waiting. Linda will help.''

"Well, really I—''

"Here. Why don't we just ask this gentleman? I'm sure he can tell you. Excuse me, we're looking for Bath Street.''

"That's easy. Just along this way—come on, I'll take you there."

Alice's heart sank. The "gentleman" had a thick, piratical black beard and wore a grease-stained overall. The woman smiled at her encouragingly. "There you go, dear." And a few minutes later she found herself safely delivered to the corner of Bath Street, where she recognized the yellow building. "Thank you," she muttered, hurrying toward it.

Angie flashed her a dazzling smile and asked how they were finding things, and if they'd had a pleasant weekend, and had they managed to see anything of Dunedin yet? She seemed in no hurry to get back to her typewriter, and Alice found herself telling about their visits to the botanic gardens. "Oh, yes? But you must see it when the rhododendrons are in bloom. They've got special tours come here just for the show. It's fantastic! Mind you, I've heard Florestan's almost as good. He used to collect rhododendrons from all over, Mr. Fairchild did. Never seen them myself, but Mr. MacInnes has—you ask him. That'll be the end of October."

Alice nodded, not saying that if she had her way they would no longer be in Dunedin at the end of October. Fervently she hoped that by then they would be well on their way back to Cambridge.

"So Miss Fairchild's coming back on Thursday. Mr. MacInnes says she's not been well. She was in before she left—I've only met her two or three times. She's quite something. Between you and me"—Angie leaned conspiratorially toward Alice, who noticed she had a smudge of lipstick on one of her front teeth—"I think Mr. MacInnes is rather afraid of her! Now Mr. Clem—" The telephone rang and she broke off to answer it. Alice picked up the brown envelope addressed to Mrs. Christine Jenkins and edged toward the door. "Yes, certainly, Mrs. Everard, we'll check on that for you. Yes, it is. I can let you know." She rolled her eyes at Alice and waved.

The post office, she remembered, was on a main street. Being careful to appear confident, she set off, this time looking around a bit. Angie's chatter had dulled her anxiety a little.

The same woman was behind the *post restante* counter, and when Alice approached, her face lit with recognition. Triumphantly she produced two letters, as if she were pulling a rabbit from a hat. "There you are, love! That'll please your mum, won't it? Both from England— one's been all around the barn getting here."

The top envelope was addressed in Gillian Evans's clear italic; Alice barely glanced at it. The second one was battered and smudged; someone had scrawled a large green question mark on it. Someone else had written "GPO Dunedin" in red, under the stamps. The original postmark was too blurred to make out, but the Auckland one was 14 August, and there was another from Upper Hutt dated the nineteenth. No return address, but the stamps were British, and sliding untidily down the front was "Mrs. Leonard Jenkins, c/o CPO Auckland, North Island, New Zealand" in Len's familiar handwriting. Alice's fingers itched to rip it open immediately, but someone had stuck down the flap with a large piece of tape, and the letter only had Christine's name on it. The woman was watching her, inviting her to stop and talk. "Thank you," Alice said, echoing her mother's discouraging politeness.

"I hope it's good news for you after all this time."

"Oh, yes," said Alice, "of course it is." Then she added, "I'm sure it is," feeling the prick of uncertainty. But suppose Len was writing to tell them he wasn't coming? Maybe he'd decided he was better off on his own, not anchored to a wife and a stepdaughter. Suppose he simply didn't want to travel halfway around the world? The letter could say, "Don't expect me—I'm staying in England." Suddenly it seemed dangerous; perhaps that was why the tape was there: to imprison the bad news until it reached Christine. Alice thrust the two letters deep into her pocket and turned to go, then remembered the other part of her errand.

Another woman, with straight, bobbed brown hair and a string bag full of oranges, had come up to the counter in the meantime. "G'day, Mrs. Andrews," said the clerk. "What can I do for you this morning?"

"I've got it on a bit of paper somewhere. I'd forget my head if it weren't screwed on!" said Mrs. Andrews cheerfully. She put her oranges on the counter and rummaged in a shabby plastic handbag.

Taking advantage of the distraction, Alice said quickly, "Excuse me, but could you arrange to have any other letters for Jenkins delivered to Florestan, please? Just until further notice," she added, trying to make it sound as temporary as possible.

Both women turned to look at her. "Jenkins?" said Mrs. Andrews, and "Did you say Florestan, love?" asked the clerk.

Alice sidled toward the main lobby. "It's on Lennox Street."

"Bless me, yes! I know where Florestan is, right enough. Your mum's never the new housekeeper up there, is she? I wouldn't have guessed it."

"Well, actually—" said Alice, beginning to feel hot.

"But I thought the old lady was still away—off on one of her gallivants," said Mrs. Andrews.

"She's coming back this week," said the clerk wisely. "Taken ill, she was. There was a telegram this morning. Dickie Murdo took it up—delivered it to your mum, he must have. I didn't think there was anyone in the house. Except Arthur Tatlock, of course," she added with a twitch of her eyebrows.

"Mind you," Mrs. Andrews said, "I wasn't surprised when Janet Mofford left. I said to my husband she wouldn't last long in that house. Well, no one does these days, and no wonder—the size of it, and the isolation. And there are easier people to get along with than Emilia Fairchild." She gave Alice a keen look. "I hope your mum knows what she's let herself in for."

Alice's fingers tangled themselves in her hair. "Actually," she said, rather louder than she'd intended, "actually, my mother's been hired to help Miss Fairchild write a book." She knew how much Christine loathed being discussed by other people, but suspected that even more she'd loathe having it put about that she was Miss Fairchild's new housekeeper.

"Write a book." Mrs. Andrews looked suitably impressed. "It'll be about her travels, I suppose. Always off to the most outlandish places, she is. Where was it this time, Susan?''

"Somewhere in India, I think. Though why anyone would want to go to India—so hot and crowded and dirty. Geoffrey's cousin Alec was sent there for almost a year. Poor Grace could hardly bear the heat, and all the beggars. I don't wonder Miss Fairchild's been taken ill. You don't know what's in the water.''

Mrs. Andrews shook her head disparagingly. "She's an odd one. I can't imagine why anyone would choose to stay in that house alone, either. Just to spite her brother, my husband says. Such a shame, him being carried off so sudden—before they'd mended their quarrel. The only family she's got left in Dunedin is her nephew, Clem, and she won't let him in the door. It's a terrible thing to be left alone in your old age. My mam used to say she's her own worst enemy, Emilia Fairchild.''

Curious in spite of herself, Alice asked, "What did they quarrel about?''

"Oh, it was the house,'' said Mrs. Andrews decidedly. "What was to become of it once Mr. Fairchild passed on. Her brother wanted to sell up, but she wouldn't hear of it. Family quarrels always come to money in the end, don't they?''

"My aunt Florence used to work up at Florestan,'' said Susan. "She helped in the kitchen before she got married. That must be forty years back now. She'd tell us stories about the goings-on up there—the parties they had, even during the Great War. And the presents he'd buy for his wife—make your eyes pop. She was there when they brought the piano—she said it was Austrian, that piano. How he ever got it in those days was a real mystery. They almost wouldn't deliver it. And everything modern? Never mind the cost. Central heating and *four* bathrooms with hot and cold. 'Course you wouldn't think much of that now, a girl like you, but it sounded like fairy stories to us in those days. Four of us in the same bed, a tub by the fire, and the loo out back.''

"Goodness!'' said Mrs. Andrews. "It must be fifteen or sixteen years since I clapped eyes on Florence Higgenbotham. She keeping well, is she?''

"Yes, thanks. She's still in Nelson. When Ernie came back from the war, they went up there.''

"Are you from far?'' Mrs. Andrew asked Alice.

"She's from England,'' said Susan, not waiting for Alice to answer. "Only just come, haven't you, love?''

"Well yes, we—''

"My husband's youngest sister, Martha, went to live in England. She's in Shropshire. Or is it Sussex? I can never remember, but it's such a small country, isn't it. You wouldn't be from Sussex, would you?''

"No,'' said Alice firmly. "From Cambridge.'' She remembered the letter, ticking away in her pocket. "Mum's expecting me back.'' She turned and fled. Outside, the air was cool and moist against her hot face. She took deep breaths of it, collecting herself. Oh, crikey! What had she done with the envelope from Mr. MacInnes? Had she left it on the counter? For an awful moment she saw herself going back for it. She *knew* they'd be discussing her. But no, there was the envelope after all, under her arm where she'd tucked it when she took Len's letter. Limp with relief she turned toward the Octagon.

— 7 —

Interview at Saint Kat's

"Well?" Alice gripped the edge of the table to keep herself from jiggling in anxiety. "What does he say?"

Her mother's eyes ran back and forth over the single sheet of lined notebook paper. She came to the end and let out a long breath. "Read it yourself. Here."

"Is he coming?" Alice made no move to take it. "He isn't coming, is he?"

"Of course he's coming. Haven't I told you that all along?"

Studying her, Alice realized two things: the first was that her mother really did want Len to join them; the other was that in spite of everything she'd said, she hadn't been absolutely certain he would. The knowledge gave her an unpleasantly shaky feeling. Her mother was always sure of everything. Refusing to think about this, she asked quickly, "When? What does he say?"

"He doesn't give a date. You know your stepfather—he's always been vague about details. I expect he'll just turn up one day. Go on, read it, Alice. If you can."

The writing was crammed into the top third of the page, running downhill, ignoring the lines. There was no date; there was no return address. "My darling Chrissie—" Alice glanced at her mother. Christine disliked being called Chrissie; she thought it sounded childish. But she had turned away and was busy at the sink. "By the time this reaches you Ill be well along on my way to New Zeland! Cant believe it. Seems like forever since I saw you—I miss you very much—but as I said in my last letter I got delaid. Its cleared up now. I hope you and Alice are well and I cant wait to see both of you again. Love to my girls—Len."

"So he did write before this. What could have happened to the letter?"

"Almost anything. You mustn't forget, Alice, your stepfather has an extraordinarily good imagination."

"But he says—do you mean you think he made it up about the other letter?" asked Alice in disbelief. "Why would he?"

"Oh, *I* don't know. It's a long way from England to New Zealand— perhaps the post office lost it somewhere in between. This letter's been donkey's years coming. For all I know, Len and Miss Fairchild may arrive on the front doorstep at the same moment."

"Thursday!" cried Alice, filled with hope. "Wouldn't that be wonderful!"

"It would not," declared her mother. "I don't want to have to explain them to each other, not right away. Miss Fairchild and I must come to an understanding before Len arrives and complicates things."

But Alice knew he wouldn't complicate things, not for her. She longed to see him—the sooner the better. "They were talking about her at the post office. She doesn't sound very nice."

"Who were talking about her at the post office?"

"The woman behind the counter and Mrs. Andrews."

"Mrs. Andrews? Who on earth is Mrs. Andrews, and why were they talking about Miss Fairchild? Even more to the point, Alice, why were you listening?"

In an injured tone Alice said, "I only told her what you said, about sending our letters up here. She already knew about Miss Fairchild because of the telegram. They started asking me questions, Mum. I couldn't just leave, not without being rude.''

"You know I don't like gossip, Alice.''

"There wasn't anything I could do. Besides, why shouldn't we know what everyone else knows about her? We'll be living in the same house. Did you know she had a fight with her brother and he died before they could make it up? Mrs. Andrews says it was about money—about selling Florestan. He thought she should and she wouldn't.''

"Mrs. Andrews seems to know a great deal about other people's business," said Christine tartly.

"She said she wasn't surprised when Mrs. Mofford left," Alice pressed on, resolved her mother should hear the rest. "Mrs. Andrews said people never stay long at Florestan. Miss Fairchild's very difficult. She said—''

"I haven't time to listen to any more tittle-tattle, Alice. Come and help me get Miss Fairchild's room ready for her.''

"Do you know which one it is?''

"The poky little one at the end of the corridor, Mr. Tatlock says.''

Alice was surprised. "Why would she choose that one? It looks like a nursery.''

"You can ask her. I've no idea.''

"What about the room next to it—the locked one?''

"According to Mr. Tatlock, it's her study.''

Giving her mother a sideways look, Alice said, "He was drunk, wasn't he?''

"No, he wasn't. Not this morning, at least.''

"I thought so.''

"What Mr. Tatlock chooses to do on his own time is no concern of ours," said Christine firmly. "I've made an appointment for us to see Miss Sallet tomorrow morning at ten.''

"Miss Sallet?" Alice was instantly distracted. She felt the clammy fingers of apprehension creep around her throat. "Who's Miss Sallet?''

"The assistant headmistress at Saint Katherine's. Mr. MacInnes spoke to her about you as he promised, and she's looking forward to meeting you. She sounds very nice. And you needn't look stricken—there's practically a whole term left before the summer holidays. You can't not go to school."

"Why? No one will care if I miss a term. It'll be horrid, starting new at the very end. I won't know anyone."

"If you start now you'll be that much to the good at the beginning of the new year," said her mother reasonably. "Besides, what would you do if you didn't go to school? I'll be busy once Miss Fairchild arrives, and I don't want you moping about by yourself. You'll be far better off at school, with girls your own age, Alice. Of course it'll be hard at first, catching up, making friends, learning your way about. But you'll be glad you made the effort, I know you will."

It amazed Alice that her mother didn't choke on what she'd just said. She didn't see how Christine could actually believe any of it. By this time in a school year all the desirable friends were taken; the only ones still willing and available would be the girls no one liked much, and those more interested in studying—and anyone unfortunate enough to be new. Coming from England, Alice knew she would be examined and discussed, but it was unlikely that she'd be invited to join any of the established groups. She'd seen it happen before, at Woodhall. She'd even spent a miserable two terms there being new herself. The best she could hope for was to be so unremarkable that after the initial flutter, people would forget about her and leave her to be new in private. But thinking of Susan and Mrs. Andrews at the post office, Alice guessed she had no chance of being ignored. Her connection to Florestan and Miss Fairchild doomed her to notoriety. "But if she's coming on Thursday," she said, trying one last hopeless argument, "and you've so much to do before, I shouldn't think you'd want to take the time to see Miss Sallet. School can wait until next week, Mum; that's only a few more days."

"There's nothing to be gained by putting it off, Alice," said her mother, closing the discussion.

The school record Christine had brought for Alice from Woodhall was a very good one, Alice knew. Of course, no matter how hard she worked, her mother was always urging her to try harder, to apply herself. Christine wanted to be sure Alice would be admitted to one of the two oldest women's colleges at Cambridge: Girton or Newnham. "A university education will give you choices, Alice, choices I never got. You'll be able to do anything," she'd say passionately. "Without it, your life will be limited no matter how clever and competent you prove yourself. Believe me, I *know*." Alice, with no particular future in mind yet, let her mother's words wash over her like water in the river Cam. She liked school, and the idea of university appealed to her, so her reports had always been satisfactory, and she didn't doubt that the assistant headmistress of Saint Katherine's would find her acceptable.

Miss Sallet's study was on the ground floor of a blushing pink Victorian bungalow, two streets below Florestan. The house did not look in the least official. If anything, it looked like an elaborate playhouse with lacy white trim and sudden, steep gables. At precisely five minutes to ten Christine rang the bell. The door was opened by a stocky, red-haired girl in a green uniform, who shook hands politely and introduced herself as Ann Ashby, a form six prefect. "Miss Sallet asked me to look out for you. She didn't want you to think she'd forgotten you were coming, but there's been a crisis at Castleton. She'll be back as soon as she can."

"Crisis?" Christine's eyebrows twitched.

"In the library," said Ann. "There was a scorched kind of smell and sparks and the lights went out. Nothing serious. She said to make yourselves comfortable. If you'll be all right"—she showed them into Miss Sallet's room—"I'll leave you and cut on back to class."

"Thank you," said Christine.

The study was unexpectedly personal, furnished with well-worn, comfortable chairs and a carpet in softly faded blues and greens. Over the ash-filled grate the mantel was cluttered with photographs, not of lacrosse and hockey teams or girls posed in class groups, but informal snapshots: girls on holiday, babies, toddlers, portraits of young women in academic robes, wedding parties. Wherever the walls of the room were not hidden behind books, they were covered with framed prints of scenes that looked suspiciously English. Next to the fireplace stood a moon-faced grandfather clock, its tick measured and soothing. The desk was heaped but orderly, and there was a pot of lavender hyacinths on one corner, tingeing the air with a thin sweetness.

The minute hand of the clock had just passed three when Alice heard the sound of quick steps. The door opened and in came a short, energetic person with a face like a currant bun: smooth, plump cheeks, a round chin, and black, bright eyes. "Mrs. Jenkins! Alice!" She beamed at them. "Apologies for not being here to greet you. I trust Ann took care of you?"

Christine had risen. "She said there was a crisis." Alice got to her feet.

"Oh, yes. There's always a crisis! We live in a *state* of crisis at Saint Katherine's. Nothing that can't be sorted out, you understand. But these houses—well, they weren't designed to be used so hard, and it's always a question of money, isn't it? Never enough to really *fix* things, just enough to stick the bits back together for a little longer. Sometimes I feel like that Dutch boy with my finger in the dike. But goodness—this isn't what you're here for, is it?" She gave a rueful laugh. "Do sit down, both of you. I've been looking forward so much to meeting you. Mr. MacInnes says you've come to us from *Cambridge*. I was at Girton myself—that was before the last war—and I did so love it. I always promised myself I'd get back again one day, but I haven't managed it yet. Mrs. Jenkins, you were connected with the university, is that right?"

"With the University Press," said Christine carefully. "I had been working with Dr. Raymond Inchcape. Perhaps you knew him?"

"The architectural historian? That Dr. Inchcape? Good heavens! I've heard him lecture, of course. Not exactly my field, but allied . . ."

The talk of Cambridge swamped Alice with homesickness. At Woodhall a new school year would be just starting. By this time Audrey would have promoted somebody else to fill the vacant position of best friend—probably Jane Winter. Jane's father was "in insurance" and traveled a lot on the continent, always bringing back expensive presents. Jane had an older brother too, Thomas, who was in his second year at King's College. Audrey had begun to pay attention to details like that. Privately Alice found it worrying; Thomas, and others of his kind, seemed to her to belong to a foreign country. She didn't understand the language.

Once or twice since arriving in New Zealand she had thought of writing to Audrey. She could tell her about Christopher Turbott, the boy on the steamship. If she did it right, Audrey would certainly be interested, perhaps even envious. Christopher was almost nineteen. He had spent a good deal of time seeking sympathy and comfort from Alice, who at first had been flattered, at last just the tiniest bit bored, though she didn't like to admit it. Christopher was being sent by a callous father to "toughen up" on his uncle's sheep station in Australia for a year or two, when all he really wanted was to settle into a civilized and physically undemanding career in banking or accounting. He was *good* with figures, he told Alice morosely. He hadn't the slightest desire to mess about with sheep in some godforsaken spot on the other side of the world. She needn't tell Audrey that he'd been seasick all over her shoes, or that his large, bony hands were damp and he chewed his hangnails. She could say that on the last evening on the promenade deck in the shadow of a life raft, he'd kissed her on the mouth, leaving out that she'd found it more perplexing and awkward than romantic. She needn't confess how relieved she'd been to disembark at Auckland, abandoning

Christopher to his term on the Nullarbor Plain, wherever that was. She'd thought about writing to Audrey several times, but she'd never done it.

Suddenly she was aware of her mother giving her a meaningful stare. She saw that Miss Sallet was holding a piece of paper—the school report—in her hand, and was speaking to her. ". . . a written examination, of course, but I shouldn't think you'd have any trouble with it, Alice. If you take it tomorrow"—she put the paper down—"you could begin with us next Monday. You won't have lost much of the term. How does that sound?"

"All right, Miss Sallet," said Alice in a hollow voice.

"It sounds fine," amended her mother. "But I did wonder, actually—"

"Yes?"

"Well, I thought possibly—if the examination goes well, naturally, I thought perhaps Alice could begin this week. Then she won't have the weekend to worry, if you see what I mean."

"I do," agreed Miss Sallet. "Are you a worrier, Alice?" She regarded her for a moment, then unexpectedly, in a broad cockney accent, she said, "Wot can't be 'elped must be endured, you know."

Christine looked startled and Alice blinked. It was a line she recognized from the story of Young Albert and the lion, just the kind of music hall turn Len was good at. She and her mother had often provided an appreciative audience for him.

"Ah, you know it!" exclaimed Miss Sallet happily. "Stanley Holloway. One of my favorites."

"My stepfather does that one," said Alice, shaken out of her gloom. In spite of herself, she warmed to Miss Sallet.

"Oh, yes? I shall be pleased to meet your stepfather, Alice. He might even help us out with one of our programs, do you think?"

"He couldn't come out with us," said Christine. "He's on his way now."

Miss Sallet nodded. "You'll be relieved when he gets here, I'm sure. Florestan is such a monster. When it was built there was an army of servants to look after it, but now—I shouldn't want to be responsible for it on my own. My little flat's all I can manage. Janet Hobbes—one of our teachers—tells me that Miss Fairchild's returning early, did she say this week? She's been taken ill? I hope it's nothing serious."

"I don't know the details as yet," replied Christine, stiffening slightly. "I really can't say anything."

"At least she won't be coming home to an empty house. That would be so depressing, especially when one isn't feeling well," said Miss Sallet. "Now then, where were we?"

"About Alice—"

"Yes, Alice. It'll be a bit difficult, jumping in right away, but that's often best, I think. Your mother's right, Alice. And our girls will help—they're a good lot on the whole." She paused, tapping her pen thoughtfully on the edge of her desk. "There's Margery MacInnes— you know her father already. She's an interesting girl, but I think—on consideration—yes, Helen's the one. Helen Quennell. Not as complicated. She'll do very well for you to start. Her father works with Margery's. Now, if I arrange the exam for this afternoon—half past two, how's that? You can take it right here, in my room. Then I'll go over it and confer with Miss Parsons—she'll be your form mistress. You'll like her, Alice, she teaches Latin. We'd expect you then on Thursday or Friday."

"Thursday would suit us very well, Miss Sallet," said Christine quickly.

So *that* was it, thought Alice. Her mother wanted her out of the way on Thursday, and never mind all that rubbish about having the weekend to worry and not losing more time.

"Alice?"

"What? Oh. Yes, Miss Sallet," Alice heard herself say meekly.

The following afternoon Alice stood in the big bedroom upstairs, in front of a tall mirror framed in gilt fruit and dusty cherubs, while her mother sat on the floor at her feet, tweaking and pinning and telling her when to turn a bit more to the right. It had crossed Alice's mind, as she set out again Tuesday afternoon to take the exam in Miss Sallet's study, that all she need do to disrupt her mother's clever plan was deliberately fail. It would serve her mother right. She considered this seriously, until the moment Miss Sallet opened the door to her, smiled, and said, "Hello, Alice—there you are, on the button! A bit like visiting the dentist, isn't it? Never mind, it'll soon be over. And once you start, you'll find it's not so bad."

In addition to the examination paper Alice found a glass of lemonade and a plate with four chocolate biscuits on it. For no reason that she could think of, her eyes stung briefly. She turned over the paper, picked up her pencil, and set to work.

So there she was Wednesday, trying not to fidget, while her mother made adjustments to the secondhand-but-almost-new Saint Katherine's uniform she'd managed to procure for Alice from the school. Diana Morse, whose name tapes were still sewn inside, had only worn it half a year. Her father had been transferred to Singapore. She'd been field hockey captain for Cargill, one of the four houses at Saint Katherine's, a prefect: a girl of substance, it was clear. When Alice tried on the skirt and blazer, she felt as if she'd been swallowed.

"Hmmm," said Christine, studying the effect. "Still—better too large than too small. I'll pin up the skirt, and perhaps we can do something about the cuffs. That should help."

"Nothing will help," declared Alice, scowling at her reflection. "It's the color—it's a horrid green." Her neck rose thinly from the collar of the blazer, and above it her face looked sallow and lumpy, like hastily made porridge. Woodhall's uniforms had been an attractive, crisp navy blue.

"No, not your best color," Christine conceded. "But the light isn't good. And it won't matter anyway—everyone else will be wearing it too." Then, in a tone of voice Alice knew all too well, she said, "It isn't the uniform that's important, after all, it's what's inside it. Don't stand on one hip like that, Alice, I'll never get the hem straight if you do. You'll meet some very nice girls at Saint Katherine's.''

And some unpleasant ones as well, thought Alice, brooding over the top of her mother's curly, butterscotch-colored head. Every school was like that: a mix of the well adjusted and the misfits, the clever and the plodding, the kind and the spiteful. But what Christine meant by ''nice'' was girls from good, well-educated families. She considered a solid education among the right classmates important enough so that she had always managed to find the money for private school fees. She herself had attended the village school in Wroxley, then gone as a day student to secretarial college in Ipswich so she could live at home and help Alice's grandmother, who was, as she herself liked to say, a martyr to sciatica.

''You just want me out of the way tomorrow,'' said Alice, ''when *she* comes.''

''If you mean Miss Fairchild, Alice, I wish you'd say Miss Fairchild.''

''Of course I mean Miss Fairchild.''

Christine removed a pin from between her lips and positioned it carefully. ''Yes, all right,'' she said after a minute. ''That's part of it, I admit. Under the circumstances, I'll find it much easier not having to think about you while I'm getting Miss Fairchild settled. There. Turn—a bit more—stop.'' She sat back on her heels and examined her handiwork. ''But I meant what I said about not having the weekend to fret. It'll be much better to get the first day over with.''

''Mum,'' said Alice, looking down at her, ''have you told Miss Fairchild about me? Does she know you have a daughter? Mr. MacInnes didn't.''

Christine busied herself putting pins back in the pincushion. It was a fat little satin ball with sections like an orange, which Len had given her years ago because she'd admired it in a shop. ''The subject never came up, actually. There was no reason why it should—it has nothing to do with my qualifications for the job.'' She sounded slightly defensive.

"But I'm living in her house," Alice pointed out. "She'll have to know about me."

"Yes, of course. And I'm sure you'll make a good impression when she meets you."

"Do you mean," said Alice slowly, "that she wouldn't have hired you if you'd told her?"

"I didn't say that." Christine rose, gathering scissors, tape measure, and workbasket. "Here's the thread, you can stitch the hem yourself, Alice." She made it clear she had no intention of discussing the subject further.

— 8 —

New Girl

Alice was upstairs, washing her hands and face Thursday morning, trying not to see herself in the foggy little mirror above the basin, when she heard her mother shout. Hastily drying her hands on her green pleated skirt, Alice dashed out onto the balcony. The shout had come from Miss Fairchild's bedroom, on the other side of the great hall. Alice ran around to see what the matter was; her mother was not ordinarily given to shouting. She found Christine standing at one of the open windows, her arms full of pillows, transfixed by something outside.

"What is it? What's wrong?"

"Come here and you'll see what's wrong. Just look."

Joining her, Alice saw six sheep on the grass beyond the terrace, heads down, nibbling hectically. "They're sheep," she said blankly.

"Well, I *know* that!" snapped Christine. "I have seen sheep before. I want to know where they've come from. This is the middle of a city."

Looking across the rough lawn to the impenetrable dark wall of trees and shrubs at the far edge, Alice could see nothing that suggested to her that they were in the middle of a city. She shivered. The morning sun had not yet come around to that side of the house, and the breeze fluttering the faded muslin curtains was chilly. From above, the cropped patches already made by the sheep looked like moth holes in a green blanket. There was a flicker of movement at the corner of the house— a black-and-tan shape. "Mr. Tatlock!" she and her mother exclaimed at the same moment. Of course—they were *his* sheep. In a sharp, carrying voice Christine called, "Mr. Tatlock, I want to talk to you."

There was a silence, then the gruff response: "I'm very busy, missus."

"So am I," returned Christine. "Those wouldn't be yours, by any chance, would they?"

"You mean the sheep?" He stepped out on the terrace so they could see him, tilting his face up, squinting. "Nope. They're not mine."

"Then whose are they, and how did they get here? Do you know?"

He scratched the back of his neck consideringly. "Reckon I do."

"Well, look at them—they're ruining the lawn! Can't you get them off it? Who owns them?"

"*She* does, missus."

"She?"

"I look after them for her. This is what she keeps them for. Ordinarily they're penned on the tennis courts. I let them out this morning, to trim the grass."

Christine digested this information in disbelief. "You can't be serious. You don't honestly expect me to believe Miss Fairchild keeps sheep to mow the grass."

He shrugged.

"But what about the—what about the droppings?"

"People pay good money for that stuff. It's only sheep shit. This way you get your grass cut and fertilized at the same time—can't beat it. Now, you just leave them be, missus—let them get on with it. Don't you go startling them," Mr. Tatlock said severely. "They got a big job to do."

Christine snapped her mouth shut and turned away from the window, giving the pillows a hard thumping. "And what are you standing there

for, Alice? You'll be late to school your first morning if you don't hurry.
You don't want to start out on the wrong foot.''

Right foot, wrong foot—which was which? Alice wondered darkly.
As she headed down the drive, Mr. Tatlock called after her, ''And don't
leave the gate open. I got better things to do than chase sheep all over
Dunedin.'' She didn't bother to answer.

Arriving breathless with haste and nerves on Miss Sallet's doorstep,
she met a girl with fair, straight hair and a mouthful of braces. ''Are
you Alice Jenkins? You must be. I'm Helen. Come on, the bell's gone
ages ago—we've missed prayers. Miss Parsons knows you're new—
she won't be strict your first morning, but oh—*do* hurry *up!*''

''What about Miss Sallet? She said—''

''She couldn't wait,'' Helen explained, hustling her along the pavement. ''The drains have backed up in Marchmont. Grace said the smell
was simply dreadful! She couldn't sleep last night it was so bad. She
felt ill. They were afraid something had died under the floor. Here we
are—here's Lockwood. Come on.'' She pulled Alice through a gate,
up a cement path and wide front steps, into what looked like another,
grander private house. The front hall was dark with wood paneling and
lined with rows of cubbies, each with a coat hook and shelves. The
scuffed parquet floor was splashed with pools of color where the sun
shone on it through stained-glass windows on either side of the door.
Helen showed Alice where to hang her coat, then led the way up a
somber formal staircase—it was carpeted with a strip of coarse, worn
brown drugget. From the landing window Alice glimpsed a dizzying
view out over the city to the harbor and the bleached, knobbly backbone
of the Otago Peninsula beyond, but Helen was urging her onward,
knocking on a door, opening it and going through, compelling Alice
over the threshold. She was aware of rows of faces turning toward her
like iron filings to a magnet, the buzz of whispers, the tiny stings of
knowing stares. She avoided looking back. Like a moth in a specimen
case, she had already been pinned and labeled: the new girl from England, Alice Jenkins, *the one who lives at Florestan.* One of the faces

belonged to Margery MacInnes, whom Miss Sallet considered interesting but complicated. . . .

But there was Miss Parsons saying, "Welcome, Alice, we're delighted to have you with us for the rest of the year, aren't we, girls?" Miss Parsons who taught Latin—Alice looked at her and blinked. She had expected a Latin mistress like Mrs. Randall at Woodhall, as ancient and solid as the language, rolling her *r*'s and quoting Virgil. But Miss Parsons was slim and dark-haired and very pretty. She had dimples when she smiled, and a small, bright diamond ring on her left hand. Among the form three girls, Alice learned later, she was affectionately known as Cecily Parsley. "Thank you," she managed to utter. "This is Alice Jenkins, girls," said Miss Parsons, quite unnecessarily. She stood there, on exhibit, not meeting anyone's eyes, pretending she didn't care, her face hot. Mercifully Miss Parsons didn't keep her there. She directed her to the empty desk in the second row, next to Helen. Whose desk had it been? Alice wondered, sinking behind it gratefully. She was sure it hadn't been standing vacant for two terms, just so she could fill it. Gradually the rush of heat left her cheeks, she began to see the edges of things, to wind her fingers in her hair and to listen.

Saint Katherine's was a collection of what had been private houses. One by one they'd been bought up by the school and converted to classrooms, offices, a library, a refectory, a chapel, studies, as funds could be raised. Most of the students were day girls, coming, like Helen and Alice, from homes in the city. But Marchmont, where the drains had backed up, was a residence for boarders whose families lived at some distance from Dunedin. Helen's cousin Grace Ingraham was one of these. Her father owned a sheep station on the Canterbury Plains, near Mount Cook, and Grace spent her weekends with Helen's family. Although Alice had gathered that a sheep station was a kind of farm, she couldn't help picturing it all red and white, with arches and towers, like Dunedin railway station.

Alice met Grace on the way to the refectory for lunch the first day.

Grace was a good six inches taller than her cousin, with a thick braid of brown hair and a noticeable bosom swelling the front of her uniform. She had broken her nose falling off her pony when she was seven and it hadn't set quite straight. The first question she asked Alice was, "Did you ride in England?" and when Alice said no, Grace shrugged and gave her a pitying look. In reverential tones Helen told Alice, "Grace has her own horse. He's beautiful—he's called Kowhai." "Cow-eye?" said Alice, startled. It seemed an unlikely name for a beautiful horse. "Like the tree," said Helen. "K-o-w-h-a-i. It has yellow flowers," she added helpfully. "Oh" was all Alice could think to say.

Helen explained that Saint Katherine's was divided into four houses, Cargill, Grey, Burns, and Hocken, cutting across the forms, so that girls of all ages were mixed up together for games, projects, and competitions. She and Alice were in Hocken with Margery MacInnes and a whole string of other girls for whom Alice had no faces, but Grace was in Burns—"With Betty Ware and Fiona Watkins, worse luck," said Grace, rolling her eyes. When Alice asked who they were, Helen said, "Betty's father's a city councillor, and Fiona's father owns the biggest department store in Dunedin."

"They're both pills," declared Grace flatly. "They aren't that bad," objected Helen. "They are too. *You'll* see," Grace told Alice. "Helen's always making excuses for people."

The confusing thing was that none of the house names matched the actual buildings, which were named instead for benefactors and trustees. Lockwood, where form three was based, immortalized the Reverend Alfred E. Lockwood, one of the school's founders. There was a portrait of him over the fireplace in the downstairs study: a genial, white-whiskered gentleman in a frock coat and clerical collar, looking quite pleased with what he had done. The house was tall and angular, with steep gables that dripped wooden gingerbread, and windows that chattered in their frames like teeth when the wind came hurtling in across the Pacific Ocean. Classes were punctuated by loud and prolonged periods of metallic banging and clanking, which seemed to originate somewhere far below and travel about from floor to floor. Each time the noises started, Alice felt an inward leap of alarm; no one else paid the slightest attention.

She asked Helen about the noises at lunch. The girls whose parents paid extra ate cooked lunches in the refectory in the basement of Marchmont, but on Alice's first day the routine had been disrupted by the drains. Instead, the girls had sandwiches and mugs of tomato soup in the assembly hall, forced to eat off their laps in some disorder.

"Noises?" Helen was looking about for a place to set her milk where no one would knock it over. "What noises do you mean?" On her other side Grace was talking about a rugby match between two boys' schools.

"She means the wonky boiler," put in another girl, joining them. "So you're Alice Jenkins. Pa said I should look out for you."

Alice regarded the newcomer warily. She had a bush of vigorous red-gold hair and startlingly vivid green eyes in a triangular face; she wasn't pretty, but she was the kind of girl you couldn't help noticing. The Saint Katherine's uniform looked as if it had been designed especially for her, color and all. She gave Alice an interested once-over. "It's ancient, that boiler. Belongs in the Early Settlers' Museum. One day it'll explode—ka-BOOM! And there'll be bits of form three scattered all over Maori Hill—bloody awful mess. It's your father's fault, Helen."

"What?" Helen's eyebrows disappeared under her bangs. "Margery, I wish you wouldn't say things like that. Why should it be my father's fault about the boiler?"

"Because he's too mean to give Lockwood a new one."

"What about Fiona's father then?" said Grace, springing to her cousin's defense. "Or yours, come to that?"

"Helen's father's far richer than mine. Isn't he, Helen?" Margery's eyes glittered like green glass.

Helen looked embarrassed. "Are you going to sit with us, Margery, or not?"

"Not," said Margery. "It's hopeless trying to balance everything on your knees—look, you've spilled your soup, Grace."

"Only because you knocked my arm."

"I'm going to sit over there, on the floor by the wall. Oh, come on, Helen, don't be a stick. There's Miss Parsons, dangling her legs off the edge of the stage. If it's all right for her, why shouldn't we?"

It sounded sensible to Alice, but she was too cautious to say so. She didn't want to align herself with Margery MacInnes until she knew more about her; Helen was much safer. Grace solved the problem by gathering her lunch together and going to sit next to Margery.

"All right then." Helen gave in, and she and Alice followed suit. "Anyway, Alice, my father says it's just steam in the pipes and nothing to worry about. If it really was dangerous, Mrs. Sinclair would have it fixed."

Margery took a large bite of corned beef sandwich. "I wouldn't be so sure. I suspect it's all part of The Sinclair's Great Plan. Saint Katherine's is always desperate for money—things are constantly breaking down or falling apart, right? That's why we're sitting here on the floor."

"So?" said Grace.

"Well, it stands to reason—if there's a really spectacularly nasty accident one day—plenty of gore spread around, the tragedy of young lives nipped in the bud, et cetera, et cetera, Saint Katherine's will be deluged with donations from horrified parents. Enough to fix everything at once, or build a whole new school. To say nothing of memorial gifts. Your grief-stricken mum and dad paying to have you immortalized as tennis courts or a chem lab. Your father could give a new gym, Grace, just for Saint Katherine's, so we wouldn't have to share with Girls' High anymore. 'She did not die in vain—' "

"What would *yours* give?" demanded Grace.

"Probably something boring like a new chapel." Margery made a face. "It might be worth the sacrifice if Pa would build a proper art studio, with my name carved in the lintel—"

"What absolute rubbish!" exclaimed Helen with a worried smile. "Don't listen to it, Alice. You can get into trouble when you listen to Margery," she added with a trace of bitterness.

"You aren't still blaming me for the scavenger hunt, are you, Helen? That was first term—it's ancient history! I couldn't possibly have known that Miss Feeney would come back early from the concert. And it isn't as if we hurt dear little Peterkin, we only borrowed him for a few hours. If I'd been her and suffering from headache, I'd have been jolly grateful to us. All the silly dog did was yap."

"But I was the one who had to take him back and apologize. *And I* got a conduct mark. Mummy was very disappointed."

"Mummy's an Old Girl," Margery informed Alice, leaning toward her across Grace. "We all got conduct marks. In fact, Helen, I did you a favor. Parents *need* to be disappointed now and then, otherwise their expectations would get dangerously high. Don't you agree, Alice?" she asked suddenly. "What about your parents? Do they expect great things of you?"

Alice's cheeks flamed; they were all looking at her. "Well, I'm not sure—I mean, my mother's always—"

"Pa said your father hasn't come from England yet. He was surprised about that. Your mother didn't mention it," said Margery, veering in another direction.

"No," said Alice, stiff with self-consciousness. "He's coming any day now. He couldn't leave his job in time."

"What does he do?" asked Helen.

What was it her mother had said? "He's an engineer."

"My brother's studying to be an engineer—it's all maths." Grace rolled her eyes.

"Dead boring," Margery pronounced. "Pa was afraid your mother would take one look at Florestan and turn right around and go home again. I heard him discussing it with Ma. What a dog's breakfast if she had, with Miss Fairchild coming home unexpectedly and no one in the house!"

"Fancy living at Florestan," said Helen, her eyebrows disappearing again. "What's it like, Alice? It must be terribly grand."

"Most of it's closed up," said Alice, skirting the question. "It's very big."

"It's supposed to have beautiful gardens. It would be a wonderful place for a wedding, out of doors, under an arbor of flowers, with big striped tents," Helen said dreamily.

Alice thought of the sheep, even now leaving their fertilizer scattered across the grass, and suppressed a nervous giggle.

"Everything comes round to weddings with Helen these days," complained Margery. "Her sister's getting married in November. The social event of the year."

"You're jealous because you're not in it, that's all," said Grace.

"Not me," declared Margery. "Miss Fairchild's coming back today, isn't she, Alice?"

There was no point in denying it, so Alice nodded.

"Fiona says she's crazy," said Grace after a moment. "She says it's living in that house all alone that's done it."

"I don't know why she doesn't sell it," Helen said. "My father says she could make lots of money."

"But she doesn't *need* lots of money—she has plenty." Margery scowled. "It's nobody's business but her own what she does with Florestan. Her father left it to her. He left the brewery to her brother and now it belongs to her nephew, Clem. And what does Fiona Watkins know about Miss Fairchild anyway? I bet she's never met her."

"Have you?" challenged Grace.

"She came to my grandfather's funeral two years ago. Half of Otago came. We had to stand in line forever, shaking hands and listening to people tell us how sorry they were, all except for Miss Fairchild. *She* said he was one of the lucky ones. He was eighty-seven when he died and perfectly fit. He just went to sleep in his chair one afternoon with his handkerchief over his face and didn't wake up for tea."

"It was very sad," said Helen.

"Don't be soft. Miss Fairchild was quite right, he *was* lucky."

Margery grinned suddenly. "Pa didn't know what to say, though. He's always been rather afraid of her. She looked like a crow, all hard, rusty black feathers and a gimlet eye."

"She wasn't really wearing feathers?" Grace sounded skeptical.

"Girls? Girls, hurry and finish—the others have already gone back," called Miss Parsons.

"Oh golly, Latin verbs!" moaned Helen. "I meant to study them over lunch."

"The road to hell," said Margery cheerfully. Helen looked shocked.

Grace said, "I don't know why we have to waste hours and hours learning a language nobody speaks anymore."

It was a question Alice herself had pondered often. But Margery sucked in her cheeks, narrowed her eyes to sharp green slits, and in a precise English accent said, "Grace Ingraham, it is not for you to question what you are taught at Saint Katherine's. Your task is simply to absorb it—absorb every drop of knowledge as if you were a sponge. Your time here is precious and you must make the most of it or you will regret your lack of application ever after."

Grace and Helen giggled. "Mrs. Sinclair gives us the Sponge Speech at the start of every year," Helen explained to Alice.

Miss Parsons approached, her eyebrows quirked. "What was that, Margery?"

"I was only pointing out the value of Latin, Miss Parsons."

"*Mirabile dictu!* I'm delighted to hear it, Margery. I sometimes feel like a voice crying in the wilderness." Miss Parsons showed her dimples. "Are you finding your way around, Alice? I'm sure Helen's being a great help, but you mustn't believe everything Margery tells you. Unless, of course, it's about Latin." She and Margery exchanged a look Alice couldn't interpret.

"Yes, thank you, Miss Parsons," said Alice politely.

"Good. I know it's hard getting used to a new school, and I hope you'll let me know if there's anything I can do to make it easier. Now hurry, girls, before you're late—but *don't run!*"

— 9 —

No Secrets

At the end of school Helen was whisked off in a neat black car by
Mummy to see the orthodontist—she was desperately anxious lest he
decide her braces should stay on another six months, so she would
still be wearing them as a bridesmaid at her sister's wedding. Grace
shouldered a hockey stick and disappeared with three other girls, simi-
larly armed, and Margery MacInnes simply vanished. Alice, who'd
spent the last period worrying about how she could escape unobtru-
sively, found herself abandoned on the pavement outside Lockwood.
Saint Katherine's uniforms dispersed around her, in pairs and small
green clots, and Alice felt the gloom that had been hovering just above
her head all day descend on her like a wet fog.

Slowly she trudged along the streets and up the hill toward Florestan.
At the corner, a block from the front gates, there was a shop, its windows
obscured with handwritten notices: Pram for Sale, Like New. Wanted:
Bed-sitter Near University, Will Do Odd Jobs. Term Papers Typed—
Ask for Karen. Lost: Pair Football Boots Size 6½. Learn Smocking,
Experienced Teacher, and ancient, faded, flyblown packets of tea, corn-

flakes, and soap powder. There were two piles of newspapers on the pavement, one held down by an old flatiron, the other by a doughnut-shaped black-and-white cat. The door was open, letting a wedge of the afternoon into the cluttered interior. Alice fingered the coins in her blazer pocket: change left over from her bus fare the other day. In the excitement of Len's letter her mother had forgotten to ask for it. There was enough for a chocolate bar—her mouth watered at the thought. She deserved a treat after surviving the first day of school, and it would give her the strength to face whatever lay ahead. Margery's description of Miss Fairchild at her grandfather's funeral was not reassuring.

A large, solid-looking woman sat behind the counter on a high stool, knitting. She wore plastic-framed spectacles and she was counting stitches to herself. As Alice crossed the threshold, she looked up and smiled, and the light from the doorway flashed on her glasses. "Hullo, dearie. You're not one of my regulars, are you?"

Alice winced inwardly. She ought to have known she would not be allowed anonymously to buy a chocolate bar. She would be expected to hand over information with her money. And she couldn't say she was just visiting—her uniform gave her away. "I haven't been in before," she tried.

"You must be new in the neighborhood. And how are you liking Saint Kat's—?" She left an obvious blank for Alice to fill in.

Resigned, she said, "Alice. It's only my first day."

The spectacles winked. "Ah-ha. You're English, aren't you. I can hear it. My mum was English. She kept her accent till the day she died, bless her. Always singled out for it, she was. Alice, is it? Who was telling me about an Alice? Oh, yes. Arthur, wasn't it. Mrs. Jenkins, he said, and her daughter Alice. Just come to Florestan to look after Miss Fairchild. All the way from England. I said to him it seems like a long journey just for that!" She chuckled. All the time she talked, her fingers worked stitches back and forth along the needles so fast Alice couldn't follow them.

"Who's Arthur?" asked Alice, wanting to add, and why is he talking about us?

"Why, Arthur Tatlock, dearie. He comes round every morning with eggs to sell. I've got plenty of customers for them, too. You can't beat fresh, free-range eggs. His chooks are grand layers. He was telling me about Miss Fairchild being taken poorly. I *was* sorry to hear. Said she was coming home today—is that right?"

Alice nodded, feeling trapped. Their arrival might as well have been published on the front page of the *Dunedin Star*: "Mrs. Christine Jenkins, recently engaged by Miss Emilia Fairchild, and her daughter Alice, just arrived from Cambridge, England, are now in residence at Florestan." Perhaps there was a regular column devoted to the travels and health of Miss Fairchild. And when Len came, he'd be given his own story as well. . . .

". . . tell your mum she has an account here—for odd things like milk and cheese. It's handy if she's ever caught short. And here—you take these back for Miss Fairchild, Alice. You tell her Flora Draine sent them along. She's always been partial." She flashed again as she put down her needles and fished a small white paper sack out from under the counter. It smelled strongly of peppermint.

Four older girls in green uniforms squeezed into the narrow space behind Alice. She recognized one as Ann Ashby, the prefect who had met them at Miss Sallet's office the morning of the interview. Practically snatching the sack, Alice said, "Thank you," and ducked out quickly, head down, before Flora Draine could brand her publicly as Alice Jenkins from Florestan.

Walking up the long, overhung drive toward the house, Alice tucked one of Miss Fairchild's exceptionally strong peppermints in one cheek and brooded about Len. Until that moment she had been looking forward impatiently to his arrival. Now all at once she felt a quiver of doubt.

Miss Fairchild had hired Len sight unseen, when she had hired Alice's mother. Writing to Dr. Inchcape from Dunedin, she had appealed to him for help; she trusted his advice. He had, after all, known her father and visited Florestan. He must certainly understand the importance of the project she proposed: a book that would suitably immortalize Clement Roland Fairchild and the great house he had built. She wanted a couple, Dr. Inchcape told Christine: an assistant with editing experience and writing skills for the book, and a man to look after the house, keep the car in running order, serve as chauffeur when needed. It couldn't be more perfect. He urged Christine to consider applying and wrote Miss Fairchild a glowing recommendation for her when she did. He would, of course, be sorry to lose her in Cambridge, but this was too good an opportunity for her to miss. Alice knew all this because her mother had told her, after the fact, when she had accepted the job and bought their steamship tickets. It wouldn't matter if Len came later, she said, because Miss Fairchild would be traveling in India until mid-December. By the time she returned, everything would be settled: she'd find the couple she expected.

But would she? Alice wondered uneasily, sucking her mint. Back in Cambridge everyone who knew Alice and her mother knew Len. He almost never had to be explained. Alice's friend Audrey thought he was great fun—not like a parent at all, she said, more like a cousin or an older brother. Audrey's father was a doctor who wore suits and always had clean hands and very little time at home. On the occasions when she did see him, Alice found him intimidating; he made jokes she didn't understand, and Audrey would giggle and say, ''Oh, *Daddy!*'' Len was not in the least intimidating. He took them to the cinema to see the latest American westerns and bought chocolates so they'd all go home not wanting tea, or they went roller-skating together, or to the Bank Holiday fair, where he'd always want to see how the rides worked.

For years Alice gave no thought to the differences between Len and Dr. Hillyard, or Len and her mother, for that matter. It was only recently that she'd begun to worry that he might have shortcomings—to wonder at the number of times he changed jobs, for instance. Everything would seem to be going well, there might even be talk of a promotion, then suddenly he'd admit he'd given notice and look for something else. She realized that other adults, like Audrey's mother, didn't altogether approve of Len. They considered him irresponsible. In their family Alice's mother was the sensible, practical, reliable one.

Alice rounded the last bend in the driveway and there was Florestan, looming ahead of her, stony and unwelcoming. Parked in front was an unfamiliar little red car. She stopped abruptly at the edge of the trees and looked up at the second-story windows. She wondered if Miss Fairchild had been told about her yet. It gave her a quesy feeling in the pit of her stomach, not knowing, and she slunk rapidly around to the scullery door, hoping she hadn't been observed.

In the kitchen the table was littered with the reamins of tea. There were three cups and saucers and smeared plates. Surely not Mr. Tatlock—then who? Her mother had used good china—green-and-white with a gold rim—good silver spoons and butter knives with the Fairchild monogram engraved on their handles, linen napkins. There was a small heap of tea sandwiches on a plate, and half a dozen of the griddle cakes known as pikelets on another, dishes of butter and strawberry jam, and a pitcher half full of milk. There was no doubt then: Miss Fairchild was back. Alice stood absolutely still and closed her eyes, concentrating. She tried to sense a change in the atmosphere of the house, now that its owner was home. But it felt as remote and uninhabited as it had when she and her mother had first set foot inside it, a week ago.

She gave herself a little shake. The sandwiches were drying out, the thin bread beginning to curl at the edges, revealing pale, unappetizing slices of cucumber. Alice poured herself a large glass of milk, cleared a space on the table, and sat down, appropriating the pikelets. They had come from a bakery on George Street; the box was on the counter. Taking a book at random out of the pile she'd brought from Saint Katherine's, she opened it. Algebra. She gazed at it with distaste.

Sometime later, when the kitchen door swung inward and light suddenly flooded the room, Alice jumped and blinked. "Alice, for pity's sake, whatever are you sitting in the dark for? You haven't been reading? You'll ruin your eyes," scolded her mother.

Alice had no idea how long she'd been sitting there; she hadn't noticed the kitchen growing shadowy around her. She had no notion what was on the pages of the book in front of her. She felt as if she'd just been woken from a sound sleep, although she didn't think she'd closed her eyes. "I was just—thinking," she said lamely. "Whose car is out front?"

"Hmmm?" Christine began stacking dirty dishes beside the sink. "That belongs to Dr. Lattimer. He's only just left. Didn't you hear us in the hall?"

"So she really *is* ill. I mean, Miss Fairchild."

"Of course she is. That's why she's back early. Alice, did you eat all the pikelets?"

"I was hungry," Alice defended herself. "Suppose it's contagious, what she has. Did you think of that, Mum? What if it's typhoid, or yellow fever, or—"

"She wouldn't have been allowed to travel if she were infectious. She has gastroenteritis, Dr. Lattimer says. It's quite common, but she's elderly and it's been very hard on her. She was severely dehydrated when she reached Auckland."

Alice leaned her chin on her hands. "Have you told her about me yet?"

Her mother picked up a cucumber sandwich and took a bite, then put it back down on the plate, frowning at it. "No, I haven't, Alice. It seemed too complicated, what with Dr. Lattimer here as well. I decided it would keep until—"

In the passage the telephone rang. Alice looked up, startled, not having heard it before, but her mother exclaimed crossly, "Bother! She's been here less than three hours and everyone in the city seems to know. I've been answering that all afternoon. I've half a mind to follow

Mr. Tatlock's example and rip it out. Alice, be a good girl and see who it is this time. My feet ache.''

"What do I say?''

"Just tell whomever that Miss Fairchild is resting. She's had a long journey and she's glad to be home, but she isn't seeing *any*one. Ask for the caller's name so I can add it to the list.''

Warily Alice approached the telephone and picked up the old-fashioned receiver. "Hullo?'' She read the number off the dial: "Seven-seven-three-four-two-five.''

A pleasant-sounding male voice said hello back and asked to whom he was speaking.

Alice cleared her throat. "Mrs. Jenkins,'' she said, trying to sound firm and adult.

There was a pause. "Mrs. Jenkins?'' said the voice uncertainly. "Is Miss Fairchild at home, please?''

"Yes, but I'm sorry, she's resting.''

"Ah.'' Another long pause. "Mrs. Jenkins,'' he said again, as if not quite sure.

"Miss Fairchild's new assistant,'' said Alice, twisting her hair around her fingers. "Can I—may I take a message?''

"Well, yes. Yes, you can actually. I'm Miss Fairchild's nephew, Clem—Clement. I wanted to be sure Aunt Emilia'd gotten home safely. We didn't expect her back so soon—I thought she'd be away until Christmas. Malcolm MacInnes rang me this morning about her change in plan, and I wanted to be sure there's nothing wrong?''

Alice wondered what she should do about the question mark at the end of his sentence. Hadn't Mr. MacInnes told him his aunt was ill? He must be the only one in Dunedin who didn't know. Should *she* tell him? He sounded nice and concerned, but there was the argument the women at the post office had talked about—

"Hello?''

"Yes. I'm sorry.'' Alice gave the lock of hair a sharp tug. "I'll give her your message, um—Mr. Fairchild. I'll tell her you rang.''

"If you would, please. Thank you, er, Mrs. Jenkins. You could tell her I'd like to pay a call later, when she's got her feet under her again. She can reach me at home or at the brewery. She has the numbers."

In spite of the chill of the early evening, Christine had the kitchen door open when Alice returned, and was standing just outside, on the step, smoking. She gave Alice a questioning look.

"That was her nephew. He'd only just found out she was back—he didn't seem to know she's ill."

"Did you tell him?"

"No. But I wasn't sure—I mean, they are related, after all, and everyone else knows. It seems very odd, if you ask me. He wants to come and see her—he said, 'when she's gotten her feet under her.' " She watched her mother for a reaction.

Christine crushed out her cigarette with a foot, then stooped and picked up the flattened butt. "I'll add him to the list," was all she said. "Come on, Alice. We'd better do something about supper. Those sandwiches are only fit for Mr. Tatlock's chickens."

"Chooks," said Alice. She wondered if chooks liked cucumber any better than she did. "The woman at the shop down the hill calls him Arthur."

"And how would you know that? Have you been gossiping again, Alice?"

"I haven't been gossiping at all," said Alice. "There's no need to anyway. Everyone already knows more than I do about us."

On Friday Alice stuck close to Helen, doing what she was told and trying, without much success, not to worry about Miss Fairchild and the weekend ahead. How long was it possible to live in the same house with a person without that person knowing you were there? She remembered a story Len had told her once about a boy called Cotton who had lived in Buckingham Palace for months before anyone realized he didn't belong. Len swore it was true. But Buckingham Palace was huge; hundreds of people worked there—they couldn't possibly all keep track of one another. It wasn't a matter of hiding so much as pretending you knew what you were doing and had every right to be there doing it. This was different. How long was Alice going to have to skulk about Florestan, keeping out of sight?

She was so preoccupied with these thoughts, she barely listened to the others' chatter during breaks and at lunch about the rugby match Saturday afternoon. She was only vaguely aware that the discussion made Helen turn pink, Grace giggle self-consciously, and Margery look sly. When Helen said, "Are you coming, Alice?" it took her a moment to understand the question. She shook her head. "No, I can't," she said automatically, feeling relieved. She had no interest in boys' rugby.

Christine was waiting for her when she got back to Florestan after school. Tea was set on the table for the two of them: ham sandwiches this time, with the crusts on, and chocolate biscuits and a mug of cocoa for Alice. Alice eyed it all hungrily, then paused, suspicious. Her mother gave her an encouraging smile and sat down with a cup of tea.

"I'll just go and change," said Alice. It was one of her mother's strictest rules: always change out of your school uniform as soon as you get home in the afternoon. "I've got better things to do than wash and iron your clothes several times a week."

"No, have your tea first. I'd like to talk to you."

Alice was fully alert. "You've told her, haven't you? You've told her and she's fired you."

"Don't be silly."

"Have you?"

"Not yet." Her mother sounded faintly irritable. "I said I'd tell her when I thought the time was right."

"But what I still don't see is why you didn't tell her at the start, when you wrote to her."

"If you must know, because she made it quite clear she doesn't like children. I'm sure she means small children, but I thought it would be much easier to work that out face to face than in letters. Then she could see for herself that you *aren't* a child."

"I don't really know what I am," said Alice moodily. "I'm not grown-up, either."

Her mother's face softened. "Not yet, but you're growing up fast. Look at you."

Alice sat down and picked up a sandwich. "So if it isn't Miss Fairchild, what is it?" she asked to cover her awkwardness. She knew her mother loved her, but they didn't talk much about it.

Christine took a deep breath. "I've moved your things into another bedroom, Alice."

"Another bedroom? Why?" It caught her completely off guard.

"Because with all the room in this house it really doesn't make sense for us to share a bed. You need your room for studying, and with Len coming—"

"You could have waited until he got here." The thought of going to bed alone in Florestan was not at all attractive.

"—and I don't want to disturb you if I have to get up with Miss Fairchild, which I may very well. I've put you in the room right above the kitchen, by the back stairs. There's a desk in it you can use for your schoolwork and a bathroom across the hall."

Alice gazed unhappily at her cocoa, her appetite temporarily quenched. First school, now separate bedrooms, and a monster waiting for her upstairs. She looked at her mother. "You mean to stay here, don't you?"

Her mother looked back, something determined in her eyes. "Yes, Alice, I do."

"Oh, *Mum*! How can you? You said yourself, it's nothing like you expected. Florestan might have been a grand house once, when Dr. Inchcape saw it, but it's nothing but a ruin now. Everyone talks about Miss Fairchild—they say she's crazy. Margery MacInnes told me her father's actually *afraid* of her. You can't work for someone like that, Mum. We could hang on until Len comes—she'll be better by then—"

But Christine shook her head. "I came here to do a job, Alice, and I'll stay until I've done it."

"You were hired to write a book, not be a nursemaid," said Alice hotly.

"That's true, and I said as much to Mr. MacInnes. But no one could have foreseen Miss Fairchild's illness."

"What about Mrs. Mofford then? She couldn't stand being here."

"I'm not Mrs. Mofford." Christine set down her teacup with a brittle chink. "Do you know how old I am?"

The question seemed utterly irrelevant to Alice.

Her mother didn't expect an answer. She went on, "I'm almost forty-two, Alice. I've lived half my life. Until now I'd never been out of England—I'd barely set foot outside of East Anglia."

Alice couldn't understand what her mother was getting at. "Why couldn't we just have had a holiday abroad then, like normal people? In Spain, or the south of France?"

"For a fortnight, you mean? Lying on a beach and eating too much, then going home with a suitcase full of dirty laundry." Christine's voice was bitter. "Nothing would have changed, Alice. Everything would just be the same."

"But what was wrong with it? I don't understand."

"No, I don't suppose you do. When I was your age, I wouldn't have, either. I thought hard about this before I decided, you must believe that, and I realized that if I didn't do it—take this job—I'd spend the rest of my life in exactly the same place—the same house, the same job. That's all I'd ever have, and it wasn't enough."

"Well, it was for *me*. I thought you wanted me to finish at Woodhall and go on to university—that's what you've always said."

"That's right. And there's no reason why you can't still. Woodhall isn't the only good school in the world. Girls from Saint Katherine's go to Cambridge, too, you know. And it's not as if we've emigrated, Alice—we haven't come to New Zealand forever, only a year or two. When I've finished my work with Miss Fairchild, we'll go back to England and I'll find another job. This is only a small disruption in your life. You might even enjoy it if you'd let yourself."

Alice gave an involuntary shiver.

Christine's voice grew brisk. "In any event, here we are, so you'll have to make the best of it, Alice. I did not come all the way here only to turn around and go back at the first sign of trouble."

"What about Len?"

"Len?"

"You left him. You waited until he'd gone to Dover. Why?" It was a dangerous question, Alice knew, and she was afraid of the answer, but she had to hear it.

"He left us first, don't forget," said Christine carefully.

"But he told us where he was going. The job was too good to refuse. He said—"

"I know what he said. He had a perfectly good job in Cambridge, Alice. He didn't have to leave it. Don't look at me like that—he's done it before. Len doesn't like facing up to things. He never has. You remember when he went off to Scotland."

Alice was six when Len had gotten a job building roads in the Highlands. Her grandmother had died, and Christine had taken her and gone back to Wroxley to look after Alice's grandfather until arrangements could be made for him. He couldn't take care of himself; he'd had a stroke some months before.

Alice had been frightened of the old man with the crooked face in the wheelchair. He seemed always to be scowling and making loud, unpleasant noises. Her mother spent a lot of time with him. Alice had been lonely. She hadn't known any of the village children and she'd missed Len, but she believed what her mother told her and everyone else in Wroxley and in Cambridge who asked: Len had to go up north because he'd been offered such a good job he couldn't afford to turn it down. It was only temporary. And within the year they'd all been together again in Cambridge, in the house on Courtfield Road. Alice had begun at Woodhall and her mother had a job as secretary at the University Press. Len joined the university maintenance crew, looking after the heavy equipment. Granddad Pickell had faded from Alice's consciousness. He'd gone to live at a place called Stanhope Manor, where her mother went to visit him every Sunday until he died the following spring. Alice hadn't thought about him in a long time.

Christine was watching her. "Len and your grandfather didn't get along, Alice. He never thought Len was good enough. Len couldn't face going back to Wroxley with us. That's really why he went to Scotland."

Alice considered this; it made more sense to her now than it would have a year or two ago. "But if that's true, Mum, why did he go this time?"

"I suppose because I wanted things to change and he didn't."

"Do you honestly want him to follow us?" Alice asked it outright and held her breath.

"Of course I do!" exclaimed Christine crossly. "You saw the letter I wrote him—I told him where we were going and when. I even left money at the bank for his ticket."

"Why didn't you just wait for him? Wouldn't that have been simpler?"

"Because I couldn't. If I'd waited any longer, I might never have done it."

— 10 —

A Visitor to Florestan

The next morning Alice came downstairs heavy-eyed. She had not slept well; she had lain in bed feeling the whole weight of the house pressing down on her, squeezing the air out of her lungs. She couldn't bear the thought of a whole empty day, when her mother would be busy with Miss Fairchild and Alice would be for all practical purposes invisible.

"Rugby?" Her mother gave her a suspicious look. "This is the first I've heard about a rugby match."

It wasn't the most inviting means of escape, but it was the best one that occurred to Alice as she ate her cornflakes. "Well, I did mean to tell you yesterday, but it went out of my head because of the bedrooms. Everyone from school is going—"

"Everyone?"

"Helen Quennell and Grace Ingraham and Margery MacInnes. It's Otago High and Saint Mark's—" She thought she'd gotten the schools right, but it didn't really matter. Her mother wouldn't know.

"Margery MacInnes." Her mother smiled. "There you are, Alice, what did I tell you? You're making friends already. Of course you can go. Just don't hang about once it's over—those crowds can be rough. Where are you meeting the other girls?''

"Um," said Alice, "we haven't set a place yet. I said I had to ask. I'll just ring Helen now and fix it.''

Then she had no choice. There was only one Quennell in the directory, on Deskford Crescent, wherever that was. Alice fidgeted anxiously, waiting for the woman she supposed was Mummy to get Helen. "I thought you couldn't come." Helen sounded surprised. "It turns out I can after all," Alice told her brightly. "Where shall I meet you?" "I don't suppose Grace will mind. What about the newsagent's on the corner of Pitt Street. Do you know where that is? At one-fifteen." "I'll find it," said Alice with more confidence than she felt. "See you." And she hung up before her courage failed her, or Helen could express further doubt.

She set off after lunch, leaving her mother hoovering the library with an aged and asthmatic vacuum cleaner. The day was bright blue and gold; the sun put a hazy bloom on the city, and the harbor shone. Alice hoped it was a good omen: perhaps the afternoon would turn out better than she expected. It wasn't quite one when she reached the newsagent's, and she assumed an inconspicuous position inside by the front window where she had a good view of the pavement. While she waited she leafed through a copy of *Woman's Weekly,* pretending to look at the pictures. The boy behind the counter didn't seem to mind whether she bought anything or not; he was immersed in an oil-stained car repair manual, tracing complicated diagrams with a bitten fingernail.

One-fifteen came and there was no sign of Helen and Grace. Alice waited ten minutes, then fifteen. Had they been delayed, or had they forgotten they were meeting her? Was she at the right newsagent's? Maybe Grace had minded after all, and they'd gone on without her— although Alice didn't think Helen would do that. Still, she couldn't be sure; she'd only known her two days. She was just beginning to wonder if she was brave enough to go to the playing field, wherever it was, by herself to look for them—she could always say she'd been late and come straight from Florestan—when they appeared, walking along the pavement, wearing almost identical gathered skirts, white blouses, and cardigans, and sharing a bag of potato crisps. Helen awkwardly stuffed the empty bag into her pocket. Alice was too relieved at seeing them to make a point of noticing.

On the way to the match they bought sausage rolls, more potato crisps, and lemonade, in spite of the rule about Saint Katherine's girls not eating on the street. Alice hadn't enough money for an eclair and had to pretend she wasn't hungry while trying not to watch Grace lick custard from her fingers. Grace entertained them with an account of something called a gymkhana, which she and Kowhai were going to enter at Christmas. It sounded very odd to Alice: costume competitions, egg-and-spoon races, relays, all on horseback—but Helen kept asking questions as if she knew what it was about, and telling Alice it was smashing fun.

There were lots of people at the playing field, most of Dunedin, Alice guessed. "There's Margery," said Helen, pointing. "She's usually late." Margery was standing up in the bleachers, waving her arms like a windmill. "Alice Jenkins," she said when they climbed up to join her. "I didn't think you were coming. I've only saved two places. But it doesn't matter, we'll just shove up a bit. Excuse me." She smiled ingenuously at the woman next to her, who moved along just enough so the three of them could squeeze in. Alice found herself sandwiched between Margery and Helen with Grace last, braced like a bookend.

"Well?" said Margery. "What do you think?"

"Think?" echoed Alice.

"Yes, think. Of Miss Fairchild. You must have met her?"

Alice shook her head. "She went right to bed when she got back. I don't think she's been out of her room, at least not while I've been in the house. She has gastroenteritis," she added impressively.

Margery frowned and Helen said, "That sounds serious."

"The doctor's already been twice."

"Haven't you seen her, though," Margery persisted.

Grace, on the end, had been paying no attention to the conversation. She was studying the boys milling around the edges of the playing field. "Look, isn't that your brother, Helen? Why isn't he in uniform? Isn't he playing?"

"Simon?" Helen swiveled around to look. "No, he sprained a finger at practice Wednesday. Isn't that silly? They won't let him play for a week. Mummy was sure he'd broken it—it swelled up and turned purple—there they are, and there's Dougie, Grace!"

A pack of boys in shorts and striped jerseys spilled onto the field and the crowd cheered happily. Alice had only the haziest notion of what was supposed to happen. The girls at Woodhall hadn't gone in for rugby, and Len preferred snooker.

"Where is he?" Grace leaned forward over her knees and peered intently. Helen said, "Over on the left. See?" The pack on the field thundered past the stands, chasing a ball. They were an undifferentiated mob, as far as Alice could see. "Who're you looking at? Which one?" she asked. Grace hissed between her teeth like a punctured bicycle tire. "With the fair hair—the one at the bottom of the heap," said Margery, as the boys went down like jackstraws. "Grace is potty about him."

They picked themselves up off the ground, and Alice saw a lanky boy scramble to his feet, shaking the sawdust-colored hair out of his eyes. His bony knees were filthy. He wiped his hands on the back of his shorts and Grace sighed. "He has the most beautiful seat," she said dreamily. "He what?" said Alice, startled. "On a horse," explained Margery with a grin. Helen added helpfully, "His father is Uncle Geoff's foreman. He's at school with my brother Simon."

The match went on and on, sloshing back and forth across the trampled grass. Every now and then one side or the other would score a goal, though Alice was never looking in the right place at the right moment to see it. Then the crowd would roar enthusiastically and half the boys would raise their arms in triumph and strut and slap one another on the back, while the others would huddle together, throwing fierce glances over their shoulders. At one point during the game the boy with the beautiful seat—his name, Alice had learned by then, was Dougie McNaughton—paused to pull up his socks right in front of the four of them, and gave Grace a broad, freckled grin. Her cheeks turned flaming red and Helen elbowed her violently. As soon as he'd run off, they exploded into giggles. Margery shook her head disparagingly and said, "Hormones!" to Alice.

"You're just jealous," said Helen.

"Not me," replied Margery flatly. "You can go all pie-eyed over great gowks like that if you want. I can't be bothered."

Grace and Helen exchanged a look. "Is Brenda really going to ask him to the wedding?" said Grace. "If he's there, I'll just die."

Helen nodded. "Of course she is. She's asking Peter Ollernshaw too, because he's Simon's best friend. Peter Ollernshaw is *so* good-looking—I've simply *got* to have my braces out in time!"

The game ended. Alice wasn't sure which side had won—whichever side Dougie-with-the-beautiful-seat wasn't on, she thought. They walked away from the bleachers together, weaving through the departing throngs. On a busy street corner outside the gates they paused uncertainly. "You could come home to tea," said Helen. "I know Mummy wouldn't mind." Grace didn't look terribly enthusiastic.

Margery shook her head. "No, thanks, Helen. Can't. We've got Aunt Jessie."

Grace sniggered. "She sounds like a disease."

Instead of taking offense, Margery grinned. "That's what Pa's afraid of—that she'll turn out to be contagious. She owns an art gallery in Christchurch. She only represents New Zealand artists, and she's always looking for new ones to encourage. That's why she's here, fossicking for talent. She brings them back to our house for meals and Pa has conniption fits. I think he expects them to steal the silver or sit on the floor smoking opium." She swung suddenly on Alice, her eyes glittering like green glass. "Miss Fairchild's an artist, you know."

"She is? Well, yes—I guess she paints flowers—"

"That's what *he* said, isn't it?" exclaimed Margery contemptuously.

"He doesn't understand—not at all. Well, I'm off. See you Monday. You can tell us what she's like then, Alice." And she was gone, darting off through the traffic.

Helen turned. "Alice, you can come if you like."

"I promised Mum I'd go right back after the game," said Alice with more regret than she felt. She guessed that Helen and Grace would spend the rest of the afternoon discussing Dougie and Peter and the wedding and she would only feel left out, even if Helen tried to include her. She didn't understand what they found so fascinating about a gangle of loud-voiced, large-footed boys throwing themselves carelessly around a playing field after a ball.

At school Monday Alice was able to tell Margery nothing new about Miss Fairchild except that Dr. Lattimer had been again Sunday afternoon and pronounced her condition improving. A sign of the improvement was the frequency with which Miss Fairchild had begun to ring her bell.

The first Alice had learned of the bell was Saturday evening, after a scrappy, unsatisfying sort of tea: tinned tomato soup that tasted thin and rusty, grated cheese on limp lettuce leaves, and bread and butter. Christine said she was too tired to bother cooking. She asked how the game had been, but it clearly didn't matter that Alice couldn't say for certain who had won or what the score had been. She could tell her mother wasn't really paying attention to the answers; her mind was elsewhere. As they were cleaning up, a bell suddenly began to jangle somewhere in the kitchen. It wasn't the front door or the telephone; this was a shrill, imperative little bell Alice hadn't heard before that rang, then stopped, then rang again.

"Oh, bother it!" exclaimed Christine.

"Bother what?" said Alice, looking around.

"Miss Fairchild's bell. She wants something and I'll have to go and see what it is. Alice, you can finish here."

The bell was attached to a board with eleven other little bells near the door to the passage. It was numbered 9, in the middle of the bottom row. When Miss Fairchild yanked on a tasseled pull hanging beside her bed upstairs, it caused the curled spring holding the bell to leap and quiver. Over the course of Sunday Miss Fairchild rang at least half a dozen times when Alice was in the kitchen, and each time her mother had to climb the stairs to find out why. Between trips Christine was busy boiling rice, poaching chicken, and making custard according to Dr. Lattimer's instructions for the invalid's diet, and continuing to clean out the library so she could use it as an office when Miss Fairchild had recovered sufficiently to begin on the book. Alice had been hoping her mother would want to go to church Sunday morning. Unless they got right away from Florestan and Miss Fairchild, she realized she had little hope of holding Christine's attention long enough for a serious discussion, and she felt they had a lot to discuss. But when she mentioned church, her mother said, "You can certainly go if you want, Alice, but I can't leave Miss Fairchild alone, and Dr. Lattimer was irritatingly vague about when he'd stop in."

Dispirited, Alice spent the morning outside, poking around the grounds. No matter where she was, she felt the house, enormous and self-important, looking over her shoulder. Below it, tucked out of sight behind vast green mounds of rhododendron, she found the tennis courts where Mr. Tatlock kept the sheep penned when they weren't wanted for lawn mowing. The nets were gone, the posts leaning drunkenly, out of work and derelict, the court lines obliterated. On one side stood an umpire's chair with no seat, next to it a long wooden trough and a galvanized tub.

Beyond the flagstoned terrace outside the drawing room were the remains of a large, formal flower garden. The ghostly outlines of geometric beds showed under mats of weed and blackened flower stalks. In the middle was a large, shallow goldfish pond. All it held, as far as Alice could see, was dark, scummy water and dead leaves. Probably all the fish had long since died, or been eaten by Mrs. Mofford's cats. In the center was a little boy riding a dolphin. The boy's round cheeks were stained with dirt and the arm he raised over his head ended in a stump at the wrist. Alice wondered what had happened to the hand; perhaps it had fallen into the water. There was a ghost story about a hand that had crept about after it had been severed, searching for the person responsible. . . .

In the afternoon, clouds came rafting swiftly across the sky, burying the sun, and a stiff wind came up. Alice watched the trees throwing up their limbs in despair. She knew how they felt. She did her schoolwork very slowly and thoroughly, making it last as long as possible. After a bland, invalid supper of poached chicken and mashed turnips she went to bed early and read *Ivanhoe* for her English class. It put her to sleep quickly.

Monday was dismal: wet and cold. By Tuesday afternoon the rain finally dwindled to a chilly dampness in the air. Returning to Florestan after school, Alice picked her way around the multitude of puddles that had collected in the driveway's ruts. On the grass in front of the house the sheep were safely grazing in a little knot, their fleeces dark with water. When Alice appeared, they jerked their heads up and turned their blank, silly faces toward her. She was tempted to shout and stamp and make them scatter, just for the satisfaction of asserting herself over creatures more timid and less powerful than she, but the presence of a dark green Austin parked beside the steps inhibited her, and she left the sheep unmolested. The car had leather upholstery and its gleaming finish was streaked with mud.

Around back she found her mother wrapped in a cardigan, standing outside the scullery door, smoking a cigarette. She looked at Alice without really seeing her.

"Whose car is that?" asked Alice.

"What? Oh, it belongs to Mr. MacInnes. He's come on business." She crushed the cigarette underfoot, and brought Alice into focus. "He asked how you were getting on at Saint Katherine's—he wondered if you'd met Margaret yet. I said I thought you had."

"*Margery*. And I told you, she was at the rugby match on Saturday. You weren't listening." She followed her mother into the kitchen, and heard her sigh.

"Don't sound so annoyed, Alice. I've had a great many things on my mind these last few days. I'm sure you understand. There's a letter on the table you'll be interested in."

"From Len?" But it wasn't. Alice could tell as soon as she saw it lying on the table: cream-colored stationery and matching envelope, with a New Zealand stamp in the corner, and the address printed on it: Mrs. Dennis Royde, 4 Augusta Crescent, Wellington. Disappointed, Alice skimmed the note: ". . . meant to write much sooner . . . so much to catch up on . . . The Bishop took a chill . . . rather worrying . . . weak chest . . . recovering very nicely now. I do hope you're settling in . . . no longer finding things strange. Of course it does take time . . ."

Bell number nine suddenly jangled, interrupting her. "Ah," said her mother, straightening her cardigan and smoothing her hair. "That'll be Mr. MacInnes now, ready to leave. I hope he hasn't worn her out."

Alice put down the letter and followed her mother through the swinging door, down the passage to the great hall. Mr. MacInnes was just descending the staircase, a leather briefcase in his hand. "Oh, there you are, Mrs. Jenkins. I was hoping for a word with you on my way out. Quite a remarkable woman, Miss Fairchild, don't you think? Her illness doesn't seem to have dulled her spirit. Indomitable, I'd say." He didn't sound entirely happy about it, Alice thought.

"Dr. Lattimer says she's making a satisfactory recovery."

"Yes. Yes, indeed—I'm so glad to hear it." He tugged at his necktie and gave a self-conscious little laugh. "To tell you the truth, Mrs. Jenkins, she always makes me feel as if I were still in short pants. I've been her solicitor ever since my father retired—that must be all of twelve years now—but I think she still regards me as a junior clerk." He paused, but Alice's mother said nothing. "Yes, well, I'm afraid I rather put my foot in it by suggesting it might be useful to have young

Clement come and look things over here, see what needs to be attended to. He's got a good head on him, knows which way is up. After all, he's been running the brewery with great success—'' His forehead wrinkled slightly and he gave a puzzled sniff. ''She didn't take to the idea at all well. She accused me of implying she was too feeble to look after the house herself, and of course I had no intention—'' He sniffed again, frowning. ''Pardon me for asking, Mrs. Jenkins, but you don't keep cats, do you? There was a spot of bother—I think I told you— with Mrs. Mofford—''

''No, Mr. MacInnes. As far as I know, there are no cats in this house at present.''

''Not live ones anyway,'' Alice amended from the shadows.

''I'm sorry?'' Mr. MacInnes noticed her for the first time. ''I didn't quite—''

''It's the dampness brings it out,'' said Christine. ''The smell. Something really must be done about it, Mr. MacInnes. And the leak in the front bedroom—several of the window frames are rotting. In fact there are a number of things that ought to be seen to as soon as possible.''

''Mmm.'' He glanced around the great hall, his smile a shade less assured. ''It is rather overwhelming, isn't it? I mean, I haven't actually set foot in this house for some years. Miss Fairchild prefers to do her business at our offices.'' He lowered his voice slightly. ''A bit reclusive, you know. Not like her father. There were always people at the house when he was alive. When I was a boy, I'd come up sometimes with my father. Mr. Clement was very proud of Florestan—he loved to show it off. When he died, I always thought it was too bad—still. It belongs to her now. He left her the house and all its contents in his will.''

''Did you ask Miss Fairchild about hiring help, Mr. MacInnes?''

''I did mention it to her, yes. But we had so much to discuss. I didn't actually get a firm answer—''

''Mr. MacInnes, I told you that I couldn't possibly run a house the size of Florestan on my own, even supposing that was what I'd been hired to do. Which, you understand, it isn't.''

"Of course, Mrs. Jenkins. I do understand that," he said soothingly. "But given the circumstances—just until the dust has settled a bit, so to speak—"

"That," said Christine dryly, "is exactly what I mean. The dust has been settling here for far too long, I would say."

"Ah—very good, Mrs. Jenkins! A sense of humor's precisely what's needed. Keeps things in perspective, I've always said. I do take your point, however. I'm sure once Mr. Jenkins arrives—you did say he was on his way, didn't you? Once he's been able to look round a bit, we'll have a clear idea of what needs doing. In the meantime, opening a few windows, unrolling the carpets in some of these rooms should make a big difference—but then you'll know better than I. And I think, in all honesty, Mrs. Jenkins, that it makes best sense for you and Miss Fairchild to discuss the domestic arrangements between yourselves, when she's feeling up to it, of course. I'll be only too happy to help in any way that I can, she knows that—and I hope you do, too. But just at present I would advise you to go a bit carefully. She's got quite a temper."

Alice saw her mother square her shoulders and knew she was getting ready for an argument. Christine had quite a temper, too; Mr. MacInnes hadn't discovered that yet. But his attention shifted. "Hullo—it's Alice, isn't it? I was asking your mother about you. How are you finding Saint Katherine's?"

Alice resisted the temptation to reply, "Out the front gate, down the hill, and turn left." She knew her mother wouldn't be amused; it was the kind of answer Len got the sharp side of Christine's tongue for giving. "It seems quite all right, thank you," she said politely.

"I'm glad to hear it. Making friends, are you?" There it was again, thought Alice, wincing inwardly. They all did it. "My daughter Margery is always off on some adventure with her chums. I hardly see her during term time. I don't know when she manages to do her schoolwork, but she must—no one's complained about it!" He laughed to show he was making a joke. "It's no fun being a grind though, is it? You're only young once. Goodness, I must be off—I didn't realize it was so late! I told Angie I'd be back by half past three and it's gone four. No, thanks, Mrs. Jenkins, I can see myself out—" And he was gone. His footsteps echoed on the flagstones as he hurried under the pikes and banners in the hall, the door whined on its hinges, then shut firmly like a period at the end of a sentence. The silence in the house closed in, filling up the space where he'd been.

"What does all that mean?" asked Alice, after a minute or two.

"I think," said her mother thoughtfully, "that it doesn't mean anything much."

Behind the kitchen door a bell began to jangle.

— 11 —

The Terrible Two

Actually, Alice quite liked Saint Katherine's. The routine of school gave a familiar structure to her days: for seven hours, Monday through Friday, she could rejoin the real world and do normal things. There were morning prayers, rules about not talking in the halls or eating on the streets, conduct marks, French club and a drama society, lost-and-found announcements, and a curt request from Mrs. Sturtevant, the librarian, reminding girls to "please place books back on the shelves *where you found them.*" In the afternoons, when Alice returned reluctantly to Florestan, she would spread out her schoolbooks and immerse herself in them, constructing a barricade of French, Latin, the Tudor Succession, *A Midsummer Night's Dream,* algebra—the same subjects she'd be studying back at Woodhall. In some she was ahead, in others behind, but the teachers at Saint Katherine's were, by and large, interested and helpful. She didn't much care for Miss Tibbets, who taught algebra, but that was perhaps as much the algebra as Miss Tibbets. Using letters to stand for numbers struck Alice as perverse and pointless.

She thought often of Woodhall. There the school year was beginning instead of in its final term. The last days of September would be growing damper and darker, while in Dunedin they were stretching out under the warming spring sun. The sea glittered in the harbor below and everywhere flowers exploded into dazzling bloom. In the morning, or the afternoon, or walking between Lockwood and Marchmont, Alice would be overcome at odd moments with a painful longing for the smell of wet leaves and coal smoke instead of fresh salt wind and growing things.

The worst part of Saint Katherine's was being an object of curiosity. For the most part, Alice kept her head down and did her best to evade questions, hoping if she was vague and noncommittal, the other girls would decide she was boring and lose interest, but her Englishness together with her connection to Florestan and Miss Fairchild made it impossible for her to escape attention.

Helen and Grace were useful. As long as she went around with them, adults didn't worry that she wasn't fitting in, never mind that the two of them were endlessly preoccupied with Helen's sister's wedding. They were to be bridesmaids in yellow taffeta gowns—like primroses, said Helen. Everything at the wedding was to be yellow and white. Privately Alice didn't think yellow taffeta was going to make either Grace or Helen look like a primrose. She resigned herself to letting their chatter wash over her; now and then she'd smile dutifully and nod, when Helen remembered to include her. Generously Helen assured Alice that she would receive an invitation. Alice hoped not; the idea was quite alarming.

Less useful was Margery MacInnes, who was part of the same group. Helen was safe, the sort of friend Alice knew her mother would want her to have. She had nice manners and a good heart. And Grace was all right. She tolerated Alice without paying much attention to her. But Alice found Margery unsettling. She often felt as if Margery was sizing her up in an uncomfortable way. She would look up from an algebraic equation or a plate of shepherd's pie or a discussion of dyeing shoes yellow, and find Margery's green eyes fixed speculatively upon her.

Margery would smile and look away, leaving Alice to wonder what she was thinking.

Betty Ware and Fiona Watkins smiled at her, too, but that was another matter. Betty and Fiona came together in the alphabet and everywhere else. They greedily seized every opportunity to remind Alice that she was an alien and inferior. Whenever Alice was called on in class—and she took care not to make the mistake of volunteering although she often knew the answers—they smirked irritatingly at each other. Betty had already pointed out loudly that Alice's uniform was obviously second-hand. Each time they saw her, they made a show of giggling and whispering pointedly. Fiona frequently mimicked her. Knowing she was supposed to hear, Alice pretended she didn't, but she really couldn't see why someone who spoke through her nose all the time should assume superiority over someone who sounded normal. As much as she could she avoided the pair of them, especially when she was leaving school in the afternoons.

On Friday she had just collected her jacket and books from her cubby in the front hall of Lockwood, and was about to make her escape, congratulating herself on what Len would call a clean getaway, when Miss Sallet came hurrying up the front steps, practically bowling Alice over, her arms full of file folders. "Oh, Alice! Thank you, dear." She beamed at Alice, who was holding the door open. "I was just thinking of you this morning. I hope you're settling in? Miss Parsons says you seem to be doing very well—I'm delighted! I've been meaning to have a little chat with you, but somehow life gets out of hand, and here it is, the end of the week already. But you do know you can always come and see me, anytime you need—?"

"Yes, Miss Sallet. Thank you," said Alice, glancing furtively around. No sign of the Terrible Two.

But instead of continuing on her way, Miss Sallet shifted the files to the crook of one elbow and put her hand on Alice's arm, drawing her back inside, out of the flow of traffic. "Tell me, Alice, how is Miss

Fairchild? I thought of ringing your mother, but I didn't want to bother her so soon. I do hope she's recovering?''

''The doctor says she's improving,'' said Alice cautiously. She had met Dr. Lattimer on Wednesday afternoon. Just as Alice had arrived, he had ''popped in''—his words—to see how his patient was, and spent several minutes talking to Alice's mother about depression and getting Miss Fairchild ''to take her mind off herself.'' He had a habit of running his long, bony fingers through his long, limp hair in a distracted way. He did not strike Alice as a very reassuring sort of person.

''Oh, I am glad. These foreign illnesses can be so worrying. Your mother's had her hands full, hasn't she? Not exactly what she'd expected.''

''No. But she's begun sorting papers and making notes.''

''Notes? Oh, yes, of course. For the book. I'd heard Miss Fairchild intended writing a history of Florestan—now who told me? Of course, how silly! It was your mother who told me. My brain is like a sieve these days. Between ourselves, Alice, I'd much rather she'd write a book about her own life and travels instead. Now that would be fascinating. She's done so much, and it hasn't been easy for her.'' Miss Sallet frowned thoughtfully at Alice. ''I rather hoped I'd be able to persuade her to give us one of her illustrated lectures this term. I was lucky enough to hear her when she spoke about her journey to the West Indies for the Victoria League in 1952. Goodness! That was six years ago. Time just races past, doesn't it? To hear a woman talk about her travels, it was so exciting. She's done extraordinary things, absolutely extraordinary. She'd be such an inspiration for you girls. And now she has a connection with us.'' She smiled expectantly.

Alice thought she was supposed to ask what, when she realized that Miss Sallet meant her. She couldn't very well explain that Miss Fairchild was as yet unaware of this connection. ''She *has* been very ill,'' Alice hedged.

''Yes, of course she has. And I wouldn't dream of asking her now.

But perhaps you could let me know when I might call on her? Or you could ask your mother to telephone?''

"Yes, I'll do that." Alice pictured the list her mother was keeping of people who wanted to visit. They'd have to give out numbers when the time came: one through eight on Tuesday afternoon, no more than twenty minutes apiece, please. Keep the line moving, thank you very much.

"Thank you, Alice. Oh, Mrs. Woolman, there you are. You wanted to see me?''

"I need to speak to you about Ellen Blunden, Miss Sallet. I've just had the most extraordinary report about her—''

Released, Alice darted out the door only to find Betty and Fiona standing at the gate. She bent her head over her satchel, hugged it to her chest, and tried to hurry past without looking at them, but they fell into step beside her.

"You're awfully thick with old Salad, aren't you? What did she want?'' asked Betty.

"Alice has probably done something wrong. But because she's new and *strange*—'' Fiona said, ''—because Alice is *so strange,* she's being let off with a warning this time. What is it, Alice? Which sin did you commit?''

"None. She only asked how I'm getting on.''

Betty shook her head sadly. "Not very well, I'm afraid, Miss Sallet.''

"No, not well at all,'' agreed Fiona. "Alice Jenkins is much too stuck up to make friends. I don't think she likes us, Miss Sallet. And nobody can understand what she's saying because she talks as if she's got a mouthful of pebbles. Betty, do you suppose they *all* talk that way in England, or is it just Alice?''

Alice began to walk faster, eyes on the pavement. Two pairs of feet, one on either side, kept pace with her.

"I do hope you'll ask Miss Fairchild to give us a lecture, Alice Jenkins,'' said Betty. "She'd be such an example.''

Fiona giggled. "She'd be an example, all right. Of an utter nutter.''

"An example of what happens when you live all alone in a haunted house. You go gaga. My father says her mind's snapped. That's why she had to hire someone from England to work for her—no one in New Zealand would work there on a dare," said Betty.

"No *sane* person anyway. But I'll bet Alice's mother isn't sane, either. She can't be if she came all the way from England just to be a housekeeper."

"She *isn't* a housekeeper," said Alice coldly. "She's an editor. She worked at Cambridge University Press. Miss Fairchild hired her to write a book." She glanced up at Fiona defiantly.

Fiona's eyes narrowed. "You're lying," she said.

"She's writing a history of Florestan. It was built by a famous *English* architect," retorted Alice. "Mr. Fairchild wanted the best. But I don't expect you'd ever have heard of him." She hoped neither of them would ask who he was.

Betty snorted. "She'd better write fast, that's all. My father says the house is falling down—it's practically a ruin. He says it's a scandal the way she's let it go. Something ought to be done about it."

Alice almost said that as Florestan belonged to Miss Fairchild, she didn't see that it was any of Betty's father's business what became of it, but she didn't want to prolong the conversation. She only wanted to get away.

"*I* know!" exclaimed Fiona, jostling Alice's elbow. "Alice can ask us to tea one afternoon. She can give us a guided tour of Florestan and teach us all about this famous architect. We might even forgive her for being so unfriendly. Don't you think that's a good idea, Betty?"

"I'm not sure." Betty sounded dubious. "I don't think my father would let me go, not to a house where a crazy person lives. He'd say it wasn't safe."

"It must be safe. After all, *Alice* lives there."

"But that's different, isn't it? Alice doesn't—"

"*There* you are! I've been looking for you all over." Margery MacInnes deftly inserted herself between Alice and Fiona, and hooked Alice's arm with her own. "Oh, sorry, Fee—is that your foot? I'm not interrupting anything, am I?"

"Yes, you are actually," Fiona said frostily.

"No," said Alice.

"Oh well," said Margery, "I'll only be a tick. I've got to collect Flora."

"Who's Flora?" Alice was quick to seize the change of subject.

"My sister. One of my sisters. She's eight—in Sutton with the infants. Ma was supposed to pick her up this afternoon, but her meeting's run late. *Again.* I've got two sisters and a brother," said Margery chattily. "Kitty's eleven and Andrew's six. Pa wanted a boy, so they had to keep trying until they got one."

"Is your aunt still here?" asked Alice, eager to keep up the conversation.

"No, she left this morning, actually."

Betty and Fiona exchanged glances and walked away.

"Good riddance!" exclaimed Margery to their backs. "Honestly, Alice, you're going to have to be more selective about the company you keep. People will get the wrong idea about you."

"But I didn't—"

"I haven't got any time—I'm late already. Pa was talking about you last night and Ma said I should ask you to tea tomorrow. Grace and Helen are coming. We're going to the pictures first—it's some sort of horse thing—cowboys and Indians, probably dead boring, but Grace is keen to see anything with horses in it. You can tell your mum that Pa'll run you home afterward."

"I'm not sure—" began Alice.

"Of course you can. We're meeting at the cinema on Moray Place at quarter to two. I have to run. See you there."

— 12 —

Odd Socks

When she woke up the next morning, Alice thought possibly she was getting a cold. Her throat felt dry and a little scratchy. She tried coughing, wondering if that might not irritate it further, but it only irritated her mother, who told her to drink some orange juice, so she gave it up. She hadn't said anything about Margery's invitation—she considered saying nothing at all, then telling Margery on Monday that her mother had needed her help at Florestan all weekend. But the next time Mr. MacInnes spoke to Christine he was bound to mention it, and there'd be more trouble than it was worth.

She waited until after breakfast, beginning to clear the table without being asked, while her mother had a last cup of tea and read Friday's *Evening Star*. "I really don't care," she said, sounding casual. "I know there are a lot of things to do here. . . ."

"Hmmm." Christine's eyes followed the lines of print in front of her.

"I did tell Margery I probably couldn't go, that you'd want me to help—"

"Go?" Christine finally looked up. "Where do you want to go? Alice, what are you saying—I can't read the paper and listen—"

Bell number nine gave a startled leap. Christine pressed her lips together.

Alice sighed. "It's just, well, some of the girls from school are going to the cinema this afternoon, and Margery's having them back to tea afterward. I said I thought I wouldn't be able to—"

"Do you mean Margery MacInnes? How nice of her. Whyever not? Do you know where she lives, and how to get back after?"

"I'm to meet them at the cinema." Alice saw her fate sealed. "She says her father will bring me back when he takes Helen and Grace home. I expect she's only asking me because he told her to."

"Nonsense. She's asking you because she wants to. I knew you'd make friends quickly." Christine looked pleased. The bell danced on its little spring. She stood up and folded the paper neatly. "You'll have a good time, Alice. Much better than staying here. As it happens, Miss Fairchild and I are going to sort papers today. Dr. Lattimer thinks the sooner she begins to work the faster she'll recover, and heaven knows there's enough to keep us busy for years. I don't think anyone in this house has ever thrown anything out. Where's my handbag? You'll need some money." She didn't think to ask Alice what they were going to see; Alice couldn't have told her anyway, Margery hadn't given her a chance to ask.

It was a gray, windy afternoon. The sky was full of extravagant cloud shapes, pierced now and then by swift, bright blades of sun. Alice made her way down through the city, hugging her jacket close under her chin, and found Helen waiting outside the picture theater on Moray Place. Grace had gone in to save seats, and Margery hadn't appeared yet. "She's always late. Her mother's never home when she says she'll be, and Margery gets stuck with the ankle-biters," explained Helen.

"Ankle-biters?"

"That's what she calls her sisters and brother."

Margery came flying along the pavement as Alice was buying her ticket, and crowded up behind her. "Crikey, I was afraid I'd have to bring them along! Ma only just got home."

"Do hurry," begged Helen, "it's going to start and we'll never find Grace in the dark. I hate missing the beginnings."

It was an American film about a gunfighter with a mysterious past who rode into a valley, solved the settlers' problems with a villainous cattle baron, then rode out again, leaving them in peace. Alice found she had seen it before, in Cambridge, with Len and Audrey, a year ago.

When it was over, they took the bus to Roslyn, where Margery lived. Coult Hill Road lay along the crest of the hills that swelled back from the harbor, higher than Florestan and Saint Katherine's. While Helen, Grace, and Margery discussed the film's hero's name—was Shane a first name or a last?—Alice watched the great mottled carpet of roof and treetops below. She found the sensation of height and the immensity of space unnerving. Oblivious of the familiar, the others chattered around her. They'd gotten on to a discussion of the menu for the wedding reception and how the place cards were to be arranged. "I can make sure you sit next to Dougie," Helen promised. Grace groaned. "But that'll be so *obvious*! And I won't be able to eat anything." "That's all to the good," said Margery heartlessly. "You'll only spill if you do." "Well, how about the same table, then?" offered Helen, her eyebrows disappearing earnestly under her bangs.

Margery lived in a comfortable, spreading brick house called Castlebrae, set back from the road in a leafy, well-behaved garden. There were no weeds between the paving stones; the gravel drive was smooth; the gate opened easily and silently; the trim on the house was a fresh, clean white; the lawn was evenly mowed; the brass doorknob was polished. A pair of small plaster lions guarded the front steps, and a web of hazy lavender wisteria screened the veranda.

The inside matched the outside: well tended, inviting, lived-in but not cluttered. There were carpets in soft, warm shades on the polished wood floors. Alice glimpsed an enormous bowl of yellow tulips on a table in the lounge, like a splash of sun. She was reminded of Audrey's house. Castlebrae would have fitted right into the same prosperous Cambridge neighborhood. It had never occurred to Alice to feel envious of Audrey, but that was when she'd had a perfectly decent home herself, before she'd been dragged to the other side of the world and compelled to live in Florestan.

Margery took them straight through to the kitchen, where Mrs. MacInnes was in the midst of preparations for a dinner party. She was doing something complicated with chicken and vegetables. Like Margery, she was thin, quick, red-haired; but her eyes were hazel instead of green, and her hair was deliberately cut to soften the lines of her face. There was a kind of controlled tightness about her that charged the air in the kitchen. "Oh, there you are," she said, flashing them a smile. "Your tea's there on the table, Margery. Did you enjoy the film? Good." It was clear she didn't expect a detailed answer. Mr. MacInnes was out playing golf with Helen's father, and the ankle-biters, rather to Alice's disappointment, had been parceled out among various friends.

Tea was ample: lemonade, sandwiches, and assorted cream cakes. The table stood in a bay window with a view of the back garden. There were croquet hoops set up on the thick grass, and a swing hung from the lowest branch of a big old tree beside the garage. It looks so *civilized*, thought Alice with longing.

As she sliced carrots and onions and pounded pieces of pinky-gray chicken mercilessly thin with a wooden mallet, Mrs. MacInnes asked conversational questions. How was Grace's grandmother doing? Had she recovered from her fall? The elderly had such brittle bones—it was a miracle she hadn't broken anything. *Bang, bang, bang.* Had Helen's mother finished the seating plan for the reception? It must be very trying when people didn't respond until the last minute. Who was doing the flowers? *Bang, bang.* Was Mrs. Jenkins settling in and finding her way around by this time? If there was ever anything she needed, she must be sure to telephone. And did Alice like Saint Katherine's? *Bang, bang,*

bang. They were the right questions, but Alice suspected the answers
really didn't matter; Mrs. MacInnes's attention was elsewhere.

"Well," she said brightly when they'd finished, "what will you do
now, Margery? Your father should be back in an hour with Charles.
Only do stay out of the lounge, will you, dear? I've just gotten it straight.
I do wish your father hadn't asked the Stewarts for seven—"

Alice thought croquet might be fun, but Margery led the way upstairs.
Her bedroom was on the back corner of the house, with windows on
two sides. It was decorated in rose and soft green, with dainty sprigged
wallpaper and white ruffled curtains. The curtains had been tied firmly
back with green ribbons, and the wallpaper was largely hidden behind
bold, bright-colored prints: a little girl in a blue dress and button boots
in a garden, holding a watering can; a wild night sky swirling with
shapes above dark hills and a huddled village; a young woman in a
white dress sitting in the sunshine sewing; the shadowy bulk of a cathedral flecked with gold and lavender. Beside the dresser was a picture of
a sad-eyed woman standing behind what was clearly a bar covered with
bottles. Alice looked at it curiously. "Ma doesn't like that one—she
doesn't approve," said Margery, behind her.

"I don't really blame her," said Helen. "It's new, isn't it?"

"Aunt Jessie brought it. At least they're all wearing clothes. She
brought me a Gauguin last year that Pa made her take back. They're so
Victorian! But just look at the way he's painted the mirror behind her—
the way it goes back and back. Isn't it fantastic? It's the bar at the
Folies-Bergère."

"Who's he?" asked Alice.

"Manet, of course," said Margery impatiently.

"Oh, of course," said Grace, rolling her eyes. "*Every*body knows
that."

"Well, Alice ought to. The original's in London. Aunt Jessie's seen
it, and one day I will, too."

Looking about, Alice noticed that as well as the frilly matching bedroom set, there was a solid, plain kitchen table set at an angle to one of the windows, its surface piled with notebooks and drawing pads; there were rags and jam jars stuck with pencils and paintbrushes and several very used-looking boxes of paints. There was a whiff of tension in the room, as if two distinct and not altogether compatible personalities were vying with each other for dominance. On the green carpet, by one of the table legs, Alice saw a large reddish brown stain. It almost looked like blood—

"So? What're we going to do?" Grace inquired, flopping on the bed.

Margery sat down on the floor and pulled a large sheet of plywood out from under her bed. On it was a scattering of pieces from a jigsaw puzzle; someone had begun to put the edge together. Grace made a face. Helen said, "Oh, good! I was hoping you'd have a new one, Margery. Do you like jigsaw puzzles, Alice?" She did. She was quite good at them, in fact. She joined the two on the floor, relieved that Margery hadn't chosen something she didn't know how to do. "Oh, all right," said Grace, and slid off the bed.

Margery handed Alice the box of jumbled pieces. "Here, you can find the other two corners." It was a picture of the Houses of Parliament. Alice began to sift through the bits of the color and pattern.

"I still wish Shane had stayed and settled down," said Helen after a few minutes. "It was so sad when he rode off alone at the end."

"But he had to," said Alice. "I mean"—she glanced up apologetically—"he couldn't have stayed, could he? I don't think it would have worked."

"It would have been utterly impossible," agreed Margery. "He didn't fit."

"But they wanted him to stay—they said so," Helen protested. "He'd got rid of the villains. He could have put away his gun and become a farmer like everyone else."

"That's just the point, Helen. He wasn't *like* everyone else. Besides, he was in love with Marian and she was already married, and she wasn't going to leave her husband for him even if he was a twit."

"Who was a twit?" said Grace.

"Her husband, of course."

"I don't think so," said Helen. "I thought he was brave to stick it out that way."

"He wasn't as handsome as Alan Ladd," said Grace judiciously. "I wonder if Alan Ladd can really ride a horse or if they faked it. They do that, you know. Not that he had to do anything really fancy. There's too many spiky bits in this puzzle, Margery—they all look the same."

"There ought to have been someone *besides* Marian, then," said Helen. "A schoolteacher. They could have lived happily ever after."

"That would have been a different story, though," said Alice. "Look, is this the right-hand corner?"

"Exactly," exclaimed Margery. "Anyway, who's to say he *didn't* live happily ever after? Just because he didn't fall in love and get married, Helen."

Stubbornly Helen shook her head. "But he was *lonely*. Anyone could see that."

"You're hopeless. You've no imagination. You've been brainwashed into believing the only way to be happy is to get married and have half a dozen babies. Well, it's not."

"I don't think—" began Alice.

"You want everyone matched up like socks, that's what. Well, what about the odd ones, eh? There are always odd socks—it's a fact of life. There's my Aunt Jessie."

Grace sniggered. "Is she an odd sock?"

"Yes, as a matter of fact, she is. And she's very happy. She lives her own life however she wants, without having to suit anyone else."

"That sounds selfish, to me," said Helen primly. "Mummy says putting her family first is what makes her happiest. She *likes* to take care of other people. What about your mother, Alice?"

"Well—" Caught unprepared, Alice fumbled for an answer. "I'm not really sure. I mean she's always had a job—well, almost. Not when she was looking after Granddad—"

"Because she wants to, or because she *has* to?" asked Margery.

"I never really thought." Helen, Grace, and Margery were all looking at her; she felt embarrassed. It occurred to her to wonder how they would manage without her mother's steady wages if they were forced to live only on Len's rather erratic earnings, but she really couldn't imagine her mother staying at home all day, cleaning and cooking and washing floors and windows. . . . "Both, I suppose. But I think she needs to *do* something, I mean have a job."

"So does my mother," said Margery, "but Pa won't let her. She'd be much happier if she had a job."

"But she works," Helen objected. "There are all her committees. Mummy says—"

"It's not the same. She doesn't get paid."

Helen shook her head. "She doesn't *need* to, does she?"

"My mother doesn't get paid, either," put in Grace. "She works right beside my dad, dipping sheep and shearing and lambing. I'll bet she works a lot harder than your aunt, Margery. It's not really much of a job, is it—selling paintings. More like a hobby."

"Shows how much *you* know, Grace Ingraham!" exclaimed Margery hotly.

"Oh, come on," said Grace. "She doesn't even get her hands dirty."

"It isn't the same kind of thing, of course—" began Helen, looking anxious.

"Here," said Alice, trying to distract them. "This *must* be the corner."

Margery ignored her. "Aunt Jessie earns her living by selling paintings. And artists earn their living painting them—in *spite* of people like you!" Her green eyes glittered with the light of battle.

"They're all odd socks," retorted Grace.

Rashly Alice said, "What about Miss Fairchild? Is she an odd sock?"

Helen giggled. "She was engaged to be married once. Did you know that, Margery? My father said. Something went wrong."

"Nothing went wrong. She went to New Guinea instead, that's all. It was very sensible. I shouldn't have wanted to marry Robbie Armstrong, either.''

"Robbie Armstrong?'' echoed Helen in tones of disbelief. "You're not serious—you can't mean Councillor Armstrong, Margery. How do you know?''

"I eavesdrop,'' said Margery smugly. "I'm very good at it—much better than you, Helen. I know lots of things I haven't been told.'' Her combativeness had vanished.

"Who's Councillor Armstrong when he's at home?'' Grace didn't like to be left out.

"Mr. Fairchild's partner's son. Armstrong and Fairchild, the brewers. He's fat and pompous.''

"He's not *that* bad,'' said Helen, and Margery shook her head disparagingly.

"Why did Miss Fairchild go to New Guinea?'' asked Alice. "Didn't her parents approve?''

"Of course they approved. Her father arranged the whole thing. The wedding date was practically set. He was simply furious when he found out she'd done a bunk,'' replied Margery. "My grandfather was sure he'd disinherit her when he found the letter.''

"What did it say?'' Helen asked.

Margery shrugged. "What does it matter? She didn't want to get married, she wanted to do something else instead. It was her choice. As a matter of fact''—she cocked her head and looked around at them—''she wanted to be an artist.''

"Not for a living, though,'' said Grace. "She's got pots of money already—she can do what she likes.''

"What difference does that make?'' demanded Margery.

"A lot, I'd have thought.''

"Perhaps she was in love with someone else,'' suggested Helen. "Someone who didn't love her, or who couldn't. He might have been married, like the film—''

"Of he could have been killed in the war,'' said Alice, "like my father." She was sorry as soon as the words were out of her mouth. She'd drawn their attention instantly. She shifted, uncomfortable under their scrutiny.

"What do you mean?" said Margery. "I thought your father was coming to join you."

"He is." Alice fiddled with puzzle pieces. "Only it's my stepfather's coming. Len."

"You're an orphan then."

"She can't be," said Grace. "What about her mother? Unless she was adopted, of course. Were you?"

"You only have to lose one parent to be an orphan," said Margery knowledgeably. She made Alice sound careless, like James James Morrison Morrison Weatherby George DuPree in the poem.

"What happened?" Helen wanted to know. "I'm reading a book about an orphan—it's terribly romantic. She has no family at all. She falls in love with this mysterious older man whose first wife died, and no one knows—"

"Oh, belt up, Helen," said Margery. "What did happen, Alice?"

She gave a little shrug. "My father was killed at the end of the war, in Corsica, that's all. Before I was born. I was almost two when Mum and Len got married. They'd known each other for years and years—practically all their lives. They grew up in the same village. Len's really an orphan," she added. "Both his parents died when he was only three. His auntie Millie and uncle Nick brought him up."

"That's so sad," breathed Helen. "It's beautiful."

"Helen, you *are* wet!" said Margery, her good humor restored.

"I don't know why you always have to say that." Helen was pink and earnest. "I'm sorry about your father, Alice, I really am. But think of your stepfather waiting faithfully all those years. It truly is a happy ending—even you have to admit it, Margery."

"One kind, perhaps," Margery conceded.

"I think it's the best kind," said Grace.

Surreptitiously Alice crossed her fingers. Right now the best kind of happy ending would come after Len appeared, once he and she between them had had a chance to convince Alice's mother to give up Miss Fairchild and Florestan. If Len came soon, there was a good chance they'd be home in time for Christmas. It would be the loveliest season to return: the shops decorated in red and green and gold; colored lights sparkling in the early dusk; the cold air warmed with the spicy smell of baking and the sweetness of carols; the chapels lit with candles and poinsettias; everyone with armfuls of bundles and happy secrets—oh, they *must* be home for Christmas!

— 13 —
"I Don't Like Children."

"There." Alice's mother slid an avalanche of fluffy scrambled egg onto a bone china plate. "You'd better wash your hands."

"I just did," said Alice. "Before I came downstairs." Hungrily she watched her mother add the plate to Miss Fairchild's Sunday morning breakfast tray and cover it with a domed silver lid to keep in the heat. It joined a small bowl of tinned grapefruit segments, a well-filled silver toast rack, butter and marmalade in little glass dishes, and a teapot under a pale gold satin cosy. The silver shone with polish, and there was a freshly ironed damask napkin beside the teacup.

Without looking at her, Christine said, "Well, wash them again, just to please me, and do be careful on the stairs."

"On the stairs?"

"With the tray. You can take it up and save me a journey."

"You want *me* to take her breakfast?" Alice's voice rose in disbelief. "But I thought she didn't know about me."

"I told Miss Fairchild yesterday. I said you'd be helping me, at least until we can make other arrangements." Still avoiding Alice's eyes, Christine broke four more eggs into the mixing bowl one-handed.

"What did she say?" Clearly Miss Fairchild had not fired Alice's mother on the spot for deceiving her as Alice had been half hoping.

Christine added a little milk and some salt and pepper and began to beat the mixture with quick, practiced strokes. "She wasn't best pleased," she admitted after a minute. "She doesn't like children—she says they're noisy and destructive. But as I told her, Alice, you're not a child. You're well behaved and responsible. Since you're living under her roof, she wants to have a look at you. Now then. Stand up straight and tuck in your blouse—that's better. If she asks you questions, look her in the eye and speak up."

"What about my breakfast? I'm starved."

"I'll have it ready for you when you come down. The quicker you are, the sooner you'll have it."

Alice could see it was no use arguing; she might as well get it over with. She picked up the tray and climbed the back stairs and trudged along the gallery feeling nervous. The tray was heavy and she was weak from hunger. Serve her mother right if she did drop it. Miss Fairchild's door was shut. Alice stood in front of it, indecisive, her mouth dry and her hands damp. Should she knock? Miss Fairchild must surely be expecting her breakfast—she balanced the tray awkwardly on one knee and rapped. The cup rattled in its saucer.

"And about time too."

Alice supposed that meant she should go in, but it didn't sound like a promising start. Miss Fairchild was sitting up in the high little bed, propped against an untidy mound of pillows. She wore a voluminous nightgown, fastened securely at wrist and throat, and a red-and-black patterned shawl. Her gray hair was braided, the end resting on her left shoulder like a frayed paintbrush. Coarse little wisps fringed her face, which was yellowy and wrinkled, like an ancient, unironed linen handkerchief. Her mouth had a sour little twist to it. "So you're the girl, are you," she said, fixing Alice with a pale blue glare.

The room was fiercely hot and stuffy and smelled of Mentholatum. Under the front window the radiator hissed like a sleepy snake. Alice thought it no wonder Miss Fairchild's expression was disagreeable.

"Well? Don't hover in the doorway. Bring the tray here. I don't remember what she said your name is." The eyes narrowed. "You're not half-witted, are you?"

"No, I am not," replied Alice indignantly. "My name is Alice."

"Mmmp. Put it down then. What has she given me this morning?" The old woman practically snatched the tray away and burned her fingers on the silver lid. She muttered under her breath. "Is that it? Nothing but egg? I told Mrs. Jenkins I wanted sausage and tomato. It's that fool of a doctor meddling again, that's what. How does he expect me to regain my strength on a diet of boiled rice and junket? I shall waste away to nothing. Here—you—what's-your-name—Alice. Where do you think you're going?"

Having surrendered the tray, Alice had been edging toward the door. "Well, I thought—"

Miss Fairchild scowled at her. "Come back here. I want to talk to you."

"I haven't had my own breakfast," protested Alice. "It'll spoil. I'll come back for the tray when you've done."

"I suppose she's giving you my sausage. You'll sit down and wait. Sit there—you can move those."

"But—" said Alice feebly.

"Pity you didn't bring a second cup."

Feeling trapped, Alice shifted the heap of books off the only chair and stacked them on the floor. "I don't like tea," she muttered sulkily.

Miss Fairchild ignored her. She busied herself with her food, pouring out tea and lacing it liberally with milk and sugar, then spooning up grapefruit segments as fast as she could, as if expecting Alice to whip the bowl out from under her nose before she was finished. Alice wondered crossly how long she would have to sit and watch Miss Fairchild gobbling. She could at least offer her a piece of toast, but she didn't dare suggest it. When the bowl was empty, Miss Fairchild wiped the juice from her chin. "I don't like children," she said.

Unable to think of a response, Alice sat on the edge of the chair, twisting her hair between her fingers. She tried unsuccessfully to return Miss Fairchild's frosty stare.

"How old are you? Ten? Eleven?"

"I'm fourteen, actually," Alice said to the lamp on the night table.

"Hmmp. Small for your age. Mrs. Jenkins never told me she had a daughter, you know. It wasn't in any of her letters. She said she didn't think it mattered, but I don't believe her. If I'd known, I'd certainly have had second thoughts about her suitability, never mind Raymond Inchcape's recommendation."

"I don't see why. It's nothing to do with the job whether she has a daughter or not."

"So you can talk back, can you." Miss Fairchild slathered butter on a slice of toast, then added a thick layer of marmalade.

Alice's mouth watered. Boldly she said, "You must have been fourteen once yourself."

"Long ago and I have no desire to be reminded of it," retorted Miss Fairchild around a mouthful. "It's a particularly awkward, unattractive stage, when no one knows what to do with one. One is simply an embarrassment—to oneself and the rest of the world." She frowned. "Do stop fiddling with your hair—it's a very annoying habit." Involuntarily Alice unwound her fingers and slid her hands underneath her. "That's what schools are for—to keep children out of their parents' way as much as possible. All this fuss about education is nonsense. You're at school, aren't you? Saint Katherine's, I believe. I suppose you like it?"

"I've only been there a week and a half, but yes. I do like it."

"Mmmp. You can read and write?"

"Of course I can read and write."

"Well, what else do you need? All the rest of it—it's all a waste of time. Utterly useless."

Alice was shocked by such heresy. Even Len, who'd left school as early as he could manage it by fudging his age, believed in the value of education. He maintained the failure was his; he viewed Alice's academic success with awe and pride. She had inherited her brains from her father and mother; it would be a crime if she didn't make the most of them, he told her.

"What do you study? Tell me."

"Latin and mathematics, English, history, geography—"

"Geography. Do you?" Miss Fairchild snorted. "And what's your geography? Blobs of anemic color on a flat piece of paper—the British Empire all in pink. What rubbish! To begin with, the world isn't flat, it's *round*. It's covered with lumps and holes and sheets of ice and vast expanses of saltwater. What do you know about India?"

"India?" The airlessness of the room was making Alice's head feel thick and woolly. "Well, tea, I suppose," she said cautiously. "And elephants. The Ganges and the Taj Mahal. Cobras and snake charmers—*I* don't know. We haven't studied India."

"I don't suppose you've been there?"

"Of course I haven't."

"Then you can't possibly know anything about it."

"I just told you, we haven't got to India yet." The conversation—if that's what it was—seemed to have gotten stuck. Alice wondered if the gastro-whatsit had affected Miss Fairchild's brain in some way. She seemed to remember Audrey's father saying that very high fevers might do that. . . .

"When I was your age—perhaps a year or two older—my parents packed me off to boarding school in England. My father claimed he didn't want me handicapped by a provincial education, but he really only wanted to be rid of me until I was presentable. He sent me to Cheltenham. It was quite horrid. I learned nothing whatsoever while I was there except how extremely unhappy it is possible to be." She sipped her tea, her eyes gone hazy with distance. In the next room Alice was suddenly aware of a clock ticking, stitching up the silence. Without meaning to, she began to twist her hair around her fingers again. Miss Fairchild blinked and scowled at her and she hastily folded her hands in her lap. "So do you know what I did about it?"

Sulkily Alice shook her head. How could she?

"I ran away." There was a triumphant gleam in Miss Fairchild's eyes. She sat back among her pillows.

"From school in England?" said Alice, impressed in spite of herself. "Where could you run away *to*? You were already so far from home. I would have thought—"

"Precisely the point. I was so far away there was nothing my father could do about it. I wrote him that I was going to spend the holidays in France with a school friend. He sent me money. He was delighted to have me stay in Europe. It was all I needed—I traveled very cheaply, staying in little inns in the countryside and going third class on railways. When the money finally ran out, I told him I wasn't going back to Cheltenham—he couldn't make me. He sent me enough money to get by on after that—not much, but I managed. *That* was my education, girl. I got out into the real world, I experienced it for myself. I got wet when it rained, I walked until I had blisters on my feet, I ate bread and cheese, I slept on straw mattresses. Not for me sitting in a stale little room being stuffed with useless information by people who didn't know any better. Snake charmers, indeed!"

"But if you were all by yourself"—Alice tried to imagine being in New Zealand alone, not knowing anyone at all—"wasn't it frightening? What if something had happened to you?"

"I was perfectly well able to look after myself. I always have been. When I wanted company, there were people to talk to. I had my sketchbooks and a few clothes, that's all I needed. If it hadn't been for the war, I might never have returned to Dunedin at all. I was completely free. Those were golden days—I hadn't a worry. The world was very sweet." She stopped, remembering. Alice wrinkled her nose, which had begun to itch. Miss Fairchild's expression sharpened. "It isn't like that anymore. People are greedy and suspicious. Everything has gotten complicated. It's all so tiresome. Whatever is the matter with you? Can't you sit still?''

"Ib goig to sneeze," said Alice, and did.

"Where's your handkerchief?"

She shook her head, sniffing. "Haven't got one."

"No handkerchief? You should always carry a handkerchief. You never know when you'll need it. There's a spare on my dresser. You may use it, and return it washed and ironed."

Unwillingly Alice took the cambric square and blew her nose, careful to avoid the embroidered monogram in the corner. She could feel Miss Fairchild watching as she waded it into a soggy lump. "Not an edifying sight," said the old woman. "I suppose she *is* married?"

"Who?" Alice was mystified.

"Your mother, of course. She wrote to me about a Mr. Jenkins. She did not write to me about you. You're here and he isn't."

"Well, he's coming. He's on his way right now—we had a letter from him last week," returned Alice, trying to ignore the chilly little draft in the pit of her stomach. It was most likely lack of breakfast. If only people wouldn't keep questioning Len's existence.

Miss Fairchild didn't seem to be listening; her head nodded forward. Alice saw the saucer wobble and tilt in her hand, as if she'd forgotten she was holding it. The teacup slid off, onto the tray, scattering milky tea and leaves all over everything. The head jerked up. "Now look what you've made me do!" Alice's mouth flew open to object, but Miss Fairchild exclaimed, "Oh, go on, take this away. I don't want to look at it any longer. Or you, either. Tell Mrs. Jenkins that if she doesn't fix me some proper food for my dinner, I'll fire her. No, don't bother. I'll tell her myself. I shall expect her in an hour, ready to go to work—you tell her that."

"She spilled it herself," declared Alice as she set the tray down in the kitchen, forestalling a possible accusation of carelessness. Christine surveyed the debris. "She's got her appetite back at any rate, I see."

"She wanted sausage and tomato. She thinks you're starving her."

"She does, does she. And what about you? I thought you were ravenous. Your breakfast's gone cold."

"That's not my fault. She wouldn't let me leave. She made me sit there and watch her eat, and didn't offer me anything. She's very rude, I think. She told me I was awkward and unattractive." Alice took a large bite out of the single cold, tough piece of toast that remained in the silver toast rack. It was extremely chewy.

"Now, Alice, I'm sure that's not what she said—"

"Oh, wasn't it though." She put the toast down in disgust. "She's rather horrid, actually."

Her mother sighed. "She's been very ill, don't forget. And she had to travel a long way by herself when she wasn't best up to it. It can't have been easy for her. You have to make allowances, love." She frowned. "What's that sticking out of your sleeve?"

"This?" Alice had forgotten it. "It's a handkerchief. *Her* handkerchief. She made me borrow it."

"Well," said Christine after a minute, "you seem to have made a favorable impression, Alice."

"Did I?" Alice glanced at her mother doubtfully. "She asked me if you were really married," she said after a minute.

"She asked you what?"

"She wanted to know if there really was a Mr. Jenkins. She thought you might have made him up."

Christine banged a plate of eggs on the table so hard Alice was surprised the table didn't crack. "And what did *you* say? No—don't tell me. Eat your breakfast while it's hot. I'll be outside." She snatched up her cigarettes and matches.

On Monday Alice was able to satisfy the others' curiosity about Miss Fairchild. At last she had met her, had even spoken to her. She could tell them firsthand what a peculiar old woman Miss Fairchild actually was, and she made quite a good story of it, at midmorning break, describing Miss Fairchild's whiskery chin and ropey hair and faded, frosty stare; the way she gobbled her food and went to sleep with a teacup in her hand. Helen and Grace giggled appreciatively and asked questions, but Margery was unusually silent, listening with a little frown between her eyebrows. "She said school is nothing but a waste of time," Alice told them, "and she asked me if I'd ever been to India."

"*India?*" exclaimed Grace. "She *is* bonkers!"

"What did you say?" Helen wanted to know.

"I said no, of course." That sent them off into fits of giggles again. "She told me she'd run away when she was my age."

"From Florestan?" asked Helen.

Alice shook her head. "From school in England. She was at Cheltenham. She *said* she'd run away to the Continent and gone traveling all around, on her own."

"Didn't you believe her?" Margery spoke up for the first time.

"Well, I mean, really—how could she have? She'd have been only fourteen or fifteen. I can't imagine doing it myself, not all alone."

"That's the trouble with you, Alice Jenkins—you have no imagination."

"Oh, come on, Margery," said Helen. "*You* wouldn't run away."

"I would if I could go anywhere I wanted. I certainly would if I could see Europe. But here—well, there's no place worth running away *to* in New Zealand."

"What's wrong with New Zealand, then?" challenged Grace.

"Oh, use your loaf. It isn't what's wrong with it—but I want to see Chartres and Notre-Dame and Saint Peter's in Rome, the Parthenon, the Rijks Museum, the Louvre, Michelangelo's *David,* the Tate. I want to see *real* Gaugins and Turners and Morisots and Renoirs, and the Elgin marbles." Margery's eyes shone with passion. "I can't get to them from here—not now, not on my own. They're too far away. I've got to wait. But *one* day—Aunt Jessie's promised me she'll help. Miss Fairchild's spot on—school is a bloody waste of time! Of course she ran away."

"Well," said Alice, feeling as if the conversation had gotten away from her, "I'm not surprised she didn't get married. She's *very* odd."

"Maybe you're wrong, Margery," suggested Helen. "Maybe Robbie Armstrong was the one to break it off, and that's why she went to New Guinea, not the other way round."

"Oh, bollocks!" exclaimed Margery rudely, glaring around at them. She stalked off and left them blinking after her.

Helen looked shocked, and Grace gave a faintly embarrassed laugh. Recovering, Helen said brightly, "Anne's asked us to help make favors for Brenda's shower. We're going after school on Thursday. Miss Sallet's given Grace permission. Do you want to come, Alice? We're going to make parasols out of yellow paper and decorate them with blue silk forget-me-nots and yellow satin ribbons. She needs at least three dozen—"

For the rest of the week Margery paid no attention to any of them. She actually seemed to go out of her way to avoid Alice, who was mystified and hurt. She wanted to feel relief because, after all, she wasn't convinced she liked Margery that well. But instead she felt curiously deflated, as if she'd failed at something she hadn't realized was important until it was too late.

She couldn't think of a good reason not to go with Helen and Grace on Thursday. She reckoned it would have to be better than spending another afternoon at Florestan alone with her schoolwork while her mother was closeted with Miss Fairchild, sorting, cataloging, sifting important papers out of the vast, undifferentiated mass of stuff Mr. Fairchild had accumulated during his life. In fact Christine was delighted, as Alice had guessed she would be, that Helen had invited her. It was further proof, to her, that Alice was adjusting to her new life. Never mind that her mother had never met either Helen or Grace, and that they were going off to the house of a total stranger in some unidentified part of the city, Alice thought with some bitterness.

Actually, the afternoon had been carefully arranged. Helen explained that Anne was Brenda's best friend; she was going to be matron of honor at the wedding. Anne had gotten married the year before, and lived in a flat near the university; her husband, Pete, worked for the Inland Revenue. "He's very nice," said Helen, wrinkling her forehead, "but it's a boring sort of job." He had agreed to run the girls home after tea. There was absolutely nothing for a mother to worry about— everything had been taken care of; Alice could have assured Christine on every point, *if* she had asked, but she was too preoccupied.

"I had thought," said Alice diffidently as she and Grace and Helen set out from Lockwood after school, "that Margery might be coming, too."

"Margery?" Grace snorted. "Not likely. I can't see her making parasols."

"She never does anything after school," Helen said. "Or hardly ever. Her mother's always got meetings. Margery's got to look after the ankle-biters."

"At least she gets paid," Grace said. "I never get a penny for minding Sammy."

On the other side of George Street Alice said, "Do you think—I mean, she acts as if she's angry with me for something." She didn't want to ask, but she wanted to know the answer.

Grace and Helen exchanged a look. "That's just Margery," said Grace, disparagingly. And Helen said, "Oh, it's probably nothing. Margery's like that sometimes. You just have to leave her alone until she gets over it, that's all."

"Sometimes," Grace went on candidly, "I really don't like her much. She goes crook for no reason."

"She has an artistic temperament. I heard Cecily Parsley say that to Mrs. Reeves," said Helen.

"If you ask me, she's a real odd sock," declared Grace.

"I don't see why anybody bothers with her then," said Alice, feeling a little better.

— 14 —

A Tramp at the Door

"Don't snap at me, it's not *my* fault the beastly thing's gone out! Why can't she eat cornflakes? If she wants a cooked breakfast, she can jolly well come down and start the range herself."

"Alice, don't argue, I haven't got time. Just tend to the toaster, will you?"

It was Friday morning. Christine had woken late; she had purple shadows under her eyes and her mouth was drawn tight. They were behindhand with everything, and discovered, when they got to the kitchen, that not only was the range cold, but that Mr. Tatlock had paid one of his hit-and-run visits, leaving six eggs and a jam jar full of red and purple anemones. This had put Christine in a black temper. Either he had failed to notice that the range had gone out, or—more likely— he had simply chosen to ignore it. Since Miss Fairchild's arrival he had made himself scarcer than ever. Occasionally Alice glimpsed him in the distance, always going away, or disappearing around a corner, and she often heard Kipper barking somewhere out of sight. Christine was too busy with Miss Fairchild, and wrestling with domestic arrangements, to spare time searching for him. Good riddance, thought Alice.

The last thing he'd done for them before Miss Fairchild came home was to fire up the big kitchen range, and explain, with exaggerated care, how to keep it going. "He evidently thinks I'm simple," Christine had muttered when he'd left. She wielded the poker like a sword, thrusting around in the range's innards, then banging the door shut. Alice was discovering, to her surprise, that her mother really wasn't fond of kitchens and cooking. She had always dealt with housekeeping in such an efficient, matter-of-fact way, Alice had never stopped to wonder whether or not she actually *liked* such chores.

Evidently Christine had forgotten to bank the range Thursday night before going to bed, so they had to revert to the hot plate in the morning. "Len could get it going again," grumbled Alice, knowing the ice under her feet was extremely thin. Just at that moment she didn't care. The worse things got, the greater justification she felt for being miserable and hating everything; she wanted to make it obvious to her mother.

"Len!" cried Christine, waving the long-handled fork furiously. "Don't you talk to me about Len! For pity's sake, Alice, look—there's smoke coming out! Can't you even be trusted to toast a slice of bread?"

"It's the rotten toaster, not me!" Gingerly she pried it apart and out fell two charred, smoking squares. "It's dangerous, Mum. I keep telling you. We ought to chuck it in the trashbin, that's what, along with—"

Miss Fairchild's bell jangled. Christine gave the bacon a vicious jab. "Well, that's it. That's all I need. Alice, you can go and see what she wants."

"You know what she wants. She wants her breakfast," retorted Alice. "And it's not ready, so what's the point in climbing all those stairs? She'll just have to wait—unless she'll eat cornflakes. And I'm going to be late for school now, you know. You'll have to write a note or I'll get a conduct mark. Is the range going out a good enough excuse, do you suppose?"

"Alice, if you don't stop nattering and pay attention to what you're doing, you'll set us on fire."

"They'd have to accept that as an excuse. It's a good idea, actually—except that this house is too damp to burn. It would only smolder for days and days and smell vile."

Suddenly there was a loud knock at the scullery door. Alice's heart whammed into her ribs; she and her mother exchanged startled looks. "Who can that be?"

"How should I know?"

"Perhaps if we pretend we didn't hear, whoever it is will think there's no one here and go away."

"Don't be silly. He can see us through the window. He's probably looked in already. Answer it, Alice—I can't leave the bacon."

"What if it's a tramp?"

"Then I'll soon sort him out," said Christine grimly.

At least she had a weapon in her hand, Alice thought as she went to the door. She twisted the knob quickly and jerked it open as if it were a sticking plaster and would hurt less done fast. She caught the man on the doorstep in midyawn, scratching under his left arm. He *was* a tramp. He wore scruffy, ragbag clothes, had a rucksack slung over his shoulder and a dirty canvas duffel beside his work boots. He was unshaven and his hair and mustache were shaggy. For a moment they looked at each other, neither one of them moving, then the yawn turned into a broad grin. The man's teeth were very white in his thin, weathered face. She stared blankly. "Miss Jenkins, is it?" said a familiar voice.

Her throat closed, allowing room only for a ridiculous squeak.

"Leonard!" Christine dropped her fork with a clatter, and somehow she and the strange man were tangled in each other's arms, laughing and exclaiming and kissing. Incredulous, embarrassed, even a bit resentful, Alice was overcome by confusion. Her mother's hair was coming down, the tightness had vanished from her face. How had she known right away it was Len? He didn't look like the Len they'd left in England, the Len whose image Alice had clung to in her head all these weeks. He had a vaguely familiar appearance, like someone you glimpse on the street and greet by name only to discover it isn't who you thought. Never had it occurred to Alice that when he finally caught up to them, she might not recognize *Len*—

They released each other, Christine disheveled and breathless, Len's face crinkled with delight. He held out his arms to Alice. Awkwardly she took a step forward, unsure of herself and of him. "After all this time, I thought you'd be happy to see me!" he teased. But his eyes were questioning; she realized he wasn't altogether sure. She shook herself. "I am—of course I am! I just can't believe it—" He pulled her in and she hugged him, reassured by his solidity. "It took you so long to get here!"

"Have a heart, Ally," he protested, laughing. "It wasn't like catching a number ten bus from Cambridge Station, you know!"

"No," said Christine, patting her hair into a semblance of order. "No, it wouldn't be. But didn't you use the money I left for you? I told you, in my letter—"

"That was yours, Chrissie, from your dad. I wouldn't have felt right about it"—he grinned wryly—"and he'd never've approved. I earned my way." He reached around Alice and took her mother's hand, and they stood there looking at each other like a pair of moony teenagers. Even though Len's other arm was still across her shoulders, Alice felt excluded. "What's that odd smell?" she asked suspiciously.

"Hmmm?"

Christine sniffed. "Len, it's you. Where on earth have you been?"

"Smell? Oh." He smiled apologetically. "It must be the sheep. Don't notice it myself. I got a lift down from Blenheim yesterday afternoon with a lorryload of them. No chance to wash up. D'you know, Alice, I counted the blighters all night and still didn't get any sleep! No breakfast, either. Is that bacon?" he added hopefully.

"Oh, blast!" exclaimed Christine. "Well, it was—once. You can wash your hands and face at the kitchen sink—there's a towel on the hook. Alice will char you some toast; she's had lots of practice."

"That's not fair," protested Alice. "It's not me—it's the toaster." Her mother was already laying rashers of bacon in the skillet, and Len was running water. "In all this time we've only had one letter from you," she told him accusingly. "It was written ages ago—before you left England."

"What?" Len raised his dripping face and fumbled for the towel. "One letter? You know I'm hopeless at writing, Ally—always have been. I thought about you often enough, couldn't you feel it?" He scrubbed his face dry, then ran a hand over his chin. "Pretty rough. I need a shave." He yawned again, cavernously.

"Sit down and eat first." Christine frowned at Miss Fairchild's tray as if she'd forgotten why it was there.

"It's very late," said Alice pointedly. "She's probably fainted with hunger by now."

"Corblimey! I haven't seen a toaster like that one since Auntie Millie's caught fire. I must have been nine. The fire brigade came—Dickie Wilson d'you remember him, Chrissie, with that helmet he used to wear? He did more damage with his hose than the fire—except it singed Auntie Millie's eyebrows right off. They never grew back in again. She had to draw them on with a little pencil after that." He chuckled.

"See?" said Alice to her mother. "I told you it wasn't safe. She's got enough money to buy a new one. I don't see why—"

"Mrs. Jenkins. Would you mind telling me what has happened to my breakfast? I have been ringing for the past half hour." Miss Fairchild stood in the passage doorway, a man's plaid dressing gown bunched around her middle, its hem hanging unevenly over her slippers. With her coarse gray braid and pouchy face she made a match for Len.

Collecting herself with admirable speed, Christine replied, "It's just coming, Miss Fairchild. I know you've been waiting—I'm sorry for the delay." On those rare occasions when she found it necessary to apologize for something, Alice's mother always sounded crisp.

Miss Fairchild's wintry gaze shifted to Len, who rose awkwardly to his feet, stifling another yawn. Her eyes narrowed to slits and she pulled her dressing gown cord tighter. "And who, may I ask, is this person, Mrs. Jenkins? Can you explain why he is having breakfast in my kitchen while I am being ignored upstairs?"

"Miss Fairchild, this is my husband, Leonard Jenkins. He's only just arrived this morning after traveling all night—"

"Several nights, actually," amended Len. "My transport was a bit—er—irregular. I wasn't sure when I'd get here. And I wanted to surprise Chrissie." Alice caught a flicker of embarrassment on her mother's face. She didn't like being called Chrissie in front of other people.

"Mmmp. So you're the long-awaited Mr. Jenkins, are you." Miss Fairchild looked him up and down. "I can't say I'm much impressed. You need a haircut and some decent trousers, for a start. My father would have had you escorted off the grounds immediately, looking as you do. He was adamant about maintaining standards, Mr. Jenkins. I suppose you do know something about automobiles?"

"Automobiles?" Len shot Christine a puzzled look. "Well, yes—I do—"

"I'm just finishing your tray, Miss Fairchild," said Christine. "If you'll go upstairs—Alice will lend you a hand, won't you, Alice? I'll bring it right along."

"But—" Alice protested, and her mother glared her into silence.

Miss Fairchild pursed her lips. "Very well, Mrs. Jenkins. You want me out of the way. You needn't think you can put anything over on me, either of you, just because I'm old and ill. I'll want to interview you later, Mr. Jenkins, when you've made yourself presentable," she warned Len. Christine opened her mouth, but Miss Fairchild swept on. "Fried bread, Mrs. Jenkins. Two slices, if you please. Clearly I shall need my strength."

"Everything else will get cold," objected Christine.

"Then give it to Mr. Jenkins and cook mine fresh."

"Ta very much," said Len politely. "What a smashing idea."

"I believe I shall have breakfast downstairs tomorrow. In the dining room."

"The dining room?" echoed Christine. "But it hasn't been opened—"

"I'm tired of being treated like an invalid, and I can see I shall need to keep an eye on what's happening under my own roof." With this parting shot Miss Fairchild turned and departed, her dressing gown trailing behind. It caught in the swinging door, spoiling her exit, and there was a tearing sound.

"Alice," hissed her mother, "go on!"

"All right." Alice was grudging. "But you have to promise not to talk about *any*thing until I get back." As she struggled to free Miss Fairchild from the door, she heard Len say, "What's this about automobiles, Chrissie? What exactly are you doing here, cooking her breakfast for her. And who is she?"

"Not now, Len. I'll explain everything later."

Good, thought Alice, as the door finally shut. I want to hear that.

Miss Fairchild forged ahead through the gloom of the great hall. At the foot of the stairs she paused to adjust her dressing gown; catching up with her, Alice noticed that the cuffs were frayed and there was an ancient tea stain on one lapel. Miss Fairchild gave her a shrewd look. "Your mother's full of surprises, isn't she?"

"I don't know what you mean," said Alice, who'd been thinking the same thing for some time.

Miss Fairchild snorted. "Oh, don't you?" She started up the staircase, climbing deliberately, one step at a time, hauling herself with the banister. Awkwardly Alice offered to help, but was waved off impatiently. "If you fall, it's not my fault," she declared.

"If I fall, you won't be able to stop me," retorted Miss Fairchild, panting a little. "Don't hover, girl! You're distracting me."

Alice backed down a step.

"You should always (puff) look out for yourself (puff) first. That's the basic rule (puff) of survival. You can only (puff) make a bad situation worse by (puff) getting in the way. Remember that. Assistance is useless ninety-nine (puff) percent of the time. (Puff.)'' At the top, finally, she stopped, clutching the balcony railing and gasping. Nervously Alice wondered how you knew when a person was about to pass out. But after several long minutes Miss Fairchild recovered her breath and said in a more normal voice, ''It's the most damnable business getting old. How I loathe it. I need my morning tea.''

''You could have had it in the kitchen,'' Alice pointed out. ''You could have had your breakfast there. You'd feel better if you had—I always do, after I've eaten.''

''Certainly not. Not in the kitchen and not before getting dressed. That would never do. He wouldn't have allowed it.''

''Do you mean Len? Len wouldn't have cared. He's had breakfast in his pajamas lots of times. When he was a night watchman—''

''I do not mean Mr. Jenkins. I mean Father.''

Perplexed, Alice was about to say, ''But he's dead, isn't he?''

Miss Fairchild replied, as if she had, ''That's beside the point. This is his house.'' She looked down at the great hall, slowly sweeping it with her eyes. ''It will always be his house.'' Coming back to Alice, she said, ''The Bentley wasn't running as it should when Arthur Tatlock collected me from the station. Now that I'm up and about I shall be wanting it. Mr. Jenkins can prove his skill by putting it in order, you tell him.''

Back in the kitchen Christine was adding the finishing touches to Miss Fairchild's tray for the second time. She'd even found a little cut glass vase for the anemones. ''Shhh,'' she cautioned as Alice pushed through the door. ''Don't wake him.''

Len was bent forward in his chair, sprawled across the table among the teacups and smeared plates, head buried in his arms, sound asleep. Seeing him there, Alice was flooded with relief; as she came back down the stairs, she'd been suddenly ambushed by doubt. Had she only imagined him? But there he was. Or someone was, at any rate. She studied the back of the head on the table. ''It really is Len, isn't it?''

"Of course it's Len—who else would it be?"

"Only his hair's getting thin on top. I never noticed that." And there was gray in it, mixing with the black. She chewed her lip. Perhaps it had happened since she and her mother had left Cambridge. Perhaps finding them gone like that had aged him overnight. She'd read of it happening. Looking away from Len, she noticed that Mr. Tatlock's bowl was empty. "Aren't there any more eggs? What about my breakfast?"

"You'll have to make do with cornflakes, won't you?" said her mother callously.

"It isn't *fair*." Feeling ill-used, Alice poured herself a heaping bowlful and frosted it heavily with sugar. "What did he say? Did he tell you how he got here? Why it took him so long?"

Christine shook her head. "He was far too busy eating. I don't think he'd had a proper meal for days." She gave him a fond look as she picked up the tray. "I've written you a note, Alice. It's there, with your satchel."

"A note for what?"

"To explain your being tardy this morning."

"Oh, but I *can't*—I'm not going to school today, not with Len only just come—"

"He'll still be here when you get back, and tomorrow's the weekend. You won't miss anything—I expect he'll only sleep all day. Blast— there's the bell! If I don't take this, she'll come down again. Alice, I want you gone before I'm back."

The only thing about school Alice was conscious of that day was its endlessness. For the first time since they'd come to Florestan she actually wanted to return to it. Her head was far too full of what she might be missing to allow space for mundane things like the Spanish Armada, irregular Latin verbs, or finding the circumference of circles. What were they talking about? What were they doing? Remembering the way Len and her mother had hugged and kissed each other made Alice's cheeks warm. Perhaps that was why her mother had been so adamant about school. . . .

Her mind skittered away from that, choosing a safer direction. Perhaps by the time she got back from school they'd have sorted out whatever had gone wrong between them. Once that was straightened out, they could begin to make arrangements. In a couple of weeks—a month, perhaps—they could be on their way home, back to England. She needn't bother ever again about Betty Ware and Fiona Watkins. Helen's sister's wedding was of no importance. No longer would it matter to Alice *what* Margery MacInnes thought. She could forget them all: Dunedin would be nothing more than a bad dream.

The only thing that disturbed her confidence in this happy ending was not understanding precisely what had set her mother off in the first place, all those months ago. When her mother began visiting estate agents a year ago, Alice hadn't given it much thought. Christine's friend Gillian Evans was looking for a house to buy, and whenever she had the time, Christine went along to lend support. It did her good to get out and forget about work. One of the senior editorial assistants at the University Press had quit without warning, just vanished at the crucial moment in the publication of an important astronomy text, and Christine's office had been thrown into a fever of reorganization as everyone scrambled to pick up all the pieces. For Alice's mother it meant longer hours, more responsibility, worry about deadlines, and communication with an author who spoke a highly specialized scientific dialect that required patient and skillful translation. For Alice and Len it meant treading carefully and keeping their heads down until the worst was over, and the book safely in production. Gillian's search provided a distraction; Len and Alice were grateful to her for it.

Eventually the crisis at the Press passed. Eventually Gillian found a nice little house near the river. But Alice noticed a change in her mother. Christine continued to talk knowledgeably about mortgages and interest rates, rising damp and fitted carpets, sewers, and gas heating. She had suddenly become critical of Number 15. She complained about the worn linoleum in the kitchen, the dreary wallpaper in the lounge, the antiquated fixtures in the bathroom. There was a draft in the front hall, and the front steps weren't safe: the mortar was crumbling and the bricks were coming loose. Sooner or later someone would have a nasty fall. Len shrugged and didn't say much; Alice felt her mother was being disloyal.

The argument, if that's what it was, came unexpectedly on a warm, sunny afternoon in late March. Len's bright idea had been to repair the disintegrating front steps while Christine was at work. He intended to have the job all done as a surprise by the time she came home, and he enlisted Alice's help. When Christine found them, Len had the bricks chipped out and scattered on the front walk, and Alice was mixing cement in an old washtub. Of course it was a mess. Christine wasn't supposed to see the steps until they were finished and the debris had been cleared away. It wasn't Len's fault that she'd come home early with a headache.

Instead of being pleased, Christine was angry, angrier than Alice remembered ever seeing her. Furious, she accused Len of wasting his time and money on something that didn't even belong to them. The steps were Mr. Davidson's responsibility—*he* owned the house, he should see to keeping it up. That's what they paid him all that rent for.

"But I just thought—" began Len.

She cut him off. "No, you didn't, Leonard! That's what's wrong with you—you don't think. You don't think, and you don't listen. You haven't heard a word I've been saying for weeks, have you?"

"I have," protested Len. "You've been going on about how dangerous the steps are. I wanted to do something nice for you, Chrissie, so I decided to fix them. I don't mind, really I don't."

"*I* mind, Len! That's what I'm telling you. I mind very much. I'm sick of living in someone else's house. I want a house of my own. I don't want to be a tenant for the rest of my life."

"But why?" Len sounded genuinely perplexed. "Think of the expense, Chrissie. Not just the payments, but if something goes wrong—

the drains back up, or the roof leaks, or there's termites? As long as we're only renting, we don't have to worry. Someone else'll fix it.''

''That's what it always comes down to with you, isn't it? You're terrified of responsibility, Len. You have been as long as I've known you. You run away.''

''Aw, Chrissie, be fair. What about after the war? I didn't run away then.''

''Maybe you should have. Perhaps it would have been better for us both.''

Ignored, Alice shivered. Her mother got impatient with Len, even angry sometimes, but Alice had never heard that bitter edge in her voice before. She hadn't wanted to hear any more; she stood up and dropped the trowel she'd been gripping with both hands. It fell into the tub with a clatter. Her mother jerked her head around and looked at her for the first time, then, without another word, disappeared around the house. Len sat with his head bent over his hands for several minutes. At last he straightened and gave Alice a funny little smile. ''I did try, Ally,'' he said sadly. ''You'd better go find your mum.'' Getting up, he walked away, out the gate, leaving the tools and bricks and the tub full of hardening cement. His shoulders were hunched and his hands thrust deep in his pockets. Alice had no idea where he was going.

What was she supposed to say to her mother when she found her? ''He was only trying to help, Mum. I don't understand—'' ''No. Why should you?'' Christine no longer sounded angry, only tired and discouraged. ''Can you get your own tea, Alice? I don't feel at all well. I'm going to have a lie-down.'' ''What should I tell Len?'' But her mother didn't answer; perhaps she didn't hear. In any event, Len stayed away all evening. In the morning he was there as usual, though it was clear he'd spent the night on the downstairs sofa. Neither he nor Christine said anything about what had happened the day before. Alice decided to pretend nothing had. The front steps were unusable for a week, then one day, while she was at school, someone came and put them back together. It wasn't Len, so Christine must have telephoned Mr. Davidson. Christine still visited estate agents, Alice knew she did, but she stopped talking about them, and Alice didn't ask.

In passing one day Christine mentioned that she hadn't gotten the job of editorial assistant at the Press after all—Alice hadn't known she'd applied for it. They'd hired a young woman just out of university instead. Well, said Christine, she was welcome to it, and all its complications. Within a fortnight Len told them he'd been offered work on the channel ferry for the summer season. The money was very good, he said; he'd be daft to turn it down. Unless of course Christine objected? No, she didn't object. She was busy just then locating photographs and checking references for Dr. Inchcape's manuscript on Jacobean architecture. He had another project in mind for her as well—something far more demanding. She wasn't sure she could undertake it. It would mean travel. "You'd like that, though, wouldn't you?" said Len in all innocence, and Alice assumed it would mean she'd be spending time that summer with Mrs. Hollings, next door, while Len was at work and her mother was away.

All of these pieces fitted together somehow, Alice was sure, but she couldn't see how they connected. Why should the front steps have made her mother decide to leave Cambridge for New Zealand?

"Alice," said Miss Parsons at the end of the day, "are you feeling quite well?"

"I'm sorry? Oh, yes. It's just that—" Alice almost blurted the news about Len, but caught herself when she noticed Fiona packing up her books within earshot. "I'm only tired, Miss Parsons. I didn't sleep very well last night."

"That often happens at your age." Miss Parsons reassured her with one of her famous smiles. "You must get a good rest this weekend."

"I will, thank you."

"I will, thank you," mocked Fiona's voice in the hall behind her as she escaped down the stairs, across the hall, and out into the windy afternoon. Alice didn't care. She was free—for the afternoon, for the weekend. And Len was at Florestan.

— 15 —

Excavating the Dining Room

Alice found her mother at the kitchen table with a cup of tea and a cigarette, sorting through a pile of papers. They were covered with spidery columns of figures. "Where is he? He's still here, isn't he?" said Alice, getting straight to the point.

"If you mean Len—"

"Of course I mean Len!"

"He's upstairs, asleep. I told you he'd sleep all day. There are some chocolate biscuits in the tin on the pantry shelf. Take off your jacket and tell me about school, why don't you. I've been at this so long my eyes are crossing. Mr. Fairchild kept every scrap of paper that came into this house, I swear—there are accounts here for every door hinge and curtain hook."

"I'll just change first," Alice called over her shoulder as she shot up the back stairs. She had to make sure. The door to the room she had shared at first with her mother was closed. Holding her breath, she opened it just far enough to slip through. The curtains were pulled almost shut against the afternoon light, but she was able to make out a humpy shape in the wide double bed. She tiptoed across the carpet, wincing as one of the floorboards groaned. It really was Len; he was still there, deeply unconscious, snoring slightly. Alice stood, gazing down at him, frowning as she concentrated. It disturbed her that she had not recognized him instantly that morning. She had known Len almost all her life; she couldn't remember the time when he hadn't been there, she'd been too small.

There were changes in his face since she'd seen him last—the mustache for one thing. She'd have to get used to that, though she was prepared to like it. She bent closer; there was a long, pale seam down the left side of his face. It ran from the corner of his eyebrow to his jaw. He'd never had a scar there before. He stirred without opening his eyes and flung out an arm, muttering something. She blinked. Outlined in blue on the bare skin was a heart. In the middle it said—she bent closer—it said CHRISTINE, and there was an arrow through it. That was new, too. Wondering if her mother had seen the tattoo yet, Alice backed away silently. She wasn't sure that Christine would be flattered.

Supper was a celebration. Len had succeeded in lighting the range as Alice had been sure he would, and there were roast chicken, peas, carrots, and potatoes, and a raspberry sponge with custard. Miss Fairchild sent her tray back picked so clean Alice thought she must have licked her plate. The three of them sat for a long time at the kitchen table, while darkness gathered outside, making themselves a bright, warm space in the shadowy house, and Len told stories about his journey.

It had been different—less direct—than Alice and Christine's. He'd come on freighters, working his way, taking whatever he could find that was headed in the right direction. He'd begun in Liverpool on a ship bound for Jamaica, and was lucky to find another, right away, carrying sugar through the Panama Canal. That's when he'd gotten the scar. He'd been on deck, fascinated by the operation of the locks. "You start out at the bottom of this pit, see, way down. Then the gates ahead open and the water pours in and lifts the ship, right to the top, and you go through those gates to the next. Blimey, what a job it must've been to build that lot! Think of working it all out." A cable had snapped, catching him on the side of the head and knocking him overboard. "What did you do?" said Alice. "You can't swim." "Wouldn't've made any difference. I never knew what hit me—I was out cold. Lucky we weren't at the bottom of the lock or I'd've been crushed against the side," he said cheerfully. "One of the blokes on the edge fished me out. Good thing you weren't there to see, Chrissie. I had two black eyes and my face was swollen out to here!" "You could have lost an eye," said Christine accusingly. "I could've been killed, that's what. But I wasn't. Never in all my life did I think I'd be going through the Panama Canal! Crikey! And Fiji. I was there almost a week, waiting for a ship. I met this bloke runs a little bar right off the beach. He used to drive a taxi in Cardiff. One day he was waiting outside the station there—it was tipping down rain—and suddenly he says to himself, what'm I doing this for anyway? He couldn't think of an answer, so he packed it in, took all his money, and got on the first boat that was going somewhere warm, and ended up in Samoa. . . ."

"Right," said Christine, wiping the table after breakfast. "This morning we're all going to turn to and clean out the dining room. I managed to put Miss Fairchild off until tomorrow, but the sooner she starts coming down for meals, the better, as far as I'm concerned. Len?"

"Hmmm?" He was shaving, studying himself in a mirror he'd propped beside the big copper sink. His chin was streaked with lather. "Whatever you say, Chrissie, you're in charge. I still can't believe I'm here. What do you think of the mustache, eh? You haven't said. I rather fancy it myself, but if you don't like it—"

"I do," said Alice promptly. She'd been watching him as she put the cutlery away. "It makes you look like Wyatt Earp."

"I'm not sure," said her mother. "It's very stiff. It reminds me of a scrub brush. Alice, you aren't paying the slightest attention to what you're doing."

"I don't see that it matters if there are forks in with the spoons. Anyway, if you shave it off, won't it leave a white patch? I mean the rest of your face is so brown."

"Good point," said Len. "Guess I'd better leave it, hadn't I?" He winked at Alice and rinsed his razor. Christine gave her head a shake. "Why ask me then?"

Clouds of dust fell out of the heavy brown drapes in the dining room when Christine pulled them back. As if doubting its welcome, light crept uncertainly in through the windows. "Corblimey," said Len, impressed. Everything the darkness had obscured became depressingly visible. Dust blanketed the room: the massive, thickly carved furniture was felted with it; all the knobs and finials, bunches of grapes and acanthus leaves, looked as if they had been touched with frost. The heavy silver chafing dishes, trays, candelabra, and epergnes were blotched with tarnish. The chandelier that Alice had thought was thick with cobweb was actually bundled in cheesecloth. Dim, gilt-framed mirrors overhung the sideboards, placed as if to keep a critical eye on the manners of the diners; interspersed around the walls were paintings: somber arrangements of waxy fruit and flowers, with here a lifeless rabbit, there several small game birds, their toes turned stiffly up. "Coo!" said Len again. "She's never going to eat her meals in here, is she? Miss Fairchild?"

"I can't see her joining us in the kitchen," replied Christine tartly. "It'll look better when it's clean. Len, there's a dust mop by the door. Alice, you can start by clearing off the table. Pile the newspapers in the hall and pack everything else in those cartons—carefully, mind. Don't just throw it together. It'll have to be sorted properly later." Christine set to work with dustcloths and lemon oil.

With a sigh Alice began at the far end of the long dining table. It was like an archaeological dig, she decided as she got into it. The further down she went, the older the material she uncovered. She half expected to find the bottom layers compressed and solidified like slate. Here and there she came across pockets of fossils: a box of congealed cough lozenges; a pair of spectacles attached to a piece of string; an assortment of handkerchiefs—mostly unused and yellow with age; a stiff brown leather glove like a dried mouse; three old electric torch batteries—one of them corroded and leaking an evil substance that had worked its way down to eat the finish off the tabletop, leaving a leprous patch; an ivory letter opener with a procession of tiny elephants carved on the handle. Alice rather coveted this last.

She worked her way along one side; the newspapers were brown and brittle, and many of the journals were still in their wrappers, unopened, but the piles weren't as haphazard as she'd expected. There were stacks of bills, each marked Paid in a firm up-and-down script, with a date and a number; the letters had all been refolded and stuck sideways into their envelopes, marked Ans and dated. The canceled checks were tied in fat bundles with lengths of knitting wool. There were several large piles with index cards on top labeled Solicitations; they were all requests for money, Alice saw, as she packed them away: from schools, hospitals, missions, even individuals. Everyone wanted donations. There were other piles of correspondence: from Murdoch, MacInnes & Holt, from the Bank of New Zealand, from the Armstrong & Fairchild Brewery. . . .

"Such a pity," exclaimed Christine, looking at the scar Alice had uncovered. "The whole table needs refinishing." She ran her hand over the surface. It was cloudy and fretted with cracks like old ice. "You're being awfully slow, Alice."

"I'm being *careful.*"

"Len, will you help me carry the silver out to the kitchen? It ought never to have been left here with the house empty."

At the end of the table nearest the door Alice came across a letter handwritten in elegant italic on thick, creamy paper. She noticed it especially because it had not been refolded; instead, it had been torn in two, right across the middle, and crumpled, then smoothed out again and laid face down. Curious, Alice glanced at the top half of the first page. "My dear Emilia, I trust I may still address you so, even after our misunderstanding of Monday last," it began. It was dated 29 May

1958. A love letter, thought Alice, intrigued. She remembered what Margery had said about Robbie Armstrong. But that had been years and years ago. Perhaps he hadn't forgotten.

She glanced around guiltily; she was alone.

I am sorry if I caused you distress. I certainly had no intention of it when I accepted your invitation, but you did press me for my opinion, and because I respect you, I felt it my duty to be honest. Surely you understand that for me to be otherwise with you would have been insulting! That what I told you was not what you wanted to hear, I am sincerely sorry, but I am confident that once you've had sufficient time to reflect, you will realize that I am right. I know how seriously you take your "work," as you call it, dear Emilia, and by all means, you must continue to pursue it, if only for your own satisfaction. It is, however, quite clear to me that you can only meet with painful disappointment if you persist in seeking a wider audience.

Not a love letter after all, Alice decided, frowning at it. She read on:

Many ladies derive great pleasure from painting—there is no reason why you should not be one. It is a most genteel and admirable pastime. But I have to say that I find a disturbing quality in your recent pictures that I would urge you to remedy. Your use of color has become muddied and confused. The natural shapes you claim to represent are distorted out of all recognition. Instead of concentrating on the harmonious and orderly, you seem to focus deliberately on the chaotic, infelicitous elements in your subjects.

I would strongly recommend that you return to watercolor, my dear Emilia, and reexamine those earlier paintings: the charming little pictures you did on your first tour of Europe, for instance. If you compare them to your present efforts in oils, you cannot fail to see what I mean.

Your expedition to India next month sounds quite fascinating, although I understand it is a difficult country in which to travel. I do admire your spirit of adventure and your insatiable appetite for unusual experiences. For myself, I find I am far too attached to the well-trodden paths of art and

*culture! I lack your enthusiasm for the wilder regions of the globe. In July
I shall make my fifth pilgrimage to the shrines of Venice, Rome, and Florence,
where I shall spend many instructive and delightful hours in the company
of the Old Masters. They have so much to teach the serious artist. Your
father had an extraordinary eye for painting. I envy you living as you do
among the fruits of his collecting. I wish I had had the privilege of knowing
Clement Roland Fairchild better. I was most flattered when he approached
me for one of my works to add to his superb gallery.*

*I hope I shall have the opportunity of offering you my hospitality the
next time you are in Auckland.*

*Ever most devotedly,
Charles Keating Murray, RRA*

Alice stood looking at the signature. She hadn't the faintest idea who
Charles Keating Murray, RRA, was, but she didn't like him. There was
something distinctly unpleasant about the tone of his letter, even though
the words seemed polite enough. She quickly buried the torn pages
under a stack of other papers as her mother bustled back in, making
impatient noises. As she packed papers into boxes, no longer paying
attention to what was on them, she found herself wishing she hadn't
read the letter, but there was no way of unreading it. "Mum?"

"Mmm?" Christine was applying quantities of oil to the far end of
the table, and rubbing it in vigorously. The pungent, lemony smell filled
the air.

"There are a lot of paintings in this house. Is there a record of them
anywhere? I mean, who painted what."

"Well, I suppose—nothing organized that I've come across yet, but
there may be a catalog. There are files full of letters about them, and
receipts. There are records for everything—the statues, the china, the
furniture." She sighed heavily. "Of course *eventually* there'll be a list,
there'll have to be. But that's a major project by itself. Why do you
want to know?"

Alice shook her head. "No real reason. I just wondered about a particular artist, that's all."

"You did?" Her mother sounded surprised. "Which one?"

"It's not important," Alice hedged.

"Chrissie?" Len stuck his head around the door. "There's a bell ringing in the kitchen. I don't know what it means."

"I do," said Christine wryly. "She thinks I've forgotten her—as if I could. Alice, if you've finished with that, you can polish the mirrors while Len does the windows."

Later, when Miss Fairchild was napping, and after Christine had declared the dining room fit for use the next morning, the three of them sat around the table in the kitchen and Christine explained the situation to Len. Listening to her mother's account, Alice thought she left out a great deal, but decided it would be prudent to wait until she and Len were alone before she filled in the missing details.

"Who takes care of the grounds?" asked Len around a yawn. "It's a big place, this. I couldn't believe I'd got it right yesterday morning when I came along the drive—I kept walking and walking, and then— crikey! Is there anyone else here?"

"There's Mr. Tatlock," said Alice, shooting a sideways look at her mother. "He lives in the lodge by the back gate."

"What does he do?"

"That's a good question."

"He's the caretaker," said Christine crisply. "He's quite elderly and not entirely cooperative. He's been making himself scarce since we arrived."

Len grinned sleepily. " 'Last night I saw upon the stair a little man who wasn't there,' " he quoted. " 'He wasn't there again today—oh, cor, I wish he'd go away!' "

"That's Mr. Tatlock." Alice nodded. "He's got sheep."

"Here?" Len's eyes opened wider.

"He claims they're to cut the grass," said Christine, "and they belong to Miss Fairchild."

"I'll have to meet your Mr. Tatlock—he sounds a right character."
"He's not *my* Mr. Tatlock, and you'll be lucky if you can find him."

Miss Fairchild came downstairs at half past eight the next morning, under her own steam. She wore a dark brown skirt and jacket made of some durable, practical fabric, and a high-necked white blouse. Pinned to her left lapel was a small gold watch, like a medal, that hung upside down, so she could consult it with a glance. Her hair was suppressed with numerous croquet-hoop-shaped pins in a knot like a skein of knitting worsted on the back of her head. She found Alice in the dining room, in the act of setting her place at the near end of the long table, where she'd be easiest to serve and could admire the green view through the windows Len had labored to clean. Beyond the glass the sun poured benevolence on the leafy world out of a sky softened with little feathery clouds and a breeze made the trees dance. It was a beautiful day, and Alice could hardly bear the thought of spending it cleaning another room.

"No," said Miss Fairchild, pausing in the doorway. "That's not right, what's-your-name—Alice. That was Mother's place. I shall sit on the right-hand side, just there. That's where I've always sat. You weren't to know, of course."

Alice made a face. "I don't see that it matters where you sit if you're the only one at the table." Yielding to Miss Fairchild's hard stare, she began to shift the cutlery.

"What's become of all the papers that were here?"

"They're in boxes, in the library."

"You're sure? She hasn't thrown anything out?"

"Only the newspapers. I packed the rest away myself. Mum said—"

"And the candelabra? Where are they? And the silver fruit bowl—"

"They're in the kitchen. Mum said they should have been locked away with the other silver."

"They belong in here," declared Miss Fairchild. "I can see I shall have to set some things straight with Mrs. Jenkins." She crossed to the place Alice had reset and sat down very carefully. Alice heard her knees creak as she lowered herself onto the chair. She fled back to the kitchen to tell her mother that Miss Fairchild was waiting. "Where's Len? I thought he'd be down by now," she added, disappointed. "He's not still in bed, is he?"

"He was up before you, Alice. He's outside somewhere—said he wanted a look round. And where do you think you're going? You sit down and eat. He'll be back when he's remembered he's hungry."

Reluctantly Alice did as she was told. It wasn't fair of Len to have gone out without her. Moodily she watched a patch of sun inch across the tall dish cupboard; it burnished the pale, tawny wood until it glowed.

"What an amazing place this is, Ally!" Len burst into the kitchen. "I saw the sheep. And I saw a pair of fantails—I'm sure that's what they were. Little birds with long tails. They came right out of the rhododendrons." He poured himself a cup of tea.

"How do you know they were fantails?"

"Ah, well. I've got this book, see. I picked it up in Auckland when I was getting my land legs. It's got drawings of birds and plants and that. We came right in under that new bridge across Auckland Harbor. That's a sight, isn't it? And volcanoes, sticking right up out of the water. But the real bobby-dazzler was Rotorua! You ever see anything like that before? All the hot springs, steam coming out all over—and the smell! Like rotten eggs."

"We didn't see Rotorua," said Alice. "There wasn't time. We had to come straight here." Len's enthusiasm was beginning to alarm her. Getting home might not be quite as straightforward as she had imagined. She'd only really thought as far as Len's arrival and his reconciliation with her mother. Next thing, in her mind, they were stepping off the boat in England.

"There's so much to *see*, Ally! Wouldn't my auntie Millie drop her teeth if she knew where I'd got to. First thing is to find a job—there's bound to be something I can do. Thought I'd have a look round the railyard and the wharves tomorrow, see what's what."

"Have you talked to Mum about that?"

"Talked to Mum about what?" said Christine, coming through the swing door.

"About finding work," said Len.

Christine gave him a considering look, but all she said was, "Len, you make the toast this morning—we haven't enough bread for Alice to do it."

"There's a whole loaf."

"We need it for sandwiches. I'll slice—Alice, you can butter. We'll use the leftover chicken."

"Why do we need sandwiches?" asked Alice.

"To take along on our picnic," said her mother, as if it were obvious.

"What picnic? Where? I thought you said—"

"It's Sunday and the sun's shining and we're having the day off. Len can drive us somewhere in the Ford."

"What about Miss Fairchild?"

"She wants to spend the day in her studio, undisturbed. Stop asking questions, and get a move on! Quickly, before she can change her mind."

— 16 —

"*I'm Off to My Love with a Boxing Glove, Ten Thousand Miles Away.*"

Len didn't have half the trouble Mr. Tatlock had getting the Ford to start. It hiccoughed a little, but he fiddled with something under the bonnet and it settled agreeably into a steady hum. They piled in, Len and Christine in front, Alice sharing the backseat with a basket full of lunch, two rugs to sit on, and an old straw hat her mother had found in the glory hole under the kitchen stairs. Miss Fairchild came out into the courtyard to watch them off. She had taken the padlock from the door at the end of the garage. Alice's curiosity pricked. What exactly did Miss Fairchild's paintings look like that Charles Keating Murray, RRA, found them disturbing? But the car was moving. As they turned the corner of the house, Alice glanced back and saw that the studio door was open and Miss Fairchild had already disappeared inside. She hadn't come out to wave, just to make sure they were going.

Len threaded his way competently through Dunedin. There was very little traffic on a fine Sunday morning. The Ford behaved perfectly. They headed south, and turned left on the Andersons Bay Road. Miss Fairchild had suggested they explore the Otago Peninsula, that long, crooked thumb of land protecting the harbor from the sea. It would, she said, take them most of the day to get to the end and back. It was open, hilly country: farms and beaches, rough grassland, cliffs and little settlements. At Taiaroa Head, right at the tip, there was a lighthouse and a colony of albatross.

"We saw some albatross from the ship," said Len. "We didn't get very close, though."

"I thought albatross were bad luck," Alice said, leaning over the back of the front seat.

"Only for the Ancient Mariner," said her mother, "and only because he killed one. He had to wear it around his neck."

"That can't have been much fun," Len said. "They're enormous, you know. Really huge"—he spread his arms wide—"bigger than this."

"Len!" cried Christine. "Do keep your hands on the wheel."

Steering again, he went on, "They stay out at sea for years and years—they can drink saltwater. They only come to land for breeding."

"How do you know all that?" Alice asked.

"I picked it up. The purser on the *Otaio* was dead keen on birds. He used to spend hours out on deck with his binoculars. He had this list he was keeping—said it gave him something to do. You can find birds anywhere."

"Better than a wife in every port," remarked Christine. She and Len exchanged a long look. Feeling excluded again, Alice pretended not to notice.

Surprisingly quickly they shook loose from the city. The narrow road followed the harbor, twisting along its very edge. The moving surface of the sea glinted with flecks of sun, and a fresh, damp salt wind blew into the car through the open windows. "What about my hair?" protested Christine. "It'll be wild."

"I like it curly," said Len. "It reminds me of when you were Alice's age."

"It's the wrong color." Alice inserted herself into the conversation. "And mine doesn't curl."

"Count your blessings. Mine'll be corkscrews by the end of the day and I'll never get a comb through it." But Christine didn't ask them to roll up the windows.

Len began to sing one of their favorite songs: " 'Where hast tha been sin ah saw thee?' Come on, Ally," he urged, grinning at her in the rearview mirror. She joined him on the second verse. There they were, the three of them together again at last, off on an expedition for a whole lovely day. She made up her mind to forget Florestan, Miss Fairchild, Arthur Tatlock, Saint Kat's, bad-tempered Margery MacInnes—the lot. The tightness in her stomach vanished. " 'I've been a-courting Mary-Jane! I've been a-courting Mary-Jane! On Ilka Moor bhat at, on Ilka Moor bhat at, on Il-ka Moor bhat at!' " Halfway through the third verse Christine began to sing, although she always maintained she couldn't carry a tune to save her life.

When they finished "Ilka Moor," they sang "Sospan Fach" and "Men of Harlech," and then Len taught Alice a silly song he'd learned from an American on his first freighter. "I hope it's decent, Leonard," warned Christine. "Not like the tattoo."

"I thought you'd *like* the tattoo, Chrissie."

"You did, did you."

"Anyroad, I could've sung this song to Auntie Millie."

The chorus was: "I'm off to my love with a boxing glove, ten thousand miles away," and they were all singing it at the top of their lungs before long.

They went to the end first, to see the albatross, leaving the Ford where the road stopped, and climbing up the bare knob of land to the white lighthouse with its round red hat. There was a hut on the brow of the hill, just above the lighthouse. It was a blind, explained the bearded young man in dirty trousers, gumboots, and a greenish sweater full of holes who came out to greet them. "So we can watch the birds without bothering them. Come on, I'll show you."

His name was Roger. He told them he was one of a team of volunteers who protected and observed the albatross colony during the breeding season. He loaned them a pair of well-used binoculars, but Alice found it easier to watch the birds without. On land, among the tall grasses, they were slow-moving and awkward; they rolled side to side as they walked, their expressions benign and slightly silly. But when they spread their immensely long black wings and launched themselves out over the choppy sea, they were breathtaking. They planed and swooped effortlessly on the wind. "They need a high place to take off from," Roger said. "They need the lift, see? They're not very good on land, but in the air? There's nothing can touch them." He sounded like a proud parent. Len asked questions. Len always asked questions—and Roger seemed delighted to talk about his birds. Alice leaned her elbows on the windowsill of the hut and watched the bright, blade-winged shapes against the blazing sky, not really listening, happy just being there. She had no idea how long, when Len suddenly said, "Hey, Ally, where's your mother?"

Alice roused herself and looked around. Christine had vanished. "Don't know."

"Well," said Len, sounding reluctant, "I suppose we should go find her. It must be lunchtime."

Roger shook hands with both of them. "Come back anytime," he said.

They found Alice's mother sitting in a sheltered spot in the sun, wearing the straw hat, and reading peacefully. *Sonnets from the Portuguese,* Alice saw, in a dark red leather binding that looked suspiciously like one from Mr. Fairchild's library. "I was just starting to wonder if you'd fallen over the edge," she said, her eyes bright in the shadow of the hat brim. "And how I'd get back to Dunedin if you had."

"Sorry, Chrissie. I didn't mean to be so long, but we got talking. You know."

She nodded. "Yes, I do. That's when I left you. Never mind, I had good company."

"They're fascinating, those birds. Did you know they mate for life?

Roger says he can recognize the pairs as they come back—they've got names for them. They go round and round the South Pole for the first seven years of their lives, and then—''

"What about lunch?" interrupted Alice.

After eating, they started back. This time Len took them along unpaved roads that led over the spine of the peninsula toward the open ocean, where there were cliffs and long white lines of surf curling toward the land. Sheep dotted the grassy hillsides, with here and there a patch of dark, wind-twisted trees, like an ink spot on a vivid green blotter. There were gates for Alice to get out and open so Len could drive through, then close again, and miles and miles of weathered gray stone walls, climbing the humpy fields. Each time the Ford chugged industriously up a rise, there'd be a wide blue-and-green vista revealed at the top: grass and sky and sea. Skylarks bubbled overhead, their thin, joyous songs tumbling out of the air.

In the middle of the afternoon they found a beach. Len piloted them down a narrow, rutted track. "I think this must be someone's private drive," said Christine dubiously. "Then we'll smile politely, turn round in their front yard, and go back the way we came," said Len. "After they've given us tea." The track ended in a flat, grassy space, and on the far side was a sandy path disappearing between high banks of foliage.

They'd passed a farm a few minutes earlier, off to the right: a small white house with a red corrugated roof and stone outbuildings. Although there was no one visible, sheets snapped on a laundry line in back, and Alice saw a black-and-white dog stretched out in the sun, tied to its kennel.

"I'll bet the sea's just over there," said Len. "Come on, Ally, let's go paddle."

"You're out of your mind, Leonard Jenkins. It'll be much too cold," declared Christine. She took her hat and her book, and Len carried one of the rugs, and they set off through the sand hills. It was hard walking, the sand was deep and slippery, but eventually they came out on a wide, deserted beach, bound at one end by a sudden, steep cliff, and at the other by the mouth of a small stream. "Oh!" cried Alice in delight. "It's all ours! It's beautiful!" She sat right down in the sand, warm on top from the sun, cool and damp underneath, and took off her shoes and socks. Hastily Len spread the rug for Christine, then did the same, rolling up his trouser legs to expose white, hairy shins. "Come on, Chrissie, you too," he urged. "You've never had your toes in the Pacific Ocean before!"

Alice expected her mother to refuse; it flickered across her face, then her expression changed. "All right then." They joined hands and ran over the beach to the water. It *was* cold—Christine gave a little shriek and Alice gasped. Len laughed happily. They splashed in the shallow waves, and Len waded out until a wave, bigger than the others, sloshed the bottom of his trousers. "Enough," Christine decided, and retreated back to the rug. She put on her hat again and sat down, her back against a salt-silvered log, and picked up her book. Alice began to prospect along the tide line, to see what the waves had brought ashore. "Find me a treasure," called her mother, and she waved.

"What have you got?" asked Len, coming to join her after a bit. She showed him her handful of shells and wave-tumbled pebbles.

They walked companionably to the end of the bay, where the cliff came right to the sea. Black jagged rocks stuck up out of the wet sand, their lower parts crusted with barnacles. The tide was going out, leaving pools among them, and snaky mats of weed that writhed and twisted when the waves jostled them. Alice watched them with wary fascination; they seemed alive. Len waded right in and let the slippery tentacles swirl around his ankles. Alice wrinkled her nose in distaste. "Doesn't it feel beastly?" But he shook his head. "It's only kelp. Just think, Ally—here we are on our own private beach in New Zealand! Who'd ever have thought it last year at this time, eh? Cor! Imagine a beach like this and not another mug in sight—"

Alice shook back her hair and looked all around at the sun-washed ocean and the green hills. "It isn't half bad," she conceded.

"Not half bad!" echoed Len. "Alice, you've got no soul!"

"Well, it's fine for a holiday. . . ."

They started back, walking on the wet sand where the waves slid in and out. Alice's pale bare feet were edged with rosy pink from the cold; they tingled, not unpleasantly. A milky haze was starting to thicken in the sky, and the breeze freshened.

"Ally, what do you think?" Len caught her by the arm. "Is she really glad to see me?"

"She?" Alice turned to him in surprise. "Do you mean Mum? Of course she is. Why wouldn't she be?"

"It's only—well, I did wonder a bit—I mean, when I got back to Cambridge and found you'd cleared out like that, I thought—" He stopped, searching the horizon for something.

"What?" prompted Alice. "What did you think?"

"I thought—well, tell the truth, Ally, I wasn't sure what I was meant to think. She wrote and told me she was going, but I didn't think— well, she had to mean *later*. But I come back from Dover and there's the house with a TO LET sign by the front gate, and nothing at all to say where you'd gone—"

"There was! I know Mum left a letter with Mrs. Hollings, with your things. I saw it. Didn't Mrs. Hollings give it to you?" She couldn't believe grandmotherly Mrs. Hollings would have held it back from Len.

He shrugged. "But she wasn't there either when I got in, was she? Up with her daughter in Sheffield. It was almost a fortnight before she came back. Her daughter's baby'd come early and she'd gone in a hurry. How was I to know?"

Alice stared at him. "What did you do?"

"Once I'd got my head working, I went round to see Gillian. I reckoned she'd know if anyone would. And she told me Chrissie'd gone off to New Zealand. I thought she was having me on at first. She said Chrissie told her she wanted a new life—something like that."

"Mum said she'd told you that herself, before you went away to work on the ferry. She said you didn't believe her."

"Yeah, well. She said a lot of things, Ally. And how was I to know that what she meant was emigrating halfway round the world? Be fair, Ally, did *you* know that's what she meant?''

Alice dug her toes into the wet sand, and watched the hole fill with water.

"Anyroad," Len went on, "I could tell Gillian was thinking, 'Good riddance to you, mate!' I mean, she's never reckoned me much, has she.''

Alice hadn't thought about it before, but she knew he was right. Out of the jumble of memories she had, from the time after Len had gone and before she and her mother had sailed for Auckland, a fragment of overheard conversation floated to the surface. She heard Gillian say, "I don't know why you put up with it, Chris, I really don't. What's to hold you? I could see while your dad was still alive, but he's been gone almost five years. If it was *me*—'' And her mother, sounding sharpish, "But it's not, is it. You're on your own, Gillian. You can do what you like. I've got Alice to consider. What about her school?'' "That's only an excuse, and you know it, Christine Jenkins. Where does it say Alice has to finish this particular school?'' "But if she's going on to Girton or Newnham—'' "There are lots of good schools in other places that send girls to Cambridge.'' There was a silence, then Alice's mother said, "Len's job's for the summer. By the time he comes back, it'll be too late.'' "Well, there you are then!'' exclaimed Gillian. "Don't be a wally. He picks up and goes when it suits him—he's done it before too. Why should you miss this chance, waiting for him to come home? Honestly, Chris, I've never understood why you let that man—'' In the hall, outside the kitchen, Alice had dropped a book, and Gillian never finished her sentence. When she opened the door, she found the two of them drinking tea and discussing Gillian's sister, Edwina, who had just bought a holiday caravan near Hastings.

Alice squinted up the beach. Her mother was stretched out on the rug, on her back with her ankles crossed and the straw hat over her face. "Then what happened?" she asked, breaking the silence that had grown heavy.

Len shrugged. "I hung about, did a bit of work for Jackie Ransome at the Millbridge Garage, you know. He let me doss down there, in the back room. Until Mrs. Hollings came back and I got Chrissie's letter and my things, and I knew for sure. So I skated off to Liverpool and found a freighter going in the right direction, and here I am, like the bad penny. Trouble is, the closer I got, the more I thought about it. I mean, she'd given me the address in her letter all right, even told me she'd left money so I could follow, and at first I reckoned that meant she wanted me to come on. But then I thought, maybe she'd gone so far away because she really didn't want me following her after all."

"But why wouldn't she?" said Alice, frowning at him. "I've been thinking about it, Len. I don't really understand what happened, I mean before you went to Dover."

He scrubbed a hand through his hair, making it stand up in spikes; his eyes were unhappy. "D'you know, Ally? I'm not sure I can tell you. I knew she was upset—it had to do with that job she didn't get. I didn't see that it mattered really. A bit more money would have been welcome, but I didn't see it was worth it. The job would've meant more responsibility, longer hours. And there was all that about the house— it didn't make sense. We were all right where we were—you thought so, didn't you, Ally? Anyroad, I decided maybe if I went off for a bit, took myself out of the way, like, she'd get over it and settle down again."

Alice shivered. For the first time she noticed that the sun had actually disappeared and the sky, blue a short time ago, was banked with ominous clouds, like dirty laundry. The breeze had become a wind; it gusted in over the water, laden with salt-smelling moisture.

"Hullo," said Len. "I think we'd better start back. There's a bit of weather coming in."

It arrived just as they reached Christine: sharp, wind-driven spears of rain, striking the beach, making dark spots on the sand. In a few minutes the spots had vanished, pounded into one another. Christine sat bolt upright, snatching the hat away, and stared around disoriented. "What's happened?"

"Come on!" cried Len. "We'll have to run!" He gave Christine his hand and pulled her to her feet, then bundled the rug up in his arms. The book fell out and Alice grabbed it; some of its pages were bent and there was sand between them, but she didn't pause to shake it out. She stuck her sandy feet into her shoes and stuffed her socks in her pockets. The rain came down hard and cold and the wind had teeth in it. It had all happened so fast—gone from a glittering and sunny afternoon to a furious one in the blink of an eye.

By the time they reached the Ford, they were soaked through. Len wrenched the doors open, and Alice threw herself into the backseat. The rain pounded on the roof and sluiced the windows as if someone had turned a hose on them, drowning the landscape. They were all out of breath.

"The book!" exclaimed Christine suddenly. "It must still be on the beach!"

"Here." Alice thrust it over the seat back. Its leather cover was mottled with rain. Christine took it without comment and wiped it ineffectually on her skirt.

"No use starting until it lets up a bit," said Len. "The wipers can't keep up. Anything left in the picnic basket?"

"Half a package of squashed-fly biscuits," said Alice, rummaging.

"I'm not hungry," Christine said. "What I want is a cup of hot tea."

There wasn't a chance of that for the present. They sat in silence, Len and Alice munching, Christine with the book clutched in her hands, her hair in wild wet wisps around her face. After fifteen or twenty minutes the hammering over their heads began to soften; gradually it became a steady, dull patter. The insides of all the windows were opaque with steam. Experimentally Len turned the key in the ignition and pushed the windscreen wiper switch, then rubbed the windscreen with the sleeve of his shirt, making a clearish smudge on the glass.

Cautiously he steered the car up the track, back toward the main road. The heavy downpour had washed parts out and created wide puddles; it was impossible to tell how deep they were. To avoid getting stuck, he tried to keep one tire on the ridge in the middle, the other on the outer edge. The Ford lurched and shuddered. It seemed much further out than it had coming in, but finally they reached the paved road that ran along the ridge of the peninsula and turned left, toward Dunedin. The rain had slackened, and the clouds had ironed themselves into a solid gray flannel sheet; webs of mist festooned the harbor and shrouded the hills beyond the city. It was simply a rainy afternoon.

"Isn't there any heat?" asked Christine in a thin voice. "My feet are like ice."

Len reached over and switched on the heater. In a few minutes the windows were fogged worse than ever. He hunched forward over the steering wheel, every now and then making a swipe at the windscreen. Progress was slow and no one thought of singing.

Miss Fairchild was in the kitchen when they returned, eating cold chicken and cream crackers spread with cheese and pickle. Over her skirt and blouse she wore a faded blue smock, randomly patterned with streaks and splotches of paint. She looked up from the paperback she was reading. "You didn't leave much for my tea, Mrs. Jenkins," she complained. "I've had to scratch for it. You might at least—"

But Christine walked right past her and up the back stairs, calling over her shoulder, "Alice, you'd better change out of those wet things at once or you'll catch cold."

"Had a lovely day, did you?" inquired Miss Fairchild, a malicious glint in her eye. She had turned the book upside down; A Man Lay Dead, by Ngaio Marsh, Alice read. It was dog-eared with use.

"Until it rained we did," said Len. He put water in the kettle and set it on the hot plate. "Those albatross are fantastic! The *size* of them—more than ten feet, wingtip to wingtip. The females won't be back for another week or two, he said—"

Alice left him settling in at the table across from Miss Fairchild to tell her about the ecstatic courtship display of the royal albatross, which he wanted to go back and see for himself. Her expression had shifted slightly, from irritable to bemused. When Alice came down again, she found they were still sitting there, and her mother, the damp hair fastened back from her face, was putting tea in the blue-and-white pot.

"It didn't always look like that, you know," Miss Fairchild was saying. "It used to be covered with native trees: kowhai, rimu, ngaio. Then the pakehas came and chopped everything down, stripped it, so their cattle could graze. And if that weren't enough, they brought alien plants with them—gorse and broom for hedgerows, lupin and macrocarpa. They've all gotten out of hand, of course. They're choking out everything that belongs. Bloody, meddling fools! Pakehas never leave anything alone." She sounded contemptuous.

"Alice, will you please fetch the milk?"

Alice asked, "What are pakehas?"

"Europeans," replied Miss Fairchild. "Settlers. *You're* a pakeha."

"Well, I don't want to change anything," said Alice, adding to herself, "except being here."

"Alice," said her mother sharply, "the milk, please. Len, make yourself useful and get out the cups."

Obediently Len got up and Alice went out to the pantry. She heard Len say, "Chrissie?" in an odd voice. At almost the same moment there was a dull crash, the sound of smashing china, then a thud. Len cried, "Chrissie! What's wrong?"

"What is it?" Alarmed, Alice ran back, clutching the milk bottle to her chest. From the doorway she saw her mother crumpled on the floor by the sink, amid a mess of tea, leaves, and broken teapot.

"Well, it's obvious, isn't it!" snapped Miss Fairchild, heaving herself up. "She's fainted, you silly girl. At least it wasn't the Limoges teapot. Don't stand there like a fence post, Mr. Jenkins! Pick her up."

"But we shouldn't—I mean, should we move her?" Len looked stricken.

"Of course we should move her! The only thing she's broken is the teapot! She oughtn't to lie there on the cold floor."

Len bent and awkwardly gathered Alice's mother into his arms. "She's breathing," he said in a voice faint with relief.

"For pity's sake! Why wouldn't she be breathing? What did you expect? You—Alice—go along to the drawing room and take the dust sheet off the sofa."

Alice stood rooted to the spot. "What's wrong with her?"

"I don't know, do I? I'm not Dr. Lattimer. I've smelling salts up-stairs—in the top drawer of my dressing table. A little purple vial. Run up and get them and *I'll* attend to the sofa. Go on."

Alice shook herself loose and sped up to Miss Fairchild's room, still holding the milk bottle, and Len staggered out through the door Miss Fairchild held open for him. By the time Alice had found the smelling salts, her mother was established on the hard, dark red horsehair sofa. Len was hovering over her with pillows. "No," Miss Fairchild was saying firmly. "Her head should be flat. You can put them under her knees." She practically snatched the tiny vial from Alice, unscrewed the top, and waved it beneath Christine's nose. Christine grimaced and shook her head from side to side with a little moan.

"What's in it?" Len's face was drawn and pale in spite of his tan.

"Ammonia. For pity's sake, Mr. Jenkins, stand back and give her some air. In the coat closet under the stairs you'll find a traveling rug. I'll ring Dr. Lattimer."

Alice crouched beside her mother, and saw her eyelids flutter. She blinked in a puzzled way. "Where am I?"

"In the drawing room. Miss Fairchild says you fainted. I've never seen anyone faint. You dropped the teapot—"

"Miss Fairchild?" Christine twisted her head a little. "Where's Len? Wasn't he there?"

"Chrissie, thank God!" Len was back, a brown wool rug bunched in his arms. He looked down at her helplessly. "You should've said— You should've *told* me—"

"How could I? I didn't—everything just went black. I was making tea, wasn't I?" She tried to sit up, then squeezed her eyes shut and sank flat again. "It won't stay still," she said in a faint voice. "Oh, I feel dreadful."

Alice tugged the rug away from Len and spread it over her mother, tucking it under her feet. "She's calling Dr. Lattimer."

"But it's Sunday evening," whispered Christine. "He'll never come out. If I just lie here for a little while . . ."

But Dr. Lattimer did come out, remarkably quickly. He was wearing a starched white dress shirt under his old mac, and had a little scrap of tissue stuck to his chin where he'd nicked himself shaving. "Now then, Mrs. Jenkins," he said, gazing at her mournfully from his great height and cracking his knuckles, "what's all this about?"

"Don't waste time with foolish questions, Brian. That's what you're here to tell us," snapped Miss Fairchild.

"You're feeling better, I see," he replied, opening his bag and fishing around in it. "Ah, here." He pulled out a stethoscope. "I'll just have a dekko. Fainted, did you?"

"And you"—Miss Fairchild turned on Len, who'd backed away when Dr. Lattimer arrived—"you can just clear out. Don't need you here. Go and clean up the mess your wife made in the kitchen, and make another pot of tea. You're in the way."

Visibly relieved, Len vanished. Miss Fairchild gave Alice a look that said plainly, "You too," and she followed him. Mechanically she filled the kettle and chose another teapot from the large collection in the dresser. Her mother was *never* ill. Once in a while she complained of headache, but that was from too much close reading, from working too late at night on Dr. Inchcape's manuscripts. For her to *faint*—that could only mean something serious was wrong. Suppose she needed special treatment—suppose she needed an operation? What if Dr. Lattimer couldn't find out what was the matter? He could have been mistaken about Miss Fairchild's illness not being contagious. Her mother might have some terrible tropical disease—what would they do? How would they ever get her home, where she'd have proper doctors?

"Ow! Bloody—"

She jumped. She'd forgotten about the kettle, which was spluttering—she'd filled it too full—and about Len, who was down on hands and knees, picking up fragments of blue-and-white china and mopping the floor with tea towels. He took his thumb from his mouth and a thin red line sprang up on the fleshy part. "It bit me," he said ruefully.

Alice stared at him. Tears burned behind her eyes and her mouth twisted. "*Why* did she have to come here? Why couldn't we stay where we belonged? We'd still be in Cambridge if you hadn't gone away, Len."

"Hey, Ally." He sounded surprised. "You're not worried, are you? You mustn't be. Your mum's tough as old boots. She is. That doctor'll have her right again in no time, you'll see—"

— 17 —

Nepenthes ampullaria

Worn out, that was Dr. Lattimer's verdict. Mrs. Jenkins had caught a chill on the way back from the beach, and she hadn't the energy to fight it off. She'd been working too hard. She'd need a couple of days in bed, resting, and then she'd need to take things easy for a week or two. Len was right, nothing to worry about. No, thank you, he wouldn't have a cup of tea, he was a bit rushed. He raked his fingers through his hair in a distracted.way, and promised he'd pop round the next day to check on the patient.

"Fine thing this is," declared Miss Fairchild after he'd gone. "I come home from my own trip, exhausted and unwell, only to find my household in chaos."

"That's not true." Indignant on her mother's behalf, Alice glared at her. "Mum did her best to have things ready for you, even though that wasn't what you hired her for. If she hadn't been here, there wouldn't have been anyone. The house would have been shut up."

Miss Fairchild sniffed. "That's as may be. In any event, I don't want you worrying her unnecessarily, d'you hear? She must get back on her feet as soon as possible, so I can get on with my work."

"Me?" Alice was indignant on her *own* behalf.

"Either one of you," she replied, including Len with her frosty gaze. "We were just beginning to make progress. It really is too bad. Can you cook?"

Len and Alice looked at each other. Alice felt dazed, as if someone had knocked the wind out of her.

"I'm hopeless," said Len. "I can do hard-boiled eggs—"

"*Any*one can do hard-boiled eggs." Miss Fairchild was scornful. "The only trick is not to let the pan boil dry."

Len shrugged.

"Mmmp."

When Alice woke the next morning, the house was silent. She put on her uniform and crept down to the kitchen, where the smell of charred toast lay heavy upon the air, and the drainboard beside the sink was littered with dirty dishes, evidence that people were up and about, but there was nothing to indicate where those people might have gone. The house had swallowed them, and refused to divulge any information. Alice made herself a comfortless breakfast of cornflakes and milk with an overripe banana on top, then added her bowl and spoon to the collection.

It wasn't until she was out of the gate that she remembered she really didn't want to go to school. The prospect of facing Betty and Fiona at the start of another week was dismal. Helen and Grace would be unbearable—full of plans for the bridal shower. And Alice still hadn't a clue why Margery wasn't speaking to her. As she approached Lockwood, her steps slowed, but she couldn't think of any better alternative. She didn't want to go back to Florestan, and the only other choice was to slink about the streets until half past three, trying to look inconspicuous. Seven blank hours. She turned in at the walk, and got to her desk just as the first bell went. Like a snail, she imagined herself wound tight into a shell where she couldn't be got at.

It was nearly four when she got back to Florestan, and she found the drainboard piled even higher. There was a saucepan in the sink, crusted with boiled-over milk, and the tea towels Len had wiped the floor with were a soggy, filthy lump on the edge. There were the remains of a meal on the table: a lump of cheese drying out on a plate, half a loaf of bread standing on its cut end surrounded by crumbs, a cold teapot, and a milk bottle with half an inch of lumpy, souring milk in the bottom. Everything looked the way Alice felt: abandoned, depressed, ugly. She cleared a small space for herself among the debris, sat down, and laid her head on her folded arms. A desolate wind blew through her. It wasn't supposed to be like this. Len had come; everything was supposed to be all right. She'd been so full of hope and eagerness. . . .

"Well, this is a fine mess, isn't it?" With a snap the light went on. Alice jerked up. Her eyes felt gritty and sore in the sudden glare. "And where do you suppose that father of yours has gotten to?"

"Len? I don't know—how should I? I've only just got back from school."

"Rubbish! It's nearly six o'clock."

Alice rubbed her eyes. Outside the windows the afternoon light was blurring into shadow. She had gone to sleep; her arms were stiff and prickly. Miss Fairchild was wearing her blue smock again; she'd come in from her studio. "What about Mum?"

"Resting comfortably. Dr. Lattimer left her a tonic, a particularly nasty one, I'm glad to say. In my experience the more disagreeable the medicine, the quicker the recovery." She glanced about and sighed. "It seems the only way we shall get anything to eat tonight is if we fix it ourselves. There must be *some*thing in the pantry." She disappeared into it, and Alice heard her muttering irritably to herself. She reemerged finally with two tins of peas and the steak-and-kidney pie Mr. Tatlock had provided for them the first evening they'd been in Florestan. It was on the tip of Alice's tongue to repeat her mother's opinion of the doubtful origins of such pies, when Miss Fairchild said, "Well, don't just sit there looking sorry for yourself. See if you can find a tin opener—there must be one in one of those drawers."

Len came in, whistling through his mustache, just as Alice dumped the peas into a saucepan. "Your Mr. Tatlock is a hard man to find. Hullo, something smells good!"

"Did you?" Miss Fairchild demanded.

"Did I what?"

"Find Mr. Tatlock?"

"Oh. Yeah, I did." He ran water in the sink and began to wash his hands, which were, Alice noted, quite black.

"And?"

"And?" Len straightened. "Crikey—I forgot! Sorry." He turned to Miss Fairchild with an apologetic grin. " 'Fraid I got sidetracked. He wasn't in when I found the lodge, see, so I had a look round, while I was waiting. Made friends with the dog. Then up he comes on this motorbike, and I can tell it's not firing right before I even clap eyes on it. So we got to talking. It's a good bike that, American. Just needs a bit of work. New set of sparks—"

Miss Fairchild gave him a frosty look. "Alice, you'll lay my place in the dining room, if you please, and call me when the meal is ready. I'll be in the library." She left them.

"What was that about?"

Sheepishly Len said, "She sent me to find Artie—wanted to see him in her studio, don't know what for. I forgot to tell him—it went clean out of my mind."

"Artie?"

"Yeah. Arthur Tatlock—you know. Told me his mates call him Artie. He was a bit stiffish at first, but after I fiddled with his choke he warmed right up. Tell you what, Ally, he's a fascinating bloke."

Alice gave her stepfather a disbelieving look, wondering if they'd met the same person. How on earth could Len have got sidetracked talking to Mr. Tatlock? Oh, she'd heard her mother complaining about Len's faulty sense of time often enough. He seldom got anywhere exactly when he was supposed to, or even near it; that didn't affect Alice much because it was her mother who saw to things like dentist's appointments and school meetings. She had always impressed upon Alice that punctuality was part of learning to be responsible. If you promised to be somewhere at a specific time, then you made sure you got there, no matter what, unless you had a life-or-death excuse. "But," said Alice, "what on earth were you talking to Mr. Tatlock *about*?"

"Oh, this and that. All kinds of things. The bike of course—I hadn't actually seen a Harley-Davidson like that before. He got it secondhand from a chap who had to leave the country in a hurry—I forgot to ask why." He frowned, then suddenly his eyes lit. "But, Ally, did you know Artie's father was a gold miner? Straight up. His grandda got here in 1863 and staked a claim on the west coast—a place called Skippers Canyon. His da was killed in a mine accident when Artie was twelve, so he went to live with his grandda until he couldn't stick it any longer and scarpered. Just think, Ally—*gold!* They panned for it, just like in all those western films. You ask him about it, he'll tell you." He gave a delighted little chuckle. "This is the frontier—the real thing! After all those years stuck in Wroxley—"

With an angry hiss the peas boiled over on the hot plate. Alice whipped them off and the hissing died. "There's a steak-and-kidney pie in the oven," she said in a tight voice. "You'd better take it out— I'm not sure how you tell if it's done. Here's a pot holder."

Miss Fairchild eyed her plate with distaste when Alice set it down in front of her. The peas were watery and coming out of their yellow-green skins, and the pie had refused to leave its tin in wedge-shaped pieces, so Len had dug it out with a spoon. "Do you want some bread and butter?" asked Alice, reading her expression correctly.

"I think that would be a good idea."

Sitting down to her own supper, in the kitchen with Len. Alice said with passion, "I *hate* this. I really hate it."

Len ate a forkful, chewing with a thoughtful look. "I've had better, I'll admit, but I've had far worse too. Go on, try it, Ally, it's not all that bad."

"I don't mean the food! I mean *every*thing. I hate everything—the food too!"

He frowned a little, then his forehead cleared. "I didn't tell you about the cook on the *Chekiang*, did I? He was from Singapore. Funny little chap, didn't speak a word of English. Anyroad, he'd got his own set of knives for chopping and carving things up. He kept them in a special wooden box with a velvet lining and he wouldn't let anyone else so much as lay a finger on them. Once in a while he'd go right off his loaf and wing them at the galley lads—you should've heard the screeching! He never hit one, at least not while I was aboard, but he didn't get any complaints about the grub, I can tell you! And the ship before that one, the first mate had a parrot, a scruffy old bird with an evil temper. He called it Long John Silver, even though it was green. Good thing your mother couldn't've heard it swear. It'd climb up on your shoulder and give your ear a pinch, then flap away laughing like a looney. It could draw blood. I thought I was going to have a permanent notch in this ear."

In the middle of the night something jerked Alice into sudden full consciousness. She'd fallen asleep as soon as she put her head on the pillow, diving gratefully into oblivion, too confused and unhappy to try to sort through everything. But later—she wasn't sure how much later— she broke the surface again. She lay motionless and listened, and heard nothing but the little secret noises the house made, noises that still made her uneasy, but that, she now realized, had nothing to do with her. Getting up, she padded silently along the corridor to the loo, alert for any sign that someone else was stirring and that's what had woken her; there was nothing; no sliver of light under a door, no creaking floorboard, no whispering. And she didn't really need to use the toilet, either, so it hadn't been that.

Back under the covers she butted her face into her pillow, trying to burrow back into sleep, but she couldn't stop thinking. Her brain refused to shut down. He didn't understand. Or didn't *want* to understand; she wasn't sure which. He must have known what she was talking about: Florestan, Miss Fairchild, school, Dunedin, New Zealand—*everything*, she'd told him. All this that she hadn't bargained for, hadn't expected, didn't want. But instead, he'd told her stories about his travels, the places he'd been, the men he'd met.

And it began to dawn on her as Len talked that for the past two and a half months he'd been enjoying himself. While she'd been worrying about him—what he'd do when he discovered they'd gone, whether he'd be able to find them, if something had happened to him on the way—he'd been having a good time. It was as if they'd been playing the same game but using different rules. Len had cheated, she though indignantly. He was still cheating. What was all that rubbish about Mr. Tatlock? Artie, he called him. She felt hot all over and her skin prickled. She flung herself about, getting tangled in her sheets, and after a long time the birds began to sing outside her window and the navy blue bleached out of the sky behind the trees, leaving them ragged and full of holes. When Alice dragged herself out of bed at last on Tuesday morning, she felt worse than if she'd deliberately stayed up all night, and her bedclothes were in such a muddle that she had to pull them apart and put them back together again.

That afternoon she was struggling with the rusty latch on the main gate when a brown van suddenly pulled in behind her and a man in a cloth cap stuck his head out the window. "Open it wide enough for me, will you, love? Got a delivery for Miss Fairchild."

Feeling put upon, Alice wrestled the heavy, uncooperative gate as far as she could, giving the van room to squeak through. Instead of driving on, it stopped just inside, as Alice, cursing Mr. Tatlock's sheep—she thought of them as his even though he claimed they weren't—was heaving with all her strength to close the gate. The driver jumped out and put his shoulder to it. "Wants oiling, this," he remarked cheerfully. "Hop in, why don't you?"

Never accept rides from strange men; Alice's mother had warned her not once, but with boring frequency. Of course I wouldn't, Alice retorted. Why did her mother think she would? She climbed recklessly into the passenger seat of the van; it smelled musty and there were odd coils of rope and pieces of sacking on the floor. "Bob Hammond." The driver held out his hand. It was hard and grimy. "Alice Jenkins," said Alice. "What're you delivering?"

"Crates." He pulled a wry face and put the van into gear. "She won't be best pleased when she sees 'em either. One's a real dog's breakfast—damaged in transit, as they say. I got some insurance forms for her to sign." He patted his breast pocket. He had a lean, good-humored face, with deep lines like parentheses bracketing his mouth when he smiled. As they emerged from the tunnel of foliage onto the weedy gravel circle, he whistled between his teeth. "It's really nothing much but we call it home," he said, grinning. "Never been up here before. Wullie, down at the office, told me it was worth the trip. You actually living in it, are you?"

Glumly Alice nodded. "Not by choice."

He gave her a curious, sideways look. "Anyone round to give me a hand? Don't know what's in 'em, but they're heavy old buggers."

"I'll see." Alice went around to the back. The garage doors were open and the Ford was parked outside on the cobblestones to make room for Mr. Tatlock's motorbike on the stained cement floor. The motorbike had been partially disemboweled, and Len and Mr. Tatlock were crouched together, examining the various organs spread around them. "Now that," Len was saying, "that's one of your troubles right there. See how it's worn?" Mr. Tatlock grunted and scratched his chin.

"Len," said Alice, glancing furtively at Mr. Tatlock, "there's a man here with some crates. He wants help."

"Righto," said Len, rooting through an old biscuit tin full of nuts and bolts and washers. "Tell him I'll be along in a tick."

"He's in a hurry," Alice lied crossly. "She has to sign for them too. Do you know where she is?"

Reluctantly he pulled himself away from the motorbike and stood up, wiping his oily hand on the seat of his trousers. Alice could hear her mother scolding him for that. "You ought to have overalls, or at least a rag," she said severely. "Mum says grease doesn't ever come out."

"What about my carburetor, eh?" said Mr. Tatlock. "It might have been a bit rough before, but at least it was running."

"Not to worry," Len assured him. "I'll be right back." To Alice he said, "Last I knew, Miss Fairchild was down at the end—in the part she calls the studio. Go have a look."

Alice's curiosity about the studio was stronger than her reluctance to go in search of Miss Fairchild. This was her chance to have a look inside it. The door was shut, but the padlock was gone from the hasp. Alice knocked and waited, then knocked again, louder. The door was pulled open. "Well?" Miss Fairchild was wearing her smock and had a thick, very black pencil in her hand. "What is it? I hope it's important— you've ruined my concentration."

"It's a delivery man," said Alice.

"He's got the wrong address. I'm not expecting anything. Tell him to go away." She started to close the door.

"But it's not wrong. He's got crates addressed to you. He says you've got to sign for them. One of them—" She hesitated, then closed her mouth. Let Bob Hammond tell Miss Fairchild that one of them was damaged; that was his job.

"Crates, you say?" Miss Fairchild's face pinched in suspicion. "What kind of crates?"

Alice shrugged. "I don't know. I didn't see them."

"My paintings! Of course. Why didn't you say so, you silly girl." She went back to her easel and put the pencil down in its trough. The sheet of paper on it was covered with slashing lines and smudges. Glancing quickly around, Alice saw a large, surprisingly light space. Two big, oblong skylights had been cut into the back of the sloping roof. The air smelled, not unpleasantly, of sharp, resinous things, and propped against the walls were big canvases on wooden stretchers, stacked four and five deep. There were three easels set up in various spots, and a long table cluttered with tubes and jars, rags and stacks of paper. In the corner by the door was a sink, splattered with paint. Miss Fairchild pushed her out and shut the door firmly.

The rear doors of the van were standing open and Len and Bob Hammond were maneuvering a flat wooden crate out. It was at least five feet square, with Miss Fairchild's name and address in large black letters on both sides. They hefted it and lugged it up the steps, to lean it beside the first crate in the hall.

"Be careful—don't bump the corners!" Puffing slightly, Miss Fairchild hurried after them. "Put it down gently. Don't drop it."

"There you are," said Len. Bob straightened up and looked around in wonder at the swords and battleaxes.

"You have papers for me to sign?"

"What? Oh, yeah." He pulled them out of his pocket and handed them over. "Top one's the receipt. The other one's for insurance."

"Insurance? What do you mean insurance?"

"You know, for the one that's got smashed in. You're to open it while I'm here; that's my instructions."

"Smashed in? What are you saying? Which one?" Her voice rose with each question mark. She went over to inspect the crates.

Now that Alice's eyes had adjusted to the gloom, she could see that one flat side of the first crate had been pushed in and splintered. Two of the edge pieces had been torn off, leaving double rows of crooked nails sticking out of the broken wood. It looked as if something heavy and sharp had been dropped on the crate from a considerable height. Someone had tied a length of stout rope around the whole thing, like a package, to hold it together.

"It was like that when I picked it up. I think it happened on the docks," said Bob. "Here—you look over the forms. I got a crowbar in the van."

Miss Fairchild paid no attention to the papers. She plucked ineffectually at the knots in the rope. Bob Hammond came back with his crowbar, and Len went to work on the knots. At last the rope fell off and Bob began to pry away long slivers of wood. They made groaning, splintering noises. Miss Fairchild, Alice noticed, had her hands clasped tight together under her chin, as if she were praying.

The first canvas was turned inward, its wooden stretcher broken on opposite sides, and there was a long jagged slit in the fabric that ran almost the width of it. Between them Len and Bob worked it free and turned it around. They all looked at it in silence. Flowers, Mr. MacInnes had said, dismissively; Miss Fairchild painted flowers. Alice thought of roses and chrysanthemums, bluebells and daisies, sunny bright colors, or pale pinks and blues. But there didn't seem to be any flowers in this painting at all. It was dark and turbulent, shades of green and brown writhing together. She thought it might be the floor of a jungle, matted with dead leaves and fallen branches, tangled in fern and vines. In the foreground was a huddle of swollen green tubular growths that looked as if they'd been spattered with mud. They had wide, hairy brown rims and appeared to be hollow. Behind them muscular tree trunks rose up, out of the picture. She thought of Charles Keating Murray, RRA. If this was the sort of painting he'd seen, no wonder he found it disturbing.

"Well," said Bob finally. "I'm glad it's not me has to reckon the insurance on that."

Miss Fairchild made a choking sound. She ran trembling fingers over the injured canvas; her face, Alice saw, was very white. "It's ruined," she whispered. "That was the only one—all I had time for. Destroyed."

"Steady on," said Len. "The other crate's all right—look, not a scratch."

Slowly Miss Fairchild shook her head. There were tears making snail tracks down her cheeks. Alice's mouth went dry. She had expected anger—shouting and fury, not grief.

Bob shifted from foot to foot. "If you could just sign these—"

In a thin, flat voice, she said, "There's no point."

"For the insurance. The company'll pay damages."

"Pay? A few pounds for the canvas, shillings for the paint? It can't be repaired. I can't paint it again. It's gone. I don't know why I bothered." With a spark of her familiar temper she turned on them. "You don't even know what it is you're looking at, do you? You haven't the faintest idea, any of you."

"Well—" Len frowned at the painting.

"Is it—are they—flowers?" ventured Alice. "I mean, that's what I thought—but they don't really—"

"Flowers?" Len squatted on his toes and peered closely at the cluster of objects. "Flowers, you say. *I* know—" he grinned up at her in triumph. "They're pitcher plants, aren't they? Bloke at the university botanic garden wanted some for an experiment. They eat flies. The fly goes down inside there, Ally, see? And it gets trapped by the hairs. There's some kind of acid—"

"*Nepenthes ampullaria*," said Miss Fairchild. "A perfect specimen. I spent two days in the bush painting them. Even if I could go back, I'd never find them, not like that."

"But if they're plants," said Alice, "couldn't you ask someone to send you some? Couldn't someone dig them up or pick them for you?"

"You don't understand anything, do you? No one does," said Miss Fairchild bitterly. "I'm old and tired and ill. No one cares about my work. All these years and all I've done is waste my time. Charles Murray was right."

Bob gave Alice's sleeve a gentle tug. "See—I've put my initials here. You get her to sign where the space is and send them back. The address is at the top. I'll just cut along. No hurry. When she's feeling better, eh?" He shoved the papers into her hand and faded out the door. She heard the van start up. Her eyes went back to the painting. She half fancied that when she'd looked away things in it had shifted; it was not a comfortable picture. Her skin felt clammy and she could almost hear the whine of insects, smell the layers of debris rotting in the heat. . . .

"Chop it up, why don't you!" cried Miss Fairchild suddenly. "Go ahead—use it for kindling, use all of them. They ought to be good for *some*thing! I can't bear to look at them any longer. I never want to see them again!''

"See what? What's going on?'' asked Christine, appearing in the doorway in her dressing gown. "I thought I heard voices. Was someone here?'' She looked at the pieces of packing crate strewn about, at the torn canvas, from Len to Alice to Miss Fairchild. "Len? What's happened?''

Relieved, he said, "Chrissie, you're just the person we need. Alice'll explain it. I'd better get back to Artie—I said I'd have his bike running again this afternoon.''

"Alice?''

Annoyed by Len's defection, Alice said, "It's Miss Fairchild's painting. It was delivered like that. The man who brought it said there's insurance, but—''

"I'm going up to my room. I don't wish to be disturbed. I'm feeling unwell, Mrs. Jenkins. I will not be down for supper,'' said Miss Fairchild distantly. She hobbled out of the hall, past Christine, and began to haul herself up the stairs. She seemed to Alice to have shrunken. Christine gave Alice a puzzled look, then went after her and took her arm. Miss Fairchild didn't shake her off. Alice was left alone with *Nepenthes ampullaria* in the shadowy hall, feeling flat and tired.

— 18 —

A Guest for Tea

"All right, Alice Jenkins." The voice at her elbow made her jump. "I've decided out of the goodness of my heart to give you one more chance."

Alice spun around to face Margery MacInnes. "Well, I don't see why. I mean, I don't see why I should *need* another chance. I didn't do anything wrong."

"Didn't you?"

Under Margery's glittering green scrutiny Alice felt distinctly ill at ease. "No, I didn't. Where are Helen and Grace?"

Margery shrugged. "Helen said something about a dress fitting."

"Oh." Alice started walking; Margery fell into step with her. Knots and clots of Saint Kat's uniforms jostled past them on the pavement. It was Friday afternoon and the laughter and chatter were louder in anticipation of the weekend. "Why anyone voluntarily chooses to go through all this fuss and bother for the sake of a few hours' discomfort is beyond me. What's the *point* of it?" demanded Margery.

"If you mean the wedding," said Alice, "I suppose it's so you can remember it for the rest of your life. Most people only get married once—it ought to be really special.''

''You're starting to sound just like Helen. I thought you had more sense.''

''I think weddings are beautiful,'' said Alice, who had never been to a real one, only seen them in films, and who wondered why she was arguing with Margery about them.

''Not me. When I get married—that is, *if* I get married—it'll be in a registry office. Do you? I do. Sign here. In and out.'' Her face suddenly lit with a wicked grin. ''Pa'll have seven fits! Are you going home?''

Jolted by the shift in subject, Alice almost said no, then realized Margery meant Florestan. Florestan was not, nor ever would be, home as far as Alice was concerned. Not only was it not *her* home, she'd begun to have doubts about whether it was Miss Fairchild's home, either, in the sense of a place to belong, to feel safe and sheltered and happy. But she wasn't about to try explaining any of that to Margery MacInnes, so instead she simply nodded.

''I'd invite myself along, but I've got the ankle-biters this afternoon,'' said Margery. ''Ma's at a Plunket meeting.''

Momentarily distracted, Alice said, ''What's a Plunket meeting?''

''Childcare. Don't you have Plunket Rooms in England? No, I don't suppose you do. Frederick Truby King—he's the one started them. Big cheese in Dunedin. He disapproved of schools like Saint Kat's. He thought girls ought to be learning domestic science: cooking, household management, darning and knitting—that kind of thing. We should all grow up to be dutiful wives and mothers and stay home and mind the babies. Mr. Fairchild was one of his greatest friends and supporters, did you know that? He can't have been very happy with his daughter.''

''But your mother doesn't do that. I mean, stay home and mind the babies.'' Alice wondered, as she said it, if she was offending Margery again.

''Don't I know it!'' Margery made a face. ''But it's not the same now anyway. It's mostly helping new mothers learn how to cope—making sure infants get proper medical care and good food. She's better at showing other mums how than doing it herself. Listen, I've got to cut along before Andrew starts to howl. He's a dreadful baby. I'm free tomorrow afternoon, though. You can ask me to tea.''

Alice blinked in alarm. "Tea?'' she said faintly.

"Well it *is* your turn. It needn't be anything fancy—just orange squash and biscuits out of a packet. I like the chocolate ones with orange. Oh, and you needn't ask Helen and Grace—they'll only go on and on about the boring wedding.''

"But there's nothing to do at Florestan.''

"Don't be daft! You can show me all round the house. I've told you, I've never seen inside, only from the drive once when Pa took some papers. He made me stay in the car.''

Grasping at straws, Alice said, "Miss Fairchild isn't well. She had a relapse this week.''

Margery's eyes narrowed to green slits. "It's all right if you don't want me to come. You needn't make up excuses.''

Alice could hear the edge in her voice; in a moment Margery was going to slam the door shut in her face again. "I'm not, honest. She's been in her room since Tuesday. And I can't invite you without asking Mum first—it's not our house.''

"Well''—Margery conceded the point—"you can ring me.''

Twisting her hair, Alice nodded. The notion of inviting anyone to tea at Florestan filled her with dismay. It was bad enough having to live there without being put on exhibit. But Margery was curious, just as Betty and Fiona were, and even Helen and Grace. Alice could forget the whole idea: not ask her mother, not ring Margery. On Monday she'd have to face Margery with a feeble-sounding excuse. That would be an end to it; Margery wouldn't bother with her again after that, Alice was sure. Perhaps that was what Alice wanted. She thought about it all the way back to Florestan.

She had been telling the truth about Miss Fairchild. Alice hadn't laid eyes on her since she'd watched her mother help her up the stairs. She had taken to her bed again and hardly even rang her bell. Fortunately Christine was feeling better, although there were still shadows around her eyes and her mouth had a thin, stretched look to it. Dr. Lattimer prescribed another tonic for her, and one for Miss Fairchild as well—Alice wondered if it was a nasty one. Trying to do too much too soon was his verdict. "Let that be a warning to you, Mrs. Jenkins," he said, cracking his knuckles painfully. Watching him leave, Christine had said, more to herself than Alice, "Well, if I don't, who will, I'd like to know?"

The packing crates and ruined painting were still in the front hall where they'd been abandoned, and the insurance forms, smoothed and neatly folded, had been put for safekeeping under the delft tea caddy on the mantel in the kitchen. Alice had given them to her mother when she came down from settling Miss Fairchild. "Will she be all right?" Alice had asked, surprised at her own concern. "Of course she will," Christine had replied. "It's only a little setback. She's not young. She needs a few days to get over it." Alice thought she detected the slightest note of uncertainty, as if her mother were trying to convince herself as well as Alice. Something in the balance of the house had shifted, although she wasn't quite sure what. Perhaps it was just that Christine was still a bit shaky, not yet her usual competent self.

Len didn't seem to notice. He had said nothing further about looking for work; Alice guessed her mother had explained to him about their arrangements with Miss Fairchild. He spent most of his time in the garage, operating on the Bentley: taking it to bits and putting it back together. When he came in to tea, his fingernails were outlined in black. He seemed quite content. Occasionally Alice glimpsed Mr. Tatlock outside, turning over flower beds, or wheeling one of his barrows heaped with tools or sacks.

At three o'clock precisely on Saturday afternoon the front doorbell reverberated hollowly through the house. "Blast!" At the kitchen table

Christine looked up in annoyance. She'd made a blot on the letter she was writing to Gillian. "Who on earth can that be?"

Noticing the time, Alice said quickly, "I'll go, shall I? I'll tell whoever it is that Miss Fairchild isn't seeing anyone."

"I'd have thought everyone knows that by now, given the way news travels here. Do you know where Len's got to?"

"He's always in the garage." Alice fled. She ought to have guessed that Margery would march straight up to the front door and ring the bell, instead of coming around back as she should have done. Why had she let herself be bullied into this? Alice wondered, with a mix of anxiety and irritation. Because she was tired of feeling ignored and lonely, that was why.

Far from rejecting Alice's tentative request to invite Margery to tea, Christine had greeted it with enthusiasm. "What a good idea, Alice. I've been thinking you should repay the MacInneses' hospitality. I'll order something special from the bakery." "But what about Miss Fairchild being ill?" said Alice. "She won't come out of her room. Unless you intend to race up and down the halls, shouting, she won't even know Margery's here. It'll be nice for you to have company." "It isn't me she's coming to see," Alice replied dourly, "it's the house. She's dead curious about it—they all are." "Nonsense," said her mother. "She likes you."

The front doorbell proved to Alice she was right. She unlocked, unbolted, and heaved it open. None of the doors and gates at Florestan seemed to want to be opened—they either complained loudly or refused outright. There on the step stood Margery, unusually neat in a dark green skirt and cardigan and a pale yellow blouse, everything tucked in and smoothed down, including her wild red hair, which was restrained by large gold barrettes. "Good afternoon, Miss Jenkins," she said, her green eyes dancing. "I do hope I'm not too early?"

"No, it's just three." Alice peered around her. "But how did you get here?"

"On the bus, of course. I wasn't about to tell Pa where I was going; I only said I'd been invited to tea. I expect they think I'm at Helen's."

"Oh," said Alice. "You didn't have to come to the front door. No one ever does, not even Dr. Lattimer."

"I'm not Dr. Lattimer, I'm company. I've even dressed like company—I hope you're impressed. If Ma hadn't been in such a hurry, I'm sure she'd have been suspicious. So where are your manners, Miss Jenkins? Aren't you going to invite me in?"

"Yes," said Alice. "Of course." Pushing back her hair, she said in a voice to match Margery's, "Do, please, come in, Miss MacInnes."

"Thank you so much, Miss Jenkins. How kind of you." Giving Alice an approving smile, she swept through the door and stopped, catching sight of the arsenal on the walls. "Crikey Dick! A warning to be on your best behavior, I suppose." Her eyes came to rest on *Nepenthes ampullaria* and she sucked in her breath. "That's one of hers—it's got to be. Aunt Jessie said—only *look*! What's happened to it?"

"That's the way it was delivered. It was damaged in shipping."

"Cripes! I'll bet she was furious! I'd've been. I'd've wanted him sacked, whoever he was. It's *sick*-making!" Margery was outraged.

"Alice? Who is it?"

"It's all right, Mum. It's Margery." Alice was eager to pull Margery away from the painting. She was bothered that Margery seemed to understand it instantly in a way that she didn't. The picture still made her uncomfortable.

Margery shook hands and said, "I'm pleased to meet you, Mrs. Jenkins. My father says you've done wonders for Miss Fairchild," in the best adult-approved manner. Alice could see her mother approving.

"I'm glad Alice is making friends at Saint Katherine's," said Christine, smiling.

"Oh, it's a very friendly school," Margery assured her, accidentally catching Alice in the ribs with her elbow.

"Yes, so your father assured me. Alice, I'm going up to check on

Miss Fairchild. I wish I could get her interested in her father's papers again—there's such a lot to do. If you see Len, remind him that he's taking me to the chemist's, will you?''

"I passed, didn't I?" said Margery smugly to Alice when Christine had gone. "Can we have tea first? I'm starving—I forgot to have lunch.''

"How can you forget to have lunch?''

"I often do on Saturdays. I get busy with something and suddenly it's teatime. You know how it is.''

Margery was fascinated by the contents of the kitchen cupboards. She kept opening doors and exclaiming over the quantities of china, the coffee grinders, toast racks, eggcups, teapots, colanders, and jelly molds. "There's more here than in Watkins's Department Store.'' She poked around in the drawers, pulling out curious objects. "What d'you suppose this is for? Force-feeding?''

"Close,'' said Len, coming in the back door. "Stuffing sausages, actually.''

"You're joking.''

"I'm not. You stick the casing on that end and push the sausage meat through there, by twisting that screw. You can make your bangers any length you want. This cherry tart going spare, is it?'' He took a large bite, dropping crumbs on the floor.

"Mum wants you,'' said Alice. "She's up with Miss Fairchild.''

"It may surprise her to know I haven't forgotten. I'm taking her to the chemist. See?'' he said, looking pleased with himself. "I've been out looking at the rhododendrons. It'll be quite a show when they bloom.''

"I've heard about them,'' said Margery, putting the sausage stuffer back. "Mr. Fairchild collected them from all over the world, Pa says.''

"Len, this is Margery,'' said Alice. "Margery, this is my stepfather.''

Len thrust a rather grimy hand at Margery. "It's all right—I've washed them and it doesn't come off." Alice could see Margery sizing him up as she took it. "Artie says they'll start coming out in another week or two. He says you won't recognize the place."

"If only that were true," Alice said.

"The Fairchilds used to have a garden party every spring—Rhododendron Sunday, they called it in Dunedin. They'd open the grounds and let everyone in to see them. There'd be a band playing on the lawn and little cakes and biscuits and oceans of punch, and Japanese lanterns strung in the trees at dusk. Pa brought Ma once when they were courting. Mr. Fairchild loved to show off the house and gardens. Of course," Margery added dryly, "all he had to do was stroll about being the genial host. He had an enormous staff to do all the work."

Alice's mother appeared in her coat with her handbag, and told Alice not to worry about anything, Miss Fairchild was taking a nap. She and Len were bound to be back before she woke.

Once they'd gone, Margery got down to business. "Now you can show me everything," she told Alice.

"All right," said Alice, resigned. "We'll begin with the library. It's this way." She felt like a guide in a museum. Perhaps she could invite the girls from school and charge an admission fee, earn a little pocket money. She deserved something for having to live in this place, she reckoned. But Margery wasn't really interested in the library; she gave it the most cursory look, not bothering with the ranks of leatherbound books, or the desk with its silver and onyx writing set and letter opener, or the wastepaper basket made from an elephant's foot, which Alice found both curious and repellent. She glanced with a little more attention at the paintings: ships under sail, which Alice hadn't bothered to notice.

In fact, Alice soon realized, it was the paintings that Margery really wanted to see. She ignored virtually everything else, wandering from room to room, examining the pictures in their ornamental gilt frames, making Alice turn on lights or open curtains so she could see them better.

For her own part Alice had never given the paintings much thought.

They cluttered the walls, making shapes against the wallpaper. Some she'd noticed more than others, like the still lifes in the dining room, and the long one over the massive sideboard in the great hall. Dimly she remembered seeing that one somewhere before, reproduced. It was the *Last Supper*: all the Apostles seated on one side of a table, with Jesus in the middle. It seemed to her an odd choice for decorating a room. And there was one at the foot of the great staircase that she didn't like at all: a man in a loincloth shot through with arrows, his head surrounded by an unearthly glow. His expression was unaccountably serene and blissful, considering he was full of holes. She guessed he had to be a saint.

Margery spent an inordinate amount of time over the classical landscapes in the drawing room: jagged cliffs and tortured trees, threatening skies swirled with ominous clouds, ruined temples, vast plains with ribbons of river snaking across them, figures in blowing drapery. Alice thought they were really quite boring, but Margery refused to be hurried past them. To Alice's surprise she dismissed the *Last Supper* with barely a glance. "A copy, of course. It's not bad, but it isn't the original." "No," said Alice. "Of course not." She wondered how Margery could tell, but she wasn't about to ask. The tour was not going at all as she had expected.

"But now *this* one—!" It was only a small painting of cows in a pasture with fountains of green trees against an immense weight of sky, pricked in the distance by the slim needle of a steeple. Really noticing it for the first time, Alice thought it was very nice. Margery let out an ecstatic sigh. "*Imagine* it! Only imagine—owning your very own Constable! Being able to look at it every day in every sort of light."

Alice knew about Constable. "He painted a lot in East Anglia. I went to Flatford Mill once. We had a field trip from Woodhall; Miss Armistead, the art mistress, took us."

But Margery wasn't really listening; she was gazing raptly at the little painting. "I've never seen a *real* Constable before—only reproductions."

Alice had been thinking of showing her the housekeeper's sitting room, with the stuffed cat in the bell jar. Christine had locked the door on it after that first sight, and no one had been in since. Alice had the key in her skirt pocket. She fingered it consideringly.

"Oh, Alice Jenkins, do you know how lucky you are?" exclaimed Margery, tearing her eyes away from the Constable. "You've got your own private museum. You can see all these any time you want—"

"I *don't* want particularly," said Alice with a touch of bitterness. "Museums aren't for living in, are they?"

Margery gave her a surprised look. "Well, no. I don't suppose they are," she said consideringly. "Still—" She glanced around the great hall. Alice remembered seeing Margery's father do the same thing.

"Aunt Jessie told me Mr. Fairchild bought a Stubbs, but I haven't seen it. Do you know where it is?"

Reluctantly Alice admitted she didn't know what a Stubbs was.

"You don't? It's probably a horse, though of course he did other things—"

"There's a painting of a horse in the billiard room. It's very big."

"That'll be it. Where's the billiard room?"

"It's upstairs," said Alice dubiously. "I'm not sure—we must be very quiet if we go up there."

"I *promise,* word of honor!" declared Margery, starting up the stairs. Alice followed. "Go right at the top," she commanded, not wanting Margery to go near Miss Fairchild's bedroom. She had visions of the old woman suddenly flinging open her door and confronting them in her flannel nightdress and ropey hair.

The gallery around the great hall was lined with more paintings; the lighting was dreadful and they were very hard to see, but Margery peered at each one, frowning.

"He certainly didn't reckon New Zealand artists worth much, did he? There isn't even a Frances Hodgkins that I've seen, and she grew up in Dunedin. Aunt Jessie said he was only interested in English and European painters. Wait—here's some local talent."

Alice stepped closer and squinted at the picture Margery'd stopped in front of. "It doesn't look like New Zealand to me." It was a piazza: ornate stone facades framing a square with a fountain in the middle and pigeons dotting the sky. It was bathed in an old, mellow, golden light.

"He's a New Zealand painter," said Margery, "but he doesn't paint New Zealand. Murray only paints classical stuff—Greece and Italy, palazzi and canals, temples on mountaintops. Technically he's quite good, but—"

"Did you say Murray?" said Alice with sudden interest. There were initials in the lower right-hand corner: CKM. "Charles Keating Murray?"

Margery nodded. "He must be very old by now, in his seventies or eighties. Aunt Jessie says he's not painting much these days—his eyesight's going. Fancy knowing Murray and not Stubbs. You *are* full of surprises, Alice Jenkins! Come on then, let's see this Stubbs."

"But what I don't understand," Margery said slowly as they came out of the billiard room and started down the stairs again, "I don't understand where *her* paintings are. There are none on the walls—the only one I've seen is the one in the front hall that's ruined. Aunt Jessie says she never sells them. There must be *stacks* somewhere—"

Alice shrugged. "I suppose they're in the studio."

Margery stopped abruptly; her hand shot out and caught Alice's arm. "Her studio! Of course that's where they are! So where's her studio? Is it in the tower room? That must have wonderful light."

"There's nothing in the tower but millions of dead flies," said Alice flatly.

"Then where is it? You've got to show me, Alice." Margery's fingers gripped Alice's upper arm painfully.

"I can't. Her studio's in one end of the garage and she keeps it locked."

"Oh, *damn!*" Margery let go and sat down on the step above the landing. "Damn, damn, damn."

Alice scowled at her in the gloom. "Is that really why you came? Just to see the paintings?"

Clasping her knees, Margery rested her chin on them and nodded.

"Why didn't you say? And"—Alice asked the question that had baffled her—"why were you so angry with me?"

"Because," said Margery, "because you were making fun of her. You had no right to make fun of her."

"Of—Miss Fairchild, d'you mean?" Alice hadn't thought of that. "You asked me what she was like. I was only telling you—"

"She's an artist, a real artist," interrupted Margery with passion. "She deserves respect. I hoped you'd be different—you'd be able to see that." She was silent for a moment, then she went on in a calmer voice, "Once, when I was eight she had a show here in Dunedin, in a little gallery near the university. Aunt Jessie took me. She said Miss Fairchild's paintings were extraordinary and I should see them—people didn't appreciate them. They were, too. I'd never seen anything like them. I remember those paintings so clearly—they changed my life."

"When you were eight?" said Alice skeptically.

"Yes. That's what I'm going to do. I decided right then—I told Aunt Jessie."

Alice sat down across the landing from Margery. "What did she say?"

Margery shook her hair back. "Oh, she said it would be hard. She said I'd probably change my mind in a year or so. But she said if I didn't—if, by the time I finished school I still felt that way, she'd help me. I knew I wasn't going to change my mind, and I haven't."

"You haven't finished school," Alice pointed out.

"That doesn't matter. There's going to be the most unholy row when I do, though," she said with a grim little chuckle. "Because *then* I'm going to art school."

Alice didn't think that sounded unreasonable. "Why not? I'm going to university."

"What do your parents think?"

"Mum wants me to—she's always encouraged me. She'd've gone to Cambridge herself if she'd had the chance, but her parents didn't see the good of it and they needed her at home. Then the war started and I was born before it was over. My father—my real father—was a fellow at Clare College. Mum says he was brilliant. Len thinks I should go to university, too, of course."

"Do you know what my pa would like? He'd like to see me get married when I leave school, in a long frilly white gown with lots of attendants, like Helen's sister. It would cost him a packet—he'd invite all his clients and partners and everyone he plays golf with, and he'd love every minute of it. It would be best if I married a solicitor—someone he could take into the firm, but a banker or a doctor would be all right. In a year or so he'd expect a grandchild, and then another—" She broke off, hiding her face in her knees, and groaned. "I'll tell you, Alice, one of us is going to be unhappy—and I'm determined it won't be *me.*"

Alice sat, frowning at the patch of light fading the carpet on the landing to a soft gray-green. Suddenly Margery straightened up. "Let's go *look* at the studio, Alice. Just look. What can it hurt? I promise I won't touch anything."

"It's locked. I told you."

Margery's shoulders slumped. "And she's got the key, of course. Are there windows? No—that's no good. I'd never be able to see anything. If I were brave enough, I'd just march right up there and knock on her door. I'd explain to her—I'd tell her straight out that she inspired me when I was eight and I'd ask if she'd give me lessons."

"You wouldn't!" cried Alice in alarm.

"I would—if I had the courage." Margery made a face.

They sat. Alice watched the patch of light creep across the carpet, struggling with herself. Finally she said, "Does it really mean so much to you, seeing her paintings?"

"Isn't that what I've been telling you?"

"Because"—she hesitated—"I know where the key is. Mum hung it on a hook in the pantry. She locked the door last Tuesday because Miss Fairchild forgot."

In a flash Margery was on her feet. "Well, come on, Alice Jenkins! Why didn't you say so? Quick—before you lose your nerve!"

— 19 —

Inside the Studio

With a sigh Alice went to fetch the key. The offer had been a rash one, but not altogether selfless. Perhaps if she saw more of Miss Fairchild's work, she'd understand why it excited Margery so much. Why Charles Keating Murray had reacted so negatively. Who, in fact, the old woman in the upstairs bedroom really was.

As they stood outside the padlocked door to the studio, she hesitated. "You will promise not to disturb anything? If she finds out we've been in here—"

"Yes, I promise. I told you," said Margery impatiently. "She'll never know."

Oh well, thought Alice, turning the key and slipping the padlock out of its hasp. This door, unlike any of the others at Florestan, actually opened smoothly.

Margery gazed around in delight. "It's a real studio!" she breathed.

"Didn't you expect it to be?"

Margery didn't bother to answer; she made straight for one of the stacks of canvases. "*Here* they are—Alice, do come and see!"

Leaving the door ajar, Alice joined her. She found it easier to recognize the flowers in these paintings than *Nepenthes ampullaria,* although they weren't flowers she was familiar with. But in any case, the blossoms themselves were only a part of what Miss Fairchild had painted in each picture: around them crowded trees and shrubs and vines, pressing at the edges of the canvases. Glimpses of sky shone through the foliage, sometimes turquoise, sometimes pale and milky with heat, sometimes swirled with great masses of cloud. There were rough, tumbled boulders, distant mountains, the gleam of moving water, here and there a butterfly with great spotted wings and an iridescent body, strange birds flashing in the trees with wild eyes and brilliant feathers. The longer Alice looked into the depths of each painting, the greater became her feeling of disorientation, of being somewhere else, a part of what she was looking at, in a place entirely alien to her. She could begin to feel the sun flecking the leaves with hot yellow, smell rich, unfamiliar, earthy aromas, hear the whine of insects in her ears. There was movement and light and a sense of uncontrolled growing things. She wasn't at all sure she liked the paintings, but she was fascinated by them.

"What do you think you're doing in here?"

Alice's heart leaped into the back of her throat, then sank like a stone. She turned to face Miss Fairchild. "We were only looking, honestly. We haven't—I didn't think—I mean—" She ran out of words.

"You have no business being in my studio. It should have been locked. Why isn't it locked?"

"It was. It has been." She felt rather than saw Margery pull herself together and take a step forward. "It's my fault, Miss Fairchild," she said boldly. "Alice didn't want to come out here, but I made her. I had to see your paintings."

"You made her, did you? And who might *you* be?" Miss Fairchild focused her glare on Margery. She had on the old plaid dressing gown, cinched firmly around her middle, and worn carpet slippers on her feet; her hair was in its fraying braid, and her face looked pouched and flabby, as if the flesh under the skin had shrunk.

Bravely Margery stood her ground. "My father is your solicitor, Miss Fairchild. Malcolm MacInnes. I'm Margery. I'm at school with Alice, and she invited me to tea."

"Malcolm's daughter, are you? You don't look much like him. I suppose he's sent you here spying. It's my nephew put him up to it. I shall give Malcolm MacInnes a piece of my mind, I promise you. I've got a good notion to find someone else to handle my affairs."

"Please," said Margery, "my father doesn't even know I'm here. I didn't tell him I was coming."

"You didn't? Why should I believe that, tell me."

"Because it's nothing to do with him." She sounded calm enough, but Alice noticed that her hands were clenched tightly on the bottom of her cardigan. "I really came"—she hesitated—"I came because I wanted to see your paintings."

"My paintings?" Miss Fairchild snorted. "Did you indeed. An art critic, are you? What do you think of them then? Have you seen enough?"

"I've hardly seen any. There wasn't time."

Alice wished desperately that they could all leave the studio before her mother and Len got back and found them. There'd be the most awful row. "Don't you think we should go back to the house?" she ventured. "It's rather chilly here—"

"Well, what you've seen. What do you think?" Miss Fairchild ignored her, addressing Margery.

She took a deep breath. "The trouble is I don't *know* enough. I've never had real lessons—only Mrs. Muir at Saint Kat's and she's hopeless. She teaches domestic science as well. But I saw the show you had at the Newtown Gallery in 1952—my aunt Jessie took me. Perhaps you remember Jessie MacInnes?" Margery was talking very rapidly. She let go of her sweater and wiped her hands on her skirt. "You did meet her—years ago, she told me. She has a gallery in Christchurch. It was the most important thing that's ever happened to me, seeing your work—"

Miss Fairchild gave her a scowl. "You're making fun of me. I'm an old, tired, ill woman and you're making jokes at my expense. I won't have it. Not in my own house. Your father shall hear about this."

"I'm not!" cried Margery. "Truly, I'm not. Alice, tell her."

Feeling inadequate, Alice nodded. "She did come to see the paintings. We went round the house—"

"And there weren't any of yours anywhere," put in Margery. "I saw the Constable and the Stubbs—and the little rooster in the drawing room, is it a Hals?"

There was a quickening of interest in Miss Fairchild's pale eyes, although her expression didn't soften. "You didn't see the Turner, did you? No, of course you didn't. It's over the mantel in my study. A London dealer convinced Father to buy it, but he never cared for it. Said he couldn't see what it was *about*. That's why he let me have it. It's about *light*." She gave her head a shake.

"I kept looking for some of your paintings—"

"My father was a serious collector. He bought the best that was available. He built his collection with care and discrimination. He never understood what I was trying to do with my painting. I suppose that must be because I never succeeded in doing it." She shrugged wearily. "I've tried my best, that's all I can say. But I'm too ill and tired to care about it anymore."

"You can't mean you're giving up?" Margery's voice rose, alarming Alice.

"And what's that to do with you?"

"Everything! You can't just stop believing in your work—not after all this time. It's good, you know it is. You must." Margery turned suddenly on Alice. "What do *you* think?"

"About what?"

"The paintings, of course!"

Caught off guard, Alice threw her an anguished look. "Oh, but I'm not really—I can't—I don't know anything about—"

"Go on, what did you see?" persisted Margery mercilessly.

Miss Fairchild was gazing vaguely around the studio, not seeming to pay any attention, so Alice plucked up her courage. "Well, I thought they'd just be paintings of flowers, like the ones in the dining room, I suppose. You know—decorative. But they aren't." She heard what she'd said and blushed furiously. "I mean, not that they're ugly, but they're not comfortable. You couldn't just hang them on the wall and expect them to stay in the background. You have to figure out what's going on in them. And they aren't only flowers—they're more—well, all kinds of things, wound up together. Oh, *I* can't explain, Margery— it's not fair asking!"

"Why should it matter to you anyway, what I do?" asked Miss Fairchild, her attention returning to Margery.

"Because—*I* want to paint."

"Why?"

"It's the way I see things. I want to put them down and make sense of them. I want to show other people what they are and why they're important."

"What if no one agrees with you? Suppose no one's interested in what you see? What's the point then? Why go on struggling?"

"I don't know." Margery looked troubled. "Because you have to."

"Can't you just do it for yourself?" said Alice.

"That's not the truth," said Miss Fairchild. "When you put your vision on a piece of paper or canvas you make it visible to other people. If you didn't care about them, you could just keep it in your head."

"But it changes," Margery said. "It's never the same in your head as it is on paper. I don't find out what I'm drawing until I draw it."

"Ah." The lines in Miss Fairchild's face shifted slightly; she suddenly looked less old and tired and ill. "And what about your father, eh? The pragmatic Malcolm MacInnes? Surely he doesn't approve of such nonsense?"

"No. He says he wants me to be happy, but he can't see that what makes him happy won't work for me as well."

"Do you think painting will make you happy? If you do, you'll be sadly disappointed."

"But if it's what you really want to do," said Alice, "and you do it, doesn't that make you happy?"

"Not in my experience, no," replied Miss Fairchild dryly. "Oh, it has its moments, I dare say. But you, my girl, you'd be much better off listening to your father, though it pains me to say it."

"You didn't listen to yours," said Margery rashly.

"Perhaps I should have."

"Do you really think so?"

"I disappointed Father. So did Rolly, though he tried his best not to. What difference does it make now? Father's dead, and Rolly, and here I am—"

Alice waited for her to add "old and tired and ill," but she didn't. Instead, she fixed Alice with her chilly gaze. "So my paintings aren't decorative, eh? Hmmp. I suppose that's something anyway. And, where, I'd like to know, is that mother of yours? I rang and rang and rang and no one answered. That's why I came down in the first place."

"She went out," said Alice. "She said you knew she was going."

"I certainly did not. I woke up and wanted my tea. Or if I did, it slipped my mind. What if I'd had a heart attack, or fallen on the stairs?"

"I can make tea," offered Margery.

"You can, can you?"

"And there's shortbread," said Alice.

"Well." Miss Fairchild hitched up her dressing gown. "No point standing about here. It's chilly. I'll just take that key, if you don't mind."

Half an hour later they heard the car rattling over the cobbles outside. Miss Fairchild spilled her tea a little in its saucer, but otherwise sat still. After a minute or two Christine and Len breezed through the door, bringing with them an aura of sunshine and fresh salt air. There was color in Christine's cheeks for the first time in a week, and her eyes were bright. She looked happy. But she stopped short when she saw Miss Fairchild sitting at the kitchen table with Alice and Margery, dipping a shortbread finger into a cup of very strong tea.

"So, Mrs. Jenkins, you decided to come back after all."

"I know it's late. I told you I was going out, but I thought we'd be back before this. I hadn't meant to be gone so long, really I hadn't." Christine took off her coat and folded it carefully. "I hope the girls haven't been bothering you." She gave Alice a probing look.

Alice waited, holding her breath, for Miss Fairchild to announce she'd caught them trespassing in her studio. Margery studied the teapot.

"I wanted my tea, Mrs. Jenkins. I rang my bell and got no answer, so I was forced to come downstairs, where I found your daughter and her friend. Now I am feeling quite tired. I shall go back to my room."

"You must blame me," said Len cheerfully, plainly assuming no one would. "Chrissie needed a bit of an outing. Dr. Lattimer said so, and it's done her a world of good. I took her down the coast a bit and we found Cargill's Castle. Bloke where I got petrol said we shouldn't miss it—quite a sight, he said, and so it is. Right on the clifftop, Ally, with a smashing view clear along the beach to the city. Seems a flipping waste to have it stand empty like that."

Miss Fairchild sat back in her chair with an audible sniff. "It's been let go badly since the family sold it—that was fifty years ago. Most recently it was used as a cabaret"—she spoke the word distastefully— "a place of common entertainment for all manner of foreign elements. Edward Cargill should have been spinning in his grave."

"My father's been round it," volunteered Margery. "He had a client who was interested in buying it last year, but he says it'll cost a packet to repair."

"It was never as grand a house as Florestan, and most of the original furniture and collections were destroyed by fire at the end of the last century. Edward Cargill couldn't afford to replace them. But then, he hadn't the eye my father had, everyone said so. I've always thought the house was badly proportioned, and of course the grounds are nothing without the view. Father spent a great deal of time and effort on the gardens here. He hired an English gardener on Mr. Lutyens's advice. Pettingill. Rolly used to call him Mr. McGregor because he was always chasing us away. Bad-tempered old man.''

"What about the garden parties?" asked Len. "When the rhododendrons were in bloom."

"Who told you about the parties?"

"Margery."

"They were long ago, Mr. Jenkins. Between the wars. Pettingill used to work himself into a frenzy," she said with a mean little smile. "How he hated to see all those hordes of people trampling his lawns and stepping in his flower beds. He used to complain for weeks afterward. But he was longing to show off the gardens, to have people admire his handiwork. I don't know what became of Pettingill. I haven't thought about him for years. Or the parties. This is giving me a headache. Mrs. Jenkins, help me upstairs."

At the door Christine said, "Len, you'd better run Margery home. Her parents will be wondering where she's got to."

"There do seem to be a lot of buds on the rhododendrons," Alice's mother remarked as she and Alice walked back along the driveway after church Sunday morning. They were swelling fatly at the tips of the branches, beginning to show tinges of the colors hidden behind the neat green scales. Alice hadn't paid any attention to them before, but the shrubbery was covered with them. For a short time they would transform the somber, dark banks of foliage, lighting up the gloom under the trees.

As they came in sight of the house, they noticed that the front door was open. Frowning, Christine hurried up the steps into the hall, Alice close behind. The crates were gone. "Len? Len, where are you?"

Alice lingered in the great hall, pausing to look at the Constable again. She didn't really believe that it changed color in different lights, as Margery said, but she had to admit that it didn't look quite the way she'd remembered.

"What happened to the painting?" Alice asked as they were washing up after dinner. "She didn't really have it chopped up for kindling, did she?"

"She had Len and Mr. Tatlock take it out to her studio. Len said she was in there all morning. It's as if she never spent last week in bed. What exactly happened yesterday afternoon, Alice? I never expected to come back and find the three of you having tea together."

"Oh, didn't Miss Fairchild say?" Alice hedged, thinking fast. "She came looking for you and found us instead. I thought she might be cross about having a stranger in the house, but Margery said who she was—"

"Whatever did you talk about?" Christine asked curiously.

"Painting, mostly. Margery's very keen. Her aunt has a gallery, and she knows a lot about art. She was very interested in Mr. Fairchild's collection. Did you know there's a Constable next to the grandfather clock in the great hall? And a Stubbs upstairs in the billiard room."

"Oh, Alice, you didn't take her into the billiard room."

"Just to see the painting. Her aunt had told her about it. I thought it would be all right if we just looked. She didn't mind, did she? Miss Fairchild, I mean."

"I wish you wouldn't twist your hair that way. You'll damage the ends. Miss Fairchild's taken quite a liking to your friend Margery. She says you may invite her back. She even said"—Alice's mother gave her an odd look—"she might show Margery her studio one afternoon."

"I'm sure Margery would like that," said Alice blandly. "Where's Len gone, do you know?"

"He's outside with Miss Fairchild, looking at the rhododendrons."

At supper Len told them about the garden parties. He and Miss Fairchild had spent the best part of an hour walking around the grounds while she told him what they had been like, when she was young, when her parents were alive, and her father was one of the most influential men in Dunedin, when the house was busy with servants: butler, cook, parlormaids, and Pettingill ruling the garden, terrorizing the boys who worked under him.

There used to be two garden parties on the same day, every year. The first one was early in the afternoon, when the gates were opened to everyone in the city who cared to come: all the ordinary citizens, who'd bring along their children. That was what Pettingill hated the most: kids playing tag and hide-and-seek among the shrubbery, *his* shrubbery, and shouting and chasing across the croquet lawn.

After they'd trickled away, sated with wonder and food, Dunedin society would arrive in the late afternoon, by invitation only, elegantly dressed. They'd stay into the evening, when the lanterns were lit, and the band of the afternoon had turned into a chamber orchestra playing classical music on the terrace. There would be chairs and tables scattered in little clusters on the grass under the trees, and maids in starched white aprons would circulate among the guests with trays laden with delicacies: Stewart Island oysters, smoked salmon en croûte, huge wedges of imported cheeses—Stilton, brie, cheddar—tiny cakes decorated with candied violets and marzipan fruits, brandy snaps rolled into cigar shapes and filled with whipped cream, almond macaroons—

"Stop!" begged Alice. "You're making me hungry."

"Eat your shepherd's pie," said her mother. "It must have cost a fortune, all of that. I supposed we'll find the records among Mr. Fairchild's papers. The parties certainly belong in the history."

"It seems a pity not to have them anymore," said Len. "The rhododendrons are still there."

"But the staff isn't," Christine pointed out. "And the grounds are a jungle."

— 20 —

Miss Fairchild Requests the Pleasure . . .

Monday afternoon Alice found Mr. Tatlock cleaning out the huge, crumbling urns on either side of the front door. He had a barrowload of fresh, dark earth with which to refill them. Kipper lay on the grass nearby, watching, nose between paws; when he saw Alice, he rose to his feet and ambled over to whuffle her hand in a friendly, hopeful way. Tentatively she scratched his ears, mindful of all those strong white teeth. He grinned, exposing them to view. Mr. Tatlock took no notice of her. He fished a clump of wet black stuff out of an urn and chucked it into the shrubs. About to leave him to it, Alice paused. She went a step closer instead, and said, "Is it really true what Len says, that your father used to be a gold miner?"

He pulled out another handful. "What if he was?"

"I just wondered, that's all."

Wiping his hands on his trousers, he began to shovel dirt into the urn. Then he stopped, leaving the shovel upright. "Come here."

"I didn't mean to interrupt you," said Alice hastily, stepping back.

"I've something to show you."

"What?" Two steps forward. She eyed him suspiciously. It was like dancing lessons at Woodhall.

He shoved his hand into his trouser pocket and pulled out a dented, blackened watch on a length of chain.

"That isn't gold," she said.

"You're right about that, Miss Clever Britches. Not the watch. This here. You ever seen a gold nugget?"

She shook her head.

"Well, now you have."

Disbelieving, she stared at the dull, disappointing lump on the other end of Mr. Tatlock's watch chain. "It isn't. Not really."

"Is too. My dad found that, up on Ross goldfields. Once he got started, he couldn't stop. Got him like a sickness—gold fever, that's what they call it. He used to say this was his luck. Only thing he left me—this and the watch." He held it out to her in his dirty, calloused fingers.

Gingerly she took it. "I thought it would be shiny," she said. "It's not very big."

"Big enough. A nugget that size'd start a stampede. You'd have miners swarming all over the hills, digging and panning and staking claims. I couldn't see it, myself. No kind of life, to my way of thinking, scraping holes in the ground." He shrugged. "Still, a bloke's got to choose his own poison, that's what my old granddad used to say."

"You scrape holes in the ground," Alice pointed out.

Mr. Tatlock gave a gruff little bark. She guessed she'd offended him, but when he looked at her, his eyes glinted with amusement. "I'm putting things in, though, not taking 'em out. I like to watch things grow, live things." He hunched his shoulders. "That's just a lump. A cold, dead lump. Never could understand what makes it so valuable."

Alice handed the nugget and the watch back. He put them in his pocket and picked up his shovel again.

"What are you going to put in those?" Alice asked, by way of conversation.

He grunted. "Geraniums. She wants geraniums. It's too early, I told her. Will she listen? No, of course not. Waste of my good plants, that's what. She's gone barmy, if you ask me—right off the deep end. I'm too old for this kind of foolishness, and so's she." He shifted, turning his back on Alice, dismissing her.

The garage doors were open. Len had the bonnet of the Ford up and was tinkering with its insides, but as soon as Alice appeared, he straightened and slammed it. He'd been looking out for her. "Going to need a new muffler. There's a hole starting. I taped it, but it won't last."

"Oh?" said Alice politely, heading for the scullery door.

"Ally—"

She turned, questioning.

"It's just—well, you might want to go a bit careful around your mum just now, is all. She's in a dicey mood."

"She is? Why? Is it Miss Fairchild?"

"Well, yeah. You could say that."

"What's happened, Len? She's not ill again, is she?"

He smoothed his mustache with his fingers. "No, not really. Not ill. In fact, I'd say she's feeling pretty perky. It's just"—he hesitated— "well, she's got this notion, see."

"About geraniums," said Alice. "Mr. Tatlock's out front planting them in the urns. He's not at all happy about it, I know. He showed me his gold nugget—"

"Naw, it's not the geraniums, Ally. Or it is, but that's only part. See, she decided she wants to have a garden party, when the rhododendrons come out. You know, like the ones I was telling you about—like they used to have."

"A garden party," echoed Alice. She thought of the grounds, all shaggy and weed-grown, the drive full of holes; of the house, most of it still closed up: carpets rolled, floors unswept, furniture swathed in sheets, dust everywhere. And no army of servants to set it straight. Just Mr. Tatlock, Christine, Len, and Alice. Len was watching her. "Well,

I don't see how she can. And anyway, the rhododendrons are already starting. There isn't time.''

"Yeah, that's just it. That's what Chrissie says. She's picked next Sunday, see. They'll be out full by then—they'll be a real show, Ally. All colors. It'll be a bleeding fairyland around here,'' he said with a rueful grin.

"Sunday!'' Alice grasped the crisis.

Len nodded. "She's been making up a guest list. She's writing out the invitations by hand—''

"Len, did you—you didn't suggest it to her, did you?''

"Of course not. Well, not in so many words I didn't. I might've said something about how it seemed a pity more people wouldn't get to enjoy the flowers.'' He sighed. "Your mum reckons it's my fault, though. I said to her, it's given the old lady something to think about, anyroad. It's gotten her interested again. I thought that's what Chrissie wanted, her not shutting herself away in that room of hers all day, but Chrissie's not too pleased. I thought I'd better warn you, that's all.''

"Yes,'' said Alice, nodding glumly.

"She means to send out one hundred invitations,'' announced Alice's mother that evening. "*Only* one hundred! She has no *idea*—'' "They'll never all come, love,'' said Len, attempting to soothe her. "It's such short notice, they'll have other plans.'' Christine gave him a murderous look. They would all come, Alice knew. They'd cancel their other plans. People would come who weren't invited; there wasn't anyone in Dunedin who didn't itch for a chance to gawk at Florestan and its eccentric owner. "Well,'' said Christine bitterly, "I've a good mind to give her my notice. This is not what I came all the way to New Zealand for. I can't imagine what Mr. MacInnes will have to say when she tells him tomorrow. The cost will be enormous.'' "Can he forbid it?'' asked Alice hopefully. She shuddered at the thought of being on display, part of the Florestan show. There'd be all the girls from school, and the staff as well—it would be unbearable. "It's her money," Len said. "If that's what she wants—" "It's irresponsible," declared Christine.

Irresponsible or not, Miss Fairchild was determined, and Mr. MacInnes evidently did not have the power to stop her, although he made it clear he wanted to. Margery waylaid Alice on her way to school Wednesday. "Pa was apoplectic last night—you should have heard him ranting. All about common sense and stewardship and fiscal responsibility. And there's absolutely nothing he can do about it." "Mum thinks it's a terrible idea," said Alice. Surprisingly Margery said, "It's dangerous." "Dangerous? Why?" "Because they'll all be coming to see if she's competent. That's why she's doing it, of course, to show everyone she's not bonkers. All the toffs'll be there—the mayor and the city councillors—Betty's family, and Fiona's, her nephew, Clem, Mrs. Sinclair. She told Pa she's got the invitations ready to send—they'll be in the post this morning. Everything had better go well." She sounded faintly threatening to Alice, who protested, "But there isn't any *time*. Mum says it's not possible." Margery's eyes narrowed, but all she said was, "We've got to hurry or we'll miss the bell."

By Thursday everyone at Saint Kat's knew; the invitations had been delivered. Alice felt raw all over, sandpapered by speculative attention. Giving her a brilliant smile, Miss Parsons told her how much she was looking forward to the party. Her fiancé would be down from Christchurch for the weekend—she'd be able to introduce him to her girls. Betty and Fiona, predictably, were especially obnoxious, whispering loudly to each other so Alice couldn't help hearing. "Do you suppose Alice will wear one of those frilly white caps and a little apron?" said Betty. Fiona's foot accidentally shot out as Alice walked past her desk, causing Alice to trip. "I hope she isn't going to serve the punch. She's so clumsy. She'd better practice curtseying, don't you think?" Alice longed to smack Fiona's silly face, or stamp on her toes, but she hadn't the courage.

The Quennells had been invited, of course, which meant Helen and

Grace were coming. "If only Mummy would let us wear our brides-maid's dresses," said Helen. "They'd be perfect for a garden party." "I'm sure it would be bad luck," said Margery. "That's only the wedding gown," said Grace. "Are you sure?" Margery arched her eyebrows. "There isn't time to get new frocks—what are you going to wear?" asked Helen. Margery shrugged, offhandedly. "I'm not sure I'll be there." "What?" said Alice. "Well, someone's got to look after the ankle-biters, with Ma and Pa going off." "But surely they can find someone else," said Grace. "Don't you want to go?" Margery didn't answer. Alice felt betrayed. She had counted on Margery as an ally, someone who would not be there out of prurient curiosity.

There was no respite at Florestan that week. Like it or not, Christine had plunged into a vast and stormy sea of arrangements. Every day was fraught with new complications and crises. The refreshments were a major source of contention; Miss Fairchild had firmly in mind the kinds of delicacies she remembered from Rhododendron Sundays past. Out of the question, declared Alice's mother, equally firm. The simpler the better, and they would have to be ordered immediately. Sherry, said Miss Fairchild. Absolutely not, said Christine. Tea and lemonade punch. They'd have to hire china and punch cups, and they'd need tea urns from somewhere. Miss Fairchild wanted tables under the trees. Saint Kat's would loan folding chairs and three or four long tables for the refreshments. But little tables? No, not possible.

On Thursday there was a crisis over the weather. What if it should rain on Sunday? Christine wanted to know. "It won't," Miss Fairchild said. "It never rains on Rhododendron Sunday. The sun shines, without fail." "But if it *should* rain," Christine persisted, "what will we do then? We can't have everyone in the house; there isn't time to make it presentable. Only the drawing room and the great hall will be fit to be seen, and best in a dim light at that." "What about tents?" suggested Len. "I could fancy one of those red-and-white striped marquees on the grass. It'd be festive." So it was agreed that Len would go into the city the next day—even though Florestan was in the city, they all thought of Dunedin as being miles away—and hire a marquee.

From thin air, like a magician, Christine produced Izzy Ryan, a rawboned girl of about eighteen, who worked as a chambermaid for one of the big hotels near the Octagon. She was willing, good-natured, and easily impressed, though not terribly quick. She would come on Friday and Saturday to help with preparations, then return for the party Sunday and stay overnight. Somehow, through Dr. Lattimer, Christine also found a Mrs. Truscott and her daughter, Janet, who agreed to help out Sunday afternoon, pouring tea and passing sandwiches. Alice absolutely refused. "I'll work in the kitchen with Izzy," she said. "I'll wash dishes and cut sandwiches—I'll do anything, but I will *not* go out front. You can't make me." Her mother evidently decided the point wasn't worth arguing.

First thing Friday morning, while they were still at breakfast, Miss Fairchild appeared through the swing door to announce they'd need a band or a small orchestra. Not a hope, said Christine, setting her cup down firmly. "We must have music, Mrs. Jenkins." "Right, then," said Christine, "*you* find a small orchestra between now and Sunday." But somehow, during the day while Alice was at school, Christine managed to locate a student from the university who would come and play the grand piano in the drawing room for a modest fee and all the food he could eat. They'd open the French doors so people outside could hear—which meant cleaning the drawing room rather more carefully than Christine had intended. Grudgingly Miss Fairchild acquiesced. "Father would *never* have agreed to have a student. Only professional musicians."

By Friday afternoon, the issue had become Japanese lanterns. Alice found a little drama in progress in the courtyard: Miss Fairchild and Mr. Tatlock squared off against each other, with Christine in the middle, like a referee. "Nonsense! We had dozens of them—no, not dozens— hundreds! All colors, with candles to go inside. We must have candles.

Surely you remember—you must have helped to put them up. They can't have vanished—you haven't looked hard enough, that's all.''

"You go and look for them yourself then," snapped Mr. Tatlock. "I been all through the blimin' garridge loft and there aren't any blimin' lanterns in it. But don't you believe me!''

"I really don't see," said Christine, in tones of exaggerated reason, "that we *need* lanterns, Miss Fairchild. After all, it isn't dark at six—"

"We've *always* had lanterns.''

"But if they can't be found—'' Alice heard exasperation sneaking past reason.

"Hey up!" Len emerged from the scullery door, festooned in strings of little electric lights. "What about these then? Wouldn't they do? I found them in the cellar.''

"Those are *Christmas* lights, Mr. Jenkins,'' said Miss Fairchild witheringly.

Len shrugged. "Who's to know? Artie and I can put 'em up in the ivy outside the drawing room. They'll be like stars, all sparkly. What do you think, Chrissie?''

Christine, who'd begun to shake her head, instead said, "Yes,'' with surprising enthusiasm. "I think they'd be very pretty. And much safer than candles. Now, Miss Fairchild, I need to talk to you about tablecloths. And Alex Petrof should be here shortly to try the piano—Len, keep an eye out for him, will you? Alice, go and change out of your school clothes and make yourself useful. Izzy's in the kitchen polishing silver—you can give her a hand.''

Izzy's silver polishing was slow and thorough. Alice went more for overall effect; she did three sugar spoons to Izzy's one, and when she decided she'd done her share, she went to see how Len and Mr. Tatlock were managing with the fairy lights on the terrace.

Len was up a stepladder, and Mr. Tatlock was muttering under his breath as he fumbled with the clips in the ivy. "There," said Len. "That's the last one. Alice, you can switch them on and we'll have a look. It's just behind the drapes on the left.''

In the gathering dusk the little lights sparkled and winked among the dark leaves against the house. They really did look pretty. Mr. Tatlock rubbed his chin. "No good if it rains—you'd only electrocute someone or fuse all the lights."

"Candles wouldn't do in the rain, either," Alice pointed out.

"Haven't you been paying attention?" Len asked. "Miss F says it never rains on Rhododendron Sunday."

"You tell that to my lumbago. I got to gather in the sheep. I'm not having 'em scared out of their woolly wits by the city councillors. I'm off before either of those women can think of something else that doesn't need doing."

Alice looked up at the sky; clouds were beginning to thicken it. "If it rains, maybe she'll call it off," she said hopefully. "There won't be any point."

"Tell you one thing," said Len, folding the ladder, "there'll be no living with your mum if she calls it off. Not after all this. Give us a hand, Ally, will you?"

Alice took one end of the ladder. Soft gray shadows wafted gently out from under the trees, filling the open spaces like smoke. Invisible birds muttered and chuckled to themselves; wings fanned the air as they flew in among the foliage to settle. Crossing the cobblestones, Alice heard her mother's voice through the half-open kitchen window. She couldn't make out the words, but from the tone it was clear that Christine was giving Izzy instructions. "Mum said not to expect anything much in the way of supper," Alice told Len gloomily.

"My backbone's coming through my belt buckle!" he exclaimed. "Tell you what, Ally. I could fancy Chinese take-away, what about you?"

Alice's mouth watered painfully. "Sweet-and-sour chicken wings, egg foo yong—I'm *ravenous!* But where'll we ever find any?"

He grinned at her. "Come on—you'll see."

"What about Mum? Shouldn't we tell her first?" said Alice as Len slid behind the wheel of the Ford.

"Surprise," said Len. "I've some money—we'll bring back enough for everyone—Chrissie, Izzy, even Miss F."

"I wonder if she's ever had Chinese take-away." Alice tried to imagine Miss Fairchild tucking into a plate of fried rice and beef with bean sprouts.

They hadn't been anywhere together in ages, just Len and Alice. She felt the same rush of excitement she'd felt when she was little and Len had spirited her off on one of his mystery tours, without telling her mother where they were going, or even that they were going at all. He got into fearful trouble with Christine when they got home too late for tea, but that never stopped him from doing the same thing again.

"Remember the old motorbike, Ally?" he said as they rattled over the cobblestones.

"I was just thinking about it. I cried when you sold it. I couldn't see why you did, but it was Mum, wasn't it? She made you."

He hunched his shoulders. "Chrissie never thought it was safe. She was sure you'd fall off or I'd smash up somewhere."

"But you never did," said Alice. "You were always careful. It was lovely riding on it—like flying. I was never afraid."

"Yeah." After a minute he said, "Still, she was right, your mum. She always is. It was dangerous, that old bike."

Tunneling through the inky darkness of the Florestan park, Alice felt like a mole. Their headlights were like long, pale whiskers, testing the way ahead for obstacles. Len swung left and right, avoiding the potholes Mr. Tatlock hadn't gotten around to filling. Alice didn't bother to close the gate, knowing the sheep were penned on the tennis court. Len waited for a bus to trundle past, its lighted insides full of people going home. The streetlamps were gathering strength as the evening thickened.

Once down the hill Len threaded his way confidently through streets Alice didn't recognize. She had no idea where they were going, but eventually he pulled up at the curb in front of an unprepossessing little storefront. A sign in lights over the door said, LU KY G RDEN. Behind the frosted glass window shapes moved, dim and featureless. It was like a cave inside, narrow and full of cigarette smoke and the pungent smell of frying. They huddled over a menu, making their choices, then Len pulled out his money and counted it. They had to sacrifice the pork chop suey when they placed their order. They joined the others waiting awkwardly by the door, shifting to let people through to the restaurant in back. At last Len's number was called and they collected two warm, damp paper bags.

"Oh *do* drive quickly, Len," begged Alice, clutching the bags to her chest. "The smell is making me faint."

"I'll never last, not without at least a chicken wing. Come on, Ally— a wing and a prayer, what d'you say?"

"All right—one each." She dug around in the white cardboard boxes until she found the right one. The hot, greasy meat tasted wonderful. She pulled every shred off the bones, then licked her fingers and sank back against the seat.

"Fancy coming all the way to New Zealand for Chinese take-away, eh?" said Len as they started back up the hill.

"We should have gone to China," Alice said. "It couldn't be any further from Cambridge. Do you suppose they have Chinese take-away in China?"

"Fish and chips more like."

"What's that?" she asked as they pulled into the courtyard.

"Where?" Lights shone out of the kitchen windows, but the rest of the house was dark.

"On the windscreen. There—it looks like drops."

"It'll be sap from the trees."

But it wasn't. Lifting her face, Alice could feel the tiny cool prickles. The sky was mottled with cloud reflecting the lights of the city below in a dusky rose-tinted glow.

"Mist," said Len.

"Rain," said Alice.

"Only a shower."

"She'll have to cancel it."

"Tomorrow's only Saturday."

"But everything will be sopping. The drive will be all mud. No one will want to come and look at wet rhododendrons."

Len said, "Look, Ally, all the fuss will be over in a couple of days."

"It won't. The party's only the start. People don't care a fig about the rhododendrons, wet or dry. They only want to come and stare at the house and Miss Fairchild. Everyone thinks she's bonkers, you know," said Alice bitterly. "Almost everyone, anyway—not Margery. But Margery's quite odd herself, and she won't come at all. I wish we'd have a *deluge*."

The kitchen table was covered with a dazzling array of silver: sugar bowls, creamers, salvers, ladles, cake servers, trays, spoons, and butter knives. "Where, may I ask, have you two been?" demanded Christine. Izzy looked up anxiously, clasping her red-knuckled hands together.

"We come in peace," said Len, "bearing gifts. Steamed rice and wontons! Look, Chrissie—"

The irritable lines between her eyebrows faded as they set down their offering and the smell of warm Chinese food began to penetrate the kitchen. They heaped everything on plates and took it through to the dining room, where they ate in gloomy splendor under the crystal chandelier: Len, Christine, Alice, and Izzy. Miss Fairchild had retired to her room with a tray. The disappointment Alice felt at not seeing her eat Chinese take-away was more than made up for by the fact that there was more food divided only four ways.

"It's raining," she said, scraping up the last morsels of rice.

"There." Her mother looked annoyed. "I told you we should have had them bring the tent this afternoon. Now the ground under it will be wet. What time did they say they were coming tomorrow, Len? Early, I hope."

Len swallowed wrong and choked noisily. Alice thumped him on the back. He coughed until his eyes ran. Christine offered him a glass of water, but he shook his head, gasping. "I'm . . . all right."

"I was asking about the tent."

"Yeah. I know."

"And? What time should we expect it?"

"Well," said Len. "About the tent. Look, I'm sorry, Chrissie, I forgot."

She looked at him blankly for a moment. "What do you mean, you forgot? Forgot what?"

"I forgot the tent."

"You forgot the—but I don't see how you *could*, Len! That's what you went to the city for. I said I'd ring up about it, and you said no, it would be better to go in person and talk to them. We'd be sure to get the right thing, you said."

"I know, Chrissie, I know. It's just I got sidetracked. I didn't mean to. Artie wanted a lift down, see, and it was lunchtime when we got there, and he said—"

"I don't want to hear what he said, Len." Christine's face was white, her freckles stark across her nose. "Don't say any more. You promised me. It was the *one thing* you had to do."

"Aw, Chrissie, I'm sorry—" He looked abject.

The Chinese food in Alice's stomach felt like a lead weight; she glanced from Len to Christine. She was horrified to see angry tears glittering in her mother's eyes. Izzy made herself very small; she was almost not even there.

"Of course you're sorry, Len! You're always sorry. But what *good* is it? I can't depend on you."

— 21 —

Fathers and Daughters

It rained all night, and in the morning, when Alice got out of bed, rain was still falling: a soft, settled, steady rain. There was no point in trying to postpone the day once she was awake. She dressed, cleaned her teeth, washed her face, and went downstairs, braced for whatever she might find. The kitchen was empty; she felt a sense of reprieve. The evening before had ended in strained silence. Len had taken Izzy home while Alice and her mother had done the washing up. As soon as they'd finished, Alice had escaped to her room, before Len came back. All the joy had drained out of their expedition to the Lucky Garden, and it was Len's fault. Alice couldn't understand how he could have been so careless. She was cross with him, and cross with her mother, too, for crying. The sight of her tears had distressed Alice more than she wanted to admit. And *none* of this would have happened in the first place if it hadn't been for Margery and Miss Fairchild. *They* were to blame as well.

She slammed around the kitchen, putting breakfast together. She couldn't even take much satisfaction from the fact that she had finally mastered the toaster. If she timed it by the drips from the faucet—twenty-two for pale golden, thirty drips for well-done—she hardly ever scorched a piece of toast anymore. When she was speaking to him again, she must remember to tell Len not to replace the washer in the faucet even though her mother had been after him about it for more than a week.

"Oh, Alice, there you are, love." Her mother pushed through the door, holding a sheaf of papers: lists, almost certainly. She looked tired. "We'll have to clean the great hall; there's nothing for it. We'll set up the tables in front of the hearth—she's afraid people will spill on the carpets, but it can't be helped. I only hope they don't all come at the same time on Sunday—"

"They'll go all over the house, you know," said Alice. "You won't be able to stop them."

Her mother pressed her lips together in a tight line. "We'll close the other doors; that's all we can do. As soon as Izzy gets here, we'll make a start. Alice, your toast is burning!"

She'd lost count, it wasn't fair. At that moment they both heard the rumble of a heavy vehicle in the courtyard; they looked at each other.

"If those are the tables and chairs already, I don't know what we'll do with them," said Christine. "They weren't supposed to come until this afternoon—"

"Perhaps it's a tent. Perhaps he managed to find one after all."

But it wasn't. It was neither the tables and chairs, nor a tent. Parked in the middle of the courtyard was a shiny red-and-black brewer's dray, with ARMSTRONG & FAIRCHILD in big gold letters on the side, arching over the picture of an owl, and underneath, in smaller letters: Keeping Otago on the Hops. A burly, bearded man in a cloth cap and an earth-colored jacket, dark with rain across the shoulders, swung out of the cab and addressed Christine as she stood in the open scullery door with Alice peering around her. "Where'll you be wanting 'em, missus?"

"I beg your pardon?"

"Where d'you want the barrels then?"

"Barrels? There's been a mistake, I think. I'm not expecting any—barrels of what?" she added as an afterthought.

"Three barrels of Morepork Ale and two of Armstrong Brown. To be delivered first thing Saturday morning, twenty-five October, to Florestan. You're having a party, eh?"

"Yes, that's right, we are. But we are not having beer. There *has* been a mistake."

He shook his head. "No mistake, missus. Delivery order's been signed by Mr. Clem himself. Look here—that's his signature." He handed her the paper with an encouraging grin. He had a gold tooth in front that shone the way Alice thought gold was supposed to.

"It must be her nephew," she said to her mother. "You know, the one who runs the brewery."

"That's him," agreed the man.

"Well, this is *all* I need this morning," declared Christine. "She never told me about this. We agreed—lemonade punch and tea. We've nothing to *serve* beer in. I haven't time to straighten this out now—you'd better just put it in the garage for now. There—at the far end."

"Right you are." He touched his cap and went to work, opening the back of the dray to make a ramp.

"Mrs. Jenkins? Mrs. Jenkins, what is going on here?" Miss Fairchild pushed her way past Alice. She was wearing a rusty black skirt and a gravy-colored cardigan over a beige blouse. Alice caught a strong whiff of mothballs. "What is that man doing?"

"He's delivering the beer you presumably ordered."

"I? *I*, Mrs. Jenkins? I did no such thing. Beer, indeed. Father would *never* have permitted it. Sherry is what I said."

"Well, someone must have ordered it because here it is," retorted Christine. "I certainly didn't."

"He said it was your nephew, Mr. Clem," said Alice helpfully.

"Clement?" Miss Fairchild pounced on the name. "What has Clement got to do with *my* party?"

"Perhaps he sent it as a present," Alice suggested.

"I might have known! Well, I won't have it. Never has there been beer at a Florestan garden party—Father would be scandalized. It's common, that's what it is. I know what Clement's after, he wants me proved incapable. I've a good mind to have him stopped at the gate tomorrow. He shan't succeed, Mrs. Jenkins, do you hear?"

"Perfectly, Miss Fairchild. You needn't shout in my ear. I suggest you come inside and close the door before you take a chill. It's very damp."

"And what about the barrels? They must go back—I won't have them—"

"We'll close the garage doors and no one will ever know they're here," said Christine firmly. "Mr. Snaith should be here within the hour to tune the piano. The only way I could get him to come was by promising him and his family invitations to the party."

Alex Petrof, the music student, had found, when he sat down to try the Bösendorfer, that not only was it badly out of tune, but a mouse had built a nest out of cushion stuffing on the strings.

Alice saw the day stretching endlessly ahead. She wondered if anyone would be speaking to anyone else by the end of it. Actually, she reflected, that might be something to hope for. Thirty-six more hours. Worst would be the party itself—if she could just stay out of sight . . .

"*Now* she's decided she doesn't want people parking their cars along the drive," announced Christine, coming down the main staircase. "She says it'll ruin the effect. What effect? What does she think? That all those people will slog in through the mud on foot? Alice, I hope you're dusting the legs as well as the seats and backs."

"No one's going to look at the bottom bits," protested Alice. "It's only a waste of time." She was cleaning the heavy, ornately carved, and uncomfortable-looking chairs scattered around the great hall with a dustcloth and lemon oil. She disliked the greasy feel of her fingers.

"I'll decide what's a waste of time," snapped her mother. "Where's your stepfather?"

"Up the chimney," said Alice sulkily.

Len was standing in the fireplace, his head and shoulders hidden as he struggled to dislodge the remains of what looked like an old rook's nest. Twigs and soot avalanched down on the hearth.

"Look at this mess! Izzy will have to hoover in here all over again now. Mind you don't track it across the floor, Leonard. You'll simply have to think of a way to deal with the parking. I haven't—" In the passageway the telephone rang. "Bother! I'm coming!"

The telephone had been ringing all morning. Alice had considered suggesting they pull it out of the wall as Mr. Tatlock had done, but decided against it. In the silence following her mother's departure she heard Len's voice coming hollowly down the chimney: "She—was—bee-yootiful as a butterfly (cough) and as proud as—a—queen (pause) wa-as pretty lit-tle Alice Jenkins (longer pause, accompanied by a shower of debris) of Pad-ding-ton Green!" He was singing one of their songs. She knew he was inviting her to join in, but she was having none of it. She was not in the mood. He seemed to have forgotten about the tent—for the second time in less than two days. Crossly she rubbed away at a clawed foot. What nonsense, giving a pedicure to a chair.

"Mrs. Jenkins? Mrs. Jenkins!" Miss Fairchild came heavily down the stairs, in the wake of her familiar cry, a fretful expression souring her face. "Now where has that woman got to? I was sure I heard her voice—"

"She's answering the telephone," Alice told her, feeling cross.

Len chose that moment to emerge from the chimney, hair on end, face and forearms smeared black. "You've never had a proper chimney sweep in, I'll wager."

"That fireplace hasn't been used in years; there's been no need. You'll ruin the carpets, you realize. I ought *never* to have agreed to this. I can't imagine what I was thinking of."

"Oh, now," said Len. "Everything'll be peachy, you'll see. Chrissie's got it all in hand."

Stubbornly she shook her head. "They'll only compare it to Father's

Rhododendron Sundays—it'll be all wrong. Father always said, if you can't do a thing right, you shouldn't do it at all.''

"Well, of course it won't be the same,'' said Len. "But he's not here, is he, your father?''

"Mr. Jenkins, that is not the point. My father was very conscious of his position in Dunedin and the example he set. Even now Florestan is his house. He created it and it was a great source of pride to him. You can see for yourself.'' She nodded at the painting over the mantelpiece. It was a family portrait: a man, a woman, and two children. Alice had seen it any number of times without bothering to look carefully.

But now she noticed that the house in the background was Florestan, before the trees had grown up, a Union Jack flying from its crenelated tower. Then the man was Mr. Fairchild, clearly a person of substance and opinion, used, by the look on his face, to getting his own way and well pleased with himself. He stood, resting his right hand possessively on his wife's shoulder, while she sat beside him. She had a mild, timid face. Leaning against her lap was an earnest, stuffed-looking little boy, and standing beyond him, slightly too far away to fit comfortably into the group, was a girl about Alice's age, gazing solemnly at something outside the frame. Alice stared at her, trying to match her with Miss Fairchild.

After a minute Len said, "How could he object if you're doing the best you can?''

"That's just it, Mr. Jenkins. He always thought I could do better. I was a disappointment to him—I made him very unhappy. He was never able to understand why I couldn't be what he wanted. Perhaps—I was simply too stubborn. What about you?'' She shifted her gaze abruptly to Len. "Have you made *your* father happy?''

Len shrugged. "I never had the chance to find out, did I?'' Alice knew the story: Len's parents had died in an automobile accident when he was just three. He went on, "Mam died when I was only little and Da parked us on her sister Millie, in Norfolk, my brother Bernard and me. Just till he got himself sorted out, that was, but we never saw him again. I don't know what's become of him. I suppose he's still alive somewhere.''

Alice, who had been crouching on her heels, sat down on the floor, absorbing this new information.

"So you don't remember your father, is that it?'' asked Miss Fairchild.

"Not really. Bernard did—he was seven. He never talked much about Da, though. He used to tell me about Mam. At night, when he thought I was asleep, he'd cry. Mind you, Auntie Millie and Uncle Nick were all right. They'd got five kids already. They could've turfed us out— sent us to a home or something. Da never gave them tuppence for our keep. Uncle Nick didn't reckon we'd turn out to be worth much, Da being Welsh, see. He was always on at Auntie Millie about what a bad lot her sister'd married and how it wasn't surprising she'd died young. Bernard couldn't get out fast enough. He lied about his age and joined the Merchant Navy when he was fifteen. Don't know where Bernard is, come to that. You might say I was lucky—I never had anything to live up to.''

Sitting tight where she was, Alice tried to imagine three-year-old Len; she tried to think if she remembered anything from being three herself. She didn't think so. If you couldn't remember, then it mustn't be very important—

"What about your daughter, Mr. Jenkins?''

"D'you mean Alice?''

"Who else would I mean? Unless Mrs. Jenkins has another surprise hidden away somewhere she hasn't thought to mention. What about you, Alice? Will you make your father happy?''

Alice had almost forgotten she was actually there. She blinked. "I can't, can I,'' she said crossly. "He's dead.''

Slowly Miss Fairchild looked from her to Len, then back again. "Is he?'' she said.

"You what?'' said Len. "Of course he is. I thought Chrissie'd told you. Alice's da was killed in the war—there's a photo of him upstairs.

He was called Toby Underwood. He was a real scholar, a fellow at one of the Cambridge colleges. Alice takes after him.''

"And did this Mr. Underwood look as much like you as she does?"

Len shrugged. "Yeah, well, that's always been a family joke, Ally being dark like me. Chrissie's great-aunt Jane was dark.''

"So you think that accounts for it.'' It wasn't a question. Her eyes flicked from Len to Alice. " 'It's a wise father that knows his own child,' Mr. Jenkins.'' There wasn't enough light for Alice to read her expression. She remembered the dustcloth in her hand and looked quickly away.

The door to the passage swung open. "Haven't you finished with those yet, Alice? Here's a broom and a dustpan—give them to your stepfather. Miss Fairchild—''

"I've been looking for you, Mrs. Jenkins. I've decided the dark red outfit simply will not do. I must wear the black. It would be disrespectful to do otherwise,'' said Miss Fairchild, advancing on Christine.

"But the red one's cleaned and pressed. You can't possibly—''

Silence settled again behind them as they disappeared into the dining room. This time Len did not sing. Alice looked at him. He was standing in front of the fireplace, resting a hand on the mantel, gazing into space.

"Is it true?'' she said. "You never told me.''

"What?'' He sounded alarmed.

"About your father being alive. I always thought—you said he'd been killed, same as your mum. Why, if it wasn't true?''

"Oh, that. I dunno. I guess it didn't sound very good, saying he'd dumped his own kids. It was a long time ago.''

"Haven't you ever thought of looking for him? Didn't you want to know what he was like?''

He took a deep breath and shook his head, as if to clear it. "No. No, I didn't. I reckoned he didn't want to be bothered. He knew where we were if he was interested. That's the truth, Ally. I don't remember anything about him, really. Best leave well enough alone.''

* * *

Sunday morning Florestan was wrapped in a soft gray mist. The grass was frosted with moisture, and the leaves dripped, but the rain had stopped. Alice slipped down the front stairs and out the big door. The air was still and milky, the trees blurred. Spread across the lawn were dozens of small spiderwebs, like gray silk handkerchiefs. She walked slowly around the house, leaving ghostly tracks on the wet grass. A pair of blackbirds began to call back and forth. Alice shivered in the chilly light.

Len was alone at the kitchen table, hunched over a cup of black tea. Alice frowned at him. "You look awful. Where did you go last night?"

"Aw, Ally, don't you lecture me, too," he pleaded. "I've already had it from your mum."

"But where were you?"

He gave a little shrug. "Off with Artie, that's all. We went for a pint—reckoned we'd earned one after all the work we did yesterday."

"You were gone a very long time."

"Yeah, well, we met some of Artie's mates. It got late early." He scrabbled at his hair.

"Is she still furious with you?"

"She's not best pleased."

"Well, you can hardly blame her. Honestly, Len." Alice sighed. "It's not raining anyway. That's one thing. Where is she?"

"Up with Miss F. She's having breakfast in bed—Miss F, I mean."

"Here. You ought to eat something," said Alice severely, putting a perfect slice of toast in front of Len. He was brooding into his teacup and didn't seem to notice. Deciding hot chocolate was too much bother, Alice poured herself a half cup of tea and filled it with milk and sugar.

"Look, Ally," said Len after a minute. "About yesterday—"

"It wasn't clever, Len, really it wasn't. We looked all over for you after supper. I didn't even hear you come in. The tent was bad enough—"

"Yeah, I know. That's not what I mean."

She took a bite of toast spread thickly with strawberry jam, and waited. He wouldn't look at her. Something stirred in the pit of her stomach.

"What I mean is, in the hall. You know, what Miss F said."

She chewed slowly and swallowed. She wasn't sure what he was talking about. His eyes flicked her face, then he glanced quickly away and cleared his throat. Mystified, she shook her head. "What?"

"About you. And me."

The toast in Alice's mouth seemed suddenly very dry.

"You haven't—I mean, you didn't mention it to Chrissie, did you?"

"No."

He let out a long breath. "That's all right then. Of course," he added hastily, "don't know why you would, anyroad. Wouldn't make any sense, would it. We'll just forget it, all right?"

"Forget what?" said Christine, coming down the back stairs with Miss Fairchild's tray. Absently Alice noticed that this time she'd barely touched her breakfast. "You," said Christine, putting the tray down with a rattle that made Len wince, "*you* had better run your head under the cold tap, Leonard. I won't say any more about it. Alice, if you've finished, you'd better get dressed for church. Your stepfather isn't in a fit state to go with us. The best we can do is pray for him."

"Church?" Alice blinked in surprise. "But there isn't time, is there?"

"Yes, if we come straight back. It'll do me a world of good this morning." She turned back to Len. "The tables and chairs are coming at ten. You and Mr. Tatlock can set them up—that is, if you're capable of standing yourselves. I need to get away from Miss Fairchild before she drives me spare. Dr. Lattimer ought to have forbidden this party. She's been up all night, working herself into a state over things we haven't done."

Six impossible things before breakfast, thought Alice as she went to change her clothes. She was puzzled by what Len had said. When they got back, she would find the time to corner him and make him tell her straight out.

— 22 —

Rhododendron Sunday

Alice lay in the darkness of her bedroom, staring at nothing, listening to Izzy's soft, rhythmic almost-snores. She'd tried every position she could think of, but after a few minutes each became intolerable: the pillow was lumpy, the blankets too heavy, her elbow cricked at the wrong angle. As they'd gotten ready for bed, Izzy had been full of the party, eager to relive it all in detail, rattling on about the people she'd seen, who'd eaten *her* sandwiches—"I mean, just imagine! The deputy mayor, Mr. Sidey! And he was ever such a gentleman, Alice. He thanked me special. He said they were some of the best he'd ever tasted. They were only fish paste, but maybe he doesn't like crusts. And Alex Petrof, wasn't he beaut? I could've watched him play the piano all night—" Alex had a great deal of black hair that curled artistically over his rather frayed shirt collar, high cheekbones, and melting brown eyes. He played with emotion rather than precision: the *Moonlight Sonata*, Strauss waltzes, occasionally pieces that sounded not at all classical. He attracted a young, female audience.

Izzy didn't seem to notice that Alice had nothing to say. Alice used the wardrobe door to shield herself modestly as she wriggled into her nightgown. She slid into her bed and turned her face deliberately toward the window.

"Well, good night, then," said Izzy. Alice pretended to be asleep. Less than five minutes later Izzy really was asleep, leaving Alice stranded in the dark, feeling battered, exhausted, and sleepless.

They had come back from church to find Len and Mr. Tatlock on the terrace, setting up the tables under Miss Fairchild's direction. The sun had broken through the early morning mist, and the stones of the terrace were steaming; the long expanse of sheep-bitten grass glittered, and the air smelled soft and rich. Rhododendron Sunday would be fine and mild. Alice changed her clothes and went to help Izzy disguise the ugly institutional folding tables with linen tablecloths. There was no chance to talk to Len; he and Mr. Tatlock had progressed to setting chairs out in conversational groups on the wet grass while Miss Fairchild stumped about, supervising.

There were trays of punch and teacups to carry out and arrange, and then a crisis because they hadn't thought of flowers for the tables. Alice's mother, out of desperation, suggested rhododendron blossoms. "After all, that's what they're coming for, all these people—" Mr. Tatlock was dispatched to cut flowers from the shrubs where they wouldn't show, and Alice lost track of Len. They had a scrappy sort of lunch, mostly sandwich crusts and chunks of cheese, and Mr. Tatlock came in with two baskets heaped with enormous tissue-papery flowers. In spite of herself, Alice couldn't help marveling at the variety of colors: pale orchid to peach to bright primrose yellow, glowing crimson and creamy white. Each blossom was a whole mound of small trumpet-shaped flowers: a bouquet by itself, surrounded by a circle of oval dark green leaves. They were extraordinary; she'd had no idea there were so many different kinds. Mr. Tatlock knew the name for each one: Elisabeth Hobbie, Else Frye, macabeanum, Loderi Venus.

At half past one Alice and Izzy were arranging little crustless sandwiches on platters, decorating them artistically with sprigs of cress and parsley and thin slices of radish, before covering them with damp tea towels to keep the edges from curling. It occurred to her that she hadn't actually seen Len in some time, not since before lunch, in fact. She doubted now that she'd have a chance to talk to him until after the party. All the while she'd been doing other things, their conversation that morning had been burrowing into her brain. It disturbed her; she had to know what he meant, why he hadn't simply shrugged off Miss Fairchild's remarks. She couldn't remember exactly what had been said; she'd been distracted by the information about Len's father—if he hadn't mentioned it, she'd have forgotten all about it.

"Well, that's *all* I need!" exclaimed her mother, bursting suddenly into the kitchen. "How could that wretched woman have been so thoughtless? I'm sure I don't know—" She stopped and Alice looked around. "What's happened now?"

"That was Mrs. Truscott ringing to say she'd been putting tins away on a top shelf and missed the bottom step of her kitchen stool. She might as well have broken her neck for all the good she's going to be. The doctor's told her to stay off the ankle for a week. Her daughter's still coming, but I don't see how we'll manage—we were going to be shorthanded as it was." Christine ran a hand distractedly across her forehead. "Alice, you'll have to change your clothes back—you can wear what you wore to church."

"But *Mum*—" Alice protested, appalled. "You don't mean—I can't *possibly*—that would leave Izzy out here on her own. There's far too much—"

"She'll just have to manage. This is an emergency."

"They'll all be here, all the girls from school! I simply can't—not out there in front of them. You don't understand—I'll never hear the end of it!"

"No, I don't," agreed her mother. "And there isn't time to discuss it. I'm sorry, Alice, but I need you out front to help, and there's an end to it. Len can work with Izzy, once he's taken care of the parking. Where *is* your stepfather; have you seen him?"

Mutinously Alice shook her head.

"This would be hard enough if people did what they were supposed to—Mr. Tatlock! Where does he think he's going? Mr. Tatlock, have you seen Leonard?" she called out the window over the sink.

Caught as he was about to make his escape, he gave her a dour look and shook his head. "He borrowed my bike, that's what. Said something about an errand and went off like the clappers—didn't say when he'd be back, neither."

"When was this?"

"An hour ago—maybe two. I'd like to know where he's gone on my bike."

"Well, I'm sure I don't know," exclaimed Christine. "*I* didn't send him for anything."

"But he'll be back in time," said Alice, then frowned. "Won't he?"

"Alice, don't just stand there—look at the time! You'll have to cope with parking, Mr. Tatlock. Make them leave their cars in the courtyard and along the back drive—"

"And how'm I supposed to do that, eh?"

"Just do the best you can. Please. Alice—"

"I'm going." Heavily she climbed the back stairs. The afternoon was going to be a disaster. How could Len have done this? *Why* had he done it? On top of everything else—he wasn't coming back; her mother was sure of it although she hadn't said.

He was avoiding her, Alice. At the top of the steps she stopped, arrested by the thought. It was that conversation in the great hall that had set him off. She passed her own room and went along the gallery to the one Len and her mother shared. It was tidy as usual: the bed smooth, her mother's gray-green wool dress laid carefully across the spread, the curtains pushed back just so. Alice tiptoed across to the wardrobe, taut with apprehension. Len hadn't many clothes. They were still there: four shirts folded, two pairs of trousers hanging up, work boots underneath. Wanting to be absolutely sure, Alice opened the top drawer of the dresser, where she knew her mother kept personal papers and documents: letters, receipts, an envelope with cash in it for emergencies, the passport she and her mother shared. Len's was there as well. She let out her breath. She opened it to his photo and there he was, without his mustache, looking anxious, as if he expected the camera to explode in his face. Not a very good picture—the one in the frame on top of the dresser was much better. On impulse she picked up the other one—the garden party in its silver frame, and her mother's rosewood hand mirror, and carried them over to the window, to the light.

Once the guests started to arrive, there was no time to think about anything else. They flowed along the drive like a river in flood, dressed in best clothes: the men somber in suits, the women in bright spring frocks, many of them wearing hats and gloves, and shoes impractical for walking about on grass. Betty and Fiona were there, of course, with their parents, laughing and chattering ostentatiously, eyeing Alice with bright, malicious stares. Alice gritted her teeth and kept her head down, muttering apologies to people when she knocked into them. "For heaven's sake, Alice," her mother hissed at her when they happened to cross paths, "smile and *look* at people! This is supposed to be a pleasant occasion." "Pleasant for who?" Alice asked, but her mother either didn't hear, or pretended not to.

The terrace quickly filled with people, milling about, greeting one another, remarking on the weather and the glorious rhododendrons, looking avidly around at the house and grounds. Alice felt herself come under scrutiny, being discussed, identified—"Oh, that's Alice Jenkins. Her mother works for Miss Fairchild." She hated it.

In the thick of the gathering was Emilia Fairchild herself, a dumpy, regal figure, wearing the dark red dress after all, clasping a silver-headed cane, her steel-wool hair wound tightly into a knob on the back of her head, her pale eyes fierce with pride. She dared anyone to make a disparaging remark about anything.

At one point a nice-looking, sandy-haired man to whom Alice offered lemonade punch remarked that Miss Fairchild reminded him of the widowed Queen Victoria. "Not that I ever saw her in person, of course. Only in photographs. But I'm sure Miss Fairchild is every bit as intimidating, too." He accepted a cup. "I had rather thought she might be serving something stronger this afternoon. After all, she is related to Armstrong and Fairchild—" He sounded regretful. "There's tea," said Alice, feeling it to be inadequate. He nodded.

Later, when she went into the kitchen to replenish the plate of petticoat tail shortbread, she found the same man standing next to Izzy at the big copper sink, his jacket off, his sleeves rolled up, drying punch cups as she washed them. Izzy's face was pink and her eyes bright, and they seemed to be having quite a good time together. "Here, let me help," said the man, hastily clearing space on the table for Alice's plate. "I don't think we've officially met." Alice gave him a blank look. "I'm Clement Fairchild—Clem. Queen Victoria's my aunt." He grinned. "Oh," said Alice, taken aback. "I believe we've spoken on the telephone," he went on. "You must be Mrs. Jenkins." She had the grace to blush. "No, actually. I'm just Alice. It seemed easier—" He shook hands with her. "Well, just Alice, I'm pleased to meet you. I honestly didn't see how Aunt Emilia could pull this off—without your mother she never could have. D'you know, it's been years since I've set foot in this house. Nothing's changed, though—it's exactly the way I remember it." "We didn't have glasses for the beer," she said, by way of apology. Clement Fairchild wasn't at all what she'd expected. "No, I don't suppose you did," he agreed.

She left him, still drying up, and went out bemused by the encounter. More and more people arrived. Alice had been right—there were far more people than Miss Fairchild could have invited. They ate sandwiches and cakes and shortbread, and drank gallons of punch and tea. Some of them actually wandered down to admire the massive banks of rhododendrons that framed the lawn. Quite a few found their way inside the house, where they peered into various rooms and examined the furniture, paintings, and clocks, the tapestries and porcelain figurines. Alex Petrof's audience in the drawing room included many girls from

Saint Kat's, Alice noticed on her way through. She saw Helen standing close to the Bösendorfer, turning pages for him, her eyebrows puckered in concentration. He smiled at her and nodded when he was ready, and she turned as if her life depended on it. Alice could imagine Margery's derisive snort.

But Margery wasn't there. Mr. and Mrs. MacInnes were. "How nice you look, dear," exclaimed Mrs. MacInnes, spotting Alice. "Thank you. I'll just have one of those—they do look delicious. I'm so sorry Margery couldn't come. She stayed home to mind the little ones. She was so disappointed—" Alice knew it wasn't true: it had been Margery's choice.

"Look, there's Alice Jenkins," said Betty Ware in a carrying voice. "Bring me some of those little cakes, Alice. I haven't had one yet."

Pretending she hadn't heard, Alice dodged away, slipping in between two couples, and came face to face with Miss Sallet, Miss Parsons, and a tweedy man in spectacles. "Alice, dear, there you are!" cried Miss Sallet. "What a splendid occasion this is. Such a treat. Have you met Miss Parsons's fiancé? No? This is Mr. Crichton—Alice Jenkins. She's one of *our* girls, Mr. Crichton. She's just begun with us this term."

"You've adjusted very well, Alice," said Miss Parsons with her smile. Mr. Crichton smiled back at her, making his rather plain face quite attractive.

"Alice and her mother live here at Florestan with Miss Fairchild," explained Miss Sallet. "I was just saying what a pleasure it is to see her restored to health. She is a most remarkable woman, isn't she?"

It was after seven before the last of the guests finally straggled off into the twilight. Alice, collecting punch cups from the terrace, realized that no one had remembered to turn on the fairy lights. Len would have, but Len hadn't come back. Her stomach gave a nasty lurch. She didn't want to think about Len.

Tired but triumphant, Miss Fairchild made her way slowly across the great hall and up the stairs, leaning on Christine's arm. Her hair snaked out of its knot, and the hem of her dress drooped unevenly on the right.

When she reached the landing, she paused to recover her breath, and caught sight of Alice with her tray. "Well, Mrs. Jenkins. It went very well, I think. Wouldn't you agree?" Alice heard her mother say, "Yes, it was a success. And that dress was exactly right. Many people commented on how well you looked."

Alice turned her pillow over, trying to find a cool place for her hot cheek. She curled up on her left side and squeezed her eyes shut so tightly she saw bright flashes behind her eyelids. Her heart beat heavily in her ears, and she felt as if she couldn't breathe deeply enough. School would be unbearable: nudge, nudge, whisper, smirk, giggle. Helen and Grace would be mooning over Alex Petrof. And Margery—Alice felt a surge of anger.

But what made her hollow inside was Len. Her mother said he'd lost his nerve. When the time actually came, he'd cut and run because he couldn't face all those people. He crumbled under pressure.

As her mother locked the scullery door after sending Izzy upstairs to bed, Alice said, "What about Len? What if he comes back and can't get in?"

"Serve him right," said her mother, but without heat.

"Suppose something's happened to him, Mum. Have you thought of that? He might have had an accident." She found herself hoping it might be true, that there was another explanation for Len's failure to return.

But Christine shook her head wearily. "Nothing's happened to him, Alice, except that he's too ashamed of himself to come back tonight. He'll turn up in the morning, full of apologies, when he thinks it's safe. I ought to have expected something like this, really. He's never been any good at public occasions, your stepfather." She gave Alice a rueful smile. "Go on to bed, love, and don't worry about him."

But it wasn't Len she was worried about, it was herself. She felt as if she'd been cut adrift; she didn't know where she was. Ever since she'd been old enough to understand, her mother had told her she was

Toby Underwood's daughter. He was still alive in Alice, and it was Alice's responsibility to help keep him alive. She must do with her life some of those things he had not been given time for. Christine made Toby real for Alice, even though Alice had never known him as a solid, walking-around, talking, breathing human being.

Since before she could remember, Len had been her stepfather—more like an older brother, as Audrey said, or maybe an uncle or a cousin. He was someone Alice played with. They went to the cinema together, they joked and sang silly songs, went on mystery tours, got into trouble. Christine scolded Len at least as often as she scolded Alice. Len never scolded Alice. If she needed a grown-up, adult opinion of something, if she had a weighty problem to solve or a serious question, Alice went to her mother with it. Christine was the one who took care of all the things parents were supposed to take care of: school conferences, dentist appointments, setting examples, shopping for new shoes, seeing that Alice had proper meals and went to bed on time. She was strict, but generally fair; Alice did not always agree with her mother, but she had never doubted her.

Her life had been built, brick by brick, upon the foundation Christine had given her: her father was Toby Underwood, fellow of Clare College, Cambridge. She made it not matter that they hadn't been married: the war was on, there wasn't time, they snatched what they could. All over Britain it was the same. Young men had gone off to fight—men with their lives ahead of them, their wives and sweethearts left at home to wait—and thousands of them had never come back. They left widows and orphans, they left fiancées, they left babies they didn't even know about. Alice and Christine were not alone. They were luckier than many, in fact, because *Len* came home. He married Christine and adopted Toby Underwood's daughter, making her Alice Underwood Jenkins. She had a place in the universe.

Was it possible that her mother had made a mistake? Alice lay on her back, feeling the night press down on her chest, the weight of the house, the darkness, the silence, her pulse throbbing in her throat. Could someone make a mistake about *that*? The details were not all clear in Alice's mind, but she knew the basics. She and Audrey had poured over the illustrations in one of Dr. Hillyard's medical books. The text was clinical and complicated; it talked about sex in a way that had nothing to do with passion or romance. It didn't even sound as if it had to do with people. But the diagrams—Alice found them fascinating in a repellent sort of way. Afterward she wished she hadn't looked, but it was too late; she couldn't unsee them. Human figures without clothes on, so you could see all their parts and how they fit together. Audrey saying matter-of-factly, "*That* goes in *there*—see?" Audrey had two brothers, one older and one younger. She *knew*. And Alice contemplating it in shocked silence. She found it hard to grapple with in the abstract; but harder still to imagine her mother actually *doing* it with her father. But she had: Alice herself was the proof, as Audrey bluntly pointed out. Given what she'd seen, Alice found it impossible to believe that her mother could have gotten it wrong about her father.

Not unless she'd done it intentionally. Scouring her memory, Alice could not recall catching her mother in a lie. Not ever. Nor could she imagine why Christine would lie about this, of all things. She'd never asked anything from Toby Underwood's family. She hadn't even told them about Alice. When Alice was old enough to ask why, her mother had taken her to the chapel at Clare College and shown her his name on the Roll of Honour, with the names of all the others who'd died in the war. "I didn't want them to think I only wanted money. I was too proud," she had said, gripping Alice's hand so tightly it hurt. "He'd meant to take me to meet them his next leave, but he never came back." It was one of the few occasions when Alice had seen her mother cry. Christine's voice had been perfectly steady, but her cheeks were tracked with tears. It was a late Saturday afternoon in winter and Alice remembered the chill striking up through the soles of her shoes from the floor. There was a tall, spare woman in a yellow smock arranging rose and white chrysanthemums on the altar, and someone was practicing on the organ, playing the same phrase softly over and over.

That was all she had: the name on the wall, what her mother told her, the photograph. But that afternoon, when she'd looked at the photograph—really looked at it—she couldn't help wondering. Toby Underwood was only a tiny figure with an indistinct face, one of half a dozen people scattered on the grass. He was nowhere near Christine Pickell; he wasn't even looking at her. It was only a casual snapshot, of course, unposed, not awfully good. . . .

For some reason Len had paid attention to what Miss Fairchild had said, about a father knowing his own child. We'll just forget it, he'd told Alice later, and by saying that, he'd made it impossible. But she couldn't keep it locked inside herself; already it was threatening to suffocate her, pushing, squeezing. She had to talk to him about it, but he had taken off because he didn't want her to. The party wasn't what he couldn't face, it was Alice. He'd left so she couldn't ask him.

And he didn't want her to say anything to Christine. She wasn't bound by that—she hadn't promised. Still, if her mother had told a lie all those years ago, why would she admit it now? Alice imagined herself saying to her mother, over cornflakes at breakfast, "Oh, by the way, Miss Fairchild doesn't believe Toby Underwood is my father—"

She couldn't sort it out by herself, but who did she have to help her? What could she do? Her eyes stung with tears of self-pity. She turned her face into the pillow and wept.

— 23 —

Desperate Measures

The next thing Alice knew there was daylight coming in the windows and Izzy was shaking her. "Your mum just thumped on the door—she said it's gone eight. I couldn't think where I was for a minute. I opened my eyes and everything was strange—then I remembered about the party. Wasn't it a beaut! And Mr. Fairchild bucking in with the washing up? I thought he'd be ever so posh, but he wasn't—not at all. He's not a bit like his aunt, is he?"

Alice grunted as if she wasn't really awake, although she'd surfaced instantly, all at once, a plan of action clear in her head. Izzy's chatter was a faint, annoying buzz she scarcely heard, like a fly against a pane of glass. It stopped when Izzy went down the hall to the lavatory. Alice climbed hurriedly out of bed, grabbed her satchel from the table where she did her schoolwork, and dumped everything out of it: books, notebooks, pencils, the history report she'd half finished. Sweeping the clutter together, she stashed it in the bottom of her wardrobe, out of sight in a back corner. In its place she packed her plaid skirt, red wool cardigan, and a change of underwear; then she added the paperback copy of *Rebecca* Helen had pressed on her the week before. She hadn't had a chance to start it. By the time Izzy returned, Alice was buttoning her school blouse. "Tell you what," Izzy confided, working a comb through her thick, springy hair, "it'd give me the shivers being alone in this house. It's got a crook feel to it." Alice yawned widely at her in the mirror.

Izzy wadded up her nightdress and stuffed it into the worn carpetbag she'd brought, and Alice went to clean her teeth, taking a long time over it. When she was sure Izzy had gone downstairs, she stole around the gallery to her mother's room. It was empty, the door half-open. Alice looked hard at the double bed; she had no way of knowing whether it had been occupied by one person or two the night before. There was nothing of Len visible: no discarded socks, no crumpled shirt. He hadn't come back, she was sure.

Everything she needed was in the dresser drawer. She hesitated over the passport she and her mother shared, but decided not to take the risk. It was an official document, and if she lost it there'd be real trouble. When Miss Fairchild had run away, all those years ago, she'd gone to the Continent. She'd only had to cross the English Channel. Alice knew she could never leave New Zealand: it was too far from anywhere. She had no intention of trying. She wasn't even really running away. She took the envelope containing her mother's emergency fund: there were a five-pound note and two ones folded inside. It wasn't stealing, she assured herself; this was an emergency and she needed the money.

Stuck in with other papers she found a railway timetable—Dunedin to Christchurch, that's what she wanted. Catching her breath, she scanned it—there was always the chance she'd be too late, the train would have gone before she could get to the station—but there it was, number 144. It came up from Invercargill and left Dunedin at 11:55. She exhaled in dismay. *Three hours!* She'd have to wait three hours. Would it be possible? she wondered. But the only other train wasn't until 5:30 and that was out of the question. She shook herself; no good standing there frozen. She didn't have to decide on the spot—what else did she need? Quickly she searched through the sheaf of letters and found the one she wanted: heavy, cream-colored stationery with the address and telephone number printed in brown across the top. The last line read, "and of course the next time you find yourselves in Wellington, I shall be *delighted* to see you!" It was signed, "Affectionately, Anna Royde."

Alice shut the drawer. Her eye rested briefly on the photographs. If she took the one of Toby Underwood, frame and all, her mother was bound to miss it, right off, but if she left the frame . . .

She crouched, shivering in the depths of the rhododendrons. Just the other side of the gate the sound of traffic came muffled through the densely woven branches. The ground was very damp. She sat on her satchel, clasping her knees, her eyes fixed on the face of the little travel clock she'd nicked from her mother's bedside table. It was the only way she could think to keep track of the time. The hands moved with agonizing slowness. She had thought at one point that the clock must have run down—perhaps her mother had forgotten to wind it? But when she shook it and held it to her ear, she could hear it ticking away confidently to itself.

She had gone downstairs not completely sure about what she was doing, poised on the brink, but ready to step back. The kitchen was a shambles: every surface covered with dirty china, serving plates, punch cups, teaspoons. Mr. Tatlock's chickens would be feasting on half-eaten sandwiches and stale tea cakes for a week or more, by the look of it. In the midst of the chaos was Alice's mother, organizing stacks of crockery beside the sink. She looked tired and rather grim. Barely giving Alice a glance, she said, "I've rung the chemist about refilling one of her prescriptions. It would be a help if you could stop on your way home from school this afternoon and collect it, Alice."

"I don't suppose you've heard from Len," said Alice, willing her mother to turn and look at her, to smile, to say something sympathetic or encouraging.

But she was squirting Fairy Liquid into a sinkful of steaming water. "No, I haven't," she replied, as if that was an end to it. She did not want to discuss Len.

Wrapping a lock of hair around her fingers, Alice tugged on it. Desperately she said, "I could always stay here today and help, if you want."

"I can hardly keep you out of school to wash teacups, Alice, now can I? I should think you'd be all too happy for an excuse to get away. No. Off you go. I've got Izzy."

Alice didn't know what else to say. Her stomach was too tight and small to welcome food; she forced down a slice of bread and butter, feeling ill. Izzy came rattling through the swing door, her tray laden with punch cups. "We'll never find them all," she announced cheerfully. "They're everywhere—behind curtains, on the grass outside, on the stairs—it's like an Easter egg hunt!"

"Oh, Izzy! Don't try to carry so many at once. What if you tripped?" scolded Christine. "Alice, clear a place on the table so she can put them down before she drops the lot."

Miss Fairchild's bell sprang to sudden life. Alice jumped, Izzy dropped a cup, and Christine said, "That's exactly what I mean."

"I didn't mean to—" Izzy's face crumpled in dismay.

"I couldn't get her settled until gone midnight—it took her *hours* to calm down. I was sure she'd sleep all morning—what can she *possibly* want? Alice, you'll be late—"

"I'm just going."

"If you see Mr. Tatlock on your way out, remind him about the chairs. They're coming for them in an hour. Izzy, it's all right. Don't stand there looking like a frightened rabbit, just clean it up!" She pulled off her apron and threw it on a chair.

Alice didn't wait for more. She snatched her satchel and fled. There could be no stepping back.

So there she was, burrowed deep in the shrubs by the front gate, hiding until there was just time to hare down to the railway station and buy a ticket on the train to the ferry at Christchurch. By tomorrow morning she'd be in Wellington. Mrs. Royde was the only person she could think of to go to for help; Mrs. Royde knew Alice, and she knew Alice's mother. She'd sort this out if anyone could; calm, efficient, sympathetic—just the thought of Mrs. Royde eased the knot under Alice's breastbone.

It was Mrs. Royde who had organized things for the Jenkinses on the ship. She had arbitrated the squabbles between Brian and Freddy Hudson when Alice couldn't distract them and their mother had looked ready to throw them over the railing. Comfortable and reassuring, she had sat in her deck chair knitting pairs of socks, one after another, for her husband's mission, always ready with good advice and companionship, administering weak tea and dry toast during the height of the storm on the Indian Ocean.

On their journey south to Florestan Mrs. Royde had met Alice and her mother in Wellington and whisked them limp and grubby, off the station platform, to a cooked breakfast and hot baths. With yearning Alice remembered the house, full of sunshine and potted plants, perched on the side of a steep hill overlooking the harbor, she wasn't quite sure where, but that didn't matter. Once she got to Wellington, she had more than enough money to hire a taxi to take her to the address on the letter.

Reminded of money, Alice fumbled in her blazer pocket for the envelope. Seven pounds seemed like a fortune; she'd never had so much in her hands before and it made her nervous. It would be better, she decided, not to keep it all in one place, so she folded the five-pound note small and tucked it into the pocket of her school skirt.

At twenty-five minutes past eleven she stood up. Her legs were cramped and stiff and her left foot had gone to sleep. She took off her skirt, folded it carefully, and put it in her satchel, taking out the plaid one. She could carry her blazer, inside out, so the Saint Kat's crest wouldn't show. Leaves slapped her face and twigs caught at her hair as she fought her way out of the shrubs. Once outside the gate she brushed herself off, then set out, her heart slamming behind her ribs, her fingers damp on the handle of her satchel. It was extremely difficult to walk as if it was the most natural thing in the world to be out of school on a Monday morning. The streets at that hour belonged mainly to women with prams or shopping baskets. Guiltily, Alice avoided looking at anyone, sure if she did someone would stop her.

At the Octagon she turned down Stuart Street. There was the railway station, blazing red and white in the sunlight; its big clock said 11:47. Her breath caught in her throat as if she'd been running. Just down the street were the law courts—briefly she closed her eyes and uttered a fervent little prayer that Mr. MacInnes might be safely shut up in his office with a client.

Breathless with nerves she arrived in front of the ticket window. The man behind it glanced up and a spasm of pain crossed his face. He sat perfectly still for a moment—Alice's mouth went dry—then suddenly he exploded into a red handkerchief with an enormous sneeze.

"God bless you," she said automatically. She swallowed, and in a louder voice said, "I'd like a second-class ticket to Christchurch—to the ferry, please." She could hear the impatient noise of a steam engine outside.

"Blimin' cold!" The man mopped his nose tenderly. It matched his handkerchief. His eyes were puffy and watering. "Christchurch, eh?"

Alice nodded. "Is that the train?" Oh hurry, oh hurry, oh hurry—

He nodded and gave a hollow cough. "Tell you what, I oughta be home in bed. D'you say return? Under fifteen, are you?"

"Single." She pulled at her hair distractedly. Here was the first crisis—she wasn't going to get away with it. "I'm sixteen," she blurted, her voice sounding unmistakably false in her ears.

"Pity. You'll have to pay full fare—thirty-three shillings and sixpence."

It was a stupid mistake. Angry with herself, she pushed the two pound notes under his grill. If she'd said she was fourteen, she'd only have had to pay half. *"Please—"*

He slid a ticket toward her. She seized it and started for the platform. "Hey up!" She froze. "You've forgot your change!"

Snatching the coins, she stuffed them into her blazer pocket and said, "Thanks," in a squeaky voice. His shoulders shook with another violent sneeze, and he buried his face in his hanky.

Outside, the train was quivering to be off. A conductor walked along it, slamming carriage doors shut. Alice made a dash for the nearest one and flung herself up the steps. She made a desperate grab for the brass handrail. Her legs felt like limp string. Behind her the door swung to with a decisive snick, and a minute or two later the train began to move. She watched the station slide past unbelievingly. She'd done it. Exultation rose in her throat, nearly choking her.

— 24 —

Carried Away

She waited in the vestibule, clutching the rail, until she was breathing normally; then she unclamped her sticky fingers and opened the door into the carriage. Most of the seats were already occupied—there seemed to be a lot of people going to Christchurch. Anxiously she scanned them: no one else her age, quite a few smaller children traveling with their mums, a number of men, most of them occupied with newspapers. Alice hesitated, feeling shy and conspicuously alone. The train jumped on a rough bit of track and she almost lost her balance. Halfway along on the right were two older girls—at least nineteen or twenty, she guessed—sitting across from each other by the window, deep in conversation.

"Is anyone sitting here?" asked Alice timidly.

The blond one glanced up. "Not that I can see."

Self-consciously Alice perched on the edge of the closest seat.

"I told her," the blond said to her companion, "I said—'I wouldn't stand for it if I was you, Patsy. He takes you for granted, that's what.' It's the third time he's done it this month. She lets him walk all over her."

"She's terrified to lose him, if you ask me," said the other girl. Her hair was pulled back tight from the sides of her face, her bangs curled like a sausage on her forehead.

"Yeah, well—there's nothing there to lose. He's no great prize, Joyce."

Out of the window, beyond their heads, Alice saw the outskirts of Dunedin disappearing, and swallowed hard. The ice under her feet was holding, but she was aware that just below it were the cold, dark waters of panic. In spite of everything, she honestly hadn't expected to get this far, but there she was—on her way to Wellington. Her knuckles on the handle of her satchel were white. Surreptitiously she looked around and saw that no one in the carriage was paying the slightest attention to her. She made herself sit back against the seat. The worn plush prickled the backs of her knees; she let out her breath. It was a long way to Christchurch; eight hours, it took. There was nothing more for her to do until she got there, and then—well, she'd worry about that later. Through the windows on the other side of the carriage she glimpsed sun-dazzled water. The track ran along the edge of the harbor as far as Port Chalmers. Squinting against the light made her eyes ache, so she rested her head against the top of the seat. She was suddenly very tired.

The squealing of brakes wrenched her out of a thin sleep, and she blinked and rubbed her eyes. Her neck was cricked. One of the girls was shaking out her jacket, standing up to straighten her skirt. The train lurched and she fell against the other, and they dissolved into giggles. The blond hunted through her handbag for a compact; she studied her reflection intently, applied a slash of dark red lipstick, rubbed her lips together, and blotted them on a tissue. "Oh, do come on," urged Joyce. "You're beautiful enough for Palmerston!" "Palmerston's not ready for me," declared the blond. "Got everything?"

They brushed past Alice, who hooked her feet underneath her. Laughing together they joined the queue in the aisle waiting for the train to come to a stop. They didn't look back. Alice envied their cheerful self-assurance. With a sigh she slid over next to the window and squashed herself into the corner, putting her satchel on the seat beside her, and folding her blazer on top.

A great many people seemed to be getting off at Palmerston, she noticed. They climbed out of the train and crowded into the station. Alice wound her hair around her fingers. Suppose they knew something she didn't? Suppose she had to change trains at Palmerston? The conductor would surely have announced it, but she'd been asleep. Perhaps she'd missed hearing. They hadn't changed trains on the way south; she'd have remembered it. That seemed so long ago. She shut her eyes, hearing the ice crack. When she opened them again, she saw that a few people were trickling back to the train, reboarding, carrying little greaseproof paper packets. Yes, that was it: there was no buffet car on the trains in New Zealand. Her mother couldn't understand it. If you were hungry, you got out at one of the stops and bought something in the railway café. The thought of food caused Alice's stomach to ask a hopeful question, but she didn't dare leave her seat. It was too late. Eight hours. She'd starve.

Then it occurred to her, if she got off now—right this minute—she could go across the platform and take the next train back to Dunedin. No one would ever need to know what she'd done. She could turn up at Florestan at the usual time and her mother would assume she'd been at school all day. Miss Parsons probably thought she'd been kept out to help clean up after the party. Len was bound to be back that evening— perhaps he was already. She could pretend nothing had happened; they'd never refer to any of it again, she and Len. But if she went on, nothing would be the same afterward.

Tempted, she reached for her belongings, but at that moment a woman and a little girl took the seat opposite her. The girl looked about eight— Flora MacInnes's age. She had hair the color of a new horse chestnut, shiny and smooth. Her mother's was a curly, unremarkable brown. She smiled at Alice and patted the green wool skirt over her knees. "Nice day for traveling," she said. "Are you going far?"

"To Christchurch," Alice answered without thinking, then wished she'd bitten her tongue. "I'm going to stay with my aunt," she answered awkwardly.

"We're going home to Ashburton, aren't we, Meggie?" The little girl nodded, her hair swinging. "We've been visiting Gran at Glenpark. I'd hoped we'd bring her back with us, but she's stubborn as a fence post. I'm Pru McKay, and this is Meggie."

Feeling mean, all Alice gave in return was her first name, but Pru McKay didn't seem bothered. The train gave a series of little jerks, disconnected at first, then settling into a steady rhythm: tooo late—tooo late—tooo late—toolate—toolate—

By the time the conductor came through checking tickets Alice knew that Pru's husband, Peter, was a builder, and they had three sons as well as Meggie. Alice handed up her ticket and waited for the conductor to challenge her, to demand what she was doing traveling by herself all the way to Christchurch, but he didn't. He smiled all around and said, "Beaut day, isn't it?" then moved on.

Alice fumbled with the buckles on her satchel and pulled out *Rebecca;* she didn't want to risk talking anymore. When she opened the book, she found the photograph she'd taken from its frame. All the figures in it looked very small and far away. She studied them. She couldn't even really be sure which of the women was her mother; she wouldn't have known if she hadn't been told, she realized. And as for Toby Underwood—if he wasn't her father, then she had no idea who he was, only a stranger who had nothing at all to do with her. She didn't want to think about him; it made her feel hollow. She thrust the photograph in between pages near the end of the book and made an effort to focus on the words in front of her.

Mrs. McKay took a book out of the basket she'd set on the floor. Out of the corner of her eye, Alice saw Meggie lean cozily against her mother as Mrs. McKay began to read aloud. " 'Chapter Five. Arrietty had not been asleep. She had been lying under her knitted coverlet staring up at the ceiling. It was an interesting ceiling. Pod had built Arrietty's bedroom out of two cigar boxes, and on the ceiling lovely painted ladies dressed in swirls of chiffon blew long trumpets. . . .' ''

The words stole into Alice's ears, and the familiar story wrapped itself around her, drawing her in. The world of *Rebecca*—Manderley and the second Mrs. Maxim de Winter vanished, and she turned her face to the window as if she were absorbed in the landscape while she listened as Pod and Homily told their daughter Arrietty about the dangers for a Borrower in the world upstairs. Alice was swept with yearning. She didn't want to be Meggie; she wanted to be eight again. She hadn't understood how simple life was then.

The train rattled up the coast, through towns with a strange mixture of names, some English, some foreign. She guessed the foreign ones were Maori. But even the towns with English names looked alien. There were clusters of little shacks along the shore, on the other side of the train. She couldn't imagine that people actually lived in them; they looked like something the sea had brought in on a high tide and left stranded. Beyond her window a road ran beside the tracks, so close she could see people in the cars and lorries and on the motorbikes; they waved and sounded their horns in a friendly way as they caught up to the train and outdistanced it. The settlements were low and flat, full of the same solid, heavy architecture as Dunedin, but without the softening of trees. And stretching away inland were vast open spaces, here and there a huddle of little farm buildings, pitilessly exposed under the enormous weight of sky. There were occasional tufts of dark green trees, or a row of tall narrow poplars planted as a windbreak, and fence posts marching endlessly across the tussocky plain. Fields of brilliant green grass were splattered with tiny white sheep.

The conductor came through again, calling the next stop. It sounded to Alice like ''Wammaroo''; the sign on the platform said OAMARU when they got there. Her courage deserted her. She was hungry, and beginning to need a loo, but if she got left behind here, she was afraid she'd vanish into the landscape, never find her way out. Other passengers piled off the train with utter confidence while Alice watched, her fingers embedded in her hair.

"You can share our lunch if you'd like, Alice," offered Mrs. McKay, closing the book. "Granny's put up enough for a shearing crew—she always does. We've got plenty, haven't we, Meggie?" "Have we?" said Meggie, sounding doubtful. "Of course we have, pet. You saw Granny packing the basket." "I'm *very* hungry," declared Meggie.

"No, really," said Alice, hastily standing up. "It's all right. I need to get off for a minute. I'll get something in the café." She didn't want to share their food. She'd feel obliged if she did; at the very least she'd owe Mrs. McKay conversation, and that was dangerous. She might say too much, or not enough.

"Well, if you're sure." Mrs. McKay gave her a smile. "Leave your things—we'll look after them."

Alice hesitated. Mrs. McKay certainly seemed trustworthy, and it was hard to believe anything bad of a person who read *The Borrowers* aloud to her daughter, but almost everything she possessed was in that satchel: clothes, money, the travel clock. She decided to risk it. Tensely she folded her blazer over her arm and joined the mob surging into the station. First she looked around for the Ladies' Restroom. When she came out, feeling much better, she found the café full of people actually sitting at little tables, eating proper meals. She looked at them enviously as she queued at the counter. It seemed to take forever to get to the front; she kept expecting the train to pull out, but there were people behind her—the train would wait for them, it must. Finally it was her turn and she bought a meat pie—never mind where it came from—a bottle of ginger beer, and then, on extravagant impulse, a chocolate bar. It left her with only four shillings and threepence from the two pounds. She fingered the coins in her blazer pocket nervously. The money worried her; she wished she knew how much the ferry to Wellington cost, but on the way south her mother had bought their tickets while Alice and Mrs. Royde waited beside the suitcases. It had never crossed her mind then that she might want to know the fare. Still, there was the five-pound note hidden in her satchel—that *must* be enough. But what if it wasn't? What would she do? She hated having to worry about it. It was Len's fault, she thought angrily. It had to be someone's, and if Len had stayed, had been willing to talk to her instead of doing a bunk, she wouldn't have to be in Oamaru, alone and anxious, at that very moment.

Back on the train she found her satchel just where she'd left it, with *Rebecca* lying on the seat beside it. Meggie and her mother had unpacked their picnic basket. They had blue-and-white checked cloths spread on their laps, and Mrs. McKay had opened a packet of greaseproof paper revealing a stack of sandwiches: slabs of pink ham between thick slices of wheat bread. There were carrot sticks and hardboiled eggs, lemonade for Meggie, and a flask of milky tea for her mother. Alice tried not to watch them eat as she made her stodgy meat pie last as long as possible, chasing every crumb. "We've a sandwich and a half left," said Mrs. McKay. "Or would you fancy an egg, love?"

Resolutely Alice shook her head. "No, thank you, I've had plenty," she lied.

But when Mrs. McKay offered her a piece of gingerbread, her resolve crumbled. She could smell it, rich with molasses and spice. "No one makes better gingerbread than Meggie's granny," Mrs. McKay said comfortably, and Alice had to agree. Once the basket had been packed again, Meggie settled to listen, and Mrs. McKay took up the story of Arrietty, Pod, and Homily. Alice listened, too, not bothering with her own book this time, but leaning her head against the window and closing her eyes so it would seem she was asleep. Arrietty wasn't afraid. Arrietty wanted to explore the world above the floorboards, she wanted to go outside and see what was there. And Arrietty was the same age as Alice: fourteen. That's what she told the boy when she met him for the first time. . . .

It was almost six when they reached Ashburton. Meggie had gone to sleep just after the boy had taken the roof off the Borrowers' house, and

Mrs. McKay had put the book away, to Alice's disappointment. It had been four or five years since she'd read *The Borrowers* to herself; she knew what happened—that they'd been discovered by the villainous Mrs. Driver, and they'd escaped out the grating, across the fields—but she wanted to hear it all again, she wanted to hear Mrs. May's comforting description of the home they'd made for themselves Outside. Mrs. McKay took a half-finished Fair Isle vest out of another of her bags. The pattern seemed immensely complicated to Alice, who watched through her eyelashes, but the knitting needles moved quickly and without hesitation. Every time the train crossed the road, Alice's heart gave a lurch as the engineer sounded the whistle. It made a loud, prolonged braying like a demented donkey. Meggie never stirred.

When the train began to slow, Mrs. McKay roused Meggie and carefully stowed her knitting. "Here we are, pet, home for tea." Meggie rubbed her eyes and peered out the window as they pulled into the station. "I can see them! I can see them—look! There they are, Mummy!" She waved excitedly. "Well, of course," said her mother. "I told you they'd be waiting, didn't I? There's your dad. Well, come on, get a move on!" Mrs. McKay smiled indulgently at Alice. "He's probably left me a sinkful of dirty dishes and heaps of dirty laundry, as a welcome-home present. Never mind, we'll soon sort things out, won't we, Meggie? I hope you have a good visit, Alice. Christchurch is ever such a lovely city, with the river running straight through the middle, and the gardens. Enjoy yourself, love."

Alice felt suddenly abandoned. She watched Mrs. McKay and Meggie being met on the platform. Mr. McKay was a stocky man, beginning to bulge over his belt, and going thin on top, with a bushy black beard to make up. He swung Meggie off her feet, and Mrs. McKay gave the smallest of the three boys a hug, while the other two hefted the basket and the suitcase the guard had lifted down for her. Alice's eyes stung. There'd be no one waiting on any platform to meet her, not in Christchurch, not in Wellington. No one to give her a hug and take charge of her. She was on her own. What if, she thought for the first time—what if Mrs. Royde wasn't at home when Alice finally got there? There was no reason why she should be; she had no idea Alice was coming. She could be out for an hour shopping, or the morning at a meeting, or even away for days, visiting her son in Masterton. Then what? The water was icy and very, very deep.

She blinked. A big, rumpled-looking man suddenly loomed over her. He hoisted a much-traveled suitcase and limp overcoat onto the luggage rack overhead, then lowered himself onto the seat across from her, where Meggie and Mrs. McKay had been. His brown suit was creased and weary, the pockets lumpy, and the shoulders flecked with white. He wore a paisley tie in startling green and gold, and he had a cigar clamped between his teeth. The odor of it made Alice's nose itch unpleasantly. Beside him he laid a battered black case. "Samples," he said, grinning at Alice around the cigar. "Sheep-dip, worming tablets, cattle drench—that's me, the farmer's best friend." He fished a little white card out of one of his pockets and handed it to her. She didn't want to take it, but she was too overwhelmed to refuse. "George Smithers, Barton & Fosdyke, Agricultural Supplies, 431 Dee Street, Invercargill," she read.

"Pleased to meet ya!" He held out a very large hand, the first and index fingers stained a yellowy brown.

"Um," said Alice faintly, withdrawing her own hand as quickly as she dared without being rude, "um—Meggie McKay." It was the first name that came into her head.

"How's it goin', Meggie." His voice was flat and loudly jovial; she couldn't meet his eyes. If she'd had the nerve, she'd have gotten up and looked for another seat. . . .

"Hi, Trev! Right here! I've got a seat for ya, mate. You don't mind sharing, do ya, Meggie? Tiddler like you? Plenty of room!" Before she could say a word, he'd swung her satchel up next to his suitcase. Then he bent toward her, the cigar smoke making her eyes water. "He's in rough shape, is Trev. Got toothache something wicked." Alice gazed up at the scuffed leather of her satchel with wide, horrified eyes. Her hand crept out and snatched *Rebecca* and her blazer quick, before they disappeared as well. Oh, why—*why* was she doing this? Why hadn't somebody stopped her? Why hadn't Mrs. McKay stayed on the train all the way to Christchurch? Why hadn't she moved when she had the chance?

A second man dropped heavily onto the seat next to her. He let his dusty rucksack fall to the floor between his feet. On his rough, plaid woolen jacket he brought with him chilly, damp air and a strong, sweet smell—a smell that bothered Alice as much as George Smithers's cigar, although she couldn't quite place it. Covertly she glanced at him. His appearance was far from reassuring: stubbly, blue-black jaw; puffy, unhealthy-looking face; black bristling hair that looked as if it had been sawed off rather than cut. He was hunched deep in his jacket, cradling the left side of his face with his hand. He groaned as the train gave a forward jerk.

"That's Meggie McKay, Trev," said George, by way of introduction. "Goin' up to Christchurch, are ya, Meggie?"

Miserably Alice nodded. "My aunt—she's expecting me," she managed to get out. It wouldn't do to let him think she was on her own.

"Bit of a holiday, eh? Good on ya. Christchurch is a beaut city, innit, Trev? I'm always glad to come up this way. Better'n Dunedin, I'd say. More going on, livelier like. Wouldn't ya say, Trev?"

"Aw, stow it, will ya, George," came the muffled reply. "Leave us alone."

"Gonna have it pulled," George confided to Alice. "Got so his mates wouldn't put up with him anymore. Said he either had to have it yanked, or they'd take him out back and shoot him. Toothache makes a fella mean. Tell ya what, you wouldn't think a big bloke like him would be afraid of the dentist, would ya, Meggie? I've been telling him, nothing to it these days—he won't feel a thing. 'Why not get 'em all yanked while you're about it, Trev,' I said. 'Get a shiny new set of gnashers on the National Health, eh? Never have to go back.' "

"Quit narkin' me," snarled Trev thickly.

George shrugged. Alice shrank back into her corner as far as she could and opened *Rebecca*. Glueing her eyes to it, she read half a dozen pages without the faintest idea of what was on them, simply following the words across the paper and turning the page when she got to the bottom. She might as well have been reading Greek for all the sense it made to her. She was aware of George, taking a newspaper out of his sample case and shaking it out. Every now and then Trev gave a low moan and shifted in his seat. At one point he fished something out of his pocket, something flat and silver. Clamping it between his knees, he unscrewed the cap and took a long swig out of it, still holding his jaw.

"Here," said George, looking up. "How 'bout a share, eh?"

"It's medicinal," growled Trev. "I need it. You don't."

"Just a short one, mate."

Grudgingly Trev passed the flask and George took a hearty swallow. Alice knew what the sweet smell was; her hands were clammy. George sputtered and winced a little as he handed the flask back. "Crikey! What's in there, mate? Sheep piss?"

Not bothering to answer, Trev returned it to his pocket.

Alice was suddenly afraid that the journey was going to go on forever. It was her punishment for having run away; she was doomed to ride for the rest of her life on this train with George and Trev, trapped. But beyond the window she noticed that buildings were beginning to shoulder each other along the tracks. It was getting dark quickly: the sky was low and dirty. Along with the empty spaces they had lost the fair weather. She recognized the dismal outskirts of a city: warehouses, garages, builders' yards, waste areas strewn with rusting equipment, old tires, derelict cars. Then there were rows of houses with strips of yard behind them, washing on lines, a few kids out playing, sheds, bits of garden, rubbish heaps. Traffic thickened on the streets. Dingy little shops, milk bars, launderettes, rattled past, a playing field deserted by everyone except a man and a dog on a leash, lunging at gulls.

Alice gazed out on Christchurch, realizing there was not one single person in it she would recognize. Thousands of people living and working and going to school in the city, and not one of them knew of her existence. If only what she'd told George was true: that there'd be an aunt smiling and waving on the platform. But she didn't have any aunts, anywhere. Never had she felt so alone.

"Christchurch!" called the conductor. "Central station. Christchurch. All change!"

Alice's muscles tensed.

"Come on, Trev, stir your stumps!" exclaimed George, giving Trev's knee a shake.

Trev muttered something that Alice was glad she couldn't understand.

The train slowed, hissing, and stuttered to a halt. George stood and flung his overcoat across one shoulder, heaving his suitcase down. He pushed it into the aisle, treading on Trev's foot and earning a deeply felt curse. Alice got to her feet, anxious to escape, wondering if she was going to have to climb over Trev. Just as she stepped forward, he heaved himself upright. The train gave a sudden lurch, he lost his balance and fell onto Alice, throwing his right arm around her shoulders to steady himself. His face was only a couple of inches from hers, his sour-sweet breath overpowering. He muttered at her. Frantic, she wriggled out from under, tripped, recovered herself, and fled, pushing past the people clogging the aisle, her blazer hugged tight against her chest.

"Hey!" shouted George behind her. "Wait up, Meggie!"

— 25 —

Now What?

Alice shuddered and burrowed ahead, finally reaching the door. She had to wait while the conductor helped an elderly woman down the steps. All the while she kept expecting to hear George right behind her, to feel his hand close on her arm. But then she was out. The air was cold; it smelled—blessedly—of coal smoke, not cigars. She sucked in a great lungful and glanced about. It was dark, the lights were on. She wasn't sure what to do next. The station didn't look familiar to her at all. Where was the ferry?

"Meggie!"

Her heart lurched sickeningly. George was in the carriage doorway, waving at her. He was coming after her—it was a nightmare. First she had to get away, then she could find someone to tell her how to find the ferry. Without looking back, she ran, dodging people and luggage trolleys. Inside the station her eyes lit on the Ladies' Waiting Room. There were lights inside, and two women sitting on the benches. They couldn't follow her in there—she'd be safe. Paying no attention to the surprised looks the women gave her, she bolted through to the washroom beyond. She found an empty cubicle, latched the door, and sat on the toilet, breathing hard. She'd just wait there until she was certain that George and Trev had gone—they wouldn't hang about the station looking for her, surely they wouldn't. They'd lose interest when they found she'd vanished. Feet came and went, shuffling, clicking, squeaking on the tile floor. Doors banged shut, swung open, toilets flushed with whooshing, gulping noises. Water ran in the washbasins. The towel squeaked on its roller.

Alice bent almost double, wrapping her arms around her knees, wishing she had a watch so she could tell how long she'd been there. She was terrified of leaving too soon, but she had the ferry to catch. It was like waiting in the rhododendrons, when minutes seemed like hours, and hours went on forever, but then she'd had the travel clock.

Oh! She closed her eyes in anguish, and saw her school satchel, lying in the rack over her seat on the train, where George had put it—and she had left it. For a blank, whirling moment her brain refused to function. She rocked back and forth, clutching her knees for dear life, to keep from flying apart. What should she do? Risk going out to see if the train was still there? Or if the conductor had rescued her satchel from the rack? But he wouldn't know it was hers; he'd assume it belonged to someone staying on the train. Staying on to where? To the harbor, she thought, her heart dropping still further. The harbor—the ferry—must be further down the line; that's why she had no memory of this station. She and her mother hadn't gotten out here; they had only passed through it. She'd misunderstood the conductor and done it wrong. If she'd only asked back in Dunedin station, she'd be on the train at that moment, with all her belongings, leaving George and Trev behind.

Cold with misery, she sat upright and reckoned what she'd lost: her school skirt and good cardigan—her mother'd be furious about them—*and* the travel clock, a change of underwear, and her toothbrush—her mouth tasted stale and furry. The money. All she had now—she fumbled with her blazer, her fingers clumsy—was four shillings and threepence. Nowhere near enough for a ferry ticket, not even enough for half fare back to Dunedin. She stared, unseeing, at the pathetic handful of coins. What should she do? It was late—it must be eight o'clock anyway. She was in the middle of a strange city; she had almost no money. What could she do? She felt hot, then cold all over. She wanted to burst into tears, but she was too scared even to do that. So she sat still and took deep, shuddering breaths, trying to calm herself. She wouldn't be able to think straight unless she could calm down. Gradually the panic subsided, but it took great concentration to keep it under control.

She could go to the man at the ticket counter and tell him. Tell him what? That she was lost. Well, that wasn't strictly true. She knew where she was, sort of. Tell him she'd left her schoolbag on the train from Dunedin and it had the rest of her money in it. She'd give him all she had, and beg him to sell her a ticket on the ferry. She'd promise, word of honor, to pay the rest later.

But at the thought of the ferry, the ice broke under her again. She'd be on it alone this time, surrounded by more strangers—people like George and Trev. Out on the dark, uncertain ocean. There'd be no escaping once she was on board; it would be a thousand times worse than the train. She and her mother had shared their tiny cabin with other, unknown passengers, who groaned and coughed all night. If she survived, she'd land at Wellington docks in the morning without a penny, still having to find her way to Mrs. Royde's house.

Her mouth was dry and her head pounding; she couldn't do it. All right. If she couldn't face that, forget it. What else? She could beg the man to sell her a ticket back to Dunedin. She'd promise the rest of the fare when she got back to Florestan. There was the panic again: Florestan. She'd have to explain what she'd been doing and why. She'd have to go back having solved nothing, only having made it all worse. Closing her eyes, she saw her mother's face, the freckles vivid across her nose. She'd be furious—as angry as she'd ever been. By this time she'd have missed Alice. She'd have rung the school and learned that Alice had been absent all day. She'd have rung Mrs. Quennell and Mrs. MacInnes to see if Helen or Margery knew where Alice was. When they said no, she'd probably have got on to Mr. MacInnes, maybe even the police—

She could go to the police herself, Alice supposed, feeling no joy at the thought. They'd guess she was a runaway. They'd telephone to Florestan, and make Alice stay until her mother came to fetch her. She pictured herself spending the night in a cell: iron bars and a cot with a sagging mattress and a thin, stale-smelling blanket, like the jail in a western. That made her think of Len, and for a moment the panic was consumed by the heat of anger. This was Len's fault. It was all his fault that Alice was at that moment huddled in a station loo in Christchurch, alone and scared and without money.

"Bloody hell," she whispered. Then she said it again, out loud, with feeling. If God wanted to strike her down for swearing, this was as good a time for Him to do it as any she could think of. And if He didn't, she felt better anyway. Not a lot better, but even a little helped.

Margery swore. She'd told Alice she'd learned it from her aunt Jessie, and she was very careful not to let either of her parents hear her. She couldn't afford to have them disapprove of Aunt Jessie any more than they already did. Aunt Jessie was too important an ally.

Alice caught her breath. Her heart began to race. Aunt Jessie lived in Christchurch. Somewhere in Christchurch. She wouldn't have the faintest idea who Alice Jenkins *was*, but if Alice Jenkins simply turned up on her doorstep, alone at night and in desperate need of help, surely she wouldn't refuse.

At least it was something to do, and anything was better than sitting still in the loo any longer. Alice rooted through her head for any useful scrap of information Margery might have dropped. Aunt Jessie had a gallery; Alice had no idea what it was called. Aunt Jessie was Mr. MacInnes's sister: Jessie MacInnes. She'd be in the telephone directory, and there'd be a telephone booth in the station. Alice could look her up and find her address. She was halfway out of the washroom when it occurred to her that Aunt Jessie might be married, in which case she'd be Jessie Someone-else. She tangled her fingers in her hair.

Well, she'd try it anyway. Margery'd never mentioned an uncle. No, she'd said Aunt Jessie was an odd sock. The clock in the waiting room said five past eight; the two women had left, and there was a young mother changing a baby on one of the benches, too busy trying to keep all the bits together to pay attention to Alice. The main foyer was almost deserted. She peered cautiously around, but there was no sign of George Smithers. She breathed a sigh of relief. The telephone booth by the entrance was occupied. Alice had to wait, seething with impatience, while the man inside cradled the receiver against his shoulder, his face creased in a frown, and wrote something on the back of an envelope. Then he read it back to the person on the other end of the line, nodded vigorously, added a few words, and finally hung up.

Alice eeled in through the glass door as soon as he left. The air smelled warm and used. She pulled out the directory, licked her finger, and paged through it. MacInnes, MacInnes, MacInnes—there were columns of *Mc*s and *Mac*s—she always had trouble sorting them into alphabetical order. "MacInnes, Charles. MacInnes, G. M. MacInnes, Hugh. MacInnes, Jessie—" She closed her eyes briefly. God had forgiven her for swearing. She ran her finger below the line and noticed how grubby the finger was. The nail had a rim of black under it. Her hair must need combing and she probably had smuts on her face from the train. Before she went anywhere, she'd go back to the washroom and clean herself up as much as she could. Then she'd set out to find— she squinted—53 Bessant Street. She ought to write down the telephone number while she was about it, but she had nothing to write with. Some careless person had left the stump of a pencil on the shelf—just enough lead to make a mark on the inside front cover of *Rebecca*. The photograph slipped out of the back pages and fell on the floor, face up. She was tempted to leave it there—she never wanted to see it again. But she couldn't. Whoever those people were, they didn't belong in Christchurch any more than she did and it didn't seem right to abandon them there. Sighing, she bent and retrieved it and stuck it back into the book.

When she'd washed her face and patted her hair smooth, pulled down her blouse and pulled up her knee socks, she faced the problem of finding out where Bessant Street was. The woman with the baby had gone. Alice chewed her lip. It occurred to her that it might not be a good idea to let strangers know, at this hour of the evening, that she didn't know where she was going. A middle-aged woman in a brown mac, wearing flat, run-over shoes, was just locking the door to the café. Alice took a chance. "Bessant Street?" The woman shook her head. "Don't know, love. Not my part of Christchurch. Tell you what. Ask one of the taxi drivers out front. Bob or Mick. They'd know."

But could she just ask a taxi driver for directions without paying him to take her? That seemed like cheating, but she had no idea how far it was, or how much the fare would be. And suppose, when they got there, Aunt Jessie wasn't home, or wouldn't help? Alice would have used all her money. She found she was staring fixedly at the sign the woman had hung on the door that said CLOSED. She was starving again. "You all right?" said the woman. "You look a bit peaky. Someone supposed to meet you, were they?"

"Oh, no," said Alice quickly. "No, I'm fine. Really."

It was dark outside. Cars and buses had their lights on. There was a sour little wind racketing around, swirling dust and bits of rubbish out of the gutter, chivying people along the pavements. Alice shivered and pulled on her blazer; no one would recognize Saint Kat's here. There was no comfort in the thought. Plucking up her courage, she approached one of the taxis waiting by the curb. "Excuse me." The driver looked inquiringly out of his window at her. She twirled her hair nervously. "Can you tell me how to find Bessant Street?"

"Better'n that, I'll take you there, eh?" he offered.

"Is it far? I mean, can I walk?"

He stifled a yawn and nodded. "Could do. It's maybe a mile and a half. Here, look." He fished under his seat for a piece of paper and began drawing lines on it. "Turn left out of the station, see—walk till you come to a traffic light. Then you go left again and keep on straight—

seven, eight blocks? I've never counted 'em. You want Marchmont, that's a right. There's a dairy on the corner''—he made a black X—"can't miss it. Got a cow painted on the wall. So you go left and left, then right—'' He added a few more lines, then handed her the paper.

"Thank you." Alice looked at it dubiously.

"You ought to hurry," advised the driver. "It's coming on to rain. Sure I can't take you?"

She shook her head, thanked him again, and set off. As soon as she got around the first corner—left out of the station—she paused to pull the chocolate bar out of her pocket. She'd forgotten it until she'd put on the blazer. She was ravenous. She chewed and swallowed the first pieces without really tasting them, then she broke off a couple of squares and let them melt slowly in her mouth, while she wrapped the remainder and put it resolutely away. If she took the wrong turn somewhere, she could wander for hours, hopelessly lost.

The driver had told her to hurry. She began walking, counting the blocks to herself, peering at street signs. Seven. Wilson Street. Eight. Palmerston. She was lost. Cars brushed past on the street, their passengers sealed behind glass, unaware of Alice. She was just a shadowy figure standing alone on the pavement. Tears pushed at the back of her throat; her eyes stung. Perhaps she was invisible? Try one more block. He'd been vague about the number. Maybe it was nine.

She saw the cow before she could read the sign. It was larger than life: a black-and-white holstein, wearing a chain of buttercups, green grass under her hooves and blue sky above. Relief fizzed up through Alice, making her scalp prickle. She turned right, away from the main street, into a quieter neighborhood. There were cars parked beside the curb, and in almost every one of the little houses lights shone warmly. Where the curtains weren't drawn or the blinds down, Alice glimpsed front rooms: pictures on a wall, the back of a red sofa, a mirror, African violets in a pot, a lamp with a white fringed shade, a tortoiseshell cat drowsing on a sill. It overwhelmed her to think of all the lives going on, concurrent with her own but utterly independent. She felt somehow unnecessary.

At the end of the block she hesitated. Was it left-left-then-right, or left-right-then-left? She held the map to a streetlamp and decided left-then-right. The first erratic drops of rain began to fall. She turned up her collar, half ran to the next corner, and miraculously there it was: Bessant Street. The odd numbers were on the left. Slowing down, she searched for them: on gateposts, letter boxes, beside front doors. She found 37, 39, 41, then two houses with no numbers that she could find, 47, 49—somehow she missed 51 because on the next wrought iron gate was a 53. Her nerve failed her. She walked right past, to the end of the street, without even looking at the house. The rain was coming more steadily. She went back, her heart slamming against her ribs. There was a light over the door as if someone were expected, but the front room was dark. Either Aunt Jessie had guests on the way, or she'd gone out and left the light on for herself.

The house was small, set back behind a shrubby little front garden. A good-sized tree at the left corner trailed its branches over the fence into the neighbor's garden. The house was like the others on the street: bay window on the left, four steps up to a tiny porch on the right, worn rope doormat and boot scraper. Alice stood rooted to the spot, unable to make herself open the gate and go up the walk.

It had taken all her energy and concentration to find the house; she hadn't given a thought to what would happen when she did. She had no idea what to say, and her brain seemed to have gone to sleep. A boy walked past, whistling through his teeth, and gave Alice a long, curious stare. He was older than she by several years, and had a sports bag slung over his shoulder. Panicked that he might ask her what she was doing, standing in the rain in front of Number 53, Alice turned and hurried in the opposite direction. At the end of the block, she turned right, then right again, circling back. If it hadn't been raining she could have kept going around and around, until the lights went on inside, or the porch light went off, or a car drove up. But she was cold and the dampness was starting to penetrate, and she was suddenly so weary her ears began to buzz. If she went up on the porch to wait, she'd be out of the rain and she could huddle inconspicuously in a corner.

Without giving herself time to think, she slipped through the gate and up the steps, and pushed the doorbell, just in case. "My name is Alice Jenkins, Miss MacInnes. I'm a friend of Margery's." "You don't know me, Miss MacInnes, but—" Nothing happened. She was about to squeeze herself into a ball on the porch floor when she heard footsteps inside the house and froze. A light went on in the hall, shining out through panels of stained glass on either side of the door, and the latch clicked.

"Hullo?"

It was the final straw. She must have read the wrong line in the directory. She couldn't bear it. She burst into tears.

— 26 —

53 Bessant Street, Christchurch

"Oh, I say! You mustn't do that! Come now, it can't be that bad, can it? No, surely not. Come in out of the rain, and let's see what we can do—" He took her gently, firmly by the elbow and guided her over the threshold into the house. His round spectacles winked in the light. "Now then." He closed the door behind Alice, cutting off escape. "Can you pull yourself together and tell me—oh, that's the kettle! Here, just you come along with me, this way." He steered her along the hall, to a bright little room at the back, full of smooth, easy music and a mouth-watering smell. He sat her carefully on a straight-backed chair. "You just stay still for a moment, that's it. What about a nice hot drink? Yes? That's what you need—um, chocolate, how does that sound? I'll have it for you in a tick."

Alice choked and heaved, the tears pouring down her cheeks and dripping onto her locked fingers, while a woman's voice sang, "There'll be a change in the weather. . . ." Part of her was absolutely horrified at what she was doing; part of her was incredibly relieved to have let go at last. She would never have burst into tears, she realized later, if she hadn't felt quite safe. The man was back in a few minutes, setting a brown-and-green-and-blue pottery mug on the table next to her. "Here now, mop yourself up with that. Go on." He put a tea towel into her hands and obediently she buried her face in it, snuffling and gasping. He sat opposite and waited while she scrubbed at her eyes and took long, shaky breaths. "That's better, isn't it," he said encouragingly. "There's your chocolate, right by your elbow. I suppose you've had supper—it's rather late. Perhaps you'd like a biscuit?"

He got up again and went to rummage in a little closet beyond the stove. It seemed to take him a long time to find the biscuit tin, but Alice was grateful; she needed a few minutes of being ignored to collect herself. Her balance was very precarious. She blew her nose in a corner of the towel. It had tiny black-and-brown kiwis all over it, she noticed, and that helped to steady her. Putting it down, she clasped both hands around the comforting warm bulge of the mug, feeling the steam on her face and the lovely rich smell in her nose as she lifted it. Even without drinking, she felt better.

"I put some milk in it so it wouldn't be too hot," said her host from the closet.

Alice took a mouthful, postponing the moment when she would have to apologize. "It's very good," she said tentatively.

"Oh, I am glad. It does help, doesn't it? Puts heart in one." He returned with a tin box and beamed at her. He was short, only a couple of inches taller than Alice herself, with thinning grayish sandy hair. He was wearing a pale green shirt and a dark green V-neck pullover with leather patches on the elbows. She studied him over the rim of her mug as he sat down again. There was a plate of stew with a fork balanced on the edge, and another plate with a half-eaten chunk of crusty bread spread thickly with butter. A book lay open beside them. She'd interrupted his supper. In spite of the cocoa, her stomach gave a rumbling growl.

"Oh, dear! You *haven't* had your dinner, have you? You should have said. There's plenty more, you know."

"But I can't—" Alice protested feebly.

"Nonsense!"

While he busied himself fetching another plate, cutting more bread, she set down her mug and looked around. They were in the kitchen, of course. The walls were a creamy yellow and the floor tiled in reddish brown. On one wall were open shelves holding a miscellaneous collection of pottery bowls, plates, mugs on hooks, all shapes, sizes, and colors. In the window over the sink hung a planter from which an ivy stretched green tentacles like an octopus. There was an avocado pit sprouting in a glass on the windowsill. Alice recognized it: she had once grown one for a school botany project. Without warning, a large orange-and-white object suddenly landed on her knees. She couldn't stifle a little cry of alarm. She felt the merest hint of claws as it steadied itself, then folded into a faintly humming fur lump.

"I *am* sorry. I should have warned you about Vinnie. I didn't think. Do excuse him—as soon as he sees a lap he's in it. I'll take him, shall I?"

"No, that's all right." Alice was heartened to find that her voice sounded almost normal. She stroked Vinnie's back, noticing that he had lost most of his left ear. It was a ragged little stub. "What happened to him?"

"Oh, the ear. It must've been a fight. It happened before we found him—or, I should say, he found us. That's why we call him Vinnie. His full name's Vincent van Gogh." He set a plate in front of Alice, heaped with savory brown stew. "Just you tuck into that. You'll feel much better with something inside you." He had a very kind, encouraging face; Alice found it impossible to be afraid of him. "Now, if you can tell me what's wrong, perhaps we can sort it out?"

Alice sighed. "Well, for a start, I've come to the wrong house."

"Have you?" He looked at her in surprise.

"I looked it up in the telephone directory at the station, you see, and I thought it said 53 Bessant Street, only I must have gotten it wrong."

"No you haven't. This is 53 Bessant Street."

"Yes, but I must have read the wrong line."

"Well who is it you're looking for? I've a Christchurch directory here—you can try again, what about that?" Before she could speak, he'd disappeared. She shoveled two more forkfuls into her mouth, half afraid she wouldn't be allowed to finish once they found the answer. The band was playing something slow and smooth as velvet, embroidered with the gold thread of a clarinet. "Oh dear how I need one sweet letter from you—" sang the woman.

"Here, have a look at this." He picked Vinnie, unprotesting, out of her lap, leaving a warm shadow on her knees. Alice opened the directory to the Ms. She knew where on the page to look: halfway down the second column on the right. MacInnes, Jessie. 53 Bessant Street. "But it can't be," she said in dismay.

"Not there?"

"No, I mean—yes. I've found the right name, but—I suppose she's moved."

"Oh, I don't think so," he said carefully. "This house has been in the same hands for—well, more than ten years anyway. Let me see."

"There." Alice pointed.

"Ah, *that's* what it is! I should have guessed," he exclaimed happily. "She's not here."

Alice gave him a wary look, wondering how you could tell if a person who seemed normal really was. She glanced apprehensively at her plate. Suppose he'd put something in her stew? She felt heavy all over, ambushed by weariness. . . .

"She hasn't come home yet. She rang not long before you'd arrived to say she'd be late—tied up with a customer. I'd been waiting dinner for her, you see, but then I thought I might just as well go ahead and eat."

"But she does live here? Jessie MacInnes?" said Alice, wanting to be sure she had it straight.

"Oh, indeed she does. This is her house," he assured her earnestly.

"Then who are you?" she asked, vaguely aware that the question didn't sound very polite.

"I'm Humphrey Tucker." He smiled. "She just calls me Tucker—I'm quite used to it now. You'd better call me Tucker as well. I'm her husband."

"Then why"—Alice was confused—"why isn't she Mrs. Tucker?"

"It's because of the gallery mainly. Everyone's always known her as Jessie MacInnes, ever since she started it. We only got married a year and a half ago, and if she'd changed her name, she'd only have had to explain who Jessie Tucker was. It didn't seem awfully sensible somehow. Good heavens, is that the time? I'd better set a place for her. You sit tight and finish your stew—it'll be cold if you don't."

Alice did as she was told, glad not to have to think for a few minutes, and Vinnie leaped up to occupy her lap again.

"I suppose really," said Tucker, setting out cutlery, "that you ought perhaps to tell me who you are." He sounded apologetic. "Do you mind?"

Alice had forgotten she hadn't. "I'm Alice Jenkins." There seemed no point in being anyone else this time. She was going to have to tell Jessie MacInnes who she was, and it seemed ungrateful not to tell Tucker the truth after all his kindness.

"Alice," he said, nodding. " 'Jam yesterday and jam tomorrow, but never jam today.' Actually, we do have some—homemade apricot. Do you like apricot jam? It's a bit runny, but it tastes quite nice." He raised his eyebrows questioningly at Alice. "Oh, I say—you don't like apricot then, is that it?"

"N-no," said Alice, sniffing hard. "I do. It's just—only, that's the way I *feel*. Like Alice, I mean."

"Yes, well, I expect it's perfectly natural," he said comfortingly. "To do with growing up, isn't it. It made her feel extremely odd, as I recall."

Alice hadn't considered *Alice in Wonderland* that way before. "Do you think—" she began.

The front door slammed, startling them all. Vinnie recovered almost instantly, rising and stretching as if he'd been going to get up anyway. He landed on the floor with a little thud and walked into the hall, his tail held straight up with a kink at the very tip that twitched.

"Tucker? Where are you? Why is it so *dark* in here? It's like the Black Hole of Calcutta! It's getting to be a filthy night out there—the wind's come up and it's lashing with rain. My feet are wet and I am so sick of these hypocritical twits who pretend they're interested in art when all they really want is interior decoration. I mean, what *is* the point in spending hours showing important stuff—really *good* paintings—to someone who hasn't a *clue*—"

"Oh, dear," said Tucker to Alice. "Not a successful meeting, I'm afraid. Jessie," he called. "Jessie, you've got a visitor."

"Oh, *Vinnie!* Get out from under my feet, you wretched cat! You'll have me flat on my—did you say a *visitor*, Tucker? Here? *Now,* for pity's sake? All I want is a beer and a hot bath. I do *not*—I repeat *not*—want a visitor. If this is your idea of a joke, we are not amused." A tall woman appeared in the doorway, making the air around her turbulent. In spite of the fact that her short curly hair was gray, her face, angular and smooth, was young looking. She wore a slate-colored tunic of a loosely woven material over a long skirt. A large greenstone pendant hung around her neck on a gold chain. She was barefoot. Vinnie eeled around her legs, purring audibly, tail gently quivering.

"I'll just get you the beer, shall I," said Tucker soothingly. "This is Alice Jenkins, my dear. She's come quite a long way to see you, I believe."

Jessie looked from Tucker to Alice, to the table with its three places and two used plates. "So he invited you to supper, did he? Do I know you?"

"Um," said Alice anxiously. "Well, no really. I mean, not exactly—"

"Either I know you or I don't. How can I not exactly know you, eh?"

"I'm a friend of Margery's," said Alice, wondering if she really was. Would Margery have said, "I'm a friend of Alice's"?

"Margery? *My* Margery? Do you mean you've come up from Dunedin? Surely not to see *me*—what did Tucker say your name is?"

"Alice Jenkins." She expected Jessie MacInnes to say, "Never heard of you." But instead, she frowned consideringly. She had prominent cheekbones, a mouth that was a little too large, and eyes the same color green as Margery's. In the silence the music sounded suddenly rowdy; the clarinet became strident, was joined by a boisterous trombone and people clapping enthusiastically. "Tucker, will you turn that racket off!"

"Sorry," said Tucker. He turned the volume on the wireless down; it hummed very quietly in the background.

"Now then. You're the girl lives at Florestan, aren't you." It was a statement.

Alice nodded. So Margery had told her aunt about the Jenkinses. *What* had she told her, Alice wondered unhappily.

"That must be an interesting experience for you," said Jessie MacInnes dryly. "I should like to hear what you think about it."

"Here you are, my dear." Tucker handed her a large V-shaped glass of gold-colored liquid, with an inch of white froth on the top. "Missionary beer," she said critically.

"Yes, I know. I poured it too quickly," Tucker explained to Alice. "It has a collar on top, you see. He didn't buy anything, did he?"

"What?" She took a long swallow and breathed a sigh. "D'you mean Robin Lewis? Of course not. He wanted something in shades of rose, exactly thirty-six by twenty-eight, to go in his reception area. Didn't care what the painting was. Even if I'd had something that fit, I wouldn't have sold it to him. Philistine. I told him to try Woolworth's."

"You didn't." Tucker smiled indulgently.

"I did." She pulled out one of the chairs and sprawled on it, her legs outstretched. Vinnie needed no encouragement; he sprang up and began to trample around and around, feeling out the most favorable spot before condensing himself precariously in the area of her middle. "Well, Alice Jenkins," said Jessie after a few minutes. She sounded uncannily like Margery. "You'll be staying the night, I presume. I didn't see any luggage in the hall."

At the mention of luggage Alice's heart gave a sickening lurch. "I left it on the train," she said in a small voice.

Jessie and Tucker exchanged a glance. "The train from Dunedin?"

Miserably Alice nodded. "I had to get off in a hurry."

"Not to worry," said Tucker. "I expect it'll turn up in lost and found."

"Do you think so?" Alice felt stupid not to have thought of that. "Bound to."

"It wasn't much—only my school satchel. But it had—it had money in it." She was close to tears again, unequal to the task of explaining herself, especially to sympathetic people.

"Clearly the first thing to do," said Jessie briskly, "is for me to have supper. I'm much more reasonable when I'm full of food. Then, since it's nearly ten, I suggest we all go to bed and sort things out in the morning."

"There is just one thing," said Tucker hesitantly, as he gave her a loaded plate.

"And what's that?" asked Jessie, digging in. "Pass the butter, Alice, will you?"

"Alice must have been going somewhere."

"Obviously."

"I mean, somewhere else. It's rather unlikely that she was coming *here*."

Alice felt them both turn and look at her and glanced up in confusion. She hadn't been paying attention to what they'd been saying, she'd drifted away on their voices. Now, a bit late, she put the words together.

Jessie ran a hand through her hair. "Presumably someone, some-

where, is standing about on a cold, wet platform waiting for her, that's
what you're getting at?''

''Yes,'' said Tucker.

''No,'' said Alice. ''She's not expecting me. She doesn't know I'm
coming.''

''Another one. Do you often pay these surprise visits?'' asked Jessie.
Alice struggled to work out what she wanted to say.

''You weren't running away, were you?'' said Tucker, after a moment. ''I'd have said you were too sensible for that, surely.''

''If no one knew you were coming,'' Jessie said, ''did anyone know
you were going?''

Alice began to twist her hair. She shook her head.

''So. Someone, somewhere—your mother in Dunedin, at a guess—
is worrying herself frantic because she doesn't know where you are. Is
that a fair statement?''

''I suppose,'' whispered Alice. She didn't want to think about her
mother; she didn't want guilt over what she'd done to her mother to
cancel out the injustice of what had been done to her. She had to hold
on to her anger to keep from dissolving again.

''Well,'' said Tucker, ''we really can't have that, can we? I mean,
we know you're all right—''

''But it isn't *fair!*'' Alice burst out. ''I'll have to go back and it will
all be the same. Nothing will be solved. I wasn't running away, I was
only going to Wellington to see Mrs. Royde. We met her on the boat—
she said if we ever needed anything to let her know. She's the only
person I could think of—I don't know anyone else in New Zealand,
and I've got to *talk* to someone. I'd've gone back to Dunedin once I'd
talked to her, but if I go back *now*—''

''Look, Alice Jenkins, hang on. In the first place *now* is a relative
word. We're not speaking about tonight, that's clear. I'll loan you a
nightdress and I'm sure Tucker's got a spare toothbrush, he always has.
Whatever happens tomorrow, it's a long way from here to Dunedin—

not like clicking your ruby slippers together and closing your eyes. It's useless to talk anymore tonight—we're all too tired. We'll discuss it in the morning. In the meantime, after I've finished my stew, I think I'd better telephone your mother—Florestan is on the telephone, isn't it? I think of it as being a relic of the past, somehow, locked in time like an insect in a piece of kauri gum. There isn't a thing she can do until tomorrow. And that's another matter altogether. Right, Tucker?"

"Oh, yes. Absolutely. It'll look much better in the daylight, you'll see."

Alice gave Jessie an anguished look. "But what will you say?"

"What can I say? That you're here, quite safe, with Tucker and me in Christchurch. I don't know any more than that, do I? If your mother wants a character reference, she can ring my brother. Serve him right if she gets him out of bed."

"What kind of character reference do you fancy Malcolm would give you?" asked Tucker, sounding amused.

"I don't think this is the moment to go into that, Humphrey," she replied dryly.

He chuckled.

Alice gazed from one to the other helplessly. They were right: her mother did have to know she was safe. If everything had gone according to her original plan, when she'd arrived in Wellington, Mrs. Royde would have telephoned Florestan. Mrs. Royde. At that moment she didn't seem real. She was like someone in a story, a character in *The Borrowers*. No, that was Mrs. May . . . and anyway, why had she ever thought Mrs. Royde could sort everything out for her? Alice could barely remember her face. Mrs. Royde had probably forgotten Alice altogether. . . .

"See here," said Tucker kindly, "she is right. There's nothing to be done tonight, and you look all in, Alice. I'll take you upstairs and show you your bedroom. You can wash up—there's hot water for a bath, if you'd like."

"*My* bath," put in Jessie.

"That's right. I'm giving your bath to Alice tonight. She needs it more than you. You can have another beer, and pour it yourself this time, without the collar. Or better still, I'll get us each a brandy once I've got Alice squared away."

"You always were hopelessly soft, Humphrey Tucker."

Alice took a long, shaky breath; her eyes blurred and she opened them wide, forcing the tears back. Crying only gave her a headache. Somehow, *somehow* she was going to have to solve this for herself. She was just beginning to understand that. But she couldn't think about it anymore that night, Jessie was right.

— 27 —

Humphrey Tucker

As soon as she opened her eyes, Alice knew precisely where she was: in the little back bedroom, under the eaves, at 53 Bessant Street, Christchurch. There was gray, watery daylight all around, and rain sluicing down the window glass; she couldn't tell what time it was. She remembered almost falling asleep in Jessie MacInnes's bath the night before, then crawling in between clean sheets wearing a blue flannel nightshirt that drooped off her shoulders and reached nearly to her ankles. That was all. Someone had turned out the light—Alice was sure she hadn't.

Cocooned and warm, she lay still, examining the room for the first time. The walls and sloping ceiling were a very pale green. At the angle where they met and around the door and window frames someone had painted a border of vine leaves starred with tiny yellow-green flowers. The curtains were the same yellowy shade, and the rug echoed the dark green of the leaves. It was like lying in bed in a tree house. There wasn't space for much furniture: the single bed, a plank-bottomed chair, a narrow chest of drawers, and a little bookcase stuffed with miscellaneous paperbacks.

Hanging on the back of the chair, where she'd left her clothes, was a yellow toweling robe. She sat up. If her clothes were gone, then she'd lost everything she'd brought with her from Dunedin. But someone had carefully arranged the contents of her blazer pockets on the dresser: the partially eaten chocolate bar, her four shillings and threepence, and *Rebecca*. There were also a comb and a brush, and a small wooden box inlaid with bits of paua shell.

Alice sat on the edge of the bed, wondering what to do next. The only sounds she could hear were the rain and the wind outside, but it didn't feel early. She was afraid that she had made a terrible fool of herself the night before: turning up, a total stranger in a skirt and crumpled school blazer, and bursting into tears on the doorstep. Thinking about it made her feel tight and crawly inside. How could she have done such an awful, embarrassing thing?

And what had Jessie MacInnes told her mother? What had her mother said to Jessie? It was dreadful not to know, having to wrap someone else's bathrobe around herself and go barefoot downstairs to face two unfamiliar people who would have been discussing her at length, who must by this time have made judgments about the kind of girl she was, and decisions about what to do with her.

What a mess she'd made of things! Miss Fairchild would be scornful, her mother would be furious, and Len—well, she didn't care about Len. There were footsteps outside the door. "Alice? Alice, are you awake?" called Jessie.

"Yes." The word caught in her throat; she swallowed it down and repeated it.

"Good. It's just gone nine." Jessie put her head in. "I'm off to the gallery—I've an appointment I can't miss this morning. Come on downstairs and Tucker'll get you some breakfast. You'd better have my slippers—here." They were enormous and lined with fleece.

So she wouldn't have to look at Jessie, Alice busied herself with the yellow robe; it was wide rather than long, so she reckoned it must belong to Tucker. The nightshirt was Jessie's.

"Rotten sort of morning," said Jessie. "I hoped it might blow out to sea." The hall, though windowless, was washed in gray light. Glancing up, Alice saw dirty clouds scudding overhead, through the glass of a large skylight. At the top of the stairs she stopped, arrested by the painting that filled the wall over the landing. It was the inside of a forest, layered with ragged screens of foliage that pulled her in, further and further, between the smooth, mottled gray-brown trunks of trees. The trees were like stone columns, very straight, very solid; their crowns rose above the canvas, unseen. Alice gazed at the picture, aware of weight and texture and eons of time, caught up in a compelling, unfamiliar rhythm.

Jessie, who'd started down, paused and looked back. "That's my prize," she said. "One of the very few she's ever done of New Zealand. The Waipoua Kauri Forest, on the North Island. It's above Auckland. I don't suppose you've been?"

Alice shook her head.

"No, well it's worth a visit. She chose to paint a stand of mature trees instead of one of the real giants. They're thousands of years old, those."

"Miss Fairchild," said Alice.

"Who else? I knew when she let me have it—this was years ago, mind you, soon after I'd opened the gallery—I knew I wouldn't be able to find a buyer. Not just because no one would have paid anything like what it was worth. I couldn't let it go. She wanted it back—said she'd changed her mind, but I told her it was too late, I'd sold it. And so I had. I ran a hefty overdraft to pay her, and then I had to have the skylight put in." She climbed back and stood beside Alice, studying the painting. "Worth every penny. The light coming down on it makes it change. It's completely different when the sun's out. Or at night, with a bright, full moon."

Timidly Alice said, "She really is good then."

"Oh, yes," said Jessie. "She's good. Look, I shall be late if I don't get a move on. Tucker's in the kitchen." She ran down the stairs. At

the bottom she called, "Tucker, I'm off. See you later." After a minute
Alice heard the front door slam and felt a guilty relief. Jessie made her
nervous; she found it impossible to tell what she was thinking, but she
was afraid it wasn't complimentary.

She clenched her fingers, thrust her fists deep in her toweling pockets,
and went to confront Tucker. He was sitting at the table with his book
propped open against an empty toast rack. "Alice." He greeted her
with a smile. "I hope you slept well? Such a wild night."

"Yes, thank you," said Alice, her voice sounding stiff in her ears.

"That's all right then. Have you ever read *The Hobbit*? Rather an
odd book, I thought, but I quite enjoyed it—dwarves and wizards and
dragons. Very clever. This one's by the same chap—fellow I knew at
Oxford, an expert on Norse legends and early English. He's invented
this place called Middle Earth. Sausage and tomato with your egg? And
some toast, of course. Make yourself comfortable, that's it. There's tea
made, or perhaps you'd rather cocoa again?" He pottered around, getting her breakfast together, while she sat on the edge of a chair, unable
to make herself comfortable. Setting a plate in front of her, he remarked,
"I'm sorry it's not better weather for you. Christchurch in the rain is
quite as dreary as any other city. Pity really." He made it sound as if
they'd been planning her visit for weeks. Vinnie accepted a fragment
of sausage from Tucker's fingers, then butted his hand affectionately,
and Tucker nattered on about inconsequential things, while Alice did
her best to eat.

At last, unable to stand it any longer, she set down her fork and
asked, "What did Mum say?"

"Well," said Tucker, "naturally, she was anxious about you. She
would be, wouldn't she? I gather you didn't leave a note, so she'd no
idea where you'd got to. And then she hadn't the foggiest notion who
Jessie was, ringing up out of the blue. But once they'd got that straightened out, Jessie convinced her that you were perfectly all right—"

"I didn't even think about a note," whispered Alice. "I was going
to telephone when I got to Wellington—" But that wouldn't have been

until morning, after the ferry. She couldn't meet Tucker's eyes. "She must have been furious." Her fingers, acting on their own, began to crumble a piece of toast. "Did she say anything about my—about Len?"

"No, I don't believe she did. At least Jessie didn't mention anyone called Len. Your mother didn't seem to have any idea why you should have gone off that way. She was afraid something terrible must have happened. You gave her quite a scare, young Alice."

Under the circumstances it was the mildest of reproofs, but Alice felt as if she'd stepped into a hornets' nest: her skin burned and stung. Back in Dunedin it had seemed like the only thing she could do: get away and find someone sympathetic who could sort out the whole tangled mess for her. Len had cut and run, refusing to talk to her; her mother was entirely taken up with Miss Fairchild; Miss Fairchild was the one who'd started it all. She liked to stir things up; she'd been making trouble when she'd said that about Len and Toby Underwood, that's all. But Alice needed reassurance.

What had seemed so clear to her when she'd woken up, only twenty-four hours ago at Florestan, had gotten impossibly confused. She didn't see how she could ever have thought going to Wellington would solve anything, but she simply couldn't stay still. She'd had to do *some*thing. And now she knew she owed Tucker an explanation—that was the very least she owed him. But where could she begin—

"See here," said Tucker soothingly. "There's no point in worrying now."

"But what's going to happen?"

"Nothing right away. We had a bit of a discussion about it and finally agreed that the best thing would be if your mother traveled up on the train today, so you can go back to Dunedin together tomorrow morning. There's a train at 8:40. So that gives you a whole day to catch your breath and think things over. If it weren't so filthy out, I'd give you the grand tour of Christchurch, but as it is, I thought we'd have a quiet

morning, then go and meet Jessie for lunch—she's left us the car. And
perhaps afterward, if the rain lets up, we can do a little sightseeing. I
hope you don't mind having your life arranged for you this way?''

"No." Alice made herself look up. "Actually, I'm glad. I don't
much want to think about it.'' She had been dreading another train
journey on her own, and then having to face her mother at the end. This
way Tucker and Jessie would be there with her when she met Christine,
and by the time they reached Florestan, the worst would be over. Feeling
it was inadequate, she said, ''Thank you.''

"Oh, my dear girl! You've nothing to thank *me* for—Jessie's done
it all. I only made a few suggestions.''

"You've been so kind, and you don't even know who I am, not
really," Alice persisted. ''I said I was a friend of Margery's, but that's
not exactly—it's just we go to the same school. I only started a few
weeks ago—''

"Then we'll have plenty to talk about," declared Tucker. "You can
tell me all about yourself, and in return I'll bore you with my life story.
How will that be?''

He didn't want to be thanked, Alice realized. It made him uncomfortable. "There is just one thing—" she began.

"Oh, dear. You'd better tell me—you look terribly serious.''

"I don't know what's become of my clothes.''

Tucker's face relaxed into a smile. "No, nor you do! They were a
bit, well, *traveled* looking, so I've given them a brushing. Hang on, I'll
get them.''

They set off just before noon, Alice wearing an old waterproof jacket
of Jessie's that did nicely as a coat except that the sleeves had to be
rolled up. The wind was bullying the leaves and forcing rain slantwise
in cold sheets. Alice regretted leaving the snug haven of the little house;
it reminded her of home in Cambridge. Tucker had invited her to look
around, apologizing for the clutter. "It's mine mostly," he said. "I'm

afraid I'm a very cluttery sort of person. My wife used to keep me in order—my first wife, that is. Jessie's not strict enough. It's the books mostly. I can't seem to *control* them somehow.''

It was true: books had infiltrated every room, overflowing their shelves, lying in heaps on top of tables and chairs, in piles on the floor. Books on art of all kinds, New Zealand history, sets of Dickens and Shakespeare, Jane Austen, Boswell's *Life of Johnson*, Pepys's diaries, Latin and Anglo-Saxon grammars, dictionaries, biographies of Keats and Coleridge, the complete works of Lewis Carroll, Edward Lear. Very few of them were leather-bound; they were all well used and stuck with bits of paper. On the Welsh dresser in the dining room Alice found *The Hobbit.* "In a hole in the ground there lived a hobbit,'' she read. Written on the flyleaf was "To Humphrey with thanks—J. R. R. Tolkien, 8.i.45.''

The furniture was simple and functional, designed for use rather than decoration; all the walls were painted creamy white and hung with paintings. Over the squashy fawn-colored sofa in the lounge was a long picture, little more than swashes of bright, strong color: blue, white, gold, green. It made Alice think instantly of the country she had watched endlessly unrolling from the window of the train. It had seemed inhospitable, overwhelming then, but as she looked at the painting, she felt a stir of excitement. She could almost imagine the artist standing next to her, saying, "But this is what *I* see—try looking at it *my* way instead.''

There were watercolors, too, of easily recognizable subjects: a wide, toast-brown beach contained within two dark headlands; a blue clapboard cottage with a jumble of flowers dancing in front; fishing boats tied to a pier, reflecting themselves upside down in the calm water; a cat—unmistakably Vinnie because of the ear—sitting in the sun on a doorstep, his eyes contented slits, his tail wrapped neatly over his toes; a green riverbank where ducks preened themselves in dappled sunlight.

Reluctantly Alice allowed Tucker to pry her away. She would have been quite happy, curled up on the sofa, reading about hobbits, but he had made plans. They drove sedately through the rainy streets and he pointed out some of the landmarks: the university; the river Avon, which snaked through the heart of the city, lined with grass and trees, now dripping and deserted except for a few hardy souls with umbrellas; Cathedral Square, a vast, rain-swept, open space dominated by the white-trimmed gray cathedral and dozens of wet gulls. "I do wish you could see it in the sunshine," Tucker said regretfully. "It's such a lively place. Pity you haven't more time—you'd like Akaroa. It's out near the end of the peninsula. Several of Jessie's artists live there—those watercolors you were looking at—Look, there's the gallery, just along there. I'd better park and we'll make a dash for it."

The single-story brick building was neat but unprepossessing: dark red with white trim. Over the door was a sign that read CANTERBURY ARTISTS; the windows were full of pottery and wooden bowls, silk scarves and paintings, carefully arranged so that they didn't compete with one another. Tucker opened the door for Alice and a chime rang. Inside, the big room was broken up by freestanding screens hung with more prints and paintings. There were bins of unframed work and pedestals of various heights scattered about displaying glass and pottery and small sculptures. Fanning out from the wall in several places were long wooden arms hung with woven blankets, shawls, and rugs. Alice's impression was of light and color and interesting shapes.

A young woman with glossy black hair and skin the color of milky tea was polishing a collection of small carved wooden animals at a counter near the back. She looked up and gave Tucker a wide smile as he removed his hat. "Hullo, Tucker. Rotten day. I thought you were a live one."

"No. I'm afraid not. How's your cold, Patty? Better, I hope. This is our visitor from Dunedin, Alice Jenkins. Jessie's in back, is she?"

Patty transferred her welcoming smile to Alice. She had a broad, pleasant face and black, bright eyes. "I hope you can swim, Alice," she said cheerfully. "Jessie's on the telephone. Ngai's got a hole in his radiator. He's stuck out near Okain's Bay."

"Good heavens, that sounds dire. Does he need rescuing?"

"He doesn't deserve rescuing," said Patty severely. "If he'd put some money into that van instead of cobbling it together with insulating tape and bailing wire—"

"Tucker? Is that you?" Jessie pushed through a bead curtain behind Patty, making it chatter and clack like a waterfall. "Look, I'm sorry. I know what I said, but I can't leave. I've got someone coming at a quarter to one. I think it's serious this time. He wants another look at Peggy's *Puketeraki Sheep Muster*. She's desperate to sell a painting, but I've been making her hold out for a decent price. Can you cope without me?"

"We can try," said Tucker. "The only thing better than taking one lovely lady to lunch is taking two."

Jessie rolled her eyes. "Get along with you, Humphrey Tucker. I'm not as green as I'm cabbage-looking! Don't let him talk rubbish all afternoon, Alice. He will if he thinks he can get away with it."

Alice glanced at Tucker and was surprised to see him grinning happily. His feelings had evidently not been wounded. "The trouble with you Kiwis is that you don't understand old-world charm. Nevertheless I shall keep trying."

"Yes, I expect you will," agreed Jessie dryly. "I'll see you back at the house, then. I should be home by six. We'll go along after supper and collect your mother."

Alice nodded, sorry to be reminded. She had deliberately steered her thoughts away from that.

"Right," said Tucker. "We're off."

He took Alice to a busy little café near the university, full of damp, noisy students and faculty types fortifying themselves with oceans of thick, brown oxtail soup and huge plates of shepherd's pie, fruit tarts swimming in gloppy yellow custard and sticky jam sponges. "We'd have gone somewhere else with Jessie," he confided. "She doesn't really approve of student stodge, but there are times when it's very comforting, wouldn't you agree? Besides, it reminds me of home." He settled back contentedly, and Alice, who hadn't thought she had an appetite, found herself putting away an enormous portion of fried fish and chips. The café was too crowded and noisy for serious conversation, and frequently someone would stop by their table and greet Tucker. Each time he introduced Alice, but she gave up the attempt to remember names. At Tucker's urging she had caramel custard for dessert. "It's one of my vices," he told her, beaming, "and it's very nice here."

By the time they'd finished, the rain had indeed let up, so he drove out of the city, along the Summit Road, with the Port Hills on one side and Lyttelton Harbor on the other. On the windy heights he found a place to stop the car, and they got out and stood pressed against it, watching clouds sweep across the hills like huge steel gray combers, breaking in brief, vivid flashes of light.

"It's so big," said Alice after a while. "I feel very small."

"Mmm. New Zealand is like that. If you look at a map of the world, it's only a speck—not much bigger than Britain really. Odd that it should be so different—all sky and open spaces."

"You are English, aren't you," said Alice. She'd been puzzling over it for some time.

"Yes, quite right. Jessie says I'm too old to lose my accent—I'll always sound like a Pom. I was born in Sussex, not far from Brighton, actually—oh, more years ago than I like to remember. Educated at Oxford, then I taught there, at New College. English literature."

"Why did you come *here*?" Of all places, she thought, but didn't add aloud.

"Oh, goodness. Well, I did promise you my life history, didn't I? Is that a spot of rain? Yes? Why don't we sit in the car, out of this bracing wind." Once they were settled, he gave her his slightly apologetic smile. "Now where—it was four years ago last March that my wife died, 1954. She'd been ill, you see, for a long time. We hadn't any children—it might have been different if we had, I suppose. But there it is. Suddenly Jane was gone and I was on my own. I felt the way I expect you must have—that I couldn't stay still, I had to *do* something. It happens to all of us, I dare say, at one time or another." He sat silent for a minute or two. Alice felt the car shake, buffeted by explosions of air.

"Well, at any rate, when you've been around a university as long as I have, you accumulate a great many former students. It's quite amazing the number of them who go on to exotic parts of the world. Every year I'd get all these Christmas cards with messages—'Should you ever find yourself in New South Wales, be sure to let us know,' and 'Do plan to stay with us when next you're in Tallahassee—' I don't suppose any of them really expected to see me." He chuckled. "I sold up everything—not my books, of course—I packed those and left them with a friend until I could send for them. Jessie was quite appalled when the crates arrived. I'm sure most of my colleagues thought, 'Poor old fellow, he's gone right round the bend, has Humphrey.' In Oxford, you see, I was Humphrey. The long and short of it is that I needed a change. There are times when there's nothing else for it. You come to the end of something, and rather than hang on when it's over, you've the chance to leap into something quite new."

"But how did you get here? Were you visiting students?"

"I had a colleague who'd emigrated to Christchurch. He was teaching here at the university, and I thought seeing as I'd got as far as Australia, I might as well see a bit of New Zealand too. Then I was planning to go on to Hong Kong. I never did find Michael—he was gone by the time I arrived, but I liked Christchurch. That was nearly two years ago—"

"You've been here for two years?" Alice tried to imagine it. It seemed like a very long time to her. *One* year looked endless. "Don't you miss home?"

"England, d'you mean? Well, yes, once in a while I do. Bound to really. I had a very good life there for sixty-odd years. But I've got a very good life here now. I'd never have met Jessie if I'd stayed in Oxford. I'd have missed such a lot of things."

"Don't you want to go back?"

He didn't answer right away, then with a trace of regret he said, "I don't suppose I ever will. I thought about that when Jessie and I got married. Then I thought I'd go back for my books, but in the end I had them shipped. It's such a long way. And you, Alice. Are you so very homesick?"

Her throat closed suddenly and she could only nod.

"I am sorry. But you're young, you'll go back again if it's what you want. In a few more years you'll be able to decide things like that for yourself. I don't suppose you wanted to come in the first place, did you?"

"She didn't ask me. She just told me we were coming. It wasn't fair."

"Mmm. Well you see," said Tucker, "life *isn't* fair. I never have understood why we teach children to expect it to be. I don't want to pry, you understand, but you weren't by any chance trying to get back to England, were you?"

"No." Alice shivered.

"Oh, I say, you're cold, aren't you. Here, let's have some heat. Hang on a tick—it'll come." He started the engine. "I didn't honestly believe you would be—trying to get home, I mean. You seem much too sensible for that. It's just—well, whatever you were trying to do, clearly you aren't going to have the chance, at least not now."

"That's all right," said Alice, clasping her hands tightly in her lap. "It wouldn't have done any good anyway. I don't know why I thought it would. I've got to work it out somehow myself."

Tucker nodded sympathetically. "If it would help you at all to talk, I'm quite good at listening."

She looked at him gratefully, thinking what a thoroughly nice person he was. "What I don't understand," she said finally, knowing he would understand if she changed the subject, "is why Margery doesn't seem to know about you. When she talked about her aunt, she made it sound— well, as if she weren't married."

"Yes. Well, Jessie and I have a difference of opinion on that subject, actually. I've met her family once or twice, but as a friend. I'm afraid that Jessie's just the slightest bit ashamed of me."

"Ashamed?" echoed Alice in disbelief. "How could she possibly be?"

"The trouble is, Alice, that Malcolm's been after her for years to marry someone dull and respectable. Someone like me. He's always been terrified she'd marry a wild-eyed Bohemian artist with long hair, dirty feet, and unconventional habits. Malcolm's a good-natured sort really, but dreadfully conservative and just a bit on the stuffy side."

"But you're not! *I* don't think you're dull."

He beamed at her and gave her hands a pat. "Bless you, Alice. That's very kind. I rather think your friend Margery might disagree, however. And Jessie's extremely fond of Margery. She worries about her. Malcolm has such inflexible views on certain subjects—"

"But how can Margery decide anything if she doesn't know you? It isn't fair not to give her the chance."

"I'm working on Jessie. Water dripping on a stone, gradually wearing it down. It's a curious thing, but I find the older I get the more patience I seem to have. I would have expected it to be the other way round somehow, wouldn't you? Gracious! Look at the time. We must start back."

As soon as he said it, Alice's mother joined them ghostlike in the car. She was somewhere on the train at that very moment, drawing inexorably closer by the minute. She'd be with them in person that evening, demanding an explanation from Alice for what she'd done. Alice couldn't imagine what she'd say. What did you say to someone you suddenly suspected had lied to you all your life? She stared out the window, unseeing. If Miss Fairchild was right, if Len was—if Toby Underwood *wasn't*—her father, after all these years—fourteen of them, her whole life—that meant they were all of them not the people she had always thought they were. How, she wondered in a kind of panic, was she going to find out who she really was?

They went back to 53 Bessant Street and Tucker made tea. Alice laid the table for supper, and Jessie came home. They sat down and ate—but what they ate, and what they talked about, Alice could never remember afterward. It was time to leave for the station, and Alice still didn't know what she was going to say to her mother. Every time she tried to work it out, it was as if someone came along and turned out the light, leaving her head full of stifling blackness.

At the station Tucker let them out by the entrance and went off to leave the car. "Come on then," said Jessie. "It won't get any easier. Once she sees you really are safe, she'll be absolutely furious with you. That's generally the way it works. But it won't last."

There was nothing to do but stand on the platform and wait. Alice felt numb and stupid, her mouth dry, her hands damp.

"Where on earth has Tucker got to?" said Jessie impatiently. "He must have parked the car back at Bessant Street."

Somewhere down the line they heard a signal. Alice's fingers crept up and wound themselves in her hair. Just as the train chuffed into sight, Tucker came hurrying out of the station, a look of triumph on his face. "See? What did I tell you! Here you are, Alice." And he held out her school satchel. "Lost and found. The lady behind the counter wasn't going to give it to me—she said she was quite sure I couldn't be the owner. But I told her your name and there it was, on the flap inside. She made me sign for it."

"And so she should. If ever I've seen a suspicious-looking character, Humphrey Tucker—"

Alice fumbled with the buckles, managing to get them open, and looked inside. Everything was there: the clock, her school skirt—and she could feel the five-pound note in the pocket.

"What does she look like?" asked Jessie.

The train had pulled to a stop and people were leaning out of windows, unlatching the doors.

"Here," said Tucker, "you look and I'll do it up again."

Her fingers were too clumsy to deal with the buckles, so she surrendered it. Passengers climbed off and were met, or hurried away by themselves, or paused to gather up children and luggage; they shrugged into overcoats, hailed porters, jostled one another and excused themselves. Alice searched up and down, her heart beating like a drum in her ears. The crowd began to thin, and there was no sign of her mother. Christine did not miss trains. Something terrible must have happened, something to do with Len. It had to be Len. Tucker said she hadn't mentioned him. He hadn't come back. She'd been right—there'd been an accident—

"Ally?"

She spun around. "Len?" It was as if she'd conjured him up out of thin air. "*Len!* But why—what are you doing here?"

He shrugged apologetically. "I thought I'd save Chrissie the trip, see. And give us a chance to talk. You and me?"

"Where did you go? What happened to you? Why did you disappear like that?"

Len shifted awkwardly from foot to foot. He glanced away from her, his eyes sliding past Tucker and Jessie, who stood a few steps away, not intruding. "I know, Ally, I know. I couldn't help it. I just, well, I had to get away for a bit, is all. I never meant—" His voice trailed off.

Alice stared at him. Like a lightning rod he drew her anger. A sudden white flash exploded behind her eyes. It had never occurred to her that Len would come instead of her mother. Never. She blinked, shook her head to clear it. There was Tucker, watching her, raising his eyebrows inquiringly. They hadn't a clue who this man was, of course. She coughed to loosen the tightness in her throat. "This is Leonard Jenkins," she said. "My stepfather." And stopped. The word sounded strange in her ears, the way words sometimes did when you repeated them over and over so often they lost their meaning.

"Ah, Mr. Jenkins." Jessie moved smoothly into the gap Alice had left. She shook hands. "I'm Margery's aunt, Jessie MacInnes, and this is my husband, Humphrey Tucker. We'd been expecting your wife."

"Yeah, I know. It's been a strain on her, these last days. And she's got Miss Fairchild to look after, so I said why didn't I come. She said I was to be sure and tell you how grateful she was, you looking after Alice the way you have.''

"It's been a pleasure," Tucker assured him.

There was an awkward silence. "Well," said Jessie, "no point in standing about here. If that's all you've got, Mr.——"

"Len," said Len. "Yeah, just the rucksack."

"Right. Where'd you put the car, Tucker?"

— 28 —

It's Not That Simple

Tucker made them sandwiches for the journey, and Jessie took them to the station on her way to the gallery Wednesday morning. There were no elaborate good-byes, no fussing. Jessie was matter-of-fact. She said she'd see Alice on her next visit to Dunedin, no doubt. She might even call on Miss Fairchild. "Perhaps I can convince her to let me have a few more of her paintings. You never know. I should be able to do very well for her this time." "Perhaps," said Alice, greatly daring, "Tucker might come with you." She hated the thought of not seeing him again. Jessie gave her an odd look as Len shut the car door, but all she said was, "Safe journey," and then she drove off, leaving Alice and Len alone together.

Len bought their tickets and they went outside to wait on the platform. The dirty clouds had blown away overnight and the sky was a new-washed blue, hung with clean fluffy little ones. They were early; they sat on one of the benches, preserving a careful distance. By the time the train came, Alice had begun to believe they might actually travel all the way back to Dunedin without speaking. Eight hours of fraught silence. Stubbornly she resolved that she would not be the one to break it. That was up to Len. He'd said he wanted the chance to talk to her, so let him start.

By the time they had gotten back to Bessant Street the night before, it had been half past eight. By their presence Tucker and Jessie had diffused some of the tension that was humming between Alice and Len. Alice avoided direct conversation with Len altogether, surprised herself at the anger she felt toward him. Len made it easy by spending an hour straightening out the connections on Jessie's Hoovermatic washing machine, which had spewed soapy water all over the kitchen floor in their absence. Tucker was greatly admiring. "I've never been the slightest use with anything mechanical. Machines seem to see me coming," he said. "But I've always told Jessie I thought there was something wrong with an automatic washing machine that wouldn't fill itself or do the rinsing for you. Only one step removed from pounding your clothes on rocks beside the Avon, if you see what I mean."

"Trouble with you, Tucker," said Jessie sardonically, "is that you've gotten lazy in your old age."

"Yeah, well," said Len, "whoever hooked it up for you hadn't a clue."

"Very likely. Ngai's as bad as Tucker when it comes to machines. He did it as a favor."

Len spent the night downstairs, on the squashy sofa. It was clear to Alice at breakfast that Tucker and Jessie had held a conference in the privacy of their bedroom once everyone had gone to bed, because there was no discussion: everything had been arranged.

The train came from the ferry dock in Lyttelton, and many of the passengers looked rumpled and heavy-eyed, as if they had spent a less than restful night on the crossing from Wellington. Alice and Len found seats to themselves, facing one another. Alice settled into hers and glanced at Len. He was looking out the window, apparently absorbed in something on the platform, but she'd seen his eyes flicker away from her. Determined not to make it easy, she took *Rebecca* out of her satchel.

Poor *Rebecca* was as travel-weary as anyone on the train: her corners bumped and her cover creased. Alice smoothed it as best she could, thinking she'd probably have to buy Helen another copy, and opened to her bookmark. Right off she found she hadn't the slightest idea what was going on, and couldn't even remember the heroine's name. She searched for it without success, wishing she'd thought to buy a magazine in the station instead. With an irritable sigh she turned back to chapter one and began at the beginning: "Last night I dreamt I went to Manderley again. It seemed to me I stood by the iron gate leading to the drive. . . ."

"Ally?"

She glued her eyes to the page. The heroine, who by page 51 still hadn't identified herself, had just been proposed to over coffee and marmalade by the enigmatic, haunted Maxim de Winter. In spite of herself, Alice had become interested, but at the sound of Len's voice the words scattered like a flock of startled birds.

"Alice."

"Mmm." " 'One day,' he went on, spreading his toast thick, 'you may realize that philanthropy is not my strongest quality. . . .' " She read the words without understanding them.

"I think we'd better—I mean, there's things we've got to talk about," said Len diffidently.

"*I* wanted to talk Sunday morning," Alice stated without looking up. " 'Are you going to marry me?' " asked Maxim de Winter on the page.

"How was I to know that, Ally? And anyroad, there wasn't time— not with the party. You could see that."

He wanted her to say yes. She said, "You knew, Len, and you took off. You didn't even say you were going. It was a rotten thing to do."

"It was all those people—I couldn't face them. I lost my nerve, that's what."

"No," said Alice. "That wasn't it." Deliberately she turned a page. He was silent so long she couldn't hold out; she raised her eyes.

This time he flinched, but didn't look away. "I wish I knew what to say to you."

"Tell me if it's true, what Miss Fairchild said."

At least he didn't pretend not to know what she meant. "Oh, crikey, Ally, I don't know." For an awful moment she thought he was going to cry. He rubbed a hand over his face, hard, working for control. "It's God's own truth. I don't know."

"But it could be. You think it is."

He turned his head to watch the country spreading away, toward the distant jagged line of the Southern Alps, but she didn't think he was seeing it. At last he said, "I've been over it and over it in my head. It'd have to be more than fifteen years ago—"

"That's my whole life."

"Yeah." He nodded unhappily. "But think about it, Ally. That would mean Chrissie'd got it wrong, or she—" He broke off. "Have you ever heard your mum say something that wasn't true? I haven't. Not in all the time I've known her."

Reluctantly Alice said, "No."

"Well, there you are then. See?" He sat back, looking relieved.

But it wasn't that simple, it couldn't be. He'd started this now; they had to carry it through to the end, wherever that might lead them. Alice knew it, and so, she was sure, did Len. "Miss Fairchild's right, I don't look like him. Like Toby Underwood. Not at all."

"That doesn't prove anything. Lots of kids don't look like their old man."

"I look like you. It's always been a joke before, but now it isn't. What she said, about fathers knowing their children—"

"Hang on, Ally, that's not what she meant."

Oh, yes it is, thought Alice, staring at him, but aloud she said, surprising herself, "Did you know him, Len? Toby Underwood?" It had never occurred to her to ask him that before. Her mother was the one who talked about Toby, never Len. Nothing odd in that; by the time Len and Christine got married, Toby was three years dead.

"No, of course I didn't. Why would I? Well, you couldn't really say I *knew* him—I only met him the once."

"You never told me."

"There was nothing to tell, Ally. Honest. We barely spoke. It never seemed worth mentioning."

She brushed the excuse aside. "When did you meet him?"

He gave a defeated little shrug. "All right, I'll tell you. But there's nothing to it. It was a bit awkward, really. I'd just been called up—that would've made it November 1941. Chrissie had a bed-sit in Cambridge then. She was a secretary at Clare—that was his college." He appeared to relax a little, the words came easier. This was safer ground. "I wasn't too keen on going off to fight. Tell you the truth, I was scared witless. The only person I could think of would care at all, at least wish me luck and that, was Chrissie. I reckoned she'd give me a bit of a send-off. I'd been working at a garage in Newmarket, and I had some time before I had to show up, so I went to see her." He paused, studying his hands, which were clasped between his knees.

"Go on."

"Yeah, well. We went to this pub Chrissie liked—all brass and beams and full of university nobs. Not my kind of place, but the beer was all right and I didn't care where we were so long as I was with Chrissie. So anyroad, there we sat, the two of us, having a quiet drink, and your dad—well, he wasn't then, of course—Toby Underwood comes in with some of his mates. They're all in uniform—officers, the lot—and he spots Chrissie and stops by for a word with her, that's all."

"I don't understand. Why was it awkward?"

"She introduced us—we shook hands. He was polite enough, but I could see what he was thinking."

"What?" Alice frowned, impatient.

Len sighed. "Well, the war was on and people didn't reckon you much if you weren't in uniform by then. They figured you for a coward. Chrissie explained about it being a kind of farewell visit, that I'd just been called up, but that only made it worse. He'd joined up right off, see. Hadn't waited to be nobbled. Not that it mattered really. I didn't think I'd ever clap eyes on him again, and I never did. Tell you the truth, Ally, I forgot all about Toby Underwood after that, until years later.''

"When the war was over and you came back to England," Alice supplied. She knew the story from there, how Len had returned from Italy, astonished to find himself still in one piece, and sure that by then Christine was happily married with a kid or two. She had the kid: Alice, eighteen months old, but no husband, and instead of a house of her own, she'd been forced to go back and live with her parents, in their tiny bungalow in Wroxley. She was struggling to save enough from her wages as the local doctor's receptionist so she could get out from under and make a life for herself again.

Len, not believing his luck, shot off to Cambridge and got a job doing maintenance on the city buses, and eventually found a little flat he could offer her, over a newsagent's near the station: shabby but decent. Then, despite Mr. and Mrs. Pickell's warnings and openly expressed disapproval, Christine had accepted Len's proposal of marriage. She'd packed up her baby and gone to Cambridge with him, and he'd become Alice's stepfather. He always joked that it was because Christine would rather her daughter be a Jenkins than a gherkin. It was some years before Alice was old enough to understand that.

And now Len had just presented her with a new piece to fit into the familiar story, but instead of completing the picture, it made her realize there were others missing. If he hadn't told her about meeting Toby Underwood, what else hadn't he told her? She had to work out the right questions; she guessed he wouldn't just volunteer the answers. She was aware that he was watching her.

He said, "She told me, straight out when I went round to see her. It was a Sunday afternoon, after dinner. We were all sitting in your grandparents' front room—they weren't best pleased to see me. Your grandda'd been having a kip, I remember, he didn't like being disturbed. Anyroad, Chrissie told me right off who your dad was and that he wasn't coming back. That he'd been killed in Corsica before you were born, and that she wanted you to know about him when you were old enough. She'd forgotten about the pub, but I recognized the name.''

"Before that," said Alice slowly. "You'd seen her while you were in the army, hadn't you? I mean, after the pub.''

"Well—" he hesitated, looking away from her. "Well, I might've done. Once or twice. I had leave, so I'd stop round to say hullo, see how she was getting on.''

The pieces were starting to appear. Studying his face, she knew she'd got it right. She waited, unsure of the next question.

Finally, reluctantly, he said, "I had a leave, just before they shipped me out to Italy. Two days, that was all." He clasped and unclasped his fingers. "There wasn't anything said—about after the war. You know, what would happen—''

"About getting married," said Alice.

Len gave her a lopsided smile and nodded. "One of the few times I didn't ask her. Well, I was dead sure I was never coming back. All that mattered then was those two days we had. Nothing that happened to me after could take them away. I didn't know about him—your dad. She didn't say and I never asked.''

Alice digested this in silence. "Well," she said at last. "There's one way to find out for certain. I'll ask Mum, straight out. She'll have to tell me the truth.''

On the instant Len's expression changed. "Aw, Ally, you can't do that!''

"Why not?" she demanded, her voice rising. She forced it down again. "I've the right to know, Len. Don't you want to know? Suppose Miss Fairchild's right? Suppose you're my father?" She'd said it.

He gave her a stricken look. "Oh God, Ally. What if I am? Does it really make a difference now? We're all right as we are.''

"How can you say that? If it's true, she's been *lying*.''

He pulled himself together. "Not your mum. Not Chrissie.''

"Can you swear, word of honor, that Miss Fairchild's wrong then?"

"It's not that simple."

"Why isn't it? Either you're my father or you're not, Len. Either Mum's told the truth, or she's lied."

"Look, Ally. When I was in Italy, sure any minute I'd be blown to bits, I used to dream about Chrissie. I'd pretend she was my girl, see. I'd imagine how it'd be, going back to her—me with a medal or two, something to be proud of. She'd open her door and there I'd be, standing on the step, and she'd throw her arms around me, and I'd carry her off into the sunset. Just like in a film. I knew it wasn't going to happen, not really. But I had to have something to hang on to, just to get on day to day."

Stubbornly Alice shook her head. "I don't understand what you're saying."

He made a face. "I'm no good at this—but your mum, Ally. She had a hard time, too. She wanted to go to university—well, you know that. When we were in school in Wroxley, she used to talk about it. 'When I'm at Cambridge,' she'd say, and go on and on about all the wonderful things she'd be able to do. Me, I couldn't wait to get out. Not Chrissie. She's clever, your mum. She's got real brains. She could've gotten a grant, but her dad said that was foolishness, nothing but a waste of time for a girl. What she needed was typing and shorthand, so she could keep herself until she got married. And of course her mum wasn't well. Chrissie reckoned she'd got to stay home and help out, and then it was too late—there was the war—"

"I *know* all of this. What's it got to do with anything?" Alice suspected Len of trying to change the subject.

He dropped his head in his hands and scrubbed at his thinning hair. "Well, he was part of all that, your dad. What she couldn't have, wasn't he? Like me pretending she'd be there when I came back, waiting for me. Thing is, see, *my* dream came true."

Alice took the photograph out of *Rebecca*. Her hand shook as she held it. "He's nothing to do with me then. Perhaps they barely knew each other, that's what you're saying. That's why she never told his parents about me." A round, dark spot fell on Toby Underwood's feet. Angrily she brushed at it. She wanted to crumple the picture, tear it to bits, destroy it.

"You don't know that, Ally." Len leaned forward and gently took the photograph from her, as if he guessed. "It might not be that way at all. It could be just what she said. Can't you just let it alone—go on believing what Chrissie's told you all these years? Where's the harm? She's given you a good father."

"But he's *dead*. He's been dead all my life. It's not *fair*, Len." As she said it, she heard Tucker's voice: "Life isn't fair. . . ."

Len was silent for several minutes, visibly struggling with something. Then he looked at her. "I'll tell you, Ally. Straight. If Chrissie'd opened the door that Sunday and said to me, 'Leonard Jenkins, this is your daughter,' I'd've been shattered. I've been thinking about it since Saturday, wondering what I'd've done. Most likely I'd've cut and run—just like my da. Your mum knew me better than anyone, than I knew myself even. She had me pegged right from when we started school together. Maybe she guessed. I only went to look her up, see she was all right, no more than that. I wasn't going to bother her again, I'd made up my mind. I'd clear out of her life for good. It never crossed my mind that I might—well, about a kid. What did I have to give a *kid*?"

"But then why did you marry her? Why did you adopt me?" Alice's voice was unsteady.

"That was different. I didn't have to worry about being a father, not a real one. See, I did have *some*thing to give you, Ally—I had a name. And I could help Chrissie get away from Wroxley. I rang the doorbell and it was just like in my dream, only better. It was a bleeding fairy tale, Ally, ogres and all—you know, her mum and dad."

He was trying very hard to make her smile, but she couldn't. She felt hopelessly confused, lost. All her landmarks were gone, swallowed up as if there'd been an earthquake. The landscape of her life was irrevocably altered. She had no idea how long she sat frozen, but gradually the numbness receded a little. "So you haven't told her anything."

He shook his head.

"Why does she think I left?"

"She thought it had to do with her making you pass sandwiches at the party. Oh, not just that, of course—other things as well. She's afraid you've been unhappy ever since you got here, and she's been too busy— well, you know. When you didn't come back after school Monday— I've never seen her that upset. I tried to make her believe it was my fault, about the tent and then cutting out like that on Sunday. I said if she let me fetch you, I could maybe patch things up a bit. It took some convincing. She really does love you, Ally."

"Oh, Len." She blinked furiously. "What am I going to do?" She wasn't asking him, and he didn't try to answer. She thought of him, sitting stiffly in the front room in Wroxley, in his uniform without any medals, the smells of Sunday dinner still heavy on the air, her grandparents, whom she scarcely remembered, regarding him with unfriendly eyes, while her mother told him about her baby—about Alice. It's not that simple, Len said, but why couldn't it be? It *should* have been—

"Ally, I haven't any right asking you a favor. I know that—"

She wanted desperately to be angry with him. Anger was something she could grasp: hard and sharp, solid. But instead she felt desolation; it stretched away from her on every side, deep and shoreless, like the gray ocean from the *Cassiopeia*. Only this time she was alone in the middle. There were no fellow passengers for company, no captain for guidance. She had to find her own way.

"Don't tell her. Please don't. It'll only cause pain."

She laced her fingers in her hair and pulled fiercely, wanting it to hurt. Cause her mother pain, that's what he meant. She could accuse him of being a coward—he'd only agree. But it was more than that, it wasn't that simple. Taking a deep, shaky breath, she said, "You haven't even asked me where I was going."

"No. I didn't think I had the right to, not after Sunday," he said humbly. "See, I just wanted you to come back, so we could be like always—Chrissie and you and me. That's all that matters, Ally, isn't it?"

— 29 —

Telling Stories: 1976

"So in all this time you've never asked your mother," Margery said.

"No. I almost did—several times. But something always stopped me." Alice looked at her friend, reflecting that she'd have known Margery MacInnes anywhere, in spite of the fourteen years they'd been apart.

Margery stopped the car and they got out. They stood together on the rough, grassy spine of the Otago Peninsula, beside the Soldiers' Memorial, where there was a wide view of the city. It caught Alice unexpectedly, this sight of Dunedin. Her eyes devoured it with a hunger that surprised her. She had wondered how it would feel, returning after all those years, most of them spent in Montreal. Only too well she remembered her fourteen-year-old self, how hard it had been for that Alice Jenkins to adjust to New Zealand. She had been afraid that coming back would prove a mistake, but her heart lifted as she gazed out over the marbled blue-green of the harbor, to the city sprinkled like sugar crystals on the hills beyond, under the astonishing vastness of the sky. "I've missed Dunedin," she said, only then realizing how true it was.

"You couldn't wait to get away. You were off as soon as you left Saint Kat's," Margery pointed out dryly.

Alice nodded. "I know. I felt I was being squeezed by everything. That I would never be able to find myself unless I could escape, put as much distance between me and Mum and Len as possible. As long as we were together I couldn't see us clearly. But it's time does that, not space." She drew in a deep breath of the iodine-smelling air. "What I did escape from was Florestan. It wasn't a happy house to live in. After Emilia died and Mum wrote me she'd willed it to Dunedin as the Clement R. Fairchild Museum, I remember thinking, good, no one will ever have to live there again."

"And now that you've had a guided tour?" asked Margery.

"The odd thing is," said Alice slowly, "that nothing's changed. Oh, the grounds are smaller, of course. They sold a lot of land for an endowment. The tennis courts and Mr. Tatlock's sheep are gone, and the lawn looks beautiful. There's a lot of fresh paint and the lighting's better, and Mum would approve of the tearoom in the garage, but it doesn't *feel* any different from when we lived there. It was a museum *then*, Margery. One that had been closed up for years, probably since Mr. Fairchild himself died."

"Interesting," said Margery. "They've taken almost all of Emilia Fairchild out of it. Her paintings are in the gallery at the university, and they've got her journals and letters as well. She wouldn't recognize her study if she could see it now—except for the Turner." She grinned.

"Yes, but they've kept some of her earliest stuff for display. The first sketchbooks, when she was painting pretty little Bavarian villages and Italian farms. They've also still got the incomplete manuscript of the book she and Mum were working on—the history of the house. I'll have to spend some time at Florestan, sorting through it. And, of course, she grew up there. If I'm going to write her biography—" She broke off, then said, "I don't know how Mum stood it, living there for ten years, especially after Len died. The Patersons were a help. She said Mr.

Paterson was very handy, and Mrs. Paterson did most of the cooking. At least she and Emilia weren't up there all alone.''

"I was sorry about your stepfather. I liked him.''

Alice gave her a lopsided smile, a familiar lump rising in her throat. "I'd've come back in spite of classes, but with an accident like that there's no time. It happened so suddenly—not like an illness. I never imagined when I left I'd never see him again. I wished so often—'' She bit her lip. "There were so many things we didn't talk about, Margery, and then it was too late. I was convinced he was wrong.''

"About being your father?'' Margery was frankly curious, didn't attempt to hide it.

"No, not about that. I'm sure he was. He would have guessed it right away if he'd let himself, but he didn't want to. It was easier for him to believe what Mum told him. I thought he was wrong about my not asking Mum.''

"I don't see why you didn't just have it out when you came back from Christchurch. You could have cleared the air once and for all. That's what I'd've done.''

"I'm sure you would,'' said Alice with a little laugh. "But I couldn't, because of Len.''

"It wasn't fair of him to make you promise.'' Margery sounded judgmental.

"He didn't. He only asked me not to. It isn't as simple as that.'' Hearing an echo in her memory, Alice caught her breath. "It was because he was honest with me. When he came back from the war, Mum told him what he needed to hear, whether it was the truth or not, and he stayed with us. Maybe he would have stayed anyway, I don't know, but I think there's a good chance he would have disappeared. We could have managed on our own, Mum and I, but in the end I realized that I would far rather have known Len as my stepfather than not have known him as my father. He could be infuriating—he never hid his faults the way Mum did hers. All the same.''

Silent for a minute, Margery said, "Afterward, though. When your mother went back to England, why didn't you ask her then? It wouldn't have mattered to Len. Well, I mean—" She stopped, aware of being indelicate.

"You're right. He'd been dead more than three years. But there didn't seem any point," said Alice slowly. "It's taken me a long time to appreciate what Len was trying to tell me that day on the train, about people giving themselves the stories they need in order to survive. Life must have been pretty awful for Mum when I was born—she'd had to give up her job and go back to live in Wroxley. She had a baby and no husband, which was bad enough in a village like that, and my grandparents never made a secret of what they thought of Len. He wasn't good enough for their daughter, not by a long chalk. Out of desperation she picked Toby Underwood. She knew she was safe because he wasn't coming back. She'd never met his family—I don't think she even knew where they lived. She convinced everyone he was my father. By the time Emilia fired off that quotation from *The Merchant of Venice*, about wise fathers, Mum had long since come to believe her own story. When I was fourteen, I refused to believe that was possible. Either a thing was true or it was a lie. I must have been a real little snot."

"You and everyone else," said Margery sagely. "It's a stage of life you get through any way you can, and then, if you're lucky, you forget it."

"That's what Emilia Fairchild said to me the very first time I met her. She looked me in the eyes and told me how much she disliked adolescent girls. 'The best way to deal with them' "—Alice imitated Miss Fairchild's voice—" 'is to send them away to school—*far* away—until they grow out of it.' "

"Well, and so she did, didn't she?" said Margery, laughing. "She sent you to McGill in Canada. My father was dumbfounded, you know. He was sure she'd gone bonkers, finally and irreversibly."

Grinning back, Alice said, "I can imagine." Then she grew serious again. "It was Len. He had a lot to do with it, though I never knew exactly what. She hinted at it in her letters. You know she wrote to me?''

"Yes. We discussed you."

"My ears used to burn. Now I know why."

"What I never understood though was why Canada? I thought you were dead set on Cambridge."

"Because of Mum. *She* was dead set on Cambridge. She believed it was heaven on earth. For a while I actually considered not going to university at all, just to spite her, until I realized I'd only be spiting myself more because I really did want to go. So instead I chose a school as far away as possible that wasn't Cambridge. Miss Sallet was super. She suggested McGill and finally managed to convince Mum it was all right."

"And now look at you: Dr. Jenkins. How very grand! Your mother must be ecstatic."

"Yes, she's pleased, but oddly enough it doesn't matter such a lot to her anymore. She's got a job doing research for the BBC, did I write you? She loves it. They're filming a series on the great private houses in Britain, all art and architecture and titled families. And she's bought a comfortable little flat in Highgate Village with the legacy Emilia left her."

"Good," said Margery warmly. "She earned it, putting up with Emilia all those years. Even Pa thought so. But then he owed your mother a tremendous debt himself. If it hadn't been for her, he'd have had to deal with Emilia."

"But Margery, she's happy. Really happy. I think for the first time since I've known her."

"What about Len?"

"She misses him. She really did love him. But she's in control now. Her life's what she wants it to be. Look, Margery, didn't you say you had to be home by four?"

" 'Strewth—that can't be the time! They'll have murdered one another if I don't get back and feed them their tea. They're dreadfully bloodthirsty—you don't know, really you don't. They were on their best behavior yesterday for Aunt Alice's arrival.''

"Ankle-biters," said Alice. They smiled at each other.

"If you'd gone to Helen instead, you could have had peace and tranquility. Her household's extremely well regulated, not a bit like ours.''

They climbed back into the car, Margery backed it around, and they bumped down the track to Highcliff Road. She turned right, away from Dunedin, toward Macandrew Bay. Margery and her bearded, bulky, imperturbable doctor husband, Robin Doyle, lived in a house perched above the settlement, with three small children, two dogs, innumerable cats, four goats, and a shaggy blond pony. There was a big stone studio out back that used to be a barn. There were heaps of muddy boots by the kitchen door, dog hair on all the carpets, books and games strewn everywhere, dirty mugs in the sink, and a basketful of clean, unironed laundry on the upstairs landing. Alice, used to the calm, self-centered arrangement of her own apartment in Montreal, found Margery's house chaotic, but she liked it. The air was charged with energy. Margery'd invited her to stay until she could find a furnished flat somewhere near the university, convenient to Emilia Fairchild's paintings and papers. The university accommodations officer had written Alice a very encouraging letter before she left Montreal.

"Well," she said tentatively, "I'm sure I still could. I mean, if it's inconvenient for you to put me up. Helen said I was welcome and I know they've got lots of room—''

Margery flashed her green eyes on Alice, ignoring the road for a perilous moment. "If you're serious, Alice Jenkins, I may never speak to you again.''

"You haven't spoken to me in fourteen years," Alice reminded her. "You've barely written. I get most of my news from Tucker. *He* sends regular letters.''

"Tucker's a peach," agreed Margery warmly, swerving away from the stone wall that suddenly loomed ahead. "I've never been a peach.

Anyway, you two are writers. Jessie and I are *visual*. That's why we all agreed you were the one to write Emilia Fairchild's biography.''

"I'm longing to see them again. They wanted me to stop in Christchurch on my way down from Auckland, but it seemed better to fly direct to Dunedin and get settled first. Tucker says Jessie can't keep your paintings in the gallery, Margery. They sell as soon as she hangs them.''

"Well, of course. I'm good. I always said I would be, didn't I?''

"Yes, you did.''

"What are you laughing for? I've worked bloody hard at it—Emilia made me. She was a terrible teacher, mind you—tyrannical, inflexible, egotistical, and that's not the half. After a couple of hours in her studio I'd leave Florestan blinded by tears of rage and frustration. But I learned from her. And she'd never have bothered with me if I hadn't had talent, you know.''

"She liked you,'' said Alice. "From that first afternoon, when she caught us in her studio. I envied you because of it, did you know? I always felt I disappointed her, letting Len bring me back to Florestan so tamely. If I'd had any spirit at all, I'd have run away properly, the way she did.''

"You said you weren't running away.''

"What about your father?'' asked Alice, changing the subject. "Has he come round at all now that you're famous?''

Margery gave a snort. "He still thinks my painting's a waste of time, if that's what you mean. But he shut up after I married Robin, who, while he's not a solicitor like Helen's husband, nonetheless has a respectable profession.''

"I wish I'd been at your wedding. I'd love to have seen you in a long white gown, Margery.''

"They ganged up on me—even Jessie. She said where was the harm in making him happy? If he wanted to spend all that money, let him. I'd never have to do it again. If you want to see photographs, you'll have to ask Ma. She's got them done up in a white satin album with pink roses on the cover. I'd never have gotten married at all, you understand, if it weren't for Emilia. It was her fault. When Dr. Lattimer went kiting off to teach in Auckland and she had the stroke—''

"Mum said Robin was very good with her.''

"Oh, he has the patience of a saint,'' agreed Margery wryly. "A real martyr complex, Jessie claims, taking on Emilia first, then me.''

"He's nice.''

"He's all right.'' Margery sounded offhand, but her expression betrayed her. She stopped the car and Alice got out to open the gate with a sign on it that said DOYLE. "I'll walk up,'' she called, waving Margery through. Margery nodded and drove past.

Alice latched the gate carefully—the goats made her think of Mr. Tatlock and his sheep, all long gone—and stood leaning against it. Overhead, gulls wrote invisibly on the sky and she could hear sheep bleating far away, down the hill. The air was damp and fresh with salt, and the sun felt good on her head and shoulders.

The next few days would be busy. Friday there was Helen. Alice had spoken to her on the telephone the night before, and she'd invited Alice and Margery to lunch. She told Alice that Grace was out of the country at present. She'd married a racehorse trainer in Hamilton—not Dougie McNaughton, he of the beautiful seat—and she and her husband had taken two horses to Australia for the Melbourne Cup. When they returned, there'd be a grand reunion, Helen promised. Grace's daughter Lucy was at St. Katherine's with Helen's Eleanor. Lucy spent her weekends with the Ollernshaws, just as her mother used to spend them with the Quennells. "Well, what else would you expect?'' Margery had asked when Alice hung up.

Miss Sallet was still at Saint Kat's, still assistant head. She must not have been as old as fourteen-year-old Alice had thought. She was looking forward to seeing Alice, too, as soon as she could visit.

And there was the matter of the flat. The accommodations officer promised several leads—nothing extravagant. He understood about stretching grants as far as possible. The book Alice had come all this way to write would be a challenge. She would need all the time she could manage in order to puzzle out the truth about Emilia Fairchild's life.

And whose truth would it be finally? Truth wasn't a single, simple thing: Alice knew all too well.

But first, tomorrow, there was Len. He was buried in the same cemetery as Emilia and her family, on the hill above Florestan. Alice turned up the unpaved track. Tomorrow she would go and find him.

LIBRARY
TELLURIDE M/H SCHOOL
725 W COLORADO
TELLURIDE, CO 81435